WAKE MY HEART

JASPER FALLS BOOK 1

LYDIA MICHAELS

BAILEY BROWN
PUBLISHING

WAKE MY HEART

A Jasper Falls Novel

LYDIA MICHAELS
www.LydiaMichaelsBooks.com

WAKE MY HEART
Jasper Falls Book One
© Lydia Michaels Books 2020

eBook ISBN: 978-1-7354677-4-0
Print ISBN: 978-1-7354677-2-6

Written by Lydia Michaels
Published by Bailey Brown Publishing
Cover Design by Lydia Michaels
Edited by Theresa Kohler
Oxford Comma Editing

❀ Created with Vellum

For D.D., my courageously beautiful friend who inspires me to never take life for granted and reminds me to celebrate the journey.

WAKE MY HEART

Jasper Falls 1

Written by
Lydia Michaels

PROLOGUE

*T*heir laughter echoed into the night as Maggie fumbled with frozen fingers to find the house key, the heat of Nash's body seeping into her side. Long savannas of protected land stretched into the mountains at her back, as the damp March wind cut through her clothing. While their little house was nothing special, the magnificent view was something to behold, especially under a dusting of new fallen snow. But it was the love they shared within, that truly made their simple house a home.

"I want you," Nash murmured, nibbling at her jaw and making her giggle as anticipation nipped at her insides.

After a night out with Maggie's sister, enduring yet another uncomfortable meet and greet with Perrin's newest love interest, it was no surprise Maggie and Nash were trashed. They had done everything necessary to survive the awkward get-together, and in the process, they kicked a fifth of Jameson.

It was St. Patrick's Day, so they were technically honoring a family tradition—being O'Malleys and all. And, as the saying went, whiskey made her frisky, so her horny husband didn't have much patience left—knowing he had a sure thing ahead of him.

Maggie fumbled for her house keys, distracted by the weight of Nash's hungry touch as it disappeared beneath the bulk of her jacket. Warm breath teased across the back of her neck as his lips found her thrumming pulse.

"Hurry."

Why did she have so many keys? She didn't know what half of them opened. "You're not making it easy."

Nash nibbled her ear and chuckled, the sound low like thunder. "Me?

You're the one making things hard." He nudged her forward, showing her exactly how hard *things* were getting.

The key glided into the old lock, but before Maggie could turn it, Nash twisted her to face him, capturing her lips in a kiss that promised she'd be his the moment they crossed the threshold into their house.

Center County didn't have much of a local nightlife, and being that their neighbors were all in their late seventies this side of town, the world belonged solely to them. On nights like this, after more than a few drinks and too many teasing comments on the ride home from her sister's, she didn't put it past Nash to take her right there on the front porch for the entire town to see.

Breathless, she pulled her mouth away, her gaze drifting up to the windows of her nosey, elderly neighbor's house. "Mrs. Nanomaker's probably watching us."

He chuckled against her throat, slipping his tongue over her pulse. "That saucy old minx. She gets her jollies from spying on us."

Maggie bit his lip and nudged him back so she could get the door open. "Doubtful. She was the wife of a preacher."

"They're the ones you have to watch out for." Nash caught her hips as the lock gave way.

The old latch stuck, and she moaned. "We need a new doorknob. This one needs more finessing than a virgin bride."

With one hand buried inside her coat, he used his other one to jostle the handle. Cold fingers grazed her flesh, and she sucked in a sharp breath. The faint scent of snow clung to the air. They needed to get into the warmth, because knowing her husband, she only had about thirty seconds before he started pulling off her clothes—freezing temperatures be damned.

"You have to jerk it to the left."

He chuckled. "I was gonna say the same to you."

"Focus. It's starting to snow again."

"I am. This damn door…"

She glanced at the street, soft flurries falling onto the already icy roads. "Light would help."

"Don't start."

She'd only asked him to replace the porch bulb a hundred times. It was a constant on their to-do lists, sort of a joke at this point. No matter how many times they went to the market, they always forgot the damn lightbulbs.

He yanked the knob and the door gave way. "Now, get inside so I can get inside you."

The moment they crossed the threshold he spun her to face him and yanked her coat halfway down her arms. Pressing his lips to the slope of her shoulder, he caught her hips and corralled her toward the stairs. He worked the button of her jeans, jerking the denim open. They weren't going to make it to the bed.

"Upstairs," she insisted. "In the bed."

"Oh, Mrs. O'Malley, lack of furniture isn't going to stop me." The sweet scent of whiskey on his breath teased the fallen hairs around her face as his finger slipped between her hot folds and filled her. "I need inside of you, now."

The first stroke of his touch filled her lungs with a gasp. Her lashes lowered as her body melted in his arms. No matter how many times he touched her, it always felt like the first time. A swarm of butterflies tickled her insides as he caressed and kissed her, casting some unbreakable spell over them.

The jangle of his metal belt buckle falling open barely registered as he stripped away her clothes. It had been this way since they were fifteen. Hot, explosive, and necessary. Every time. No matter where they were.

Nash was a part of her, and she belonged solely to him. He was her husband, her best friend, and the other half of her soul.

He pressed her back into the stairs, and while she knew there would be bruises in the morning, the consequences meant nothing as he filled her. Her knees clung to his hips, her fingers scraping up his back. Had they even closed the front door? The cool draft teasing her heated skin warned they had not.

Breathy sighs caught in a tangle as their moans broke the silence. Peeking past his shoulder, she stared at the open door and across the black plains. The sky lay like a blanket of stars over all of it. Everything they knew and all that they were, existed in this place in time. Their imperfections, their secondhand furniture, their brightly painted walls, their burned-out lightbulbs, none of it mattered as long as they had each other.

"God, Maggie…" He breathed against her ear. "I could have you like this for an entire lifetime, and it still wouldn't be enough." He thrust hard, taking her passionately and filling her soul as much as he filled her body.

"I love you, Nash."

His mouth devoured hers, stealing her view of the night sky and overwhelming her soul with a mind melting kiss. "You're mine, Maggie. Only mine."

"Only yours."

"Forever."

She nodded, having made the promise a thousand times before. "And ever."

CHAPTER 1

 *wo Years Later*

SNOW PACKED against the wet mud, dampening Maggie's jeans as she kneeled. Her hands cradled the thermos of coffee, stealing warmth from the metal and drawing her shoulders in against the cold March wind.

"I finally paid the water bill." Her gloved finger brushed the numb tip of her nose as she sniffed. The air still held the metallic scent of snow, and she worried there would be more before the end of winter. "Tom came by to fix the hose bib. He said I should leave it dripping so it doesn't freeze and burst again. That little trickle sure hikes up the bill, but it's better than having to repair a busted pipe in the dead of winter."

She always allowed time for a reply that never came.

"The dryer finally broke. I got one of those folding rack things. I need to go to McGinty's and pick out a new one, but I don't want to inconvenience anyone. Can't carry a dryer home, so I'll need someone with a truck to help me drive it back. Unless they deliver. I should call."

She sipped her coffee, letting it warm her chest. "I can't wait until this weather breaks and I can hang things on the line. I think there are hooks out back. I'll need something to reach them."

Her mind immediately went to the shed where Nash's ladder stood, tipped against the wall, his work gloves still sitting exactly where he left them. She didn't have the heart to disturb them. Her step stool from the broom closet would probably reach.

Did McGinty's sell clothesline? She should stop at the hardware store in town first. She pictured herself buying the rope, and imagined Mr. Montgomery giving her a sympathetic smile as he placed the rope in a brown paper bag. He'd offer to send the stock boy over to help, and she'd politely turn him down. Then she'd go home and cry.

The simplest thoughts could sometimes overwhelm her. Thinking too many steps ahead, often caused her eyes to prickle with tears.

"Maybe I'll just keep using the rack."

Her head dropped, her gaze falling to a patch of matted down grass where the snow had melted. She should plant flowers as soon as the ground thawed.

Her throat tightened as she considered which flowers he'd like best. A wall of tears blurred her vision, and she blinked, brushing away a salty drop as it cascaded down her wind-chilled cheek. She sat up a little straighter and sipped the coffee.

"I know I promised not to cry as much, but it's March. This month is always a little harder than the others. It's been two years, Nash. How did that happen? Where did the time go?"

Her gloved fingers swept over the patch of exposed earth. Blades of grass clumped in stiff tufts, frozen in time by frost and snow.

"I wish I went with you."

She sniffled, her tears gathering again as she stared out over the cemetery. Several O'Malley tombstones surrounded the area, but his was the only one carved into a guitar. Her hand trembled as she traced the engraved shape of his name.

"I miss you."

She would give anything to hear him say it back. To hear his laughter or the sound of his voice. Their home had always been such a musical place, filled with his many instruments.

Now, it was mostly silent. Her favorite songs too painful to hear, too reminiscent of a time when life was perfect.

Tightness coiled in her chest, twisting until she could no longer draw a full breath. The metronome of her heart no longer beat properly. It hadn't since the day he left her, the day her world broke into a thousand unfixable pieces.

Vivid flashes of that day raced through her mind, and she flinched at the grotesque reality of the nightmare that became her life. The scent of ice and snow mixed with the burn of rubber. The flash of red lights against the trees. The sight of blood, and his blank, unblinking eyes. The scream that shattered her world when they told her he was gone.

Totaled, the car never returned home, only a few personal possessions left on the driver's seat that the emergency responders had salvaged. Meaningless, but oh so significant. An ice scraper, his cell phone, and a box of lightbulbs for the porch.

She could hardly breathe for months, every inhalation a serrated reminder that she was alone, and he was gone. She'd passed an entire year in tormented surrealness. Her reality didn't make sense. They were

Maggie and Nash. They were going to start a family. They were happy. Ridiculously happy. This wasn't the way things were supposed to go.

Her lungs seized as she covered her mouth, smothering a sob. She hated to cry in front of him. Not that he was there. It was a graveyard. But she always felt like he watched her whenever she visited the cemetery.

Her gaze turned to the gray sky, and she blinked back her tears. "Sorry."

Pushing up from the cold ground, she ignored the damp stains on her knees and pressed a kiss to her fingers where they poked out of her cutoff gloves. She traced her fingers over his name.

"I love you."

She waited for the silent beat to pass, giving him plenty of chance to say it back from wherever he was. Turning away, she lost the fight against the choking sobs and bundled her arms deep in her jacket pockets.

Taking brisk strides toward her bike, she sniffled, trails of tears chilling her chapped cheeks. Adjusting the wool beanie cap on her head, she placed the thermos in the basket of her bicycle, then pivoted in the direction of her house.

She hadn't driven since the accident. With their car totaled, the idea of driving terrified her. There were the rare occasions she accepted lifts from others, mostly when snow made it impossible to ride her bike home from work, but she was never easy about traveling in cars.

Center County was known for its brutal winters. She used to love the snow. Her affection changed when a small patch of ice stole her husband's life and her future.

Cheeks frozen, she peddled around the bend and her shoulders tensed at the sight of her sister Perrin's small blue car parked at the curb. Great, Maggie thought, brushing her gloved palm over her cheeks to erase the tracks of her tears.

Mrs. Nanomaker's house stood vacant on the corner, the FOR SALE sign an unceremonious declaration that someone could buy the house at any time, though no one had attended the many open houses that took place shortly after her neighbor's passing.

Maggie had adjusted to the quiet of their block. She preferred the solitude, but her peace was not impenetrable. When outsiders came to visit, the slightest noise caused the greatest disturbance. Her sister was no exception.

Turning her bike into the driveway, Maggie hopped off just before the shed, the pedals still spinning. Perrin waited on the back porch, two cups of coffee from the local café in her gloved hands.

"You're out early."

Maggie mimicked her sister's smile with a brittle one. Her sister knew where she'd been. It was no secret she visited Nash's grave every morning.

"Where were you?" Perrin held out a paper cup of coffee.

Maggie accepted the cup and unlocked the back door. "You know where I was."

Her sister made no comment and followed her into the kitchen. Maggie leaned her hip into the corner of the counter and waited. Perrin's gaze scanned the unchanged interior of the house, seeking a point of small talk or silently judging the lack of *progress*.

Progress was one of those fancy buzzwords regular people liked to throw around as if they had some secret intellect on the stages of grief. Another two cent term was *closure*. Everyone was so concerned about her progress and closure, as if it were that easy.

Didn't they know her heart had been ripped to shreds? Sometimes things were too messy to simply close.

"Do you need something?" She plucked off her hat and stuffed it in the front pocket of her jacket.

Her sister's manicured brows pulled together in a familiar look of concern. Her short, windswept blonde hair at complete odds with Maggie's long, straggly brown waves.

"Do I have to need something to stop by, Maggie?"

No, but there was always a motive, always a sense of obligation that she "check" on her poor brokenhearted sister.

Maggie sighed, trying hard to reel in her cynicism. "Sorry." She waved a hand toward the table. "Wanna sit?"

Perrin lowered herself into a chair. The fur lining of her hood matched the gold hues of her hair. Only she could manage to keep a down jacket so pristinely white all winter long.

Maggie pulled off the bulky layer of her thermal hoody, made for warmth more than any sort of vanity. It was what everyone wore in the sub-zero supply store where she worked. Static electricity assaulted her hair as she stripped off the added layer. She hung the outerwear on the hook by the door next to Nash's leather jacket.

As she sat, her sister watched her, like an animal at the zoo in a new exhibit. Used to such scrutiny, Maggie popped the top off her coffee and took a sip.

Her eyes closed as she recognized the savory flavor of quality coffee. "This is good coffee. Thanks."

"It's from the café in town." Perrin's lips pressed tight. "I know the anniversary's coming up, Maggie."

"Yup. That's the funny thing about anniversaries. They come every year."

March would forever be the month he died. April commemorated their first official date. May was when he asked her to move into his apartment. July was their wedding anniversary. September was the month they bought their house. October was his birthday. December was all together brutal because no one did Christmas like Nash. January marked the day he proposed. February was the month they first kissed outside the gym during a school dance. And then, it was March all over again.

"Maybe it's time for you to get back out there—"

"Don't."

She didn't want another speech about how young she was or how many fish still swam in the sea. She'd been with Nash since middle school. He was her first everything. She couldn't remember who she was before he'd come along, and without him breathing life into her soul, she felt no urge to keep on living. She had no desire to pretend that the mundane social bullshit other singles did to waste time and distract them from their lonesome, meaningless existences was actually worth her time.

Perrin nodded and backed off but then announced, "Bran's mom knows a therapist that just opened a new practice in town. Maybe you could call. He's doing free consultations."

Every time her sister mentioned Bran, Maggie had to remember this person had become a fixture in her sister's life. But to Maggie, he was no one. Another stranger. She didn't care what he or his mom had to say.

She reminded herself that her sister was only trying to help. "Thanks."

"A therapist could help. Maybe he could fix some things in your life."

Her lips formed a thin line. People used terms like fix because she was so obviously broken. No one wanted to acknowledge that some breaks were permanent and unfixable.

"Perrin, I'm mourning. My husband died. Grief takes time. I'm sorry if my inability to *get back out there* is hard for you, but trust me when I say, it's harder on me. I'm the one who's broken, and sleeping with someone else isn't going to fix me."

Her sister recoiled at the verbal slap. "I'm only trying to help you, only suggesting you talk to a therapist. I'm not suggesting you have sex with someone. But I think you need to socialize more, Maggie. All you do is go to work and the cemetery. Socializing, even with a professional, could help your progress. You have to get out of this house."

"I like it here."

Perrin's head turned, her gaze traveling over the unchanged signs of Nash. "It's dark and quiet. Why don't you turn on some lights or play some music?"

"I like the quiet." She dropped her gaze to her coffee cup.

Perrin slid a business card across the surface of the table, into Maggie's view. "I just think it would help if you talked to someone."

"I talk to people."

"Who?"

"Well, you're here. And I talk to people at work. I had to buy some things in town the other day. I was polite and said hello to those who waved."

"But maybe it's time to talk about the things you're afraid to say." Perrin slid the card another inch, until it nudged Maggie's fingertips peeking from the clipped edges of her wool gloves. "Just think about it."

The black ink beveled under her fingertips, raised to the touch. *Dr. Alec Devereux*. Sounded pretentious. "I'll think about it."

Her sister smiled, and she hated giving her false hope. "Thank you."

Maggie stood and pinned the card on the corkboard above the trash can where the house keys hung. Her gaze swung to the window where the FOR SALE sign in the neighbor's yard stood, and she did a double take.

"What's wrong?"

"Nothing." She squinted at the sticker proclaiming the property had SOLD. Her quiet little corner of the world was about to change, and she panicked at the unknown.

"Is someone out there?"

Not someone but there would be someone there soon. "The Nanomaker house sold."

"That's good. I don't like you living here alone without neighbors."

"The new owners could be serial killers."

Her sister chucked her empty coffee cup in the trash bin. "In Center County? Please. Nothing that interesting ever happens here."

The china in the cabinets rattled as a truck barreled down the street. Her house was at the very edge of town, so only people who had business in this area drove by.

She and Perrin craned their necks to see the truck. It turned the corner and pulled into the neighbor's driveway, which faced her backyard.

"That was fast." Perrin laughed. "Maybe we should try manifesting a winning lottery ticket next."

Maggie chuckled and stared at the windshield of the truck, her view inhibited by the morning glare of sun. The idea of pretending to be normal and cheery for a perfect stranger exhausted her.

She glanced out the other window at her raggedy lawn. "I have to cut the grass."

"You should hire someone to do that stuff for you."

"I'm not helpless."

Leaves gathered along the shared fence and the plants she hadn't trimmed back had turned to straw. She and Nash used to spend a full weekend doing yard work at the start of every spring and again at the end of fall, mulching the beds and hosing off the lawn furniture. He used to love sitting around the firepit with his guitar.

"I know a guy who owns a landscaping business. I'll give you his number."

Her sister kept chatting as she dug through her purse, but Maggie's attention locked on the truck. Who were they? A family? Newlyweds? Would their palpable happiness be her undoing?

"I think you'll really like him. I know him through the salon. He's a big, friendly guy, really sweet and funny."

She frowned and turned away from the window, missing whatever Perrin had just said. "What?"

"Randy's number."

"Who?"

"The lawn guy. Weren't you listening to me?"

Perrin shampooed clients at the local salon, so she had insider gossip and a contact for everyone. "Thanks, but I can mow my own lawn."

Unlike her sister, Maggie had always been a bit more hands-on. Her sister loved dainty things, pretty, girlie things. Maggie, on the other hand, preferred activities that left a little dirt under the nails and the taste of sweat on her skin.

"I know you're not helpless, Maggie, but it isn't a crime to accept assistance from others. You can afford to pay someone to help around here if you don't have the time or energy to do it yourself."

She didn't want help. She wanted solitude and a long nap. "I'm not hiring a stranger to do things around here that I'm capable of doing myself."

"Then let me help you. That's what family's for."

Nash was her family. He didn't offer contacts, he offered hands-on help. They were supposed to have four little kids that never had the chance to exist. Their rooms were all empty, just a hope chest of hand-me-downs she'd wished to one day share with them and a list of beautiful names she'd never get to call.

"You're right," Maggie said, stepping closer to the door in hopes that her sister would follow. "Text me the landscaper's number." She wouldn't use it, but if it satisfied her sister's need to fix a broken piece of her life, she didn't see the harm in humoring her.

Glancing at the door, Perrin's expression shifted with understanding that this was a dismissal. "Oh, I… It's early. Bran's working until tonight." She shrugged. "I was thinking we could do something together."

"I can't." The response came automatically without actual consideration of her schedule.

Perrin frowned. "Why, what are you doing?"

"I…" Maggie's mind scrambled for any solo activity that might work as an excuse. "Have a dentist appointment."

"Oh. Maybe after?"

"I have to run errands in town."

"I could come with you."

She was a horrible sister. "Perrin, I just... It's not a good day." It never was.

Understanding flashed in her sister's eyes, reflecting an effort not to take her rejection personally, but the hurt was evident. "I know. I'm pushing for too much."

Maggie let out a breath, the pressure to be something she wasn't ready to be lessened the second her sister backed off. Her brow puckered in apology. "It's not about you."

"I know that, too. I just wish we could go back to the way things used to be."

A sharp knife lodged in her chest. "So do I."

Every day Maggie wished she could turn back time, but there was no undoing the past. She remembered how it felt to be happy, but the foundation of her happiness was gone. And after such a painful loss, she saw no sense in forming or maintaining other attachments. Life was temporary, but grief stayed permanent because love was permanent. It didn't ease with time. And what once brought pleasure, now only brought pain.

"You have people that love you, Maggie. If you'd just let us be here for you..."

Perrin might love her, but since losing Nash, any level of affection hurt. Her mother couldn't fathom the loss, because she never truly respected their marriage. Her dad had attended the funeral but never once offered words of condolence. Between his coldness and her judgement, Maggie couldn't bear their proximity. Perrin was a part of them by default. Even though she saw Maggie's grief for the trauma it was, she'd never fully grasped the totality of it.

Maggie swallowed and dropped her gaze. "It's better if I'm alone." If she learned to be alone, it wouldn't hurt as bad the next time she lost someone. "I have to get to my appointment."

"Can we do something next weekend? Even if we have a crappy time, let's do something."

"Like what?"

She shrugged. "Let's go shoe shopping."

Maggie's face scrunched. "I hate shopping."

"We could get makeovers."

"You must have me confused with someone else."

"Fine." She glanced around the kitchen. "What about house shopping? We could get you a new couch."

Sharp possessiveness spiked inside of her. "What's wrong with my couch?"

"Um, it's old and hideous."

"It's not old," Maggie said with a bite of defensiveness. "We bought it when we got our apartment."

"Maggie, that was almost ten years ago."

"So?"

"So, it's outdated. Buy yourself something new. Brighten up this place."

"If I want to brighten things up, I'll buy a lamp. I'm not getting rid of my couch."

She and Nash had picked out that couch. They spent weeks shopping around and sitting on various styles. It was their first big purchase after deciding to move in together. They'd made love on it countless times, built forts around it, and had pillow fights on it. She used to lay there with her eyes closed and listen to him play the piano.

"Maggie, you're never going to move on if you continue to live in the past."

Feeling under attack, she dumped her coffee down the drain. Everyone thought they had a solution she was missing, like replacing her sofa could somehow heal the ache in her heart or the splinters in her soul. She tossed the cup in the garbage and turned, crossing her arms over her chest.

"I was *happy* in the past. Maybe I like it there."

"But you're not happy now. There's so much more out there, except you refuse to open your eyes to new possibilities. *This* isn't living, it's sleepwalking."

"I'm living!" she snapped, jabbing a finger toward her chest. "If I wasn't alive, this wouldn't hurt so much."

"I know you're in pain, but hiding behind that pain won't protect you from future loss. Life changes, Maggie, and one day you're going to need family again, but you'll have chased everyone who cared about you away."

"Maybe I just want to be left the hell alone!" she snapped and silence fell over the kitchen.

Perrin's brow pinched with regret. Her shoulders shrank as she let out a breath. She lowered her head. "Well, I better go."

"Thanks for the coffee." The words shot out with more accusation than gratitude.

"You're welcome." Her sister faced the door and hesitated. They used to hug all the time, and Maggie sensed her sister needing that contact now.

She couldn't bear the intimacy. Nearness had a way of choking her.

Guilt tightened her insides, forming a physical nausea. "I'm sorry I snapped at you."

"I shouldn't have pushed."

"I know it's out of love, Perrin." But love had become a terrifying thing since Nash left.

Hope flashed in her sister's eyes as she looked back. "If you change your mind and want to do something later…"

Maggie crossed the kitchen and opened the back door, using it as a sort of shield between them. "Drive safe."

"Call me later."

"I will." She wouldn't.

"And call that therapist."

She nodded, not vocalizing any promises.

Perrin's smile didn't reach her concerned eyes as she glanced back at Maggie. "Love you."

"Love you, too." That one was free. Losing Nash had a way of making sure she never missed the opportunity to tell someone they were loved, even if her heart didn't know how to receive those emotions from others anymore.

At the sound of her sister's car pulling away, she plucked the pushpin on the corkboard free. Dr. Devereux's business card fluttered into the garbage bin below.

"Sorry, doc. We're just not meant to be."

CHAPTER 2

*R*yan Clooney pulled the string of the hanging light in the basement, then Luke whistled, the sound echoing off the cinder block walls. "You could make an awesome bar down here."

Ryan grinned at his cousin's suggestion. "That's what I was thinking. I just have to redo the floors and paint—maybe add some sheetrock if I wanna get *fancy*."

Luke approached a wall of exposed studs that divided the laundry area from the rest of the basement and gave the wood beams a shake. "Looks like the previous owners thought about finishing it at one time but got sidetracked."

Ryan gave one of the two-by-fours a kick with his boot. "This will probably come down. It's not like it's a load bearing wall or anything."

His cousin inspected the craftmanship. "If you sheetrock it, you could close off the laundry area. That way if clothes pile up you can still entertain down here."

"True." Though Ryan didn't know who he'd be entertaining aside from his two thousand cousins.

Part of the reason he moved to this side of town was to get away from his many, often prying, relatives. His big, Irish Catholic family was literally *everywhere* in Center County. Anyone who wasn't a Clooney, McCullough, or an O'Leahey, was usually married to one or related by marriage. It made the dating pool a very narrow, shallow place to swim.

"I'd definitely tile down here." Luke's inspection had moved on to the water heater beneath the stairs. "Basements have a tendency to get damp. I have a tile cutter. We could bang this out in a day with Tristan's help."

Tristan was Luke's husband, who also happened to be Ryan's best friend from college. After a nasty falling out with his family in Texas,

15

Tristan followed Ryan back to Center County and became a sort of surrogate brother. Luke, Ryan's cousin and childhood best friend, instantly clicked with him. It took years for the two to come out, but when they did, no one was surprised. They were ridiculously happy and now the proud fathers of a beautiful little girl.

"Yo!" Speak of the devil. Tristan's heavy boots traveled down the wooden stairs, kicking dust into the musty air. "Am I unloading this crap by myself?"

"We're coming. We were just talking about what a great bar Ry could make down here." Luke grinned. "I'm seeing a huge flat screen on that wall." He framed the space by holding his hands out, his thumbs and forefingers shaping a square.

Tristan stood on the lowest step, holding on to the cement overhang, as if afraid to get sucked into the space. "That would be awesome, and we can talk about it later. Right now we got a truck full of boxes that needs unloading, and Alexia has a dance class in a few hours. It's our turn to take her."

Alexia was their daughter. Luke and Tristan had initially been turned down for adoption, so they'd gone the less traditional route. Alexia was biologically Tristan and Sheilagh's kid. They all shared custody and somehow made it work.

Alexia, poor thing, had three dads, Tristan, Luke, and Alec, Sheilagh's husband. Boys wouldn't stand a chance when she reached dating age. Luckily, those days were a long way off.

Ryan followed Tristan up the stairs into the kitchen. "We can get the truck emptied quickly and then you guys can go do your dad thing. I appreciate you giving me a hand on your day off."

Tristan clapped a heavy hand on his back. "That's what family's for."

Not always, Ryan thought, remembering the guilt trip his mother laid on him the day he announced he'd bought a house. Apparently, moving beyond a mile from an Irish mother's womb was a capital crime in their culture.

The woman lit about twenty candles and said eight rosaries for him in the past week. It was perfectly normal to leave the nest at his age, but his mother saw it as some sort of betrayal.

Why couldn't he stay home and save his money? He should wait until he met a nice girl to marry, wait until he was ready to start a family. On the verge of turning thirty, he wasn't sure that would ever happen for him.

Ryan was finished waiting for his life to start and sick of watching everyone pair off around him, so he decided to plan for a future alone. And he was fine with that—or so he told himself on a regular basis.

All his cousins were now married and having children. Christ, even some of his cousins' kids were starting to date. He needed breathing room.

Ryan and Tristan carried several more loads into the house, plopping boxes in the empty room he assumed was the dining room.

"Luke!" Tristan snapped as they passed through the kitchen with another armful of boxes. "I'm not going to be late for Alexia's class. Get your ass up here and help."

"I'm coming!" Luke barked from the basement.

Metal screeched from below and Ryan paused at the kitchen door, his brows lifting in concern. "Should I be worried?"

"Nah, Luke knows how to fix just about anything. He's probably just giving your boiler a proper inspection."

Ryan nodded and followed him into the dining room. Tristan stomped off toward the truck as Luke came up the basement steps, wiping oil off his hands with a smudged rag.

Watching his husband leave in a huff, Luke rolled his eyes. "He's going to give himself a coronary if he doesn't chill out. He's becoming one of those helicopter parents we used to make fun of."

Ryan smiled, knowing full well both men were equally protective of their daughter. Of all Alexia's parents, Sheilagh was probably the most laid back of the clan.

They made several trips in and out of the house unloading boxes. Ryan left the heavier stuff for his cousin, since he often bragged about being the strongest male in the family.

Luke had always been an athlete and his body reflected his rigorous training over the years, which showed in the breadth of his shoulders and his remaining strength when it came to moving extremely heavy objects, whereas Ryan's days of playing sports in high school had only left him with a lean body. His muscles had softened from working in the office at the lumberyard, sitting at a desk five days a week.

Maybe he should think about turning the basement into a gym. Nah, a bar would get more use.

Tristan climbed to the back of the truck and hauled the headboard and bed frame onto the driveway. Leaning the furniture against the truck, he paused to guzzle a sip of water.

"What's going on with the house next-door?" he asked, following Ryan's stare.

Ryan glanced at the property, noting the mismatched shed. A gray exterior wall clashed with the other three red ones, as if someone had started painting the shed and never finished.

"Don't know. Whenever I drive by, I hardly ever see any lights on over there. But the bike moves from time to time."

It was an old beach cruiser with a basket—the sort a woman would ride. He'd been hoping to catch her on one of his drive-bys before settlement, so he could introduce himself, but no such luck.

"No car?"

"None that I've noticed."

Tristan lifted a brow. "Better hope it's not squatters."

"Squatters?"

"Yeah. Homeless people see an abandoned house and figure out a way in. They'll stay until the proper authorities have them removed. Sometimes it's impossible to get them out."

"I don't think Center County has a high population of homeless people."

"Every town has homeless people, Ry. We're all just two crises away from bankruptcy."

"Good God, is that true?" As a new homeowner, with thirty years of debt ahead, those were not the uplifting stats he wanted to hear.

Tristan shrugged. "No one's bulletproof." He took the last swig of water and tossed the bottle in the empty recycling can the previous owners had left. "Just keep an eye on that house. Maybe invest in some motion sensor lights."

Tristan carried the headboard inside, and Ryan stared at the neighbor's yard. The house didn't appear abandoned, just a little neglected. Maybe the owner was older and sickly. Once he settled in, he'd do the neighborly thing and knock on the door to introduce himself.

His house occupied the corner lot, putting their driveways perpendicular from each other. From his back porch, he had a clear view into their little back yard.

The knee-high lawn on the other side of the neighbor's fence lay in snarls of wet leaves and leftover snow. The overgrown beds of dry plants needed tending. Spring was coming.

Maybe the owners were waiting for the weather to break to clean up their yard. He could offer a hand if the owner wasn't up to the challenge. Although, they were well enough to ride a bike.

He grabbed the box spring and dragged it through the back door. The truck was unloaded within an hour. Two days ago he thought he had too much crap. Now, looking at it dumped in the middle of an empty three-bedroom house he wondered how he would ever furnish such a place.

"Well, we gotta take off. Alexia has—"

"A dance class. I know."

Tristan flushed. "Sorry."

Ryan laughed. "Don't be sorry. You're a proud dad. I'd be the same if I were in your shoes."

Tristan gave him a knowing look. Ryan had suffered countless failed relationships, and Tristan and Luke had been there for every single fallout.

"It'll happen for you, man." His friend cupped a hand on his shoulder, offering an affectionate squeeze. "Not living with your mother is step one."

Ryan threw his head back and laughed. "I'm telling her you said that."

"I'll deny it. Don't try to put a wedge between me and Rosemarie. I'm her favorite."

Ryan laughed again. "I don't doubt it, especially with my recent abandonment. At least Pat left home to become a doctor. I have no excuse."

"You left to find yourself. It was the right move. Your mum will get over it. She loves you too much to stay mad at you."

Luke rolled his eyes. "You're a kiss ass, Tristan. It's not that easy for the rest of us. Ryan's got his work cut out for him. An Irish mother's guilt can bring a grown man to his knees. You have my sympathy, Ry."

"I have a feeling I'll be overdosing on pizza before she forgives me."

"Well, you know how fast word travels in this town. Eat out enough and eventually she'll see it as a reflection on her mothering. Then she'll send you a home-cooked meal. The women in this family are too territorial to let their sons eat someone else's cooking for too long."

"Especially if you're filling up on Italian," Luke joked. "Ask Italian Mary to cook for you. That'll get right under Aunt Rosemarie's freckled skin."

Ryan laughed. Italian Mary was fifty pounds wet and older than God, but she terrified all of them. "I don't want to upset my mum any more than I already have."

In all honesty, he was sorry his moving out had upset her at all. She always took care of him and was his greatest champion. But it was time for him to find his independence. His mum, however, saw this as surrendering to the permanent life of a bachelor.

"You're supposed to meet your wife first, then *buy the house together,"* she would say, as if there was only one way to move out. And she'd usually follow that up with something like, *"If your father had bought our house alone, it would have been covered in buck skin, pistachio shells, and taxidermy. No woman wants that."*

A crush of disappointment punched low in his gut as he wondered if he was giving up and getting set in his ways too soon, but he quickly pushed that worry aside. He wasn't buying a house with the woman he planned to grow old with. So what? He could still find her.

There came a time in a man's life when the waiting game felt more like an excuse than a probability that Mrs. Right would eventually show. He'd done cyber dating, small-town fix ups, and even horribly awkward blind dates with friends of friends. Nothing stuck and he needed to get out on his own.

Maybe it was him. But he didn't think he had any screaming flaws. He had a longstanding job at his family's lumberyard, which he'd eventually take over with his cousin Finn once their fathers officially retired. When his cousin Kelly needed a hand, Ryan also took shifts at O'Malley's Pub, the town hangout. He was respectful to women. He carried groceries for the older residents whenever he saw them leaving the market. And he even fixed Mrs. Waldron's flat tire when she'd been stranded and unable to reach AAA.

Not that he wanted some sort of Boy Scout award for being a good citizen, but it would be nice if some of the single women in Center County appreciated these qualities the way the older, married women seemed to. His mum and aunts couldn't understand why he was still single, and honestly, he didn't get it either.

In the past year he'd started feeling like the family's charity case, getting pity invites here, and relatives pointing out pretty women there. His single status had become a glaring mark on his chest, and he needed a change of scenery—a change of audience.

As Luke and Tristan pulled away in the moving truck, Ryan stared up at the old house and grinned. This was *his* house. A wave of pride swelled in his chest. He should celebrate.

His mouth twisted to the side as he glanced at the empty driveway of his neighbor's home, doing a double take when he noticed the bike missing. Whoever it belonged to must have taken it when they were busy unloading. He was sorry he missed them.

He returned inside, greeted by silence and boxes. The open space and lack of furniture overwhelmed him. He supposed he should pick a place and just start unpacking. First things first, he needed music.

He grabbed a work radio from his truck, and Elton John christened the house with a live rendition of *Rocketman* as he used a box cutter to open boxes and deliver them to the proper room.

Music acted as a constant companion in his life it broke up the day, got him out of his head, and lifted his mood when the loneliness overwhelmed him. He'd grown so used to his relatives constantly popping by that the quiet seemed more tangible than usual. In such silence, he could physically feel the absence of people in his life. He rolled his shoulders and turned up the volume of the song.

Having never lived anywhere but home and a college dorm, he mostly had bedroom and bathroom stuff. His old college futon and TV made up the guts of the living room for now. He didn't remember the futon being so small and uncomfortable. Maybe, after almost a decade in storage, it shrunk. He flipped a cardboard box and used it as an end table to hold his beer.

As he carried the last of the bedroom boxes toward the upstairs, he surveyed the hall, which divided the dining room and den at the front door and led to the kitchen at the back of the house. He caught himself smiling at the vacant space. It was a simple little house, but he had no doubt it would make a good home.

His smile faded as a tinge of emptiness whispered through him. Maybe the void he felt only had to do with the missing furniture. In time, he'd fill the vacant space. Life was a process, not a destination.

CHAPTER 3

*R*yan carried the box up to the second floor. This was *his* home. He could make it a bachelor pad. He'd do what Luke suggested and make a bar in the basement. He could decorate it in paraphernalia from his favorite teams—one of the perks to not having a woman around to fill the house with ruffles and frills. Maybe if he kept finding the silver linings of situations things wouldn't seem so dreary after a while.

He paused at the top of the stairs where a window faced the house next-door. The homes mirrored each other in style, only separated by the neighbor's driveway shooting off the adjacent road. Like his house, the siding on the neighbor's home was faded from the beating sun, and the windows hadn't been renovated since the 1970's.

He glanced at the gutters and frowned. If they didn't clean out those branches and leaves soon, they would have roof issues.

Once all the boxes were flattened and his bedroom furniture was put together, he carried the trash out to the shed. It was a small garage with French doors. A compact car could fit inside but not his work truck.

A light flashed and his gaze lifted to the neighbor's second floor window. If squatters lived there, they wouldn't have electricity. He didn't see the bike, but that didn't mean it wasn't in the shed.

The light on the second floor flickered again, concerning him and relieving him at the same time. Was it too late to knock and introduce himself?

The sky faded to shades of purple as the sun dipped behind the mountains in the distance. They might be settling in for dinner. Speaking of dinner, what the hell was he going to do for food?

This was why he never minded picking up an extra shift at the bar whenever his cousin asked for help. He'd rather pick at bar food while taking drink orders and appearing busy than sit in a booth dining all alone.

He withdrew his phone and scrolled through his contacts, hitting up each cousin as he worked down the long line of McCulloughs and Mosconis.

Since Luke and Tristan had Alexia, Sheilagh and Alec were out on a date. Colin had something at the church. Braydon was doing family stuff with Becca and the kids. Kelly had an art show this weekend that sent him out of town and left Ryan's mum and Aunt Colleen in charge of O'Malley's Pub, which took the bar off the option list for dinner. And Kate and Anthony were visiting colleges with Frankie.

"Yo, Ry," his cousin Finn answered. What sounded like a dozen rowdy kids shouted in the background. "How's the new place? All settled in yet?"

Ryan grinned. "The house is great. You should come by and check it out." A loud boom rattled and someone shouted. "You at a party?"

"Nah, just hanging at home with my brood. They only have one volume, and it ain't quiet."

Ryan laughed, thinking it must be nice. Finn had four kids, two dogs, and now rabbits from what he'd overheard from the aunts' gossip. "I was about to order a pizza and pick up some beer. If you're looking for an escape, consider this a lifeline. Think Mallory would mind if you took a few hours off?"

"Escape sounds incredible. Let me just let Philly know and I'll be on my way. Text me the address so I go to the right house."

"Cool. See you soon. Tell Philly I said hi." Mallory, Finn's wife, came from Philadelphia, hence her nickname Philly.

Some people were just lucky, he thought as he hung up the phone. Finn, who also happened to be Luke's twin brother, was one of the luckiest guys he knew. He had a beautiful wife, a family, the seat at the head of the family business once his Uncle Frank finally retired, and he was always smiling.

In a way, he and Finn had a lot in common. They both showed little interest in leaving Center County, so it made sense for them to be the next generation of men to run the family business. Finn handled the fieldwork, and Ryan took care of the business end. So why had Finn managed so much more than him in the same amount of time?

There was only one pizza joint in town, conveniently located a mile away from his new pad and run by the Marcellis, related to him by marriage on his cousin Kate McCullough's side. Ryan tossed a generous tip in the jar on the counter, certain they'd be seeing a lot of him. They fought him about paying for the pie, but he insisted.

The Chain by Fleetwood Mac rumbled from his truck speakers as he drove home, the delicious scent of Italian sauce and oregano filling the air. An ice cold six-pack sat to his right on the center console, the perfect complement to a hot pizza.

He loved that his house was on the corner lot. Finn's truck idled at the curb as Ryan pulled into the driveway. In that moment, he decided the back door would be the main entrance. It made sense, since it was closest to where he'd park.

He shut off the truck and his headlights poured over the neighbor's shed. Something moved in the shadows and he squinted. A small figure parked the bike against the fence and climbed off. A female, small, possibly a teenager. Blocking her eyes from the beaming headlights, she stared at his truck.

Her face turned and he noticed her small upturned nose with a spattering of freckles on otherwise pale skin as she looked back at him. Her lips were full and eyes large. Her wavy, brown hair streamed from beneath a gray wool beanie cap.

He hit the switch to kill the lights but regretted his decision the moment her figure nearly vanished in the dark. As she moved a few steps, the narrow frame of her shoulders bundled in an oversized hooded sweatshirt caught the moonlight.

There was something familiar about her. Of course, there weren't many mysterious residents in a town with a population under four thousand. But who was she? Had they met before?

The passenger door jerked open, startling him out of his trance. "This place is great," Finn said in greeting, grabbing the pizza off the front seat. "Smells good. You get this from Vincenzo Marcelli's?"

Ryan glanced back at the bike, and the woman was gone. He returned his stare to Finn. "Yeah. Did you see that girl?"

"What girl?" Finn followed his stare. "Someone over there?"

Had he imagined her? He grabbed the beer and climbed out of the truck. "I must be seeing things." But he could swear he saw her.

He led Finn through the back door. "I don't have any furniture yet, so we'll have to rough it."

"I'm sure we'll survive. This is really nice, Ry."

"Thanks. Tomorrow I'm heading to McGinty's to see about getting some furniture."

They each cracked open a beer. Finn flipped a cardboard box over in the center of the living room and used it as a coffee table for the pizza. The warm mozzarella and hot marinara sauce seemed the perfect end to a great day.

"How're Mallory and the kids?"

"Can't complain."

"And did I hear you now have rabbits?"

Finn laughed and groaned. "I think the one's pregnant. I could shoot Philly for agreeing to let the kids get them."

"Fertile land you come from. And you know what they say about rabbits…"

"That they have a libido only second to McCulloughs?"

~~Ryan laughed. He was probably right,~~ being that there were now something like thirty-five of them living up on what the family referred to as McCullough Mountain.

"Something like that."

His cousin grinned. "That rabbit isn't the only thing packing heat."

Ryan stilled, a warm mouthful of sauce and cheese forgotten on his tongue. *"Mallory's pregnant again?"* He stared in shock.

Finn's smile stretched from ear to ear. "Guilty."

Ryan swallowed with a gulp. "Holy crap. That's five kids, Finn. *Five!* What the hell are you gonna do with *five* kids?"

He shrugged and happily reached for another slice. "Maybe start a minor league baseball team or form the next band of junior river dancers. We could call ourselves the Irish Von Trapps." He laughed. "We'll just make it work. Just like my parents did. It all comes together in the end."

"You're going to be overrun by redheads and bunnies."

Finn laughed. "It's great."

"And how's Mallory feeling?"

"Exhausted, but happy."

"Aunt Maureen must be thrilled."

Finn held up a finger. "She doesn't know yet. We just found out on Wednesday and Philly wants to tell everyone after the morning sickness ends, so don't tell your mum until then."

"She's not speaking to me at the moment, so your secret's safe."

"Baloney. I heard she's got a freezer full of casseroles for you. With Pat so busy doing his residency and Tristan preoccupied with family, you're her number one. She's just pouting and enjoying the sympathy. It'll pass in a few days once she misses you. Besides, there's no way she's going to let you decorate this place without meddling. The women in our family don't know how to back off. Believe me, she's happy for you."

"Well, she sure has a funny way of showing it."

"She's an O'Leahey woman, Ry. They're all insane. But Aunt Rose has always been the most logical of the three, so she'll come around. Maybe stop by Ashlynn's Farmers' Market and pick her up some flowers or something. Sort of a peace offering." He tossed his crust into the box with the other bit off pieces. "Either that or have fun watching Tristan eat all your dinners."

Ryan laughed. "He's such a kiss ass."

"No kidding. Even my mum swoons whenever he comes by. It's that damn southern charm."

He gave Finn the grand tour, and when the six-pack was gone, he walked him out. Finn was a great cousin, a great business partner and supervisor at the lumberyard, and an even greater friend. Since their dads were on the verge of retirement, the responsibility of the business fell into their laps. Together they made an unstoppable team, Ryan thought.

"Thanks for coming by."

"Thanks for the invite. It's a great place, Ry. You should be proud of yourself."

He grinned. "Yeah, I am."

That night, he lay in bed thinking about all the items he needed to buy. Good thing he padded his loan from the bank, because he basically needed everything from new faucets to curtains. Tomorrow was going to be a busy day.

CHAPTER 4

$\mathcal{D}$eafening silence surrounded Maggie like a hand curled to her throat. The louder the stillness grew the more it choked her.

Pressure built in her chest as she battled to breathe. The urge to do *it* again gnawed at her nerve endings. Moisture gathered on her palms.

No more...

She'd done it over thirty times tonight and that was too much, even for her. Like an addict, she quivered as an internal war wreaked havoc on her insides. Her will battled with her heart, but both parts felt lost.

A cool sweat broke over her skin as her gaze jerked about random objects that turned shadows into curious shapes. Sometimes, if she let the laundry pile up on the chair it looked like he was sitting there, watching her in the dark. Tonight, the chair was empty.

She lay perfectly motionless in their bed, her body still favoring the right side, much like an amputee would still reach with a phantom hand. If she could just fall asleep, the need would go away until tomorrow. She could beat it if she outsmarted it. But her mind kept jolting awake, as if bargaining for an infinite second chance.

Just one more time and I'll go to sleep...

Liar...

No, I mean it.

You never mean it.

You're weak. Weak!

"Fuck." Her fist punched the pillow. Her other hand squeezed the case of her cell phone.

She should break it. Throw it away.

Her heart whipped against her ribs and plunged into the pit of her stomach as she fell into an absolute panic. No, no, she would never break it. This was all she had left.

Her phone illuminated and she hit play. Her eyes squeezed shut, her heart finding solace in the familiar rumble that broke the silence.

"Hey, babe. It's me. Call me when you get this."

Her mouth curved, baring her teeth as a sob gutted her. Hot tears pushed against her lashes as overwhelming relief slowed her racing panic. One more time.

"Hey, babe. It's me. Call me when you get this."

Her body curled around his pillow, breathing in the scent that had long since faded. She cradled the phone to her chest. Some nights she needed to hear his voice more than others. Tonight was one of those nights.

She couldn't explain this new layer of panic. She couldn't shake the sense that something was coming, something ... life altering. It terrified her.

Lately, it felt like an invisible force was pulling him away, more than destiny already had. She worried that one day she might wake up with half as many memories and no one to blame. Irrational, yes, but terrifying all the same.

She kept the light off, listening to the voicemail several more times until she fell asleep. When she woke the next morning, her phone lay in the curve of her palm.

Every day became a game with herself. How long could she go without listening to his voice? How many minutes could she make it without thinking of him? How many hours could she survive without falling completely apart?

To some, she might look like a first-class basket case. But she noted progress every day. The fact that she could go an hour without bursting into tears was huge.

In the beginning, she could barely make it through a minute. Keeping busy was key. Her need for privacy, however, added a challenge.

She hadn't always been an introvert. But when Nash died, the pitying looks followed, and it made it impossible to socialize. First, she didn't want to talk, but she knew healthy humans interacted with each other, so she did her best. Unfortunately, people only wanted to talk about her loss.

They'd tip their heads, pucker their brows, and look at her with pitying eyes. "How you holdin' up?" they'd ask.

Like there could be any answer other than terrible. But that wasn't what they wanted to hear.

If she made it to any social occasion, she was having a better than usual day. But people's questions made her grief inescapable. She forced herself to get out of the house and try to appear normal. But in the end, everyone only saw a poor widow, which was exactly how she felt most days. She was a poor pathetic widow, who had no clue or desire how to live without her best friend.

Like every other morning, she dressed, filled her thermos with coffee, and threw on her hooded sweatshirt and hat. It was the same routine every day, and while others might not understand, it worked for her. Knowing she'd get to talk to Nash seemed the only motivation strong enough to get her out of bed and moving.

A fog blanketed the cemetery as she parked her bike, making the gravestones difficult to see, but Maggie knew them by heart. She dropped to her bottom in front of Nash's headstone and opened the thermos, pouring a small amount of coffee into the lid and placing it at the base of his slab. She sipped her half from the container while steam coiled from his into the cool March air.

"Someone moved into the old Nanomaker house. Maybe a few some-ones. All guys. Remember the lumberyard at the top of the mountain? The one at the end of town? I think they work there. They all have trucks that say McCullough Lumber."

She didn't know how she felt about a bunch of young guys moving in next-door. If they were cool, she was cool. But last night the one pulled up blasting music. She preferred the silence.

"I need to buy a new rake. I can't find ours."

She passed the better half of the hour making small talk and sipping coffee. When his portion stopped steaming, she knew it was time to go.

Her fingers pressed a kiss over his engraved name and she stood. She had a rule that every weekend she had to do something productive. Yesterday, she cleaned out the hall closet. Today, she'd do the flowerbeds.

It was important to keep up on the house, because too much neglect attracted the concern of others. Concern provoked house calls, and house calls led to unwanted advice and business cards with the local shrink's name and number embossed on the front.

On the way home, she stopped at McGinty's to pick up a rake. Trans-porting it on her bike wasn't the easiest task, but she managed. By the time she arrived home, the sun was high overhead and the day had warmed, which was a lovely change from the typical damp and rainy air this time of year.

After bagging the leaves, she dragged out the old lawnmower, filled the small tank with gas, and gave the cord a hard pull. The mower clicked, sputtered and then seemed to burp at her, as if to say *I don't think so.*

"Come on, you old piece of crap." She yanked again, greeted by another gurgle.

She stabbed her finger into the starter button three more times and gripped the bar. Angling her body, she jerked the cord as hard as she could. The mower released a congested *vrummm* that quickly disappeared.

"Having trouble?"

Maggie sprung back and stumbled over her feet as she spun on her heels. A man stood on the other side of the picket fence separating her driveway from the neighbor's yard.

He held up his hands in a signal of peace. "Sorry. I didn't mean to sneak up on you."

She'd have to adjust to having neighbors again. Was this guy her neighbor? She recognized him from the day before. Where were the others? Did he have roommates?

"Is your mower not working?"

Realizing she'd been staring silently for over a minute, she blinked and dropped her gaze back to the lawnmower. "It's old."

He placed a hand between the pickets and leapt over the fence with surprising dexterity. "I can take a look if you want."

She swallowed, unsure if she wanted to invite a complete stranger into the reserved sanctum that was her yard, but he was already across her driveway that acted as a buffer between their homes, and opening the gate to her private backyard, so she didn't seem to have much of a choice.

Stepping back, she asked, "I'm sorry, who are you?"

"Ryan Clooney, your new neighbor." He smiled and a dimple formed a divot in the gold stubble along his jaw. "You live here, right?"

She nodded, trying to decide if she'd call his hair blond or red. Maybe strawberry blond?

"Do those other guys live with you?"

He looked over his shoulder then turned back to her and frowned. "Other guys?"

"The ones here yesterday. I thought I counted three of you."

"Oh, they're my cousins. No, it's just me living here. They were just giving me a hand. They live up on the mountain."

She frowned. People lived up there? She always assumed it was just the lumberyard and a bunch of windmills. There were so many trees, she supposed a house or two could be hiding in the forest. Mountain folk.

Then it occurred to her. "Clooney as in *Liam* Clooney?"

He smiled again, showing off a mouthful of perfectly straight teeth. Another dimple. "That's my dad. Do you know him?"

The Clooneys had been involved in the notorious card game that lost Nash's grandfather his pub. Not since the death of Wild Bill Hickok had there been a more famous hand of poker than when Liam Clooney beat Caleb O'Malley and stole the bar the very next day, in the biggest brawl Center County ever saw. Nash would have hated living next to a Clooney.

"No, I don't know him."

He frowned. "But you recognized the name?"

She shrugged. "It's a small town. Everyone knows the story about Liam Clooney stealing O'Malley's Pub."

"He didn't steal it. He won it fair and square in a game of poker. Old

O'Malley went back on the bet though, so my dad and my uncles had to strongarm him a bit." He grinned as if it were some sort of rite of passage, the kind that put hair on a boy's chest and made him an instant man.

She supposed there were two sides to every story. As an O'Malley by marriage, it was safer if she didn't take one, especially with a rivalry as ancient as the one that forever changed the fate of O'Malley's pub.

His head tilted and he squinted at her with remarkably bright blue eyes. "You look familiar. Did you go to school around here?"

She really just wanted to cut her grass and get on with her day. "Yup. Go bears." She unscrewed the gas cap and added a touch more fuel to avoid eye contact. Her finger poked the starter again.

"Careful you don't flood the motor." He stepped closer, and she stepped back when his hand curled over the bar of the clutch. "What's your name?"

She hesitated. She wasn't looking for new friends, and she really didn't want to encourage people to poke around in her private life. But, being neighbors, he'd learn her name eventually.

"Maggie ... Harris."

It was the first time she gave her maiden name in years, and she didn't understand why. Maybe because he was a Clooney, and Clooneys and O'Malleys rarely got along. No need to form animosity where there wasn't any.

"Maggie Harris," he repeated, searching for a taste of familiarity in the sound. "Maggie... Maggie, Maggie, Maggie." He clicked his fingers and she flinched. "Mrs. Sheffield's biology, right?"

The name of her senior science teacher blasted her into the past. She suddenly recalled the scent of the lab and the view from those old metal-rimmed windows that barely let air in or out. Most of all, she remembered Nash sitting beside her, sharing her microscope and making her laugh when they should have been working. They both scarcely passed bio, but neither of them cared.

She looked at her neighbor again, waiting for a twinge of recognition. What was his name? Ryan? Yes, Ryan Clooney. Nothing.

"I had Sheffield, but..." She shrugged.

"I knew you looked familiar. We graduated the same year. What a small world."

Too small. She rubbed the back of her neck then shot a thumb over her shoulder. "Well, it was nice meeting you—again—but I gotta get back to work."

"Oh. Right." He turned his inspection to the lawnmower, which at least took the attention away from her for a moment.

She was brutal when it came to social graces, but the normal back and forth that came so easily to others proved excruciating for her, especially since Nash died. It seemed the longer she lived alone, the worse she became at interacting with others.

"Is this the first time you've used it this winter? Sometimes if they sit awhile, they take some cajoling to start back up." He flipped the mower on its side to inspect the undercarriage.

"I'm sure I can figure it out."

He paused and glanced over his shoulder. "Really?"

No, not really, but if he fixed her lawnmower, she'd feel indebted to be friendly in return. She'd have to wave and be extra neighborly. What was wrong with her? Like waving was some incredible hardship.

Her mouth formed a tight-lipped smile. What she lacked in congeniality and manners, he had in spades. The grass wasn't even that long. She just wanted to clean up the scraps she couldn't get with the rake.

"It's old. I should probably just put it on the curb." *Never.* That lawnmower had been a gift to Nash on their first wedding anniversary, the same year he got her a pair of turquoise earrings—earrings she never wore anymore.

"I think it's salvageable. It might just need a new—"

"It's fine," she blurted, her anxiety spiking out of her in disproportionate panic. "It's fine," she repeated more calmly and forced a more convincing smile.

He slowly tipped the mower right side up on the grass as he stood. "Okay." He took a cautious step back. "Well, I'm right next-door if you change your mind."

She nodded and turned her back to him, bailing on the niceties she couldn't manage. Sensing his lingering presence, she tried to ignore him and the mower. She raked a tumble of leaves from the corner of the yard, but there seemed nothing left to do aside from cutting the grass.

Giving her nosey neighbor enough time to go back to his side of the fence, she raked a while longer, then tried the lawnmower again. Head down and focusing strictly on willing the damn thing to work, she gritted her teeth and gave the lawnmower cord three more yanks.

"You stupid piece of crap, *come on!*" The cord whipped back, and this time not even a gurgle escaped. Kicking the metal base with her boot, she growled in frustration. "Damnit!"

"Let me give you a hand."

"Jesus!" She nearly sprung out of her skin when her neighbor reappeared, as if he'd been watching her the entire time. Hadn't he gone away yet? "It's no use it's—" Her words cut off as he marched back into her yard and grabbed the cord. Intrusive much?

"Sometimes it's just a matter of reach." He wrenched the cord and the fickle mower came to life, purring like a kitten. He offered an apologetic smile and shrugged. "I have longer arms than you."

Another joyous part of being vertically challenged, she thought. "Thanks."

He tipped his head toward the clutch as he held the bar to keep the motor running. "You wanna grab this?"

She glanced at his large hands, roughened by work and freckled at the knuckles. She hadn't looked at a set of male hands in forever. Strange how she forgot the way hair dusted the backs. Nash always had callouses from fingerpicking his guitar. She hadn't thought about that in a long time and shouldn't think about it now. Her fingers closed around the bar, the spring lever pressed into her palm as he let go of the tension.

"Let me know if you need help with anything else."

She hadn't needed help in the first place. He just barged in and took over. Of course, now the mower was working, but she would have fixed it eventually.

"Thanks."

This time he didn't linger. He hopped the fence into his yard and disappeared into his house. As she zigzagged over the lawn making quick work of cutting the grass, her gaze kept returning to his back door. Maybe she should get a privacy fence.

She hadn't always been so antisocial but people came with emotions, and she preferred to feel as little as possible these days. Having no attachments safeguarded her heart against future loss. If she had nothing, she had nothing to lose, which was exactly why she pushed people away, including her sister.

She used to be a happy, easygoing person. Her monotonous days kept her moving without the pressure of others' expectations.

She was breathing. She was moving. She interacted here and there. And while her family viewed her isolated existence as a tragic shift from what it was, they would never know how much the slightest effort took out of her.

There was a fine line between living and giving up completely. Most days it was a battle to get out of bed. That's why she started taking daily trips to the cemetery. If she could trick herself into thinking she could spend the morning with Nash, share a cup of coffee with him, and talk about her boring life, she had a sliver of something to look forward to. Otherwise there was nothing. Just emptiness.

She didn't want *other* people to fill the void. She wanted Nash and he was gone. He would always be gone, and now, she would always be alone.

Maybe that wasn't healing, because the pain pretty much stayed the same. But she also wasn't spiraling, as she never did anything to risk the pain getting worse. Her static life gave her a sense of control that she could handle. She didn't care what others thought she needed. This was the only way she knew to survive.

She raked up the grass clippings and hauled the bags of debris to the curb. Nash loved when the weather broke, and they could use the firepit again. He loved strumming his guitar and staring across the flames at her while he sang classics like Johnny Cash or Bob Dylan or The Stones.

She dragged both lawn chairs out of the shed—*his and hers*. Her eyes filled with unshed tears as she sat in hers staring at the empty one on the other side of the stone firepit. Empty. Everything was empty.

Her throat grew tight as she forced herself to sit there, feeling the void in some masochistic attempt at acceptance. Her fingers traced the cold stones that formed a ring over the scorched earth, and she stared blankly at the ash and leaves gathered in the hollow cavern.

She'd give anything to hear his voice in that moment. Her eyes closed as she slowly rocked her shoulders. Birds squawked in the distance, and she could almost hear his voice pitching over Neil Young's lyrics as he alternated between the acoustic guitar and harmonica.

"Keeps me searchin' for a heart of gold..." she whispered, her voice cracking over the lyric. *"And I'm getting old..."*

Her gaze lifted to the gray sky, her eyes seeking some form of acknowledgement from whatever god existed above. Cynicism mingled with anger as a tear slid into her hair. Grief formed an icy web in her chest.

Why had the universe taken him from her? Why not take someone evil? Nash was good. He was everything to her. He was the other half of her soul. Without him, she was broken. Incomplete. Lost. Nothing.

When the sun set, the temperature dropped and she moved inside. She had a habit of forgetting to eat, so she indulged in her first meal of the day, a cold ham and cheese sandwich on white bread, chased by half a fifth of whiskey.

Once the alcohol dulled her senses, she ended up sitting at his piano. Her body curved under the weight of her grief, all the sharp, broken pieces of her heart cutting into her in ways even alcohol couldn't numb.

Her head hung low as she traced her fingers over the worn keys. The soft plunking *ping, ping, ping* of a single white key filled the silence, the sound lonely and all too fitting.

"I can't remember if I cried, when I read about his widowed bride..." Her hand slid off the keys falling into her lap. *"...something touched me deep inside ... the day the music died..."*

A soft sob shivered out of her. She knew better than to sit at his piano.

Their home had never been a quiet place. Nash *was* music. He played, sang, and constantly listened. Music filled every corner of their life. Everything about him screamed rhythm and blues. When he died, he took the joy of music with him. Now all her favorite songs only brought sorrow in his absence. And all the things that he used to sing sat like dusty relics in a painfully hollow room.

She pressed the key again, and that solitary sound punched into her soul like a bullet. Sometimes she wished the shock of her pain was enough to knock her out cold, but there would be no sleeping for her on a night like tonight. When she let herself slip this far down the rabbit hole, the only peace she found came in drunken oblivion.

Taking her trusty bottle of whiskey, she dragged herself up the stairs to bed, passing out sometime around four in the morning with her phone in her hand and Nash's recorded voice filling the darkness.

CHAPTER 5

"What is the world coming to?" Ryan's mother cried, falling into an empty booth at the pub and dabbing her eyes with a paper napkin. She sniffed and unscrewed the lids of several ketchup bottles gathered on a round tray. "I just can't bear it. We're all getting so old. Who will be next?"

Ryan, trying to earn his way back into his mum's good graces and perhaps get his hands on the meals she supposedly had earmarked for him in her freezer, attempted to match her devastation with appropriate sympathy.

"He had a good, long life, Mum. Try to think of how happy he was all those years up on the mountain."

Angering the red, creped skin under her eyes with a stiff napkin, she nodded. "I know he seemed rough around the edges, but he really was a sweet boy. We all loved him so much, you know, even if we didn't always show it." She sniffed and shook her head. "I should have told him more often that he was a good boy."

"I'm sure he knew, Mum." Ryan bussed a table and carried the tray to the kitchen, returning a moment later with a damp rag. "He's in a better place now."

She formed the sign of the cross just as his Aunt Colleen showed up with a box of cabbage. Ryan quickly relieved her the burden and took it to the back.

"Thanks, love. I'm growin' feeble in my old age." Colleen slid into the booth across from his mum, rattling all the ketchup bottles.

"You're like an ox in a china shop," his mum snapped, stilling the teetering bottles before they fell. "Do you mind?"

Aunt Col stuck her tongue out at her sister. "Quit your complaining.

Ryan, love, be a dear and fetch your favorite aunt a beer. Something dark."

He filled a pilsner at the tap and delivered it to the booth. "Mum, you want anything?"

"Only my youth back."

Aunt Col rolled her eyes and took a sip of her beer. "Kelly has another art show this weekend, and Maureen and Frank are planning to check it out. That leaves us in charge of St. Paddy's Day, and there's no way I'm luggin' all that corned beef and fifty pounds of potatoes to and from my car. You'd think we'd have half the brains to figure out a menu that was easier to transport by now."

"That's the menu, Colleen. That's always been the menu." His mother sniffled, topping off the ketchup bottles. "Besides, you love having everyone fawn all over your corned beef."

"I do make it the best." Aunt Col frowned. "You're covered in hives, Rose. What the heck have you been doing?"

"I've been crying. I just can't believe he's gone."

His aunt's eyes went wide. "*Who's* gone?"

His mother let out a whimper and waved the question away as she blew her nose into the crumpled paper napkin.

Ryan cleared his throat and rolled his eyes. "Rufus."

Aunt Col's green eyes bulged. "You're crying like this over a dog?"

"Oh, you wouldn't understand. Such an unfeeling wench you can be."

"I am not unfeeling. The dog was older than Stonehenge, Rose. Maureen isn't even this broken up over it. Get a grip!"

"You were never an animal lover."

"I love animals just fine." She grabbed a rag and wiped down the refilled bottles of ketchup. "The silly dog was missing a leg. It was lucky Frank took pity on it all those years ago. It had a fine life, and now it's time to move on."

His mother scoffed. "I suppose we'll say the same thing when you go. Oh, well, she had a fine life, and now it's time to move on."

"Go ahead. I've got no complaints."

"Oh, please, that's all you do is complain!"

"Yes, and when I'm gone, I'll finally be gettin' some peace and quiet."

Ryan left the two bickering sisters and did a quick inventory in the back but not before he heard his aunt hiss, "We all know you're only using this as an excuse to cry over something else. Every mother eventually has an empty nest, Rose. Be glad your son still lives here."

"All the way on the other end of town!"

Ryan was keeping a list of questions to run by Kelly and jotted down a note about condiments. St. Patrick's Day was one of the pub's busiest nights of the year, and this would be his cousin Kelly's first time missing it since he took over the bar. Luckily, his mum and aunt knew what they were doing. They had run the bar back when he and all his cousins were still kids.

He poked his head out of the kitchen window. "How many kegs do you think we'll need for Tuesday?"

"Twelve."

"Two dozen."

He added a question about beer to his list for Kelly.

"Twelve won't be enough," his mother argued. "You'll go through a keg an hour. And that's just the dark stuff. Then there's the shite you have to dye green for all the rookies."

"Two dozen is absurd. Not everyone wants a pint. Don't forget to stock up on your Irish whiskies and creams," Aunt Col shouted and he added another question to the list.

"What the hell kind of party do you think this is, Colleen? People aren't comin' to have cordials. They're comin' to get pissed."

The two continued to quarrel hardly paying any attention to him as he mumbled, "I'll call Kelly."

He dialed his cousin and got his voicemail. "Hey, Kel, it's Ryan. I know you're busy at the studio, but when you get a sec, give me a call. I want to go over the bar order for Tuesday."

His aunt and mum had moved on to other topics as they refilled the saltshakers. He should run some errands for the things he knew they needed while they were here to cover the bar.

"What time does Restaurant Supply close?" he asked.

"Eight."

"Nine."

"Lord, give me strength," he mumbled. "I'm taking a ride to get the meat and potatoes. I shouldn't be long."

"Take the company card." Colleen dug in her oversized pocketbook and produced the O'Malley's Visa. "Don't lose that. Kelly trusted me with it."

"I won't. Call me if you think of anything else." Relieved simply to get away from their bickering, and in no real rush to get back, he took the scenic route through town.

Center County was a straight shot off the mountain. A cleverly titled central street, named Main Street, hosted all the local businesses. They weren't fancy and everyone knew everyone else's business, but there was something special about living in a small town, something that felt like home even when outsiders visited for the first time.

Restaurant Supply was a mile outside of town. The large warehouse sold everything from handcarts to crème brulee. It catered to diners and local colleges. By no means was it a place regular people grocery shopped, but the women in his family sort of lived there. One, because they had a membership through O'Malley's. And two, because their family dinners consisted of over fifty ravenous Irish men, women, and children. The mums only shopped in bulk.

He parked beside several food trucks boasting local restaurant names from nearby towns. Knowing very little about the food service business, he observed everyone else when he entered.

Rather than shopping carts, patrons pushed oversized handcarts. He found one by the automatic doors and steered it inside.

His shoulders lifted at the instant temperature drop. It was an ice box. He should have worn his coat, but he'd left in such a rush he only wore a thin thermal shirt and jeans.

Wanting to avoid freezing his biscuits off, he pushed the cart quickly along the outer aisle, reading each hanging sign. The meat department was the coldest aisle yet. He loaded the cart with over eighty pounds of salt-cured brisket. Then he went in search of potatoes.

The checkout seemed chaotic. Clerks moved around carts with wireless scanner guns, ringing each customer out and sending them to a counter with a tallied receipt to pay. He awkwardly followed what others were doing and tried not to look out of place.

A large man, with wrinkles carved from a permanent grimace, scanned his items. "That all?"

"Yup."

The man stared at him expectantly. "I need your membership card."

"Oh." Fingers frozen to the bone, Ryan could hardly pull the plastic card from the folds of his wallet.

The man scanned the membership card and waved him out of the way. Ryan raised a brow, never understanding perpetually grumpy people. Was *have a nice day* such a difficult sentence to manage?

His thoughts jerked to a stop as he recognized the small woman ringing out customers, and his mouth curved with a grin.

Perched on a battered wooden stool, bundled in a bulky thermal jacket, sat his neighbor, Maggie. Her fingers were partially covered in wool gloves with the tips cut off and her head was in the same beanie cap she'd had on the other day.

A rosy flush tinged her cheeks, and from what he could tell, she didn't wear a speck of makeup. She looked nothing like the girls he knew, which might be why he found her so captivating.

He steered his cart forward, waiting for her to finish ringing out the man ahead of him and make eye contact. He used the time to study her. She didn't flounce her hair or bat her eyes. There was nothing stereotypically girlie about her, yet he found her unquestionably adorable.

She seemed to have a gritty stubbornness about her. If he hadn't insisted on helping her the other day, she'd have stayed out there battling that lawnmower until dark. Headstrong seemed a fitting word for her.

It made sense that she'd work in a place that employed mostly men. Maggie Harris was a class A tomboy by the looks of it. The job fit with her no-nonsense attire and cosmetic free appearance. He wondered if she hated when one of her coworkers pulled out a chair for her at a staff meeting or held a door for her.

He glanced back at the guy with the scanner. Maybe she worked here because these guys didn't do those things.

The customer in front of him pushed his overloaded cart toward the automatic doors and her gaze lifted. Only she didn't smile when she recognized him. In fact, she did the exact opposite.

He probably just caught her off guard. "Howdy, neighbor." He pushed his cart closer to her register and handed her the bill.

"What are you doing here?" She glanced at his cart. "That's an obscene amount of potatoes."

"St. Paddy's day is coming up. It's for the bar."

She frowned. "The bar?"

"Yeah, O'Malley's. Remember?" Had their conversation been that forgettable?

"Oh. Right." She scanned the bill.

He tried to think of something interesting to say. "You know, it's actually reading the white space in between, not the black lines."

She stared at him in confusion, frown lines etched between her brows. "Huh?"

"The barcode. People think the black lines are the code, but it's the negative space actually." He tapped his temple. "I'm a fountain of useless knowledge."

"How ... lucky for you."

He handed her the O'Malley's credit card. "Do you like trivia? We have trivia night at the bar in the spring."

"Not really." She swiped his card.

"You should come by next Tuesday. I'll be working. Neighbors get a green beer on the house."

She frowned. "So, did you take it over after your dad?"

"No. It's sort of a family business, but my cousin runs it. He's been traveling a lot for his other business lately. I'm helping out. He's a local artist. You might have seen his work around. His name's Kelly McCullough."

"Never heard of him."

She never heard of Kelly? That was a first. He didn't know a girl in Center County who hadn't dated his cousin or at least had a crush on him, especially someone in their age group. Before settling down and marrying Ashlynn, his cousin was the town player.

The charge went through, and he wished the process took a while longer so he could talk to her more. When she handed back the card and receipt, he noticed how tiny her hands were. Nails, bitten down to nubs, peeked from the cutoff tips of her gloves.

He hesitated, carefully folding the receipt into his wallet. "So, you work here?" He inwardly winced. There were a million other things he'd rather ask, but everything seemed too personal. Best to keep it superficial.

"Yeah. This is my glamorous life."

The corner of his mouth hitched into a partial smile. He liked her dry tone, sensing the sarcasm was strong with this one.

"You probably get a good discount."

"Ah, yes. A girl living alone always needs meats and paper products in bulk."

He perked up. Had she intentionally mentioned she lived alone? "I hear you. Well, now that we're neighbors, maybe we can barbeque together some time. I can handle my fair share of beef."

Her expression shuttered, and the energy shifted, telling him he'd crossed a line. But he wasn't clear how.

"Vegetarian?" he asked, uncertain what offended her. "I grill a mean vegetable kabob, too."

Her brow lowered. The energy still wasn't right. Where had he gone wrong?

He laughed nervously. "I'm just kidding."

She looked for the next customer, as if willing them to arrive sooner. "I like working here, because I don't have to deal with people. Customers are usually in and out."

As far as hints went, it was anything but subtle. "Got it." So much for being neighborly. "Well, I guess I'll see you around."

She gave a tight-lipped smile. "Probably."

Had he done something to make a bad impression or was this her norm? He wanted to watch her interact with someone else to see how she behaved with others. For a tiny thing, she sure had her guard up, and by guard, he meant huge freaking fortress.

He shoved the cart away, glancing back to see if she was watching him. She wasn't.

The bulky coat swallowed her figure but not enough to hide the way her posture slouched as she massaged tension from her neck. She moved her head from side to side, and when she let out a breath, a cloud of vapor passed her lips.

He frowned, wondering what would make her so overwrought?

That night when he got home, he found himself searching out his neighbor on social media, but Maggie Harris didn't exist online. Her mysterious secret identity only peaked his interest.

He found himself peeking out windows, trying to get a glimpse of her. He looked for any clue to fill in the puzzle. Around eleven that night, just as he was lying down for bed, a dim flash caught his eye. And then another.

He stood and went to the window, staring at Maggie's dark house, seeing nothing out of the usual. He was losing his mind.

Turning away, something flashed again and he pivoted back to the window. A light from the second floor illuminated lace curtains then the window went dark. Ten seconds later, it flicked on again—then off.

He frowned. "What the heck?"

On, off, on, off, on. It flickered back and forth every thirty seconds.

Should he go over there? Maybe it was faulty wiring. Was she even home? He didn't see her bike. What if she was home and something was wrong and she was sending a signal for help?

He knew the pattern for SOS in Morse code and that wasn't it, but maybe...

It went off again and he waited. The window stayed dark for some time, making him believe everything was fine. He needed to mind his own business and get some sleep.

Returning to bed, he mentally added curtains to his shopping list. Lying back in the dark, he folded his arms on his bare chest and stared at the ceiling. He should get a TV for up here.

The light flickered again, just as he was about to pass out. "All right, what the hell is going on?" He sat up and scowled at the window as the light went out. Was this going to happen all night?

He went downstairs and shouldered into a flannel shirt he'd tossed over the railing. Using the front door, something he rarely did, he skipped down his front steps and nearly broke his neck trying to manage his way up hers. Did she know her front porch light was out?

He knocked, glancing at the fixture. Maybe she couldn't reach the light to change the bulbs.

"Come on," he grumbled, stuffing his fists in his pajama pants and huddling into his flannel against the wind. He knocked again and the door opened.

Maggie looked up at him and frowned. "Yeah?"

"Are you okay?" He hadn't meant to snap, but it was colder than a witch's tit outside.

"What?"

Shivering, he jerkily pointed toward the second floor on the side of her house facing his. "I saw your light flickering. I didn't know if you were trying to get my attention or needed help or something."

Her freckled cheeks tinged with pink. It was the first time he saw her without her wool cap, and he couldn't help but admire her dusky brown hair that tumbled far past her narrow shoulders. There was so much of it. It swallowed her petite form, exposed in a worn white tank top and a pair of baggy cargo pants. No bra.

"I'm fine. Sorry if I woke you." She moved to shut the door, and he caught it with his hand.

"Wait. You should really have lights out here. I almost broke my neck coming up your steps." He noted her short height. "Do you have a bulb? I could replace it in thirty seconds."

All the color bleached from her face, and she gaped at him, as if he'd said something horrible like he ate puppies. They stared at each other for a solid minute. He would have laughed at the awkwardness, if she didn't look so distraught.

He was really screwing this up—and he wasn't sure how. He figured at this point he had no game with women, but game aside, he still had to live next to this chick.

"Uh, did I say something wrong?"

Her head shook but barely. He wasn't buying it. This girl did not like him, and he'd been nothing but nice.

"If we somehow started off on the wrong foot, Maggie, I'm sorry. I'm not some sort of neighbor from hell, so if I gave you that impression..." She was just staring at him. He sighed. "Can we start over?" When she said nothing, he held out his hand. "Hi, I'm Ryan Clooney."

Her brow crimped and she blinked, her gaze turning to the side and dropping to the floor. He definitely wasn't coming off the way he'd hoped.

His hand dropped once it was clear she didn't plan to shake it. "Look, I'm sorry if I somehow offended you—"

"You didn't."

"Are you sure?"

"I'm just not used to anyone living next-door."

He didn't buy her excuse. Someone lived there before him. There was something weird between them, and he couldn't figure it out.

"It's cold," she announced, drawing his gaze to her exposed arms and her barely covered chest. She abruptly crossed her arms, restricting his view.

"Sorry."

"I have to go."

"Sure. Goodnight." He was more confused then he'd been a few minutes ago.

This time when she shut the door, he didn't try to stop her. He turned and blindly guessed his way down her dark steps. He should write a letter to the township about getting some street lights out here.

When he returned to his bed, he made a decision. He'd be polite to his neighbor, but he wouldn't go out of his way to be friendly.

It actually made perfect sense. He thought she was cute, so of course there would be something off about her. He'd yet to find an attractive woman in Center County that was single, not his relative, and sane. Why should that change now?

between the two Irish families had been something her in-laws took very seriously, a betrayal they said they'd never forget.

But did anyone really care anymore? Caleb O'Malley Senior, owner and sole proprietor of the bar before it was lost in a poker game, now resided in an assisted living apartment and suffered severe dementia. Surely if he didn't remember the grudge, no one else would. However, it had been his son, Caleb, who lost the hand of cards and therefore, lost the bar.

Still debating her loyalties and the significance of vendettas half a century old, she pushed through the pub door and froze. Her in-laws' grudges vanished as blaring Irish music and half-drunk Irish men and women, painted every color of Ireland's flag, yelled from one end of the pub to the other. Bodies packed the place from wall-to-wall and the potent scent of sloshing beer assaulted her senses.

This was a mistake.

She quickly pivoted toward the door, but a hoard of patrons pushed in, driving her deeper into the pub like a stampede of thirsty caribou.

"Excuse me," she shouted against the current of the mob. A wall of green shirts drove her closer to the blaring music. "Pardon me. I'm trying to leave."

Her short legs stumbled backwards as the crowd corralled her toward the bar. No one heard her from her low altitude. *"Excuse me!"*

She ducked under a heavily tattooed arm and squeezed past a set of glittering green breasts smooshed into an orange tube top. Something knocked her headband loose, but she quickly caught it and righted it, scowling.

This had to be some sort of fire code violation. Didn't these people work? It was a Tuesday afternoon for crying out loud!

The entire parade seemed trapped between these walls. Long tables, bedecked in kelly green, skirted the back wall of a room mostly occupied by pool tables. Steaming chafing dishes covered every surface and patrons loaded their plates with Irish fare.

"Did you want to eat, love?"

Maggie turned, stunned someone finally acknowledged her presence in the tornado of chaos. Staring at the woman, Maggie's eyes widened. She looked to be in her last month of pregnancy and carrying triplets. What the hell was she doing in a rowdy bar?

"Sure," Maggie said, more out of pity for the woman's condition than any sort of hunger for corned beef and cabbage. "How much?"

"Five bucks and it's all you can eat until the food's gone."

Maggie dug out a five and paid. The woman tucked it into a small metal cash tray and handed her a plate, then stamped her hand with a green Celtic cross.

"*Lá Fhéile Pádraig sona duit!* Come back if you need another plate."

Maggie held her green paper plate to her chest and blinked wide-eyed at the wall of patrons lined up for food. A small redheaded child sprang through the crowd, her curly hair cascading down her back in flaming ringlets and her dress like that of a leprechaun's.

They let children in bars?

The girl, who couldn't be more than five, lifted to her toes that were encased in black dance shoes that laced up her calves and shouted in the pregnant woman's ear, "Mum *th*aid to get *th*omething to eat. *The'll* be out in a minute."

The pregnant woman nodded. "Can you watch the cash box?"

The little girl smiled with no front teeth, scooted into the booth, and clutched the box, dragging it close to her body. "Do I get to *th*ell the plates?"

"Yes, you get to sell the plates. Five dollars, okay?"

The little pixie-like creature stuck out a thumb. "Got it, Aunt *Th*ammy."

Maggie's heart fluttered at the little girl's sweet lisp and red curls. She found herself inexplicably smiling, her eyes slightly damp but not with tears of sadness. There was just something precious about the woman and child and the whole exchange.

"I'm starving," the pregnant woman said, stepping behind Maggie and speaking to her, as if the purchase of a plate somehow made them friends.

"Oh, you can go ahead of me," she offered.

"You sure?"

Maggie nodded and followed her to the food line. "I'm Sam McCullough. I don't think I've met you before."

"Maggie … Harris." It was the second time she'd given her birth name rather than her married name, but it felt right, being that they were in O'Malley's Pub a place where O'Malley's didn't typically visit.

Sam smiled. "I highly recommend the Irish soda bread and colcannon soup. My mother-in-law makes both, and I swear she adds crack or something to the recipe. They're totally addicting."

Maggie loaded up on both. "So, you're a McCullough? Your family owns the bar?"

She nodded. "My brother-in-law, Kelly, runs the pub, but he's away right now so we're all pitching in. It's sort of a family-owned business."

She thought about the girl she met that morning. "Are you related to the girl who works at the café, too?"

"Tallulah?" Sam's smile beamed with pride. "That's my daughter."

She could see it now in the shape of her nose and the angle of her eyes, but the younger girl's coloring was more olive. Sam was all ivory skin and freckles. "She's a beautiful girl. I bought a scone from her earlier."

Sam laughed. "Those scones are out of this world, aren't they? My mother-in-law makes them, too."

Maggie recalled how delicious the pastry was and found herself more excited to taste the pub food. She glanced back at the line, wishing she'd grabbed more Irish soda bread.

"Your mother-in-law can definitely bake."

Sam's eyes twinkled with laughter. "She'd love you on the spot if she heard you say that. Come on, we have a reserved table up front. You won't find a seat anywhere else at this point."

They passed the little girl minding the cash box. Another little girl had joined her, this one also dressed in an Irish dance costume but with blonde hair. A striking woman with red hair smiled at Sam as they passed by the table.

"Take your time, Sammy. I've got this covered for a while." The redheaded woman said as they waited for the crowd to shift.

Sam paused at the table. "Thanks for relieving me, Devil." She pointed to Maggie. "This is Maggie Harris. Maggie, this is my sister-in-law, Sheilagh."

"Another McCullough?" Maggie asked, shaking her hand. "Nice to meet you."

"Guilty. Well, I'm actually a Devereux now, but I bleed kelly green."

"Do you need a stamp?" the little girl with red curls asked.

"It's my turn," the small blonde girl argued.

"Alexia, give Gianna a chance," Sheilagh said, pulling the ink stamp free from a small-handed wrestling match.

Sam held out her hand to the child called Gianna. "Here, Gi, I need a stamp."

The little girl smeared the stamp across Sam's hand.

Sam smiled at the green smear on the back of her hand. "Perfect. Thank you, sweetie. Is your mum here?"

"No," little Gianna answered. "She's sick, but she said not to tell Aunt Col or Aunt Rose because they'll tell Mum-mum."

Sam and Sheilagh's eyes widened and their mouths curved into matching smirks, as if they shared a secret. "Really? Well, you tell your mum that her secret's safe with us, and we hope she feels better soon."

Sheilagh snorted. "Yeah, like in about nine months. I swear, those two can't share a toilet seat without procreating."

"Be nice," Sam said to her sister-in-law. "Poor Mallory probably wants to castrate Finn. She barely finished nursing the last one. Come on, Maggie. Let's eat."

Everyone seemed to get out of their way when an enormously pregnant woman waded through the crowd. "You're like Moses parting the Red Sea."

Sam grinned over her shoulder. "I shamelessly use my condition to its full advantage. Here we are."

Maggie blinked. This wasn't a table. It was an assembly. More than a dozen gorgeous men and women crowded around two cluttered banquet tables. Blue-eyed little boys and curly-haired Irish dancers dangled from knees and ate off green plates while their parents sipped jars of whiskey and beer.

A man with dark black hair and bright blue eyes stood, offering Sam his seat. The way he lovingly brushed her cheek with a kiss told Maggie this man was her husband. The blond next to him rose as well, waving Maggie to take his place.

"Oh, that's okay—"

"I insist," the man yelled over the music.

The overwhelming welcome to eat with a family she'd never met before should have felt awkward, but some inexplicable force propelled her to join them. Her usual nature would have commanded she bolt out of there. Everything about this day seemed off.

"This is Maggie Harris," Sam shouted to the group as a whole. "Maggie, this is my husband Colin, my brother-in-law Luke, his husband Tristan, my other brother-in-law Finn, then Alec, Becca, Braydon, Kate, Ant, Pat, Rosemarie, Paulie, Colleen, and these little ones are the offspring. I'd tell you their names, but chances are you won't remember."

Holy. Crap. She blinked, already confused about who was who. "You're all related?"

"Aye," a man with red hair and a charming smile confirmed. "Irish Catholic too, so we tend to breed like rabbits. Speaking of which, are you here alone?" He flinched when someone threw a crumpled green napkin at his face.

"Careful, love, we're a potent bunch. Share a spoon and you might find yourself in the family way," a voice whispered in her ear, but when she turned she only caught a glimpse of broad shoulders walking away.

The redheaded man sidled his way to the table, holding a beer mug and resting heavily on his elbow. "In case you missed it, name's Patrick." He gave another charming grin. "And today's my holiday."

A nervous smile twitched to her mouth. "Nice to meet you, Patrick." There was something familiar in his eyes, but she didn't want to stare and give the wrong impression.

"Pat's completing his residency at Penn," Sam informed. "You'll have to excuse him. When he visits home, the others tend to celebrate his return by buying him enough shots to tranquilize a rhino. He's been here since nine and wasted since ten."

Maggie made a silent *oh* and picked at her bread.

Sam grabbed the shirt of the blond man who gave Maggie his seat. "Stop right there, Finnegan. I was just speaking to *the informer* in the back."

The man, Finnegan, laughed. "And what news did my darling daughter spill?"

"She said Mallory's sick." Her knowing gaze met his. "Is she, or did you give her the family bug?"

He smirked proudly. "Guilty."

Sam smacked a kiss on his cheek. "Congratulations! Send Mallory my love."

He lowered an affectionate hand to her protruding belly. "They'll be best friends."

Sam smiled and Maggie's heart fluttered with something close to envy.

Though she was only a fly on the wall, for a brief second her heart wondered what it would be like to belong to such a family so surrounded by love and acceptance. It was tempting to pretend.

And just like that, a draft cut through the enveloping warmth. Her body chilled. Her fork stilled. The salty taste of corned beef turned to ash on her tongue.

They could have had this. It would have started with their children and grown from there.

She looked at the two older women occupying the head of the table. Twin heads of faded copper hair tinted in silver, leaned together as they laughed at something their younger relatives said. One glance and Maggie identified them as the matriarchs of this clan. Grandchildren, nieces, and nephews hung on their every word as they told stories and teased the younger generations.

She'd never known such a lovely sight, never saw family come together in such living color where flaws were unhidden and love seemed the only code. There was no struggle here, no pain, no loss, only togetherness. And she didn't belong.

Her chest tightened. She couldn't stay here.

A wave of emotion churned from her belly, burning up her throat like acid. She feared suddenly bursting into tears. Her hand noticeably shook as she placed her fork on the plate.

"Excuse me," she muttered, pushing up from the table and abandoning her seat before she fell apart in front of a bar full of strangers.

"Maggie?" Sam looked up, her eyes brimming with concern.

"I'm sorry. I have to go." The words choked out painfully as she swallowed down a sob.

Disoriented by the smothering crowd, she pushed through the throng and tried to find her way to the front of the bar. She couldn't see past the bodies crowding her and lost track of the stage since the band was no longer playing and ordinary pop-music filled the bar.

Speakers pumped from every corner. Voices buffeted every wall. So turned around, she couldn't discern which way led to the exit.

Her vision wavered as she spun in place. Where was the door? She couldn't breathe. She was going to lose it if she didn't get somewhere quiet soon.

"Do you have a stamp?" the little blonde girl called as Maggie stumbled back towards the pool table room.

Sheilagh frowned as she noted her distress. "Maggie? Are you okay?"

She nodded and rushed past the food line toward a back hall and what she hoped was an exit. A crowd gathered in a narrow corridor. Women waiting to use the restroom leaned into the wood paneled wall. Men filtered in and out of the door labeled LADS. The door at the end of the hall said PRIVATE. No exit in sight.

The walls closed in on her, and panic climbed through her like spiders. Strangers stared and whispered as she twisted, trying to go back the way she came but finding her getaway blocked. Shallow breaths left her lungs shortchanged as she frantically searched for an escape and resisted the urge to scream.

Losing it, her fingers tunneled through her hair and found her scalp sweaty. More people piled into the lines at the bathrooms, and as a man exited the men's room, she stumbled out of his way, sinking deeper into the narrow hall until her back hit the door labeled PRIVATE and it opened.

She pivoted and came face-to-face with familiar blue eyes.

"Maggie?"

Bewildered, she stared up at her neighbor as he held a box of commercial paper towels. What was his name? Her labored breathing lifted her chest.

Another man exited the men's room and bumped her shoulder. Her neighbor frowned as she caught the wall, a tear jostling past her lashes.

"Hey, watch it," her neighbor yelled at the drunk patron. He shoved the box to the floor and caught her elbow. "Are you drunk?"

She shook her head. Drunk would be so much better. "I can't … breathe."

He looked over her shoulder, searching the congested hallway. "Can't breathe like you're having an allergic reaction and I need to find an EpiPen, or can't breathe like you're having a panic attack?"

"Get me the fuck out of here," she practically sobbed and he nodded, bolting into action.

Gripping her upper arm, he used his body as a shield between her and the crowd and barked out orders at the drunks standing in their way. "Move!"

Her short legs moved double-time to keep up with his longer strides as he towed her through the congested hall. People stared, but they were moving too fast for her to register their faces.

When they reached the pool table room, the heat from all the chaffing dishes of food hit her like a wall of steam. She drew back at the multiplied voices and screeching music.

Her neighbor cursed when he saw the swelling mob. "This way. I'll get you out."

He plucked a set of keys out of his pocket and pulled her down the hall toward the end of the bathroom line. Unlocking a nondescript wooden door, he pulled her inside.

When he shut the door behind them, her eyes adjusted to the dark. The music and voices muffled, her jagged breathing suddenly too loud as she drew in a shallow breath of stale air. Then she caught the clean scent of his clothes.

"Watch your step." His hand lowered from her arm to her hand, and his fingers laced with hers. "There's a flight of stairs."

She followed him up a narrow staircase, and he flipped a switch when they reached the top. An old lamp flickered on and she blinked, her eyes adjusting to the dim amber light.

It was some sort of a loft. A drafting table sat in the center of the room. A couch was shoved in the corner. Canvases, draped in dusty white sheets, piled against every wall.

"What is this place?"

"It's an apartment above the bar. Don't worry. No one lives here. My cousin just uses it to store his art."

He released her hand and went to the wall where a cabinet stood beside a large wash sink. She caught her breath and lowered to the small love seat.

He returned, holding two glasses, one filled with clear water, the other filled with something darker. "I wasn't sure which you'd want."

"What is it?"

"Tullamore Dew."

She took the whiskey and swallowed it down in one shot.

He cautiously sat beside her. "Did something happen—other than that asshole crashing into you down there?"

She shook her head, trying to remember what insane impulse made her come here today. "Can I have some more?" She held out the empty glass.

"Are you driving?"

She frowned, then remembered normal people drove. Only she didn't. "No, I walked."

He retrieved the bottle, bringing it back to the couch and topped her off. "That's a pretty far walk. Do you have a car?"

She shook her head and sipped the whiskey this time. "Not anymore."

"Did you lose your license?"

"No, I lost my car." And her entire world. "I prefer walking or riding my bike."

She felt him staring but kept her eyes on the floor, her hands folded around the glass. He tapped one of the shamrocks attached to her headband. "I like this. You didn't strike me as the kind of woman to get into the holiday."

She shrugged. "It's sort of a tradition."

"I've been here for every St. Paddy's Day since I was a kid. But I think this is the first time I've ever seen you here."

Maybe it was the whiskey or getting away from the crowd but something about his voice soothed her. She felt safer here and only slightly petrified of having to go back through that crowd to get out.

"This is my first time in O'Malley's," she confessed.

"Really? Yet, you drink whiskey like a seasoned veteran."

She had a lot of practice. Probably too much.

"How come you waited all this time to check it out?"

If she told him who she really was, would he ask her to leave? "Can we stay here for a few more minutes?"

"As long as you need." He added another finger of Tully to her glass.

Her lips pressed tight, and she took another sip. "My name isn't actually Maggie Harris. Well, it was, but no one's called me that for years."

He drew back, and only then, did she realize how close they were sitting. "Are you married?"

"Widowed. My name's Maggie O'Malley."

His face slightly paled. "Oh, shit…"

"Thanks. And thanks for..." She waved a hand at the empty apartment.

"Any time, neighbor."

She smiled and it seemed as sincere as it was beautiful.

A strange fizzy sensation came over him, and he had the urge to lean down and kiss her. His head lowered and her eyes widened.

She staggered back. "What are you doing?"

Jarred by the panic in her voice, he stilled. *Totally inappropriate.* What was wrong with him? "I'm sorry. I just... We were talking and the lights are dim. I wasn't really thinking about anything other than how pretty you look, and now I can see I'm only making things worse. I swear, I'm not some creeper you have to worry about. It's just been a really long time since..." He forced his mouth to close before he totally emasculated himself. "That was really pervy of me, wasn't it? God, men suck, don't they? I'm totally embarrassed. I just had a temporary lapse of judgement." He swallowed. "Please say something."

Her mouth opened but no sound came out.

Voices from the bar below broke the silence as the door at the bottom of the stairs opened. "Ryan, are you up there?"

His spine stiffened at the sound of his mother's voice. "That's my mum."

Maggie stepped onto the cement landing. "I don't want anyone to see me."

"Especially her," he agreed. His mother would automatically assume something was going on if she found him up here with a woman. Footsteps sounded behind him. "You'd better go."

She nodded and mouthed, *Thanks.*

"Ryan? Who left the bloody light on?"

He smiled at Maggie and hissed, "Run."

She darted down the steps, and the back light kicked on. He shut the door just as his mother made it to the top step of the loft.

"Hey, Mum."

"For Pete's sake, Ryan. We asked you to go for napkins twenty minutes ago. Everyone's down there lookin' like a bunch of dirty vagrants. The kids have meat drippings running down their necks, especially that one with the weak chin. What the hell are you doing up here anyway?" Her eyes dropped to the bottle in his hand. "Hand it over."

He passed her the bottle, and she twisted off the cap, tipping it back to her lips for a long sip.

"*Whooo!* That'll add a bit of bounce to your tits. I'm keepin' this."

He followed her downstairs and gathered the box of paper products he'd left by the office. The band was once again playing and the crowd was lit.

His cousins crowded around the front tables, every one of them toasted except poor pregnant Sammy. He searched for Mallory but didn't see her.

A loud cheer erupted as his Aunt Maureen and Uncle Frank appeared, back from their trip to visit Kelly's art show. His mother and the aunts typically did everything together, so whenever one of the three sisters left town for more than a few hours, they celebrated their return like V-J Day, only with less soldiers and fewer people kissing in the streets.

"What the hell happened while I was gone? You're all a mess!" Aunt Maureen gathered the plaid shawl around her arms and used it to wipe Declan's mouth. "Lachlan, you're worse than your twin brother. Get over here so Mum-mum can clean up your face. Finnegan, what do you mean letting my grandbabies walk around with their wee cherub cheeks filthier than landfills. People will talk!"

"Sorry, Mum." Finn turned to him. "Took you long enough." Snatching a package of napkins out of the box, Finn tore them open and began wiping down the greasy faces of his four kids. The other cousins did the same with their children.

Ryan sat for a few minutes and managed to shove down a plate of food while listening to his aunt regale the others about their adventure to the city. Kelly's art show seemed to be going great, which pleased and frightened Ryan.

What if Kelly decided to stay in the city? Who would run O'Malley's? He didn't mind taking a shift here and there, but this managing stuff was for the birds. He got his fill at the lumberyard. Working here was only supposed to be temporary—a favor to his cousin.

Besides, Kelly's wife, Ashlynn, ran a farm and the town market. They couldn't do that from Philadelphia. Ryan was overthinking things. Eventually Kelly would return to Center County and everything would be back to normal.

His family lingered at the bar until late that night. The women were the first to fade, and Uncle Frank acted as the designated driver this year, carting everyone's drunk asses home. All the grandkids were sleeping at the big house with Aunt Maureen, who said a week away from her grandbabies was simply too much to bear.

The pub closed at two on the dot. Ryan should have known better than to suggest he might get out earlier. Not that Maggie had taken him up on his offer. She hadn't. The woman couldn't have been less interested. *And* he tried to kiss her.

His face flamed every time he relived the humiliating moment in his head. The fact that he was still thinking about her, despite her disinterest, only proved how out of touch with the opposite sex he'd become. *Get a clue.*

Beer and green flair drenched the floors. Sue, the lead bartender, closed out the register as he used the push broom to sweep a disgusting pile of beer battered crap into the center of the floor. They worked until three in the morning, deciding the rest could wait until daylight.

By the time he drove home, the roads were empty. He had work at the lumberyard in four hours.

Pulling into his driveway, he parked and rested his eyes for a moment, trying to dredge up the strength to make it into the house and up to his bed. He sighed and frowned when something moved in the shadows.

Narrowing his eyes, he leaned forward and squinted at Maggie's backyard. What the hell was he looking at?

A fire smoldered in the stone ring in his neighbor's yard, mostly glowing embers that should have been extinguished hours ago. But that wasn't what caught his attention. He was more worried about the collapsed body on the lawn.

"What the...?" He hit the high beams. "Oh, boy."

She lay on her back in the grass, wrapped in a wool blanket. A bottle of something clutched in her hand. Possibly passed out.

He killed the engine and hopped out of the truck. This couldn't be good.

CHAPTER 8

"*Maggie?*" Ryan hopped the fence into her driveway and entered her backyard. "You okay?"

"Hmm?" Her head turned and she grinned at the sight of her neighbor. Ryan? She thought his name was Ryan. "Hey, neighbor." Whoa. The world tipped sideways then quickly righted itself. "Did you feel that?"

He crossed her lawn and looked down at her. He was really tall. "What are you doing?"

She held up the bottle of Jameson and nearly clunked herself in the head. "Lookin' at stars."

"It's three-thirty in the morning."

"It is?"

"Yeah. And about forty degrees out here. You're going to get sick."

"But look how pretty the sky is tonight."

He grabbed a log from the pile, tossing it into the firepit. Hot, red embers danced into the air like fireflies. She smiled, appreciating the added warmth.

He rubbed his hands together and crouched beside her. "Did you go out tonight?"

"I bought bananas and beer." Just like Nash wanted.

He tugged the wool blanket around her shoulders. "Your cheeks are freezing."

"It's okay. They're numb, so I can't feel them anymore."

He sat beside her, chafing his hands and blowing on his fingers. Popping the collar of his coat, he held out a hand. "Can I have a sip?"

She handed him the bottle and he laughed.

"Figures, you're a Jameson girl."

"It's an O'Malley thing. You wouldn't understand."

She watched him tip it back, drinking right from the mouth of the

64

bottle. His hair looked more blond than red at night. She liked his beard. Was it a rule that lumberjacks had to have beards? "Are you good at climbing trees?"

He laughed. "What?"

"You're a lumberjack, right, for McCullough Lumber?"

"I'm a junior partner. I run the company. My cousin runs the lumber-jacks, though we never actually call them that." He rolled to his back and lay beside her. "What are we looking at?"

She pointed. "I'm trying to figure out if that red one is a plane or a planet."

"Has it moved?"

"They're all moving at this point."

He screwed the cap back on the whiskey. "No more booze for you."

She leaned closer to him. He was so warm that his body heat seeped through the blanket covering her.

Then she realized what he said and scoffed. "Who are you, the booze police? That's *my* bottle and don't think I won't kick your ass to get it back. I may be small, but I'm scrappy."

"I have no doubt you'd win in a fight. Here." He handed over the bottle, but she wasn't thirsty now.

The stars were so bright over Center County. Sometimes it looked like they were right on top of the houses. She and Nash used to stare at the sky all the time. It had been forever since she'd spent a night out here.

"Do you think that's where we go when our spirit leaves our soul?" she mumbled, her stare softening as she looked at what might be the Big Dipper.

"Maybe. I don't know."

Her body relaxed in the chilled grass and her mind settled. She could fall asleep out here. Probably catch pneumonia but still. It was peaceful.

She softly hummed a familiar tune, not realizing what it was until the words fell out. *"And I think it's gonna be a long, long time..."*

"Till touch down brings me round again to find..." Ryan's voice followed, soft and unobtrusive. *"I'm not the man they think I am at home. Oh no no no..."*

Her head turned, her hair pulling in the damp blades of grass as she smiled at him. *"I'm a rocket mannn..."*

His mouth pulled into a half smile, the fog of their whiskey-scented breath mingling between them. *"Rocket man burning out his fuse up here alone."*

"Where did you come from?" she whispered, her thoughts jumbled and lost somewhere between her memories and reality, between here and outer space.

"I just got here." His stare held hers like a hug, warming her from the inside out.

"I feel like I know you."

He chuckled. "I live next-door."

Her head shook. "No, more than that." She felt herself leaning closer to his body's warmth. He seemed to be leaning in as well. "I feel like we knew each other before."

"We didn't. Not really. Just saw you around school."

"Oh. That's kind of sad."

Warm breath fanned her cheek as he chuckled. "Why?"

"Cause I think you're nice."

"I think you're nice, too."

"Ryan?"

"Yes, Maggie." He said her name in an almost teasing manner.

"Were you going to kiss me earlier tonight?" His eyes were so blue.

He looked away. "I was being stupid."

"No." She bumped his shoulder with hers and met his stare. "You were being nice."

His gaze dropped to her mouth, and a forgotten sensation swirled in her belly. "It's getting late," he said, voice rough like gravel.

"No one's kissed me in two years."

He broke eye contact again. "Maggie…"

"'S—okay. I can't kiss you anyway."

His head turned and his brow pinched. "You're drunk."

"Yup. It's nice."

"You should go to bed. It's late."

Unspoken rejection curdled her stomach. "'Cause I'm drunk?"

"Yeah."

"And you don't want to kiss me anymore?"

He looked into her eyes, and for a moment, she thought she could hear the stars moving closer to watch what might happen next. "Do you want me to kiss you?"

She never kissed a man with a beard before. "Do you want me to want you to?" Did she say that right? "Do you?"

He laughed. "Part of me wants to kiss you. But I think you don't know what you want right now."

She told her head to nod but wasn't sure if she moved. "Maybe that's okay, because right now, I don't care about what's good for me or what consequences will come. It's lovely."

"You're sure?"

"As rain."

"I don't think that's a saying."

She smiled. "It should be. Will you try again?"

A battle waged in his bright blue eyes, the silence stretching long enough for embarrassment to nip through her drunken haze, until he finally rasped, "Stay still."

Slowly closing the distance, his lips brushed hers, warm and soft. Her lashes lowered, and she pressed into the kiss, remembering how sweet the act could be.

The weight of his large hand curled around her hip. Warmth unraveled low in her belly as she breathed against his lips and softly licked at his tongue. She missed this. It had been so long.

The crinkle of his facial hair registered against her frozen cheeks. Facial hair? She jerked back and opened her eyes. Crushing guilt shoved her shoulders to the ground. Unfamiliar blue irises watched her. What was she doing? And on *this* day of all days!

She sat up, disgusted with herself and woozy from moving too fast. She fumbled with the cap of the bottle, needing to wash out her mouth. Oh, God, how could she?

"Hey…" He touched her back, and she tensed, angling away from the contact as she took a long swig of Jameson. "Maggie, you might want to slow down."

She didn't need someone telling her how to—

The trees swirled and swooped as her belly flipped. She dropped the bottle onto the grass and rolled to her hands and knees, scrambling away as fast as she could crawl. She only made it a few feet before tripping over her arms and vomiting.

"Shit." He crawled next to her and gathered her hair behind her shoulder. "Get it out."

"You should go," she groaned and then threw up her spleen. She should have eaten more than two bites at the bar and a banana today. She had nothing inside of her but whiskey, and her stomach wanted to throw everything out.

"I'm not leaving you like this."

She shivered as another dry heave ripped through her. Sweat beaded her body from straining. No more. No more. Her mind clumsily begged her stomach to settle, but she felt the pull of another purge.

She wretched again, dry heaving and spitting into the lawn. Where was her blanket? If she got puke on it, she'd have to wash it and then it wouldn't smell like Nash anymore.

Oh, God, Nash. What time was it?

It was almost time. What if he was watching?

Her stomach lurched and her face crumpled as she started to cry. "I'm so sorry…" She was a horrible wife.

"You don't have to apologize. We've all been there."

Why was her neighbor still there? Wiping her mouth on the back of her arm, she staggered to her feet. Thank God, the blanket was nowhere near the puke. She gathered it to her chest and took a jerky step away from him. What had she been thinking?

"I have to go."

"Let me walk you in and get you situated. You need to drink some water and probably eat a piece of bread or something to sop up the—"

"No." This had to end here. "I'll be fine."

He stood. "Maggie, I'm sorry about the kiss. I thought you wanted me to—"

"I have to go." She rushed inside, not wanting an account of her despicable behavior. Locking the door, she slid her back down the wall, pressing her face into the blanket as she let her tears freely fall.

Wiping her nose on her sleeve, she cried promises to herself. To Nash. To the emptiness that was her life.

"It didn't count. None of that was real. Nothing happened. Nothing happened. It didn't count. I'm sorry."

CHAPTER 9

$\mathcal{M}$ aggie awoke the following morning on the kitchen floor. "Oh, God." She winced as she tried to move but everything hurt.

Everything always hurt on March eighteenth. The weight of the day seemed lodged right on top of her chest. She already doubted her strength to survive the next twenty-four hours. Maybe she should just start drinking now, nip this hangover in the bud with a little hair of the dog and just get mind-numbingly wasted. That was a plan.

She pushed herself off the floor and guzzled a glass of water. Only one hour until work and she needed to get moving.

She rushed through her morning routine, making coffee and taking a quick shower. After swallowing down two aspirin, she filled her thermos and bundled up for the ride in. When she turned the knob the door didn't budge. Her brow creased with confusion, and she winced, her whiskey-soaked brain still sore from the night before.

She never locked the back door. Her sister lectured her about leaving the house open constantly. Her stare moved to the backyard. A tickle of unease crept up her spine.

She unlocked the door and walked down the back porch steps, looking for some clue to why she felt so … off. Puddles soaked the grass, but the driveway was bone dry. Did it rain over half the yard?

She looked inside the firepit and stilled. The ashes were shoveled out, and all signs of last night's fire were gone.

"What the hell?"

She checked the trashcans by the shed. The empty bottle of Jameson sat on top of the damp ashes. Who did this?

Her gaze lifted, taking in the familiar view of her neighbor's house, and her hand flew to her mouth as she remembered him kissing her last night. "Oh, my God."

Her gaze shot back to Nash's empty chair. Her heart raced as she struggled to find a way to make this sickening feeling inside of her go away.

He kissed her! Or she kissed him? She couldn't remember. But there was a kiss. She was going to be sick. She had been sick!

Her gaze darted to the lawn. Not a trace of puke. Did her neighbor clean up her shame vomit? That was incredibly disgusting and equally sweet.

No! She would not think of him in any favorable manner. He was her neighbor. And he was intrusive. Nosy. Why had he come over last night?

She couldn't remember, and her head pounded whenever she thought beyond her natural reflexes.

But he'd rescued her at the bar. He *was* sweet. Still, they were going to live next to each other. He wasn't renting the house. He owned his home as much as she owned hers. Her behavior yesterday was unacceptable. She'd make sure nothing like that ever happened again, nothing to threaten the safety of her only sanctuary.

Glancing at the time on her phone, she winced, already running late. Today was not a day to get lost in overthinking things. Today was a day for autopilot.

Tossing her thermos into the basket of her bike, she started peddling toward the cemetery. It was a dry morning, nothing like the snowy mess it had been two years before.

The ride across town helped soothe her aching head. She hopped off her bike, leaning it against the wrought iron fence that lined the cemetery but staggered just before the gate, her guilt chomping at her steadiness.

Did he know what she'd done? Her views on heaven and any afterlife jumbled the moment he left her. She stopped believing in any sort of God when the universe stole her husband, taking him to a place she couldn't follow.

But what if there was a heaven? She convinced herself there was, on most days, simply so she could make it through, selling the promise that they might someday meet again. However, if there *was* an afterlife and Nash could somehow see her, he'd know what she'd done last night.

The weight of the thermos grew heavy in her hand. She only had ten minutes to have coffee with him if she planned to be on time for work. Her throat repeatedly swallowed. Maybe she should just confess what she'd done and be done with it. It wasn't like it meant anything.

Did it?

She hadn't thought of kissing anyone aside from Nash since the fifth grade when Danny Darushak dared to spend seven minutes in heaven with her. Nash hated Danny.

What possessed her to kiss her neighbor? Alcohol and gut-wrenching sadness wasn't a recipe for good choices, so she needed to chill with the drinking.

Wiping her clammy palms down the front of her hoody, she forced herself to walk to his grave. The entire time her mind went back and forth on what she might say to him when she got there.

"What the hell?" Her thoughts derailed as she spotted a patch of purple hyacinths surrounding his headstone. She dropped to her knees. "Who did this?"

Leaning forward, she breathed in the unique scent. They smelled like spring. She remembered he used to buy his mom hyacinths every Easter Sunday before they met the rest of the O'Malleys at church.

The thought of her mother-in-law filled her with more guilt. There was one other woman on earth who felt the loss of Nash as deeply as Maggie, and that was his mother, Caitlin O'Malley. She must have had the flowers special ordered to get them this early in the year.

"Your mom was here," she said, brushing a loving hand over the small purple petals. "I haven't talked to her in a while. I should probably stop by for a visit."

Nash's relationship with his father ran hot and cold. He never fully supported his son's dreams to become a musician. Like Maggie's mother, his father objected to them getting married so young. But Caitlin always saw so much talent and hope in her son. She believed their marriage was an inevitable part of their future so marrying young didn't make a difference.

How wrong his mother had been. They had no future. "I can't imagine what this is like for her."

Maggie met Nash in kindergarten when he asked if she'd trade her chocolate milk for his apple juice. She hated apple juice and had an addiction to chocolate, but on that day, there was something about the little boy asking her for an unfair trade, something that made her give away her prized chocolate milk for a crummy juice box. That might have been the day she fell in love with him.

But his mother loved him since birth. She carried him inside of her, loved and protected him since the day he was born. Maggie couldn't compete with that. And she couldn't bear knowing his mother's grief might be greater than hers, when hers remained so all consuming. It was simply more sorrow she couldn't manage, so their relationship had faded like many others.

She slid the lid of black coffee onto the base of the headstone. "Today marks two years."

Did time matter where he was? Or did time simply stop?

"There wasn't a parade yesterday." She bit her lip. "I went to O'Malley's." Another betrayal. "I met the people who own it now. Well, some of them. There's like a hundred of them. They didn't know who I was. I told them my last name was Harris. But they were so nice to me, Nash. You would have liked them no matter what happened between your families."

She sipped the coffee from the thermos. "There's something else."

Her stomach knotted. "Remember that neighbor I told you about? His name's Ryan. He's a Clooney, and his dad was there when they took O'Malley's."

Maybe that was enough. Did it really matter if she said it out loud? For all she knew, she was just a crazy widow who talked to herself every morning in a cemetery.

No, she needed to hear herself say it, or the guilt would eat her alive. "I had a panic attack yesterday. I haven't had one in over six months, but it was a bad one. It happened at the pub in front of a bunch of strangers."

Remembering how awful it was, she took a deep breath and reminded herself it was over. "I almost lost it completely, but my neighbor was there. He works there, and he got me out of the crowd before it got too bad."

Her voice lowered as she thought back to how kind Ryan had been. "I don't know what would have happened if he hadn't shown up. Things probably would've gotten really bad."

She swallowed against a lump in her throat. "Then last night ... I drank ... *a lot.* He came by to check on me, I guess, and..."

She looked away. What did it prove if she said the rest? Nash was dead. He was gone. No confession or shame could bring him back.

Her regret shifted to anger and frustration. She resented how many mornings she spent talking to herself, knowing there was a very real crazy part of her that still hoped one day he'd answer.

Two years. It had been two excruciating years, and her life was just as broken as it had been the day he left her. It wasn't supposed to be like this! She wasn't supposed to be alone!

"You said you would get new tires on the car that Christmas," she snapped.

Her chin trembled as the accusing words tumbled from her tight lips. "I think of that all the time. You knew those tires weren't safe for winter, and you just kept putting it off. Then you bought that damn Fender guitar—like we needed another instrument. We needed tires!"

She hadn't meant to come here and yell at him, but she couldn't navigate the swift shift from guilt to resentment. "I need my husband and you're gone! You just left me here, and I don't know what the hell to do without you."

She sniffed and dashed away her tears. Her confession didn't matter. None of it did. He didn't matter anymore and neither did she.

Snatching the lid to the thermos, she sloshed the coffee onto the grass and screwed the top in place. Standing on shaky legs, she glared at his tombstone.

"I'm dead inside. People look at me, thinking they can somehow bring me back to life, but there's nothing left anymore. Everything I was, died with you two years ago. All because of a burnt-out lightbulb and shitty fucking tires."

With that, she marched back to the gate and threw her thermos into the basket. She had one leg over her bike before crushing guilt consumed her. Her vision blurred as the tightness of her ribs suffocated her.

Dropping the bike to the ground, she raced back through the gate, careening onto the ground in front of his headstone and crushing several hyacinths as she pressed her frozen fingers to her lips and pushed them over his name.

"I'm sorry! I didn't mean any of that. I'm so sorry. I'm a fucking mess. I don't know why I said that stuff. I don't know what's happening to me."

She spent several minutes crying and apologizing, trying to fix the flowers she'd trampled. Like always, no reply came. The comfort she always hoped to find there never existed. And it never would.

She spent countless mornings talking through the emptiness. There was nothing there for her, yet she continuously returned with the hope that something might change. Wasn't that the definition of insanity, doing the same thing over and over again and expecting different results?

She couldn't go on like this. Nash wouldn't want her to live this way. He'd be the first to tell her it wasn't living.

When she got back to her bike and picked up her thermos, which had rolled into the grass, she called out of work. She needed a day to herself, not to drink but to heal. To open herself up to the grief and truly mourn her husband. She needed *a dark day*.

She had people she could go to, but none of them would understand. They all watched it happen from their safe positions on the outside of her and Nash's world. They grieved and moved on, but their grief had never been gutting like hers. Theirs was simply sympathy. Pity. Sorrow that something so traumatic would forever change her from the daughter, sister, and friend she had once been.

She often caught hope in her friends' eyes, awareness that Nash's death complicated the simplicity of their easy going relationships, and often, they decided some friendships weren't worth that sort of work. For most of her friends, her grief was too real. They waited for her to return to the girl she used to be, but that girl died with Nash. She was gone as permanently as he, and eventually people stopped waiting around for things to go back to the way they were before.

So in times like this, when she felt the truth stabbing in and sanity slipping away, the last people she wanted to call were those who could measure all the ways she'd changed. All the ways she was less *now* than she'd been before. Half. Fractured. Broken.

If she didn't do something soon, she'd be ringing in the third, tenth, and twentieth anniversary cursing her lost life all the more. She did a quick online search and held her breath as she made the call she'd been putting off.

She couldn't go on like this. She didn't want to. Calling for help somehow seemed less complicated than checking out completely. Less tears maybe.

A female answered and Maggie choked on her words. "Hi. I, um, was wondering if it would be possible to make an appointment to speak to someone."

"Have you been here before?"

"No."

"Dr. Devereux has an opening today at four. Would you be able to make that? You would have to arrive fifteen minutes early to fill out the necessary paperwork."

Was she really doing this? On autopilot, her words agreed before her mind could form any sort of judgement. "Yes, I can be there."

She answered a few more questions and ended the call. Perrin would be proud. She should be proud. This was a big step. But all she could muster was numb acceptance.

Now she just had to make it to four o'clock—sober.

CHAPTER 10

"*H*e can see you now."

Maggie moved like a fish out of water through the small waiting room. Everything inside of her wanted to bolt out the door, but some buried remainder of hope pushed her in the opposite direction into the therapist's office.

A tall, trim man with silver hair stood and greeted her. "Maggie?" He extended a hand and she shook it.

Ah, the famous Dr. Devereux. She offered a tight-lipped smile, trying to bank her skepticism until the end. "Thanks for fitting me in."

He waved a hand at the empty chair across from his, inviting her to sit. "Of course. This was unexpected, but it's nice to see you again."

He spoke with an eloquent British accent that put her at ease, until his words sank in. "Again?"

"We met at O'Malley's yesterday. You were with Sammy."

The blood rushed from her face and her knees softened. She abruptly released his hand and dropped into the empty chair. "You're one of them?"

His expression blanked, but she noted the trace of a smile. "Not quite. My wife is a McCullough. I'm not sure you met her yesterday. Sheilagh."

She'd met a woman named Sheilagh, but that woman was young, and this guy was... Well, he was attractive, but his hair was silver. He had to be at least fifteen years older than the girl he claimed as his wife. And now he was staring at her expectantly.

Say something to make this less awkward! "I think I met her."

Thankfully, he let the uncomfortable family talk drop. "Can I offer you something to drink?"

She shook her head and eyed the office. "No couch?"

"I find most clients are more comfortable speaking face-to-face—as equals."

She thought there would be a couch. Her fingers traced over the brown leather upholstery of the chair. This was weird. She folded her hands on her lap and stared at her knees.

The doctor sat to her right and collected a leather bound portfolio with what looked like an expensive pen. "Have you ever gone to counseling before?"

"No."

"I prefer to let my clients lead the dialogue. What brings you in today?"

His pen poised over the blank notebook, the cover of the leather portfolio forgotten for a moment. But she knew, once he began writing, he'd jot down all sorts of thoughts and use that cover as a shield—like she shouldn't see how crazy she actually was.

"How long have you been..." What was the accurate title? Shrink? Therapist? Psychologist? Psychiatrist? "A doctor?"

"I opened my practice two years ago. My background's in philosophy, but I assure you, my credentials are long and up-to-date. When did you first consider speaking to a professional?"

"My sister gave me your card a few weeks ago, but it's not the first time she mentioned therapy."

"Do you get along with your sister?"

"Sort of. We used to be tight, but over the last two years things sort of fell apart. She calls a lot, but I hardly pick up."

"What changed?"

Life. She shifted, unfolding her hands then picking at a hangnail on her thumb. She slid her hands under her butt to stop fidgeting. "My husband died."

God, it still hurt to hear those words and recognize that it was her voice speaking them.

"I'm sorry. Did you have a happy marriage?"

She nodded. "The happiest. He was perfect."

"Impressive. Though, I find *perfect* to be a relative term. Would you mind telling me what makes a man perfect in your eyes?"

She chewed her lip. "Well, he was just ... *everything.* We started dating in middle school. He was there for all my firsts. He taught me how to drive, showed me how to fish, and even tried to teach me to play guitar. Nash was an amazing musician. He could pick up any instrument and make it sing. He had natural talent." She remembered how frustrated he'd become at her inability to even hold a guitar properly. "He never learned how to read sheet music."

"He sounds like a very talented musician. What was he like as a husband?"

She smiled. "Kind. Funny. Everyone loved his silly side. Sometimes he was too silly."

"Explain *too silly*. Can you give me an example?"

Her brow pinched as she tried to remember a specific time. It didn't take long for one to come to mind. "He was impossible to fight with. I'd get aggravated about something and he'd make me laugh. Everything was a joke to him."

"Did this tactic of his alleviate the need for an argument?"

"Sort of." She shrugged. "He'd defuse the situation, but nothing got fixed. So, if I was pissed that he let the laundry sit in the washer all day, I'd say something, he'd make a joke or do something to make me laugh and then it would be over. I couldn't stay mad at him. But a few days later, the laundry would be forgotten in the wash again."

"And what was the consequence of the laundry being forgotten?"

"Did you ever leave a batch of laundry in a washing machine on a hot August day, Dr. Devereux?"

"I'm afraid I have not, and please, call me Alec."

"Well, Alec, it stinks to high heaven. The fibers carry this horribly musty stench and it doesn't always wash out. If left long enough you sometimes have to throw the clothes away."

"So this irritated you because it was wasteful."

"Well, yeah. It wasted water, money, time, and clothes. But mostly it pissed me off that I brought it up over a dozen times and he still left them sitting."

"So you felt ignored."

Wait. What? Her defenses shot up. What was happening? Who was this guy to assume Nash ignored her? "No, I mean…" She frowned. Nash loved her. "He didn't ignore me. I was his world and he was mine."

"Okay."

He agreed easily enough, but she sensed he'd made an unfair judgment. She waited for him to make some sort of note in his fancy book, but he just kept looking at her.

She squirmed uncomfortably, finding the silence awkward and testing. "He brought me flowers almost every month. He always kissed me hello and goodbye. He made sure we always went to bed at the same time. My husband didn't ignore me."

"My interpretation was misplaced."

"Yeah. It was. I mean, Nash was a guy, so of course he left dishes all over the house and never put his clothes in the hamper. He lost the cap to every single toothpaste we owned. And he probably spent a solid hour every week searching for his keys, because he could never remember to hang them up by the door. But none of that matters in the end."

"Of course."

The pitch of her voice heightened. "And yeah, some nights I'd want to have a nice date night and it would be a fight just to get him to take off the silkscreen T-shirt and put on something nice, but who cares? He always took me out when I wanted. He always paid attention to me in his own way."

He leaned forward with a box of tissues, and she plucked one free. She blew her nose and held out her hands in exasperation. "He wanted to be a musician, and I always supported his dreams. He had incredible talent. I mean, I can barely yodel, but he could make music out of a pair of spoons and a shoe. Sometimes talent isn't enough, you know?"

"Could you expand?"

"Nash rarely took gigs in town, because his family has this old vendetta about the local pub. It's stupid. He could have played there every week. We could have used the extra income. It would have gotten him exposure."

"The local pub? Do you mean O'Malley's?"

"Yes, that's his family. He's an O'Malley. They don't go in there. But how the hell is anyone supposed to discover his talent if he's just playing songs in our living room and around our firepit? Two years ago, Center County only had one bar. There weren't all these other places like there are now. I told him to apply to other towns. I would have traveled with him. We were waiting to have children, because he was supposed to eventually go on tour. But how can anyone go on tour with a car that can barely make it across town? He swore he'd replace the tires. He swore to me! It was the only thing I said we needed that Christmas!"

"Did he?"

She pressed her nose into the ruined Kleenex. "No. He bought a guitar. Another instrument."

Something in her chest seemed to rupture. A volcanic burn singed up her throat, and she feared she'd get sick right there in her new therapist's office. Spreading her knees, she dropped her head between her legs and massaged her temples.

"I'm sorry," she apologized, unable to stave off her tears.

"There's no need to apologize. There's no judgment here." He held the tissues within her ducked view, and this time she took the whole box.

"If he would have just listened to me." She hiccupped, flinging her head upright. "Everything was a fight." Crumpled tissues gathered on her lap. "*One time* he replaced the lightbulb on the front porch. *Once.* Why couldn't he keep up with that stuff? I did! I went to the market every week. I made sure we never ran out of the necessities. Even when we were tight on money, I made sure the bills got paid, skimping on groceries and buying generic cereal."

"Were finances a stress point in your marriage?"

"We bought a house at auction. It was cheap, but it was still a commitment, one we probably weren't ready for."

"Do you work?"

"At Restaurant Supply. I make next to nothing, but we were never materialistic people. I was happy so long as we were safe, you know?"

"And Nash?"

The truth ground inside of her with unwanted honesty. "He always wanted more. I'd say we couldn't afford something, and he'd throw a fit about how everyone else had luxuries. Sometimes it made me feel awful. I was happy with our simple life, but when he wanted something, it became clear our small-town world wasn't enough for him. And I worried, maybe one day, I…" She swallowed. "What if one day I wasn't enough?"

"When he would express these desires for luxuries you couldn't always afford, how would you respond?"

She sniffled and dropped her gaze. The tissues littering her lap blurred behind a fresh wall of tears. "There was no point in fighting with him. I wanted him to be happy. Content. So I'd apply for a new credit card and do whatever I could do to get him that thing he needed to feel better about his life."

"Did Nash work?"

"His dad owned a shoe store, and he worked there on and off, but it eventually went out of business. Nash said it was the perfect motivation to get out there and start touring."

"But he didn't?"

"No."

He made a quick note in his book, but she lost interest in seeing what his interpretation might be. Drained from crying, she shut her eyes and took in a few deep breaths.

"How are finances now?"

She shrugged. "His parents had a small life insurance policy for him, so the house is paid off. I was able to clear up our credit card debt, too. But I don't rely on what's left of that money. I hate it."

"That may change with time."

She lifted a shoulder. "I don't need it. I need my husband. I can't imagine ever spending it on myself, so it just sits there like a painful reminder, a payment for my life and his. Sometimes I feel like we weren't worth that much."

Nash was. He was worth more. But she… Her life seemed worthless the longer it dragged on.

"When was the last time you purchased a luxury for yourself, Maggie?"

She blinked stupidly, unable to recall. "I don't know."

"Anything. Any large or small ticket item that made you happy despite the cost."

"Besides the house?"

He nodded. "Besides the house."

Chewing on her lip, she tried to remember the last time she'd been shopping. "We had an apartment after high school. Back then, I never thought much about debt. We financed our living room furniture. That was pretty expensive."

"Did you pick it out?"

"Well, the one I wanted didn't really go with the rest of our stuff. Nash really liked the red one on sale."

"What color couch did you wind up purchasing?"

She swallowed. "Red." But she loved that couch. It was theirs. She didn't see it as his because they were a partnership. "It's old now. There are stains on the cushions and feathers fall out of it all the time."

"Something to think about." He closed the cover of his book. "Perhaps using some of your saved money to make a small purchase—something for yourself—something that might bring you joy—might set some new habits into motion."

"I don't need anything."

"It's not about necessity. What do you want? Is there anything that would make you happy? We can learn a lot by choosing a gift for ourselves. It could be a revealing exercise."

Having Nash back was the only thing that would make her happy. The resounding hopelessness of that wish cut her down. "I don't want anything."

"Everyone wants something." He glanced at his watch. "Maybe think about that for the next few days. Progress comes when we identify what we want. Reflect on your current situation. Change can be frightening at times, but it's also a powerful tool. Change represents growth, and growth brings closure. You're in control, Maggie. Perhaps it's time for you to decide how your future will look differently from the life you're leading today. Decide what needs to change in order for you to find closure."

Closure. What a terrifying word. Closure seemed too final. She wasn't ready to close away her memories, because she wasn't ready to let him go, and maybe she never would be.

She made an appointment for the following week, though she wasn't sure she'd keep it. She got a lot of stuff off her chest but wasn't sure if saying any of those terrible things out loud actually helped.

She wondered why she didn't mention Ryan or the kiss or her drinking? Maybe there was just too much crap that came before those insignificant turns. But if they were insignificant, why did she keep thinking about them?

When she got home, she opened the fridge to grab a beer and stilled. Her hand hovered over the almost empty six-pack—one bottle left. It had been full yesterday. Then she remembered the empty bottle of whiskey in her trashcan out back.

If she was really going to give this healing thing a try, she needed to do it truthfully, and that meant being honest with herself.

"Time to dry out for a bit." She shut the fridge.

The temptation to self-medicate remained, but she fought it off. The house seemed more silent than usual, every few minutes her thoughts returning to the fridge.

Frustrated with the frail condition of her will, she threw on her hat and left. Who said running away from problems didn't work?

CHAPTER 11

*T*ristan entered Ryan's office at the lumberyard with Luke following. "Hey, you working at the pub tonight?"

Ryan stretched at his desk, shoving away the invoices he'd been reviewing. "No, Aunt Col's keepin' an eye on things, and Sue's got the bar." And thank God for that. He was barely keeping himself upright after only an hour's sleep last night.

"Good. Swing by our place when you're finished up here. We've got something for you."

His mood lifted. "For me?"

"Yeah. Stop by."

Luke and Tristan lived in the renovated barn across from his Aunt Maureen and Uncle Frank's log cabin on the top of what their family called McCullough Mountain, and directly next door to Sheilagh and Alec's stone farmhouse.

Ryan envied the closeness his McCullough cousins shared. Everyone but Kelly and Ashlynn lived on the Mountain. Of course there were complaints of intrusiveness, and each couple learned the hard way to lock their doors. But when they needed company, it was never far.

He parked in front of the barn, and a sudden longing to turn back and drive home overwhelmed him. While his extended family was great, he'd gone to a bitter place over the last year, and sometimes their happiness was too much to take. He loved them dearly, but their good fortune had a way of shining a spotlight on all the empty parts of his own life.

With his brother Pat completing his residency in the city, things had been lonely. Pat, though younger, had always been there, so Ryan never felt like a third wheel, or in the case of all his now married cousins, a fifteenth wheel.

He was used to being *the single one*. A few years ago everyone stopped adding a guest option to his invitations. It was just sort of accepted that he was the loner. And he didn't mind being unaccompanied—most days.

But seeing how happy everyone else was, how established and lived-in their homes were, and watching the anniversaries and birth announcements pile up... Well, it sort of killed him in a bittersweet way that made him feel like a self-centered shit.

The house he bought wasn't the only one he looked at. There had been others, three that were far away from Center County, but in the end, he couldn't bear crushing his mum by moving any farther away than the other side of town. Plus, he worked here.

Maybe he made a mistake staying because he'd already learned there was no one here for him. In a small town, everyone knew everyone. And if he hadn't yet been set up with an available, age appropriate woman living in town, there was good reason to continue avoiding them.

He'd dated all of them—or tried. Even some of the crazier ones. No one interested him. Except Maggie.

Maggie was different, or so he'd thought. And like all the others, Maggie was unavailable. She might be a widow, but her heart very much belonged to her deceased husband.

He needed to get her out of his head. Last night had been a disaster. One would think her disinterest would have set him straight when he was hosing away her puke that morning but nope.

A sharp whistle caught his attention. He quickly stuffed his pining thoughts down where no one could see, and his gaze jerked across the lawn. Luke waved to him from the garage by the big house.

Ryan climbed out of the truck and walked that way. Tristan appeared on the wraparound front porch of the log cabin, Aunt Maureen coming out after him and smiling widely.

"Ryan, love, are you hungry? I've got a fresh stew cookin' and dinner's just about ready."

"Thanks, Aunt Maureen. I'd love that."

"Wonderful. I'll set you a plate." She went into the house. Tristan met him at the tire swing by the tree in the front yard where Alexia was swinging.

"Daddy, watch!"

Tristan and Luke both turned as Alexia lifted her feet off the dusty ground, and the tire spun quickly, the thick weathered rope unraveling from the tight coil she'd worked up to the tree branch. Her wild red curls spun like cotton candy as she squealed with glee.

"She looks so much like Sheilagh."

"Except for the curls," Luke commented, smiling.

"That, and she's not evil," Tristan joked.

Ryan laughed because despite Sheilagh's reputation for being a she-devil, everyone knew Tristan had a soft spot for her. "So, what did you have to show me?"

The guys directed him toward the garage. A strong scent of lacquer caught the breeze. "We made you something."

"A housewarming gift," Tristan explained, pulling open the garage doors.

Ryan's head cocked at the sight of a long slab of wood, several inches thick. Bark covered the edges and the heavily lacquered surface swirled with aged rings. It stood on a custom-built cabinet with open shelves. The varnished gloss gave it a gleaming surface that would easily wipe clean.

Ryan didn't know what to say. "It's gorgeous. You guys made this?"

They smiled and nodded. "That's custom McCullough lumber, so you know it's quality wood," Luke said.

"McCulloughs *are* known to have the best wood." Tristan lifted a brow and gave the surface a knock with his knuckles. "Thick and hard."

Ryan laughed. "You'd know." He ran his hand over the smooth surface. "This is incredible, guys. I don't know what to say. Thank you."

"Now you have a reason to finish that basement."

"Put all those new bartending skills to use," Tristan teased.

As far as gifts went, this one was spectacular. "I'm speechless. This is over the top."

"We love you like a brother, man. We had to get you something. Buying a house is a big deal."

He cleared his throat, shoving back the emotions sneaking up on him. "Thanks."

"You can thank us by inviting us over when the bar's up and running."

"Definitely. Speaking of bars, any word when Kelly's coming back?"

The guys shared a glance that didn't give Ryan any sense of hope.

"What is it?"

"Maybe you should give him a call," Luke hedged.

"Maybe you should tell me what you know."

His cousin sighed. "He's been commissioned to do a whole new line of canvases. It's a pretty big deal, but it's going to take time to complete."

Ryan frowned. "But his studio's here."

"Right, but…" Luke glanced at Tristan and they shared a look of disappointment.

Tristan sighed. "He's thinking about selling the bar."

"What? To who?"

They shrugged. "Anyone who will buy it."

That would never fly. O'Malley's was a part of their family. His dad and uncles had been running the bar since they were kids. The aunts held every christening and reception right there in the back room.

"That's bullshit," he snapped. "It's been in our family for half a century."

"We're all upset," Luke said. "But Kelly's found his calling. This is

84

what he wants to do. It isn't right for us to assume he has an obligation to run the pub on top of everything else going on in his life."

"You guys could run it."

"No," they both said at once. "We talked about it, and we don't want to be tied down like that. We like working outdoors."

"Braydon—"

"Bray's got his architecture firm. And Finn will never give up his share of the Lumberyard, just like you. Alec just opened a new practice in town. And Colin's got too much going on with the church and school board. And Kate and Ant aren't interested."

"There is *one* other option," Tristan said, his expression setting Ryan up for a long shot.

Luke rolled his eyes. "That's not an option."

Ryan looked at them expectantly. "Who? Tell me." Their family was simply too large for there not to be *someone* willing to take over the stress of running the pub.

"Giovanni."

The garage silenced and Ryan waited for the punch line. It didn't come. "Are you out of your mind?"

"I said the same thing," Luke commented.

"What? The guy's family. He could care less about Paulie's portion of the lumberyard. Maybe he'd want the pub."

"He's a Mosconi!" Ryan snapped.

"So? Aunt Col's a Mosconi, too, and she ran the bar until Kelly took over."

"By marriage. It's different. Giovanni walks around like he's an extra on the *Sopranos*."

"Those track suits are the worst. He'd change the name from O'Malley's to Mosconi's or Little Italy or something."

"He'd change everything," Ryan agreed. "Giovanni's a definite no."

Tristan shrugged. "It was just a thought."

"We'll think of someone else," Ryan said, just as Aunt Maureen yelled that dinner was ready.

Inside the big house, they washed up from work and gathered around the large table in the cavernous kitchen.

"Smells great," Ryan complimented, settling in beside Sheilagh.

"Where's Alec?" Aunt Maureen asked.

Sheilagh filled a bowl for Alexia. "He had a late appointment today. He should be here soon."

"Oh, I wonder who it was." Aunt Maureen ladled one bowl of stew after another. "He sure keeps busy with his new practice. Who knew we had so many touched people in our town."

"They're not *touched*, Mum. They just want to talk to someone."

"Of course, dear." She ladled out a hearty helping and slid it in front of Uncle Frank. "Do you think he's getting some juicy gossip? I bet he knows who's sleeping with who and what secrets everyone's keepin'. He'll probably be the first to know who defaced the old Windsor Bridge. I honestly don't know what possesses someone to graffiti a six-foot penis on a perfectly charming bridge. Deviants."

"Maybe it was Kelly. He said he wanted to get into self-portraits." Luke snickered.

Without missing a beat, Aunt Maureen smacked Luke on the back of the head. "Honestly, Luke."

Ryan laughed, always enjoying when his aunt whacked her biggest son.

"Mum, don't say words like that in front of Alexia," Sheilagh scolded.

Aunt Maureen paused. "Words like what?"

Sheilagh looked up at her. "Like what you just said."

Aunt Maureen gasped. "Oh dear, did I say cock?"

"Mum!"

"You said penis," Luke provided, still rubbing his head.

"Luke!"

He flinched, ducking a swat from his sister. "What? She would have just kept guessing."

"Well, when Alexia starts repeating words for male genitals you can all blame yourselves."

Tristan helped himself to a second serving. "When did you become such a prude, Sheilagh?"

"It's because she's married to a Brit," Aunt Maureen mumbled. "The British are notorious for their dirty minds and clean manners. But really they're just a collection of blue blooded perverts."

"Mum, you can't say stuff like that!"

"It's my house. I'll say whatever I want. And try to deny it. I've walked in on Alec more times than I'd like to recall. I could pick his wanker out of a lineup. Can I say wanker, dear, or is that too crass for Alexia's ears?"

There was never a dull moment at his aunt's house. Dinner was delicious and Ryan appreciated the excuse not to have pizza again.

Alec arrived just as Aunt Maureen was dishing out her famous rice pudding for dessert.

"Well, it's about time," she greeted, shoving her son-in-law into a chair and filling a bowl of stew for him. "Eat up before the others finish all the dessert."

No matter how many years Alec had been living on the mountain with the McCulloughs, he always appeared slightly harassed by Aunt Maureen's brash mannerisms, which made it fun to watch. Accepting the bowl of stew, he set it aside and went to his wife who had started washing dishes at the sink. He hugged her with bone deep affection.

She turned and looked up at him. "Everything okay?"

"For the last hour, I could think of nothing more than coming home and telling you how much I love you."

Sheilagh smiled up at her husband. "Aw, babe."

"I was thinking," he said, giving her chin an affectionate bump with his finger, "that Jeep you like, the hideous yellow one, let's sign the papers tomorrow."

Her face lit with a stunned smile. "Really? I thought you hated it."

"Truly. And I do."

"What changed your mind?"

"Something reminded me, it's not about what I want. The car's for you. I want to give you something that will make you happy."

"I don't need a car to be happy, Alec."

"I know. But you've hinted enough. I know it's what you want, so we're getting it." He turned the faucet back on and returned to the table, brushing a kiss on Alexia's head along the way.

Ryan watched the exchange with warm affection and envy. As odd a couple as Sheilagh and Alec made, they somehow balanced each other in a chaotic world and made perfect sense.

That night, he drove home wondering if the world had a surprising someone reserved for him. When he pulled into the driveway, the sky was dark. Not until he climbed out of his truck did he notice Maggie waiting on his back porch.

His first thought was what a pleasant surprise. His second, more accurate thought was he'd seen that look in a woman's eyes before.

This was when she would tell him everything up to this moment had been a mistake, and they were better off being friends, which was code for strangers of increasing distance. It didn't matter that they only shared a handful of interactions, there was something between them, something she didn't like—or maybe she did like it, and that was what worried her.

"Hey," she greeted, looking small and adorable, her nervous gaze following him as he rounded the truck.

"Hey." He pocketed his keys and hung back.

"I wanted to apologize for the way I acted last night." Her cheeks slightly flushed.

"Don't worry about it." They both embarrassed themselves.

"I've been drinking a lot lately."

His humiliation shifted into concern. "Is it a problem?"

"No. Not usually. I haven't had anything aside from coffee or water today, but... March is a really bad month for me. I'm kind of stuck in a bad few years."

She didn't have to justify herself to him. They all had demons and hers were bigger than most. "Understandable."

She glanced at the fence separating their yards. He loved when she wore that gray wool cap. It showed off her face and drew his attention to her full lips. Would she mention the kiss?

"My memories are ... sketchy."

Ah. That was how she wanted to play it. "It's cool. We don't have to rehash it."

Her gaze returned to his, and she looked up at him with big eyes. "Yesterday, when you took me up those stairs at the bar, why did you do that?"

"Because you looked like you needed an escape."

"But you were slammed. You could have just pointed me toward the exit. You didn't have to wait with me."

"I thought you needed a minute to catch your breath, and I didn't want to leave you alone."

Her brow pinched. "What about what you needed?"

He shrugged. "That didn't matter at the time."

Her shoulders rounded as she folded her gloved hands between her knees. "You're a really nice guy."

"So are you. Well, woman." He took a slow step forward and then another. Without getting too close, he lowered himself to the step and sat beside her. They both kept their stares directed at his truck. "You know, if you ever need to just get out of your head for a little bit, I'm usually around. The bar thing's only temporary. I'm home by six most nights."

"Same. I sort of forget how to act around people, like I forget how to be normal."

He chuckled. "Normal's overrated. Just act however feels right."

The wind shifted and the soft scent of her hair drifted to his nose. She was back to her usual appearance of jeans, a bulky sweatshirt, fingerless gloves, and a hat. Not a speck of makeup competed with her natural beauty.

"I miss … talking," she whispered. "Everyone I know knew Nash, and sometimes that's all they want to talk about. Even when they aren't saying it out loud, I can sense their eyes screaming things at me."

"We don't have to talk about him."

"But sometimes I want to."

"Then we can."

She glanced at him. "Do you find it lonely, living here alone?"

"Sometimes it's lonelier living in the midst of so many other people's lives and feeling like the odd man out."

"Yeah, I definitely know what that feels like."

"Do you get lonely?" He figured she must. It had been two years.

"It's more than loneliness. I wonder if I'll actually atrophy from lack of human interaction. I flinch when people touch me unexpectedly. Sometimes human contact hurts my heart. But there's this part of me that knows if I can just push through the awkwardness and tolerate it a little bit longer, I'll find comfort."

He came from an overly affectionate family where everyone kissed and hugged each other all the time. While he desperately missed intimacy—sex was different—the last time he slept with a woman he found the connection hollow and unfulfilling. He missed the emotional link that came with love—or what he imagined that might feel like. In a pinch, infatuation served as a close second. He couldn't imagine going without any physical contact for as long as she had.

Skin hungered for touch. It would be horrible to never feel a pat on the back or an affectionate hug. He turned his hand over and splayed his fingers wide in invitation.

She looked down at his palm and back at him.

"It won't bite," he said with a gentle grin. "And it doesn't mean anything more than a neighbor offering a hand if you need it."

She glanced back at his palm and frowned. He waited in silence. If she didn't take it, no problem. But if she did, he'd happily be the friend she could lean on.

A vaporized puff of breath fanned from her lips as she let out a long exhalation. Her arm slowly shifted, her dainty hand covered in a tattered glove gradually filled his. Their fingers laced as he closed his grip around hers, gently holding.

Her shoulders lifted and fell with each shallow breath as she stared down at their entwined hands. If she wanted to break contact, she could. But she didn't. This wasn't at all what he'd expected when he found her waiting for him.

Her hand tightened, squeezing with surprising intensity as she turned her gaze back to the driveway. They sat in silence, simply holding hands, for over an hour, both of them savoring the quiet connection, before she let go.

CHAPTER 12

$\mathcal{A}$fter her next session with Alec Devereux, Maggie decided it was time for a bold move. Something, therapy or perhaps her budding friendship with Ryan, made her hopeful that life could improve. For the first time in two years she felt like she was making progress. Though she didn't have any concrete proof, she felt change in the wind. It was more of a gut thing.

That Friday, she stopped by McGinty's on the way home and sat on every couch in their showroom until she found one that made her smile. It was pale blue with brushed nickel buttons down the arms. It would totally clash with the deep russet tones of her living room, but she loved the contemporary feel of it. It gave her an airy, light sensation she wanted to maintain.

She purchased it on the spot and arranged for the delivery that evening. Unfortunately, there must have been some miscommunication with the shipping department, because when she turned her bike onto her property, the couch had already arrived, and the delivery truck was nowhere in sight.

"What the hell?" She parked her bike and called McGinty's from her cell while standing on the porch staring at her new plastic wrapped couch. This was not her living room, where they assured her the sofa would be delivered.

As she explained to the receptionist that the delivery was supposed to be for six that evening and the couch was meant to go *inside* her house, not the porch, the woman on the other end apologized. But the delivery crew was gone for the weekend and wouldn't be back until Monday. The most the woman could offer was a refund for the delivery fee and a complimentary carpet steaming to be redeemed within the next thirty days—like that solved her problems.

Maggie ended the call and sat on the plastic wrapped sofa occupying her porch. She stared at the field across from her house. How the hell would she get this inside on her own?

She'd have to call Perrin. And Perrin would insist on bringing her boyfriend over to help. A boyfriend who Maggie never took the time to get to know, even after two years of him dating her sister...

It was awkward to say the least.

A horn beeped and she lifted her head just as Ryan's truck turned the corner. A jolt of relief had her sucking in a breath, which she then held for a second, wondering if asking him to help her was somehow taking advantage.

Did she want to involve him? He'd probably agree to help the second she asked, because he was that nice. But what if he had plans? She should just call Perrin.

"Is this a new look you're going for?" He stood at the bottom of her porch steps, thumbs hooked into the pockets of his worn jeans and a pressed flannel tucked in at the waist. He looked too clean for a lumberjack or even the junior CEO of a lumberyard.

She flushed. Why was she looking at his clothing? "They screwed up my delivery."

"So now what?"

"That's what I'm trying to figure out."

"Well, while you think on that, why don't you give me a hand lifting this couch through the door?"

She smiled as he climbed the front steps. She didn't even have to ask.

He lifted the plastic covered arm, tipping her off the cushion and onto her feet. "Up you go."

"Are you sure?"

He rolled his eyes. "Do you honestly think I'm going to let you try to move this yourself?"

She hid a smile and unlocked the front door, then lifted the other end. Ryan held the brunt of the weight, and she helped steer.

While she navigated the piece into the house, she didn't have time to consider that this was the first time he'd been inside. They dropped the sofa in the foyer by the den, and he stretched, casually scanning the rooms and taking a quick look around.

"What are you doing with the old one?" He glanced into the den.

For some reason this made her notice all the belongings that were Nash's, things she had no real use for like his piano, bongos, and various guitars. She looked at the old red couch.

"I was going to put it in the shed." She might be ready to replace it with the blue sofa, but she wasn't ready to let it go.

"We could just put it on the curb."

"No, bulk pickup isn't for a few weeks." She had no clue when bulk pickup actually was.

"If you want, I could run it to the landfill in my truck."

"That's okay. I'll just stick it in the shed for now."

"You're sure?"

She nodded. The thought of removing a piece of her prior life permanently would probably require a solid hour of therapy, several shots of whiskey, and a good amount of tears. She had none of those things on hand at the moment. As a matter of fact, she hadn't had a drink or cried since she started seeing Alec Devereux—not counting the tears shed in session of course.

They carried the old couch to the shed, which swallowed the remainder of free space, but she needed to know it would be there if she wanted to sit on it. After quickly vacuuming the carpet, she helped Ryan slide the new sofa into place. He pulled off the plastic wrap and she stepped back to look at it.

Her enthusiasm deflated. "Well, that doesn't work." It looked horrible against the dark burnt sienna walls.

"I like it."

"You're a guy."

"So? I think it's pretty."

She laughed at his easy use of the word pretty. "It doesn't go with anything."

"So paint."

She glanced around the room, supposing the walls could use a fresh coat. Once she really looked, all the nicks and chips really came into view. Painting was probably a good idea. It needed it.

She purposely tried not to think too hard about how such a transformation might trigger panic. "What are your plans this weekend?"

He laughed and backed out of the living room, hands up in surrender. "Oh, no you don't. I've got a house full of rooms that need work."

She tried for puppy dog eyes. Painting alone sucked. But painting with someone could be fun. And it went twice as fast. "Please? I'll help you if you help me."

He paused. "Really?"

"Sure. Painting's always better when you have a partner."

His posture instantly relaxed. "Deal."

She narrowed her eyes. "That was easy."

"My house has old lady wallpaper."

She shut her eyes and groaned. "No wonder you agreed so quickly. Whatever. Tall person does the ceilings."

CHAPTER 13

The following morning, Ryan was knocking on her back door when she pulled her bike into the driveway after her usual morning coffee session with Nash.

"Hey." Maggie hopped off the seat and leaned it against the shed. "You're up early." Grabbing the thermos out of the basket, she entered the backyard.

"I…" He glanced at her house. "I thought you were still sleeping."

She hopped up the back steps and entered the kitchen. "Nope. I hardly ever sleep."

He followed her into the house. "You left your door unlocked."

"I never lock it. Do you want coffee?"

"No thanks. I was heading to the hardware store for supplies. I thought you'd want to come."

She rinsed out her thermos. "Sure, I just need to grab a pillow off the new sofa so I can match colors."

"Okay. I'll meet you in the truck."

She was halfway to the living room and he was already out the back door when his words reached her. She raced into the kitchen and stared at the empty room. A sick sticky feeling crawled through her belly, and she swallowed.

She meant to go after him, to call him back and work out a plan B. But she just stood there. Her stare bounced from the door to Nash's coat, to the spare car keys hanging on the hook.

She wouldn't be able to transport paint cans and supplies on her bike. Did the hardware store deliver? Maybe she could meet him there.

"What are you doing?" He popped his head through the door and frowned. "Where's the pillow?"

"I… I can't go with you."

He stepped back into the kitchen. "Why?"

"I..." She swallowed again. A sheen of sweat gathered on her skin. Her knees weren't locking. She should sit down but she feared falling if she tried to move.

"Maggie, what's going on?" He crossed the room and cupped her shoulders, crouching down to look into her eyes.

She blinked rapidly. "I can't drive with you."

His frown deepened. "Why not?" Then he drew back, comprehension reflecting in his concerned gaze. "Because you don't drive anywhere."

She nodded and turned her stare to the ceiling, not wanting to fall apart this early on a Saturday. She'd been doing so well lately.

"Hey, it's okay. We can walk."

"How will we get the supplies back here?" Even if they had a wagon, it infuriated her that she couldn't even pretend to be normal for a day. "You should go. I can paint my house another day."

"No way. We had a deal. We're painting your living room today, one way or another."

"But—"

"It's nice out. We'll walk and I'll run back and pick everything up afterward."

That seemed the least efficient way to get an early jump on the morning. "You don't have to do that—"

"Hey, I want to." He turned toward the door. "Besides, I need to get my ten thousand steps in. You'd be doing me a favor. Go get your pillow. I'll meet you outside."

He left before she could argue that this was silly. If she wasn't so embarrassed, she would have smiled. The sound of his truck engine silenced, and a tear tripped down her cheek, not because she was sad but because Ryan was one of the kindest, most understanding people she'd met in a very long time.

He didn't bring up her emotional baggage on their walk to the hardware store, which she appreciated. Instead, they talked about all the renovations needed at his house. Ryan was working on his basement— some sort of man cave.

"Does that mean girls aren't allowed?"

He laughed. "I can probably make an exception in your case."

She shrugged. "We'll see. I might not want to hang in your *boy fort*."

"It's not a boy fort. It's a man cave. There's a bar and I'm getting an enormous flat screen TV for game days."

"Football?"

"Football, hockey, baseball, soccer, I like it all."

"Steelers or Eagles?" she asked.

He stopped walking and stared at her, appraising her the way she appraised him. His answer could make or break this friendship. "I don't want to say."

"Say it. It'll come out eventually."

"Do you have a preference?"

She scoffed. "Yes."

He hesitated. "I really don't want to be your rival."

"Then pick the better team," she said through gritted teeth.

He laughed. "Oh, you're *really* into football."

"I never miss a game."

He met her stare, drew in a long breath, and blurted, "Eagles."

She grinned and lifted her chin. "Good. Then we can stay friends." And with a swish of her hair, she kept walking.

He hurried after her.

When they reached the hardware store, they split up to peruse paint samples. "Who names this stuff?" he asked, flipping through the various swatches. "Baby Wrist? Is that a thing?"

She scrunched her nose and glanced at the pale pink swatch. "That's not going in my house. I want something tranquil with a much less creepy name."

"So no Severed Thumb?"

She gaped at him and snorted when she realized he was kidding. She held up a teal sample. "Do you like this?"

"I don't think that goes with your new furniture."

"No, I meant for your man cave. It's Eagles green—unless you want to go old school."

He came closer and pulled another sample of the teal swatch. "That's pretty spot on."

"Well, there you go." She dropped the swatch in the basket. "You could do one wall in teal and the other three in something lighter. Do you have a lot of light down there?"

"No, just two small egress windows."

"Then you might want to counter it with a neutral."

He pointed to the gray in her hand. "What are you doing with that?"

"I like it for my living room."

He held the teal close to the gray. "They complement each other."

They did look nice together. "Well, that makes it easy. We can share." She tossed the swatch in the basket.

They loaded up on brushes, rollers, tarps, and other supplies. Ryan threw a few candy bars in at the register as well. She paid for her items and he paid for his. When he explained that he'd be back to pick up the order it wasn't as awkward as she'd dreaded, since they had to wait for all the paint colors to be mixed anyway.

Once back on Main Street, he asked, "You want to stop for breakfast? I need to eat before we start working."

She looked down the strip of stores and recalled the delicious scone she had. "Want to hit the café?"

"Perfect."

Maggie searched for scones once they were in front of the glass display but didn't see them. She debated between a blueberry and chocolate muffin.

"Hey, Ryan! What are you doing here?" A beautiful woman with long blond hair and flawless olive skin appeared from a curtain behind the counter.

"Hey, Mariella. Just grabbin' some coffee and breakfast."

The woman smiled, showing off perfect teeth and full lips. "We've got beignets today. My mom made them."

"Oh, hell yeah. We'll take a dozen." Then, as if remembering she was there, he turned to Maggie and asked, "You like beignets, right?"

"Sure?"

"A dozen beignets coming up." The woman winked and turned to fill a box with the fluffy white donuts.

Maggie, without realizing she moved, had drifted back a few steps. Ryan faced her. "You want a coffee to go?"

"No thanks." She'd already had some that morning at the cemetery.

The beautiful woman placed the box on the counter. "Anything else?"

"I'll take a large dark roast and…" He glanced at Maggie again. "You sure?"

"I'm sure."

"And that's it."

The woman scribbled *Ry* on the side of the cup and quickly made his coffee. "There you go, babe. On the house." Her smile rivaled the sun in terms of brightness.

"Thanks, love." He carried the box and coffee outside and Maggie followed.

"You know her?" She wasn't sure why she suddenly felt so out of place and forgotten, but there had definitely been a shift in her mood. She no longer felt like painting.

"Mariella? Yeah."

No explanation as to *how* he knew her. But Ryan was attractive, single, and in his thirties. She should have expected he'd have exes, and in a small town, there were bound to be run-ins.

Maggie never actually thought about the sort of women he'd dated, but seeing that beautiful woman in the café was a bit of a reality check, not that it was any of her business.

Why was she even thinking about this? Ryan was her neighbor. Who he dated was irrelevant.

Plus, it was stupid to let some stranger devalue her own sense of self. But that woman had been so beautiful some might even call her exotic.

Maggie wasn't blind. She'd stopped wearing makeup and doing her hair and didn't even bother to shop in the women's department. Most days she wore old cargo pants and men's cotton clothes that came in three packs.

"You okay?" Ryan asked as they turned the corner.

"She's very pretty." That hadn't been what she'd meant to say, but it was definitely the conclusion resounding in her mind.

Cocking his head, he shrugged. "I guess. She wears a lot of makeup."

"You don't like when women wear too much makeup?" She didn't know why she cared what he liked.

He glanced at her. "I prefer girls *au naturel.*"

"But you can't deny beauty like hers."

He glanced at her again, this time his brow knit in confusion. "Did I miss something?"

"No." She stuffed her hands in the front pocket of her hooded sweatshirt.

"No, something's weird." He frowned at her, like a math problem he was trying to solve. "You're, like, pissed off or something?"

She scowled. "No, I'm not."

"Did you want coffee? I would have gotten it for you."

"You mean *Mariella* would have gotten it?"

He laughed. "Does it bother you that I got this stuff on the house? I never pay when I go to the café."

"How come?" Her snarky tone was completely inappropriate. What was wrong with her?

"Because my aunt and uncle own the café. Mariella's my cousin."

Oh, my God. She was such an idiot.

He gave her a smug smirk, as if he knew where her thoughts had led. She scowled. "Is there anyone in this town you're not related to?"

"Yeah, you and about four other people."

"No wonder you're single." As the words left her mouth and his teasing expression blanked, she wished she could pull them back. "I'm sorry. I shouldn't have said that."

He smiled and pushed out a breath intended to be a laugh, but the sound lacked any joviality. "It's cool. If I use that as an excuse it takes some of the blame off my own shoulders."

She frowned. Why would he be to blame? "I didn't mean anything by it, Ryan."

He shrugged and thankfully they were nearing their street. "No worries. I *am* single. Believe me, it's not news."

When they reached his property, he wouldn't make eye contact. She remained standing on the sidewalk as he handed her the box of donuts and went directly to his truck. "I'm gonna head back and pick up the stuff at the hardware store. I'll see you…"

His goodbye felt unfinished, as if he didn't want to make any promises. She shouldn't have said anything about his personal life. She had no place. And for someone who valued privacy so deeply, she should have known better and been more respectful of his.

He pulled away before she could muster the courage to apologize. An apology might have only made things more uncomfortable. She couldn't shake the lump in the pit of her stomach.

She changed into an old Cranberries T-shirt and waited by her kitchen window, watching for his truck to return. Worried he might not come back or might make some bogus excuse that something came up, she annihilated her thumb nail, biting it into a short nub.

She needed to think before she spoke. She hardly ever talked to people, which made her the least graceful woman alive when it came to other people's feelings. It was why her relationship with her sister was strained, why her mother rarely called anymore, and why she preferred to work in a place where no one bothered her with small talk.

The truck returned and she let out a sigh of relief. Grabbing the box of donuts, she walked to his driveway, taking the long way because unlike him, she was too short to hop the fence without hurting herself.

"I was thinking we could do your basement first."

"That's fine." He didn't look at her as he unloaded the supplies.

He wasted no time setting up. It was her first time inside his house and he didn't offer a tour, so she felt awkward and uninvited looking around. She waited by the bottom of the basement steps as he loaded the roller tray with teal.

"Do you want me to cut in?"

"Sure."

She couldn't stand the sense that he was giving her the cold shoulder. This was not what she had in mind when she agreed to paint with him.

Her stomach knotted with guilt. Should she apologize? Too much time had gone by and bringing her rude comment up again felt cruel. She didn't know how to fix this and put things back to the way they were.

So she grabbed a brush and went to the far wall where he was prepping the roller. Without thinking, she bumped his shoulder with her hip, playfully knocking him off balance.

"What was that for?"

She frowned down at him. "You're being weird. If you're mad at me for what I said, then say so. But don't just ignore me."

He looked ready to argue, but instead, he dropped the roller and stood, dwarfing her by his size. "Fine. The single thing's sort of a sensitive subject for me. I used to date, but after a while it's like what's the fucking point? Every girl I've ever cared about cared more about someone else. It's never worked out for me. Maybe because half of Center County's my family, or maybe because there's something wrong with me. I stopped trying to figure it out a long time ago. A big reason why I moved to the opposite end of town is because I was tired of other people wondering what was wrong with me as well."

She frowned. "There's nothing *wrong* with you."

He rolled his eyes. "I'm glad you think so, but that still doesn't change my reality." He pointed the roller at the wall. "Let's make this the teal wall."

Seeing he didn't want to discuss it further, she let the topic rest. They painted in silence, neither of them bothering to speak or even acknowledge the other's presence. But she never forgot he was there.

He filled the squat basement like a giant. While she cut in the walls, working diligently along the trim, he rolled out the paint in long strokes. There was something unmistakably rugged about him, something hardy, masculine, and capable.

Historically, those were all qualities that would call to the opposite sex, so why was he single? She really had to stop thinking about it.

Maybe it was his beard. Some women liked men clean shaven. She still couldn't decide if his hair was more blond or red. In different lights it showed different highlights. His facial hair was a mix of copper and light brown. If memory served, it was softer than it appeared. Did he put something in it to make it soft?

"Music?"

His question startled her. She'd been daydreaming and getting paint all over the trim. "Sure." She quickly grabbed a rag and tried to clean up her sloppy mess. Realizing too late what he'd asked, she panicked. "Something old. No rock and roll, alternative rock, or blues."

She'd been having a better than usual day and didn't want to trigger an episode. More than any picture or scent, the sound of certain songs cut right to her heart and ripped her apart.

He fussed with his phone. "Something old, coming up."

A battered Dewalt boom box sitting on the steps kicked on and a recognizable beat filled the room. Of all the genres she expected he might choose, doo-wop never crossed her mind.

Her mouth formed a smile. "Good choice." She glanced over her shoulder and found him watching her.

"You like?" he asked, not knowing why she would be so selective of music but accepting her issues all the same.

"I like."

He grinned and lifted the roller to the wall, continuing his work. She returned her focus to the trim, only to pause when his voice cut through the basement.

"Are the starrrrsssss out tonight? I don't know if it's cloudy or bright. I only have eyes, forrrrr you..."

She laughed. He couldn't sing, but he got an E for effort.

"Don't you sing?"

"No."

"Oh, come on." He belted out the old doo-wop classic. *"The moon may be high, but I can't see a thing in the skyyyyyy..."*

Unable to resist, she glanced over her shoulder and lost it. He somehow contorted his blue eyes into those of a true crooner's as he sauntered across the basement floor in her direction.

"*I on—ly have eyes...*" He held out a hand. "Do you dance?"

She shook her head. "Nope. I'm embarrassed for you."

He smirked and prowled closer, moving like one of the Pips. "*Sha-bop-sha-bop... You're here and so am I...*"

"What are you doing?"

"Come on."

"No." She turned back to the wall, and he stole her paintbrush, tossing it right onto the cement floor. She tsked. "You got paint on the floor."

"*Sha-bop-sha-bop...*" He pulled her to her feet, and she pressed her lips tight, not indulging him in any way.

"Ryan." She stood but kept her arms stiff at her side.

He clicked his fingers to the beat, not touching her but also not caring that he was dancing by himself. "How long has it been since someone danced with you?"

Too long. "I don't dance."

"Try." He took her hand, lifting it to his shoulder, and dropped his grip to her hip, curling his fingers around her side. She tried not to flinch at the contact, but her body noticeably stiffened.

"Relax. I'll lead." He lifted her other hand and slowly turned them in a circle as the song played, each *sha-bop-sha-bop* bouncing off the bare cement walls and floor.

Her feet awkwardly followed along as her neck craned to look into his eyes. "Dancing, huh?" It was sort of nice.

"What can I say? Painting was getting boring."

She smiled, finding her rhythm and loosening her shoulders. Not thinking too hard about it, she rested her head against his shirt. As the song continued he quietly sang, the words rumbling from his chest to her ear.

Her eyes closed and for a second the world disappeared. She didn't think about the past or what would come tomorrow. She existed only in the present, alone with him. No guilt. No fear. Just safe.

The song ended and she blinked her eyes open, wishing it had lasted a few minutes longer. She awkwardly peeled her hand out of his grip, noting the way teal specks spattered his knuckles. Hers wore thicker smears.

"Thanks for the dance," she said, moving back to her wall and looking for her paintbrush. "That was nice."

Another doo-wop song came on. "We can keep going."

The Still of the Night. She knew it, and it triggered no painful memories. Maybe the genre was the key. She could still have music in her life, she just had to find music that didn't hold a memory. She spotted her paintbrush just as Ryan held open his hands, inviting her for another dance.

"O—okay." *Don't overthink it.*

She returned her hands to his and let him lead for the next three songs. What was it about music? It could relax a person so completely, excite them, or take them back in time. The right song could fill a person with hope or energy or even sorrow. God, she'd missed music.

For years, she assumed she'd never have music in her life again. What a relief to discover she could still handle certain songs, as long as they weren't linked to any memories of Nash.

After several slow tunes, the beat shifted to something faster, and he surprised her, twirling her. She giggled in a way she hadn't giggled in years, a full belly laugh, the way only a little girl could laugh when enchanted by everyday magic.

He made a charming dance partner. And he knew the words to almost every song.

Impressed by his skill, she asked, "Who taught you to dance?"

"My mother. Ready?"

"Ready for what?"

"Hold on." The chorus repeated, and this time, instead of twirling her, he dipped her.

All the blood rushed to her head. Worried he might drop her at this angle, her grip on his shoulders tightened. Her gaze latched with his and her amusement faded. The music seemed to drift away.

"You have the best laugh," he rasped, his arm cradling her back as he held her suspended, her hair trailing on the ground. His gaze held hers in an intense stare that made her feel trapped in something intimate she wasn't ready for.

"Ryan…" Her grip tightened, her fear of falling escalating sharply. Her belly flipped and she licked her lips, unsure how or why the energy had shifted.

"Did you get jealous this morning when you thought Mariella was more than my cousin?"

She hadn't expected the question, but recalling her silly behavior made her uncomfortable. She squirmed in his hold. "Let me up."

He hesitated, then pulled her back to an upright position. She let go of his hands, her heart beating too fast. The paint fumes were getting to her.

"I…" There weren't enough windows down here. "I need some air."

She raced up the stairs, hearing him call her name but too chicken to stop. Bolting out the back door, she trudged down the back steps and flung herself at the picket fence.

He was standing at the door when she turned. She couldn't get back to her yard without hopping the fence or coming face to face with him, which wasn't an option.

Breathing roughly, she wondered what the hell she was doing. She glanced into her yard, her gaze falling on Nash's empty chair by the firepit. Chin trembling, she looked back to Ryan.

He watched her closely. "Maggie, if it's something you honestly believe you can't handle, I'll accept that."

She swallowed tightly against the lump in her throat, unsure how to respond to such a comment. They were only dancing. They were friends. Just friends.

He let go of the back door, and it swung shut behind him. "But if you're pushing me away because of misplaced guilt, then I think we should talk about it."

She scoffed, her hands curling around the white pickets of the fence behind her. "There's nothing to say."

He casually descended the porch steps. "This morning, did I imagine something that wasn't there or were you jealous?"

Her lips formed a thin line. She turned her back to him and faced her yard. Maybe she *could* hop the fence. Her gaze got lost on the shed Nash never finished painting.

The emptiness she'd been keeping at bay vibrated her bones. She let it back in. The void in her heart yawned like a waking lion, and she shut her eyes, willing it to swallow her whole.

"It doesn't matter."

"It does to me." His body was closer. She could feel the heat of him at her back.

Her vision blurred. "It shouldn't. I can't be with you like that. I can't be with anyone."

"Why, Maggie? Maybe there's something more out there for you."

Her head shook. "I'm not right for anyone. Not anymore."

Nash broke her heart. Why would anyone want a broken heart? She was broken. Unfixable.

His fingers curled around her shoulder, tugging softly. "Look at me."

If she looked at him, he'd try to convince her she could have normal again. He didn't know how screwed up she was. He didn't know she had coffee with a ghost in the cemetery every morning. He didn't know she fought the urge to follow her husband to the grave on an hourly basis. He didn't know how deeply she'd always love him, and how that love had turned into a poison that crippled her from ever moving on.

She turned and blinked up at him, her eyes drowning in unshed tears. "I'll never be over him. And you're too nice of a guy. I don't want to hurt you."

"I'm tougher than I look." He brushed a thumb over her cheek, wiping away a tear.

She shook her head. "No." If she led him on or hurt him in any way, she'd never forgive herself. "I can't."

"Try, Maggie. All I'm asking is that you try."

Her lashes flicked and twin tears fell down her face. "I..." She didn't know how to be that kind of person anymore. She could hardly have a conversation without offending others, because as she struggled to manage her own turbulent emotions, she couldn't handle other people's feelings as well. "You deserve more than I can give. Please trust me on that."

And what if she tried and he changed his mind? What if something happened to him? She couldn't risk developing new feelings for anyone. She knew what it felt like to care and have her world ripped away without warning. Eventually, he'd realize how messed up she was, and he'd change his mind. Then where would she be?

"You don't know what you can give until you try. You can have it all, Maggie. You just gotta want it." His eyes brimmed with such sincere concern she couldn't bear feeling so exposed. "If it's me, fine. We can stick to being friends. But as your friend, I gotta tell you, you're too special to not put yourself out there again."

The jagged pieces of her heart flipped and all the tender edges ached. "I'm not special."

"The fact that you don't even realize how special you are makes it all the more true." He caught her chin between his forefinger and thumb. "You're beautiful and sweet, and there's this spunky little tomboy inside of you that I can't seem to resist."

Her chest quaked with a jagged breath. "You're only seeing what you want to see."

He shook his head. "I see you. I see your pain and grief. I see your struggle. And I see something that tells me you want more, but you're afraid to go after it. It's like your soul's crying to live, but you're terrified of waking a beast. Not all emotions hurt, Maggie."

Her breath hitched on a sob but she swallowed it back. "I'm a mess. If you saw the things in my head you'd run as fast as you could in the opposite direction."

He laughed softly. "My family's full of crazy women. I think I can handle it."

"But why should you have to? You're a sweet handsome man, who deserves a nice normal girl."

"But you're the one I want. If the feelings aren't mutual, then I severely misread the situation. But if I'm right, even just a little bit, the least you could do is level with me. I can be patient with you. I'm in no rush."

Yes, she'd been jealous that morning. The woman at the café was tall and strikingly gorgeous. She hated seeing her write his name and wink when she gave him his order on the house.

Maggie was short and the farthest thing from glamorous. She couldn't compete with women like that and didn't understand how she'd landed in some sort of mental competition in the first place. The only thing that made it better was realizing she completely misjudged the situation and they were cousins.

She shook her head. That wasn't the point. This had nothing to do with his beautiful cousin. They were neighbors. They barely knew each other. And she was, and would always be, too in love with her husband to care for anyone else. It wasn't fair to date someone knowing they'd always be second choice.

Her head lowered. "It doesn't matter if I was jealous or not."

"It does to me."

She narrowed her eyes and looked up at him. "Do you get jealous?"

"Of course. Everyone does on occasion."

"Then why the hell would you want to get involved with someone who's in love with someone else?"

His expression blanked and he eased back. "I'm not threatened by your love for him. He was your husband."

"Right. He was also my soulmate, Ryan. Those parts you're searching for, I already gave them away. And God doesn't give us backups."

"You really believe that? You think this is the rest of your life, living alone in a house where his clothes still hang by the door?"

She stiffened, startled that he'd noticed such personal details. And feeling slightly judged, despite the non-judgmental look in his eyes.

She didn't know what she thought, because she never got past thinking of Nash. But if this was all she saw in her future, why was she wasting her time and money going to therapy? Was she kidding herself with this new sense of progress? Maybe the reality was she'd never be healed.

"I don't know what I think." She looked into his eyes, wishing she had the answers he wanted. "All I know is that I'm really messed up in here." She pointed to her heart. "I want to be better, but it's a battle I fight every day, knowing how much easier it would be to just give up."

"Don't give up. I won't let you."

Her gaze lowered and she sniffled. "You have no idea how difficult it is to have no control over your life. This wasn't the way it was supposed to be. I had a plan. I used to have goals and dreams. Everything lost its meaning when he died—including me."

"You have meaning. He was just one part of you. Figuring out how to live without him doesn't mean you're forgetting the things you shared. No one will ever replace him, Maggie. No one wants to."

She lifted her stare. "How are you so understanding?"

"I have a very overbearing mother."

She laughed, wondering if that was any sort of explanation or just something he needed to get off his chest. "I hardly ever talk to my family anymore."

"Did they do something?"

"They love me, and I can't bear it." At least her sister did. Her parents were more complicated. "My perception gets confused. Sometimes their love feels like judgement and I'm so consumed with guilt, I have no energy left to defend my feelings, so I just push them away." She honestly didn't know if she had become overly sensitive or if they had lost their patience with her.

His brow knit. "Maybe we can work on that."

"There is no we." Her head and her heart were at war, and she was stuck in the middle. The things he asked of her were too difficult.

"Okay." He brushed the backs of his knuckles along her jaw. Despite her conflicting thoughts, she shut her eyes and leaned into the caress.

It would be so easy to give in if she could just shut off the gnawing guilt eating away at her insides. But it wasn't just the guilt. Beyond culpability hid a great deal of fear. Fear of the unknown. Fear of loss. Fear of more grief when she was already carrying too much to bear.

He took a step back, as if showing her he'd give her room to breathe. "What do you say we go back to painting and leave this for another day?"

"Okay."

He smiled and wrapped his hand around hers. Once again, his touch brought the overwhelming sense that she was safe.

CHAPTER 14

The clerk dropped the receipt into the bag and handed it to Maggie. "Have a nice day."

Outside of McGinty's, she withdrew her purchase and tossed the trash in a receptacle. This might end horribly. Or it could go the total opposite direction. She was trying something new so all she could do was hope for the best.

Straddling her bike, she pulled out her cell phone, searching for the Bluetooth setting that would synchronize her music with the new wireless headphones. Well, not *her* music. Her music hurt too much. She was trying different music—older music.

Finding the network, she connected the devices and keyed in a playlist for oldies, stuff Nash would never play, music before his time and outside of his repertoire.

The tiny headphones rested in her ears as a slow drumbeat played, followed by a group of silver-tongued crooners harmonizing to *The Still of the Night*. She smiled, her chest lifting with a lightness that could only come from the magic made by music and the memories she now associated with this song.

Slipping her foot onto the pedal, she gripped her handlebars and rode to work. She couldn't get enough. On the ride home from work that night, she took the long way, just to listen to a few extra songs and feel the wind hitting her face.

Hints of spring were finally showing in the grass and on the trees. She patiently watched for flowers to push through the soggy April ground and add color to the dreary smear of landscape left by winter. The daffodils would be the first to show, dotting the trees that lined Main Street, but none had bloomed just yet.

She used to love the snow, sledding, winter holidays, cuddling up

106

with a toasty mug of hot chocolate, but her favorite pastimes had forever changed when her husband slid off the road. If not for the treacherous winters and snow eaten highways, he might still be here.

When she parked her bike in front of the shed, she danced across the lawn and into the house. Still bopping along to her oldies, she washed the dishes in the sink and carried a load of laundry to the washer. Clean towels hung on the folding rack, stiff from drying. She transferred them to a basket and carried them upstairs to fold.

The living room was really coming together. The gray walls made the new blue sofa pop. Ryan had been a great help. She thought the change would be harder, triggering a deluge of unwanted guilt and pain but it wasn't.

The only time she semi-freaked-out was when he tried to move Nash's instruments. It didn't seem right to let another man hold his guitar. That belonged to Nash. It always would.

"Maggie!" Ryan plucked an earbud out of her ear, cutting off The Penguins' *Earth Angel.*

She screamed, her heart catapulting out of her chest as she jumped a foot in the air. "What the hell are you doing?"

"I was knocking for five minutes."

Her heart hammered against her ribs as she found her bearings. She removed the other earbud. "I didn't hear you."

"No kidding." He laughed. "What are you listening to?" Holding the headphone to his ear, he smiled approvingly. "Nice."

They'd been hanging out a lot lately, so she wasn't surprised to see him. He usually came by around six-thirty. Sometimes they went halves on a pizza. Ryan ate a lot of pizza, which was probably why he was here now.

"You must be hungry." She took out the earbuds and returned them to their wireless charging port so they'd be ready for tomorrow morning's bike ride.

He nodded, then stilled. "Unless you want to do something different. We could go out."

"Out?" She glanced over her shoulder as he followed her into the kitchen.

"Yeah." His gaze shot to the cabinets as he rubbed the back of his neck. "Like a date."

One tiny earbud flung out of her hand and across the counter. She quickly caught it and stuck it in the charger. "Oh."

"Or we could just do pizza again. Whatever."

They couldn't keep doing this. She already explained that she couldn't be more than a friend to him. She asked for time to think, but she'd finished thinking days ago. Her mind remained made up, and her heart belonged to someone else.

"I'd rather just … have pizza."

Understanding flashed in his eyes and he did a good job of masking his disappointment. She appreciated his effort and the fact that he never made her feel bad for her inability to be more than his friend, despite making it clear that he wanted more.

She wished there was some sort of compromise she could offer. "I'm sorry."

Her apology seemed to surprise him. "For what?"

She shrugged. He knew *what*.

Meeting him halfway, she suggested, "We could walk into town instead of having the pizza delivered."

"Yeah?"

She nodded, glad to see him smile. "Sure." So long as he understood this wasn't a date. "It's just pizza."

"Right. Okay."

It seemed a fair compromise. "I just need to get my sweatshirt and hat."

"It's getting dark. We could take my truck."

She stilled at the door, her heart shuddering. "I'd rather walk."

His footsteps approached, but he didn't touch her. "Maggie, you'll eventually have to drive somewhere. Why not practice small trips with someone you trust, before there's a situation that forces you to do something before you're ready?"

There had already been a few situations when she needed a ride, and they hadn't gone well. She'd rather not push herself unnecessarily. She lived in a town four miles long. Worked only a twenty-minute bike ride from her house. Everything she needed was reachable by foot. Only modern standards made her choice not to drive seem weird.

"I'd rather walk."

"Okay," he backed off, and that was why she enjoyed his company. He saw her issues, wanted to help her, but never pushed too hard when she balked.

The night was in the high fifties, which was a nice change from the damp, frigid weather they'd been having. The scent of the pizzeria, Vincenzo's, drifted onto the sidewalk as a man carried a box of food to the delivery truck parked out front.

It had been years since she ate in a restaurant. This wasn't a date, but it still felt significant.

"After you." Ryan hoisted open the glass door, and her lungs filled with the steamy scent of delicious ethnic cuisine. She thought she wanted pizza, but now she was reconsidering. Maybe she was in the mood for pasta.

Mambo Italiano played from a speaker in the corner, tucked above an old black and white photo of an unmistakably Italian family crowded around a large dinner table cluttered with enormous bowls of pasta, meat courses, salads, and other famous dishes. The kitchen walls wore a powdered dusting of dough flour, and the loud hum of employee chatter competed with the sounds coming from the dining room.

A young woman with jet black hair and full red lips came from the kitchen, brushing her hands across a sauce stained apron. "Ryan!" She practically yelled in greeting, her ruby lips splitting into a bright smile. "Hey, Angela, get out here!"

Another woman, roughly the same mid-twenties age with the same dark brown hair appeared and held out her hands. "You're kiddin' me!" She rounded the counter and cupped Ryan's face, holding him in place with an equal mix of aggression and affection. Slapping a smacking kiss on his cheek, she yelled, "We were starting to think you were being held prisoner in that house of yours."

"Yeah, Ry, you don't want to come visit us anymore? What gives?"

He actually flushed, and Maggie got a small thrill out of seeing these women pick on him. They obviously had a close connection with him. She tried to guess what that link might be without overthinking, but she couldn't figure it out. They looked too Italian to be his relatives, but then again, the woman at the café had an Italian name and she had been his cousin.

"Nicky!" the woman, Angela, shouted, causing Ryan to flinch. She turned back to him and pinched his bearded cheek. "All this hair! You're like a werewolf."

His flush darkened. "You don't like it?"

"Nah, it suits you." She made a muscle in her arm. "Rugged. Anyway, we got a nice veal cutlet today. Why don't you let Nicky cook for you? She'll start with a nice *caprese* salad." She slapped his stomach. "Eh? You need a break from all that pizza."

"Look who the cat dragged in!" A third black haired woman appeared, with similar enthusiasm, hugging and kissing him like the others had. She dragged him behind the counter and Maggie wasn't sure if she should follow. It was a whirlwind of bad dye jobs, cheap perfume, and too much gold jewelry.

"Come on. We'll get you a good table." The third woman nudged him in the shoulder with zero subtlety. "You and your *lady friend.*"

Maggie fell into step behind them as the women shoved Ryan into a booth along the back wall. They collected the menus off the checkered red tablecloth and told him to give them five minutes. Apparently, they had no say in their dinner tonight.

When the three women disappeared to the kitchen, Maggie looked at him, noting the flush of his cheeks hidden behind the red of his beard, now marked with three crimson kiss marks.

She laughed. "They're not Clooneys."

"No, definitely not."

There was something special about the pizza shop, the essence of family and acceptance with a dash of judgment that came from the deepest place of love. If she had a place to belong like that she'd never leave. Or maybe she would. She had family and still chose not to interact with them.

Not wanting to think of her own life, she focused on his. "Who are they?"

"They're my cousins-in-law. Their brother Anthony is married to my cousin Kate McCullough."

"There really isn't anyone in this town you're not related to, is there?"

"I told you, not many. If you look at our family tree, you could even trace our family back to the O'Malleys."

"Shut up."

"I'm serious." His eyes turned to the ceiling, as if he were solving a complicated calculus equation in his head. "My grandfather on my mother's side was an O'Leahey. But my grandmother was originally a Murphy twice removed from the Ó Máille generation, and everyone knows that was Caleb Senior's family's surname before they changed it to the Americanized O'Malley."

She blinked, hardly able to follow a word of that. "Do they make you study your family's ancestry as some sort of clan mentality training?"

His laughter rung out, and he looked so relaxed and perfect in that moment, bursting with such unthreatening confidence, she wondered again how it was possible that he remained single.

"Yes, but rule number one of the clan mentality club is that we don't talk about the clan mentality club."

"Here we are." One of the black haired women—Maggie couldn't tell them apart—delivered a platter covered in thickly cut buffalo mozzarella and fresh tomatoes, drizzled in olive oil and a balsamic vinaigrette, sprinkled with shavings of aromatic basil.

Maggie's mouth watered, and she unraveled a fork from the dinner napkin.

"Beautiful," Ryan praised. "Maria, this is my neighbor, Maggie."

"Good to meet you. We got a real nice antipasto platter tonight. Some paper-thin *prosciutto*, Kalamata olives, fresh baked bread, and sautéed long hots. You want me to bring somethin' out?"

"Bring it all," Ryan welcomed and the woman beamed.

"That's a lot of food." Maggie cut a sliver of *caprese* and shut her eyes as the soft cheese melted on her tongue, mingling perfectly with the vibrant blend of basil and tomatoes. "*Ohmygod*," she slurred, shoving another bite into her mouth.

"Right?" Ryan popped a slice between his lips.

"What *is* this?" The burst of salt and homemade cheese melted like a drop of heaven over her tongue.

He chewed with a smile, watching her savor the food. "I'm pretty sure it's made from the same stuff orgasms are made of."

She snorted. "No wonder I can't remember the last time I tasted something so good."

He arched a brow but didn't comment. Still, she blushed. Definitely too much information but goddamn this salad was off the charts delicious.

Another sister brought out the *antipasto* platter and cleared away the *caprese.* Ryan introduced her again. The women were very preoccupied with feeding him and paid little attention to her. Maggie didn't mind because the food was *that* good.

By the time the main dish arrived, she was painfully stuffed but couldn't seem to put down her fork. The pasta was a delicate angel hair that tasted so fresh she knew it was nothing more than eggs and flour that morning. And the veal, seared then dressed in a rich tomato sauce, had no match. It was easily the most delicate meat she'd ever tasted.

"I can't stop."

He groaned, twirling another bite of pasta on the tines of his fork and hefting it into his mouth. His eyes glazed with a sort of contentment that only came with incredible food or sex. But in all honesty, the meal might've been better than sex—she couldn't remember.

He groaned somewhere between pain and pleasure. "We have to stop."

"Have to," she agreed, dredging a mouthful of sauce with the last piece of bread and shoving it into her mouth.

"I'm gonna be sick if I eat one more bite."

The third sister appeared. "So?"

"Oh, my God, so good," Maggie said, holding her belly.

"Amazing," Ryan agreed, giving his bloated stomach a pat.

The woman preened. "Maria's slicing you a nice piece of tiramisu. How about coffee?"

Maggie was going to burst, but the thought of leaving and not tasting the tiramisu felt like some sort of capital sin. "I think I'll need coffee just to make it home."

"Two coffees."

Maria cleared the table, and a moment later a square of layered rum-scented cake dusted with spicy cinnamon sat between them with two spoons balanced on the side. He lifted his and touched it to hers.

"Cheers."

They took a bite at the same moment and both groaned, the sounds equally sexual and ripe with contentment.

"Holy crap."

"Shh." She shut her eyes and held up her hand, savoring the decadent taste. "Shut up. I'm in the middle of something."

He laughed. "You have cinnamon on your chin."

"I don't care." Her eyes sprung open when his finger brushed her jaw. He smiled. "Got it."

Maggie slowly licked her lips, unable to turn her heavy gaze away. She was in some sort of Italian food oblivion. A real carbohydrate coma. Everything felt soft and heavy and warm. That's when it occurred to her, despite their intentions, this had turned into a date.

"Um…" Realization ricocheted between them. He knew it and she knew it. Hell, the three sisters probably knew it. Maggie cleared her throat and looked down at her coffee. "So…"

"So…" he echoed.

The emptiness of the restaurant registered as did the soft flicker of the votive candles and the dainty red rose in the bud glass between them. She put down her spoon and sat back. Did this sneak up on him the way it snuck up on her? Or did he plan it all along?

Dean Martin's voice rang from the speakers singing *Everybody Loves Somebody.*

Her head lowered, realizing she'd been the one to suggest they go out instead of ordering in. Stupid. Why did she keep putting herself in situations like this with him?

"I didn't plan this," he said, seeming to follow her train of thought.

She chewed her lower lip, still tasting the sweet spice of cinnamon. "I know."

"Nothing's happening, Maggie. We had a nice meal and shared a nice night."

That wasn't true. Something else was happening. The worst part was, on some level she *wanted* something to happen.

"Are you mad at me?"

She frowned at him. "Why would I be mad?"

He shrugged. "You seem upset."

"I'm … confused."

When she was with Ryan, she was happy. He made her laugh and he kept her mind off the past. But that was the problem. She didn't want to forget about the past. It anchored her to reality and kept her safe. Yet, with Ryan she felt safe in a different way.

Time flew when they were together, because he was fun. But whenever she realized she forgot to think of Nash, the guilt would kick her ass. Maybe it was progress not to think of him so much. That was the goal, right? Progress?

First, she'd thought of him every minute, then every few minutes, then sometimes every hour, and eventually she might reach a point where she only thought of him a few times a day. She couldn't imagine. Especially when forgetting to think of him for one meal made her feel so awful.

She lowered her coffee mug and folded her hands in her lap, unable to meet his stare. "I have this fear that you'll erase him."

"What?"

Her brow pinched with regret. "The more time we spend together, the less I think of him."

"Maggie, you can't put that on me."

"I know. But it's what's happening. I like *this*. But I feel like I'm losing pieces of myself the more we do *this*."

And each night when Ryan left her, her mind worked double-time, entrenching her with memories of Nash. She drowned in guilt for forgetting to be sad for an hour, which only further proved she was crazy.

His brow creased and he put down his spoon. "We've never done *this* before. I'm not even sure I know what *this* is."

"*This*. Us. I know you like me."

"I could argue the same."

Her gaze shot to his, accusation burning her eyes, but she couldn't deny his words.

"You're not losing anything, Maggie." He reached across the table and squeezed her hand in a tight grip. "I know he was your first love and your husband and he'll always own a part of your heart. I'm not trying to take that away from you or him. I just like to be near you." His grip loosened and he laced his fingers with hers. Her shoulders buckled as fresh guilt whooshed in. "Tonight was harmless. We had a delicious meal and we laughed and neither of us had to spend it alone. Don't turn it into something ugly because of misplaced guilt. We aren't erasing anything."

She shut her eyes, envisioning Nash's brown eyes, but they quickly wavered with blue. She tried to remember the shape of his ears and the angle of his jaw, but Ryan's beard was all her mind wanted to see.

She was falling for him. What would happen when they argued about something stupid, or when he wanted something she couldn't give? He'd pull away and she'd be alone again. She was starting to remember how nice having someone's company could be, starting to want things she shouldn't want.

"You'll get tired of me."

He scowled. "You don't know that."

"Friendship's easier. Couples argue. And then they break up."

"We aren't even going out yet. One step at a time, Maggie."

"There are too many reasons not to—"

"Excuses. Not reasons." He wrapped her imprisoned hand in both of his. "And for every excuse you throw at me, I can give you two reasons why we should try. But that's not what tonight was. Tonight was just two friends keeping each other company. Don't feel bad because you enjoyed it."

She tried to shove back the blame, and a smile trembled to her lips. "It was nice." Until she ruined it with more talk about her inadequacies.

"We make each other laugh. We have fun together. There's something between us, whether we acknowledge it or not. We have chemistry. We like the same football team, drink the same beer, and I'm teaching you what decent whiskey tastes like instead of that piss you're used to. I can even over-look the fact that your last name's O'Malley because that's what friends do."

She didn't know how to respond but loved all those commonalities they shared too. "You're a real pain in my ass."

"You're not the first person to say that."

She drew in a deep breath and let it out slowly. Rather than pull her hand away, she stopped trying to move it at all. Her fingers fit perfectly between his. It was … comforting.

"Okay."

His head tipped with confusion. "Okay?"

She nodded. "Okay, I'll … keep an open mind. But you have to be patient with me."

"Always."

"And you can't ghost out of our friendship, no matter how much you might want to. I know I'm frustrating, but I need to know that you won't just abandon me without warning. Before anything else, we're friends. That can't change."

"Deal. And for the record, I would never ghost you. You know where I live."

"I do, but…" Maybe this wouldn't be so weird if they took things super slow. Dating was basically friends with…

And just like that, a wall went up and she stumbled into a world of doubt.

"Get it out," he said softly. "We might as well put everything on the table from the start."

Being anything more than friends would eventually require more than friendship. She'd never shared such intimacies with anyone but Nash. Her mind couldn't go there yet. Or ever.

"Maggie, where'd you go? You just stopped talking."

She should warn him she had major limits, things she wasn't sure she had the strength or the urge to work through. Her head was a minefield of uncertainty. "As far as…" She waved a hand between them, but couldn't bring herself to say it.

"Coffee? Food? Flamboyant hand gestures?"

"Sex," she hissed.

He grinned. "I knew what you meant. I just wanted to hear you say it."

Her eyes narrowed. "Well, as far as that goes, I'm not sure I'll ever get there." It wasn't a stipulation that necessarily included him, just a confes-sion amongst friends—one she thought he should hear.

He looked like he wanted to argue, but he kept his mouth shut.

"Told you I couldn't be what you—"

"Oh, I'm still interested."

"What? How?"

He chuckled. "Easily. And, to be clear, I'm *very* interested. But I have one rule."

"What's the rule?" She had a lot of hard limits, even in her easiest relationships, which was a big reason why dating seemed too complicated to comprehend.

"No matter what we are, we're always totally honest with each other. I'm okay with approaching this differently, because you're different and I like that about you. But I'm not a mind reader, so I need you to tell me what's going on with you if something comes up. And I want you to keep an open mind. No ruling things out until we get there."

"That's two rules."

He shrugged. "They're important."

She let out another long breath. "Okay."

His face came to life as a smile stretched his cheeks. He lifted her hand and kissed the tips of her fingers.

"I knew I'd wear you down."

"You're not wearing me down. You just got me to agree I'd keep an open mind. I still think you're a pain in the ass."

"Whatever. It's progress." They walked home and he didn't release her hand until they reached her house.

CHAPTER 15

"*Y*ou're smiling."

Maggie's thoughts scattered as Alec lowered into his chair. "Huh? Oh." She supposed she had been grinning, though she hadn't realized. "Sorry."

"Please, don't apologize. It's nice to see you happy." He collected his leather notebook and settled in across from her. "How are things?"

For the past three weeks she'd been sleeping better, eating more, drinking less, and laughing *a lot*. "Things are … good."

"Do labels like *good* or *happy* worry you?"

"No," she quickly answered. *That would be crazy*. But the more she thought about it… Her lips twisted and she sighed. "Maybe."

His eyes creased at the corners as if he appreciated her candid honesty. "What, exactly, do you find worrisome about those adjectives?"

She shrugged. "Life never stays comfortable for long. Things change."

"And you want to be prepared for that change?"

"It's inevitable, so yeah."

He nodded, as if he agreed, which sort of felt like a setup, because then he asked, "But why borrow trouble? Why not just embrace this comfortable stage and enjoy it while it lasts?"

"It's my nature to prepare for the worst."

He cocked his head. "Based on the stories you've told me about your past, I'm not sure that's always been true."

"I was young. Young people are inherently naïve." Before becoming a widow, she'd been blissfully trusting that life was fair, and the world was a safe place.

He offered a charming smile. "I'm going to let you in on a little secret. I have it on great authority that you're still considered young. But I wouldn't dare to call you naïve. In fact, your life expe-

116

riences have taught you lessons most people don't learn until their golden years. I find your perspective on life both informed and tempered."

"Thanks?"

"Just my personal observation. Which is why I'm intrigued by your reluctance to accept happiness when it enters your life again."

"I'm not *reluctant*. I just know it's temporary."

"One could argue that everything's temporary, including life."

"Exactly."

He raised a brow. "And knowing our time here is limited and growing shorter every day, you draw some sense of security from reminding yourself of this?"

"No, but I don't want to be blindsided. When Nash died, my entire world turned upside down."

"And, had you known Nash's time was running out, would you have been more prepared?"

She considered his question, wondering how things would have been different if she could have known March eighteenth was his last day on this earth, her last chance to look into his eyes, the last morning she'd wake up in his arms and hear his laughter.

"I would have wasted less time."

"When you think of time wasted, what comes to mind?"

"I guess I wouldn't have worried so much about the stupid stuff that used to drive me crazy. The petty things married people bicker about like the dishes or taking the trash out."

"And how much time do you suppose you would have spent worrying about time, if you knew when your time together would run out."

She shifted uncomfortably. "It would have consumed me."

"Knowing that, if you had the option to know when his time was up, would you take it, or would you choose to finish your time together in blissful ignorance?"

Every day they spent together had been genuine until the very end. They were both ignorant, lost in their twenties still under the delusion that they were young and invincible. She'd been so unaware of how quickly life could change, how permanent loss could be.

Losing him had been a hurricane ripping through her heart. It happened too fast for her to understand. The moment the chaos stilled and the condolences fell away, she drifted in an endless sea of confusing aftermath, where her reality resembled more of a nightmare than any version of her life before. It passed like a bad dream, and for days and weeks she hoped to wake up, hoped for her old reality to return. But it didn't.

Losing him was like a bullet cleaving through her soul, fast and over before she could process what was actually happening until her world cut away. The real pain didn't come until after he was gone, when the grieving set in.

"I wouldn't want to know," she whispered. "Knowing how limited our time was only would have distressed me. I would have been consumed with fear of the inevitable and possibly missed our last moments together. We were happy. We argued and had our moods, but we were content until the very end."

His lips formed a compassionate smile. "Perhaps it's wise advice then, to not look too far ahead in the future. Why not try to simply exist in the present and enjoy it while it lasts?"

"That's easier said than done."

He didn't disagree. "Imagine you could go back in time and speak to the Maggie who existed three years ago. You can't tell her what's going to happen, but you can give her advice. What would you tell her?"

"I'd tell her to never miss an opportunity to say I love you. To take more pictures and videos. To back up her hard drives and print things out. I'd tell her to save every love note, to record him singing, and to take more time to laugh."

All those seemingly meaningless things were what she missed the most. She didn't care about the house or the car or any of the stuff couples often stressed to accumulate. She assumed she'd have decades of cards and letters to save, so keeping his silly Post-It notes seemed foolish. Sometimes she found one crumpled in a drawer like a little treasure that survived a war.

"I'd tell her to get new tires."

He handed her a tissue. "And what would Nash tell you, if he could offer some advice?"

She wiped her nose. "I don't know."

"Try to guess. You knew him better than anyone else. You knew his strengths and flaws. What would he say to you if he knew just how limited his time was?"

She didn't like this game. Her shoulder lifted in a half-hearted shrug. "He'd probably tell me he didn't like the new couch."

"Go deeper. He's given the rare chance to address you from the beyond. I highly doubt he'd waste time commenting on your furniture choices."

He didn't know Nash. Her husband never liked anything too serious. "He'd hate death, hate that there was no punch line to his circumstances."

"Deeper. This isn't about him. It's about what he'd say to *you*."

"He'd tell me he misses me." Her voice strained against a lump in her throat, each word scraping painfully past her lips. "He'd wish he could touch me one last time. He'd tell me he's sorry."

"Sorry for...?"

"Leaving me." Goose bumps rose on her flesh. "He'd tell me to stop hanging out in the cemetery and stop being so sad."

But he wouldn't tell her how. Not even Dr. Alec Devereux could tell her that. No one could because no one knew how to turn off this pain inside of her.

Grief was the counterpoint of love. The more a person loves something, the more painful their sorrow became when that something disappeared. She loved Nash with every ounce of her being, so when he went away, he took her entire soul with him, leaving only a skeletal shell behind.

"Do you need to stop, Maggie?"

She realized Alec had asked her a question. "No. What did you ask?"

"I asked what Nash would say about Ryan?"

Her chest tightened painfully. Her head shook. "He wouldn't like that."

"You don't think he'd want to see you happy?"

"Happy, yes. But he was always very territorial. He'd hate the idea of me dating another man." He couldn't even bear the thought of her hiding in a closet with Danny Darushak for seven minutes in fifth grade.

"Let's take Nash out of it, for a moment. How do *you* feel about being with another man?"

Her head shook with more conviction. "I'm not there yet. We're barely… We're not dating. I doubt we'll ever get to a normal adult standard."

"Normal is a relative term in regard to adult relationships."

"We don't do anything. We aren't … intimate."

"Intimacy takes many forms. Intercourse is only one version. There are thousands."

"Well, we aren't doing any of them either."

"I'd like you to shut your eyes and imagine a time in the past few weeks when you were alone with Ryan. Can you do that?"

She closed her eyes and pictured them standing in his kitchen, hovering by the counter over an open box of pizza as they joked about random things and stuffed their faces. They'd done this enough that each memory started to look the same in her head.

"Okay."

"In that moment, can you recall any sense of longing? Perhaps a time when you wished he would touch you or look at you? Have there been moments like that recently?"

She recalled a moment yesterday. He'd said something funny and made her crack up. His eyes watched her closely and he smiled, slipping in a whispered compliment about her laugh. He said it was prettier than choir bells—*a perfect mix of chaos and beauty.*

Of course, at that comment her laughter drifted away and there had been a moment of silence when the energy between them stretched like glue, holding them tight to that moment of time and also filling her with the nervous sensation of being trapped in something sticky.

"Yes, but..." Ryan never crossed those lines. "He knows I'm not ready."

"Do you think it's his belief that you're not ready, keeping him at bay, or is it possibly a need to respect your decision? Who is actually controlling those moments, you or him?"

"Both of us."

"You mentioned him promising to be patient several times, but patience doesn't negate desire. If you asked him to touch you, do you fear he might reject you?"

"No. I know he wants more. But he wants me to be ready."

"And what do you want?"

More guilt scraped at her belly, clawing the insides raw. "I don't know."

"There's no judgment here, Maggie. You're in a safe space. It's just us. No Ryan. No Nash. What do *you* want? We can't live our true life until we're prepared to be honest with ourselves."

Chills raced up her spine. She couldn't look him in the eye. "I ... miss closeness. But what if the thing I'm missing is closeness with Nash. I don't want to hurt Ryan."

"Ryan is a grown man, who is capable of expressing and protecting himself. This is about you."

She swallowed. "What if I regret it? What if we do something that can't be undone, and I can't bear the reality?"

"You mean what if you create a *permanent* regret?"

"Yes."

"So, is it safe to say you're afraid of change but also afraid that nothing will change the status quo?"

That didn't make sense. She couldn't be afraid of both, could she? "No, only with certain things."

"Such as?"

"Guilt. It's unending. Loss. Absence. I'm afraid of things changing for the worse, but I accept nothing's permanent."

"Except regret. Is it fair to say you're afraid of regretting actions that can't be undone?"

"I just ... don't want to be sad anymore."

He nodded with understanding. "Uncertainty can be paralyzing when we focus on all the possible negative outcomes. But if we stay still, we don't evolve. Happiness is a byproduct of change. Yes, it's temporary, but that's why it's human nature to keep moving. Life experience is meant to be an evolution of self. We can't experience success without the chance of failure. You might discover new regrets, but you might also discover new levels of happiness."

He was right. She knew he was right, so there was no point in debating him.

After several minutes of silence, he asked, "Has stillness relieved your sadness in any way? Do you find avoidance a beneficial coping skill?"

"No."

He opened his palms, as if to say there you have it. "Perhaps grief is a wound timepiece that needs to unwind at its own pace. There are varying levels of heartache, and each person processes loss differently. For some, it might even be a permanent ache. None of us know how much time it will actually take to heal, and there's no written law that says grieving alone will hurry things up. On the contrary, the only thing that seems to speed up time is happiness, living life to its fullest potential."

"Sort of a double-edged sword because none of us really know how long we have."

He grinned. "That's why time's so precious."

"I get it," she admitted. "I know I can't go on like this forever, but it feels like it's too soon to … start over. What if Ryan's just some guy I'm supposed to know? What if everything we have is just a fling? I've never been with anyone but Nash. Our relationship grew as we grew up together. He was my life. We had a hundred dates at the middle school lunch tables before we even kissed. We shared a million conversations and a thousand secrets before we lost our virginities together. I don't know how to date a man. I don't have a clue what I'm supposed to do."

"*Is* there a specific expectation?"

She raised her brows. "Are you trying to make me say it?"

He frowned. "Do you think teenagers are the only generation to share those first emotional forms of intimacy, those curious insecurities that come with sharing vulnerabilities?"

"No, but adults screw. It's casual."

"Not to all adults."

She pursed her lips. "Fine. To *most* adults sex isn't a big deal. I've made it this enormous elephant in the room, and I don't know how to shrink it."

"You want intimacy to hold less significance? How much less?"

She lifted a shoulder. "I'd prefer a mouse to an elephant."

"Elephants are afraid of mice. Making something appear smaller doesn't always remove the fear factor."

"Which is why I don't think it'll ever happen. It'll always be a big deal, and my obsessing over it will only make things more awkward."

"Yet, you said Ryan's willing to wait until you're ready where intimacy is concerned. Knowing that, do you still feel pressured?"

She crossed her legs and then crossed her arms over her chest. Her brow scrunched as she tried to pinpoint the source. "Maybe."

"Do you know where that pressure's coming from?"

Her lips pressed tight and she bobbed her foot nervously. "I think so."

"Can you share it?"

She looked toward the windows, her frustration mounting. "It's coming from me. Okay? It's me. I like him. I like when he looks into my eyes, and I like when he holds my hand. And sometimes he touches my hair or my shoulder and…"

"It's okay to enjoy those things, Maggie."

"It's too soon."

"According to who?"

"Me." Though her body didn't seem to agree. "I don't know." Her arms tightened over her chest. "What if people think I'm dishonoring Nash's memory or assume I didn't love him as much because I move on?"

"Which people? Who has a right to the intimate details of your sex life?"

She shrugged. Perrin would eventually ask. "My sister."

"How would she know unless you told her?"

"I don't know. She'll be able to tell. She knows me better than anyone." Which was why she'd been dodging her since Ryan moved in. Too many questions.

Alec flipped to a clean sheet of paper and wrote something down. "There's a saying. It's an oldie but a goody. I'm going to write it down for you, and I want you to keep it in your pocket for the next few weeks. Read it often and try to memorize it. Feel free to repeat it whenever you're feeling unfairly judged and criticized." He tore off the sheet of paper and passed it to her.

She read his scribble. *"Butt out."*

"I know it's not the most eloquent phrase, but I find it does the trick."

She smiled, wondering what it was like for him living on that mountain with all those McCulloughs. "I bet you use this from time to time."

"It's come in handy on occasion."

"Thanks." She folded the paper and stuffed it in her pocket.

When Alec subtly closed his portfolio, she knew their time was up. She hadn't moved any closer to a decision where Ryan was concerned, but she decided to work on being more honest with herself.

Ryan was an unexpected surprise. He was thoughtful. Sometimes he brought her trashcans up from the curb. He bought her a headlight for her bicycle. He held doors for her. But most of all, he made her feel good, when for the last two years she'd felt nothing but sadness rotting away her insides. Somehow, he soothed some of her pain.

Scrubbing her palms over her face, Maggie tried to shake off the uncomfortable feelings that surfaced during their session. She stood and so did Alec. "So, same time next Monday?"

"There's one more thing, Maggie." He waited until she looked at him. "This is a bit awkward, and I wasn't sure if I should bring it up or not but I didn't want to blindside you."

"What are you talking about?"

"This weekend we might see each other at the party."

Party? She frowned. "What party?"

His expression turned confused. "It's Ryan's birthday."

"It is?"

"I assumed you knew."

"No. He didn't tell me." Crap. "Is it Saturday or Sunday?"

"I'm not sure, but his family's planning a surprise party for him on Saturday."

"I wasn't invited."

"I'm not sure anyone knows he's dating. But I assumed you'd go with him. I'm sure they've planned some sort of ruse to get him to the party."

A party meant family and Ryan had an enormous family. Would it be all of them? Where would it take place?

"I wanted to give you advance notice so my presence didn't throw you for a loop. But if me being there makes you uncomfortable, I can easily stay home. An evening without my in-laws isn't always a hardship. We see each other often."

She didn't like making waves and didn't want to cause anyone to change their plans. "No, he's your family. You should go."

"You're sure?"

"Yes." It was a small town, and they'd been in the same place at the same time before with his family. Besides, she wasn't even on the guest list, so it didn't matter anyway. "I'll be fine. It'll be fine."

"No one knows you're my client, so there's no need to feel uncomfortable."

But she knew and Ryan was very observant. He'd pick up on their connection. "Okay. Then I guess I'll see you…"

"Saturday," he supplied.

"Right. Saturday." She had less than forty-eight hours to think of a gift idea or an excuse. Maybe she was getting that bug going around.

CHAPTER 16

On the ride home from therapy, Maggie thought about possible birthday gifts for Ryan. Since he hadn't told her his birthday was approaching, she had to act like she didn't know. Why hadn't he told her? He'd bought her several thoughtful little gifts since they'd met, so she wanted to get him something special for his birthday. But what?

Alec seemed surprised that she didn't know about the party. She wasn't surprised. Ryan had moved out of his parents' house to get some space from his family. Their relationship was new and still fragile. He likely hadn't told his relatives about her. And seeing how many there were that was probably a good thing.

On the nights Ryan worked at the bar, he could get tied up until well after midnight if they were busy. With summer coming, and the college students returning home, the nightlife tended to pick up a bit in town.

That night he worked a second shift at the pub and she waited for him to come home. She constantly checked the window to see if his truck was in the driveway.

After two hours of hovering and stalking, she decided to take a ride into town and visit him. So long as the crowd was nothing like St. Patrick's Day, she would be fine.

The days were lasting longer, and it was officially spring. She parked her bike out back of O'Malley's where no one would mess with it. Then walked around the front to the entrance.

The pub appeared empty compared to the last time she'd been there. *Crimson and Clover* played from the jukebox and her breath caught. This was a Nash song, but it didn't quite paralyze her the way his music sometimes could. She scanned the bar, focusing on her other senses in an attempt to ignore the music.

A few people filled the booths along the wall, and a group of men ate at a center round table. The bar stools were mostly full, but she found an opening and climbed up. Being as vertically challenged as she was, her feet dangled like a toddler's from a highchair.

"Can I get you somethin', love?"

Her jaw fell open. All words and thoughts literally came out in one clunk of a syllable that sounded nothing like a word, more like a "*glinfdh.*"

Was she having a stroke? Her vision seemed fine. Unless she was dreaming.

"What'll it be, beautiful?" The dark haired bartender waited, but her motor skills had taken an unexpected vacation.

Her face heated and she giggled—a sort of girlie chirp reserved for playgrounds and pep squads, a sound she couldn't recall ever making before. As he stared at her with those crystal blue eyes, her face caught fire. That look was the flirtatious equivalent of a lobotomy. And she was *not* immune.

"Hey!" Ryan appeared beside the black haired Adonis, his welcoming grin a much more comfortable place for her eyes to rest. "What a great surprise. I wasn't expecting you. Did you meet my cousin, Kelly?"

Another cousin? Of course they were related. Why should she be surprised? She briefly glanced back at the bartender and regained control of her face and words. "Hi."

"You two know each other?" the blue eyed devil asked.

Maggie didn't risk more than a glance in his direction. Those eyes had tighter grips than bear traps. And sweet Jesus, his hair was a mussed disaster of bed head and beauty. Testosterone wafted off this man in consuming gusts.

Ryan rounded the bar, and she only slightly tensed when he rested his hands on her shoulders, massaging gently. "Kelly, this is my girl-friend, Maggie O'Malley."

Oh shit. The room chilled a few degrees. It was enough of a change to distract her from the fact that he'd introduced her as his girlfriend.

Blue eyes narrowed on her. "O'Malley?"

She cleared her throat. "By marriage only. My maiden name's Harris."

"Ah." Kelly tossed a coaster on the bar.

He glanced at Ryan who gave a subtle shake of his head, as if to say her marriage was an off-limits topic.

The bartender let the conversation drop and asked, "What can I get you?"

She hadn't planned on drinking, but now a beer sounded like a good idea, so she ordered a Guinness. As Kelly stepped away, she pivoted on her stool to glared at Ryan. "Thanks for that."

"What? It's your name." He pressed a kiss on her cheek too fast for her to object. "Missed you today."

Her gaze reflexively scanned the patrons, looking for any familiar faces. But she supposed the pub was a safe place to show affection, free of her O'Malley in-laws.

Not that she was doing something wrong. She wasn't married anymore.

Why did she continue to need such reassurance? Reminders, though painful, helped her remember she wasn't breaking any rules, but they also slid over her like razor blades, seemingly smooth yet slicing her open.

Was dating just a way to figure out how to bleed silently, or would the hurt eventually ease? Or, as a widow, would it cut every time?

One minute. It took only one minute for her thoughts to cycle into a place she didn't want to go. Shaking off those depressing thoughts, she focused on the present and Ryan's words clicked.

"You missed me?" Her chest warmed. Her mouth formed a genuine smile, which it often did in his presence.

"Since the minute you left." He had a way of making her feel special every time they were together.

"I missed you, too." So much so, she rode her bike here when she'd usually be getting ready for bed.

Kelly returned with her beer then left to take other orders. "So, is he the one that owns this place?"

"Yeah. Well, he runs it. The deed's still in my dad and uncle's names. But that's all changing. They're selling it."

"They're selling the bar?"

Disappointment flashed in Ryan's eyes. "Kelly's an artist on the side, but his art's become such a big deal he doesn't have time to do that and run the bar. No one else in the family wants the responsibility."

She noted the frustration in his voice. "You don't want him to sell it?"

"No, but I can't afford it. And I have a job at the lumberyard. The double shift thing's a killer. My other relatives are all too busy with kids and family to run the business." He shrugged, as if it wasn't a big deal, but he appeared unmistakably sad. "It's the end of an era."

The bar was clearly a nostalgic part of his life. "I'm sorry. That stinks."

"Tell me about it. I love this place. And if one of us doesn't keep it, it'll probably get torn down. Next thing you know, it'll be a bank or a pharmacy or some other dime a dozen commercial pop-up store."

"Maybe someone in town will buy it. People need a watering hole." The O'Malleys were the only ones who avoided the pub. Everyone else practically lived there.

"It's been in our family for fifty years. The value's in the nostalgia. Once inspectors and realtors get involved, they'll probably condemn the building until renovations are made. Add that to the price of the lot and the added cost of buying the O'Malley's name..." He shook his head.

"Even if someone did buy it, it wouldn't be the same. It makes more fiscal sense to tear it down and build something new."

He seemed really broken up over the decision. "Change is hard." She could sympathize.

Since the town elected a new mayor and been awarded a federal grant for some revitalization projects, Main Street had been growing. They used to be a county with one salon, one pub, and one place to buy tractors, which also happened to be the same place the townsfolk bought their jeans and flannel. It was neat watching new stores appear as the town modernized but also weird.

"I heard they're petitioning for a new town name." She sipped her beer.

His brow furrowed and it was clear he hadn't heard. "What? How? Changing the name to what? Center County's always just been Center County."

She tried to remember what she'd overheard the guys saying at work. "It has something to do with the revitalization projects happening. With the town attracting so much new business, the council wants to try for more government grants. But Center County's large and we're all sort of lumped together with neighboring towns. If the county's sorted into districts, our numbers look better on paper for funding." She shrugged, because it didn't make much difference to her. "It makes sense. I mean, there's an extreme difference between our neighborhood and the next town over."

"But what would they call it?"

She shrugged. "They're voting on names. The article I read said the idea is to represent small-town charm. The town off Exit 6 just petitioned to change their name to Ryder Creek."

His frown deepened. "Not the pig farmers?"

She nodded. "They're probably tired of being referred to as *the pig farmers*. A big inn is opening up, so I imagine it has to do with tourism. It's kind of smart."

"I guess. But it just seems like everything's changing. What was wrong with the way things are?" His hand ran over the length of bar in front of him and affection reflected in his distant stare.

"Change is hard," she repeated. "Especially when it's unexpected."

"Yeah. Not to sound like a pussy, but it gets me really upset. This place has been a part of our family for generations. It's where our family celebrates weddings, birthdays, and sacraments. But it won't be there for my family, if I ever end up having one of my own."

She hated seeing him sad, especially when he was so good at cheering her up whenever she needed it. "Will it make you feel better if I let you beat me at darts?"

He barked out a laugh. "*Let me* beat you? Honey, I could give you every advantage in the world and you wouldn't stand a chance at beating me."

"Oh, game on." She chugged the rest of her beer and hopped off the stool. "Are your legs feeling okay? Strong? Because after this ass whooping you won't be able to sit for a while."

All sadness evaporated from his stare and he smiled widely. "I'm sorry, did you say something? I couldn't hear you from way down there."

"Har, har, har, you're so funny. Bring it, stretch. Now, I'm really gonna kick your ass."

He led her to the back of the bar where the dartboard hung on the wall. Ryan plucked the darts from the cork and handed her half. On the chalkboard beside the target, he scribbled their names.

"Nice," she commented, seeing he'd written *Ryan Dart Legend Extraordinaire* vs. *Wee Maggie.* His smack talk wouldn't intimidate her. "Should we put a little money on it to make it interesting?" He should know from the beginning she had a fierce competitive streak.

"Well, do you want to bet money or make it interesting?"

"Is getting beat by a girl half your size not interesting? Or does that happen all the time?"

He laughed. "Feisty. I like it. But since you're so confident, how about we bet something a little more valuable than money?"

"Such as?"

He walked back to the line on the floor and prowled around her in an attempt to psych her out. "If I win, I get to kiss you—the way I want."

Oh, that was how he wanted to play it? "And if I win?"

"Name your mark."

She tried to think of something really good. "If I win, you clean out my gutters."

He scoffed. "You're on."

She tipped her head with the cockiness of a dart master. "Since your ego puts you at a disadvantage, you can throw first."

"Oh! She's a shit talker, folks." Lining up his shot, he displayed good form and let the first dart sail.

"Not bad."

He threw the second. Another great shot, earning him sixty points right off the bat. But by the third he got a little too smug.

"Too bad." She tsked, waiting for him to write down his score.

"Seventy-three is the score to beat." He sounded rather proud of himself.

She stepped behind the line and sketched out her shot with practiced form. The weight of the dart left her hand, hurdling toward the board and sinking in the center of the bullseye.

Ryan stilled as she threw the second dart. Another bullseye. There wasn't much room for the third, but she managed to squeeze it in. Smiling broadly, she wrote down her score.

"One-fifty. Make sure you wear gloves when you come to do my gutters. They're real dirty with goop and bugs and stuff."

"You brat," he whispered. "I see how it is."

The game continued, but no matter how much Ryan tried, he couldn't beat her. Still, he was a good opponent.

"I can't believe you're gonna win."

She had it in the bag. One more bullseye and she'd take the game. He needed over a hundred points. Glancing over her shoulder at him, she smirked. "I told you, I'm short but I'm scrappy."

"I think you cheated."

"How did I cheat?"

"You distracted me with cuteness. I'm used to playing against ugly, hairy men."

"I bet they kiss you real nice when you win."

"We play for money."

"Ah, interesting." She threw the dart and gasped. Well, that was a wash. The damn thing didn't even sink in.

"Oh! What happened?"

"Shut up and let me concentrate." She lined up her second shot.

One bullseye, that was all she needed. She drew back and Ryan smacked her ass. The dart lodged into the wood paneled wall, and she turned to scowl at him.

"Hey! Penalty!"

"I'm afraid light tapping is permitted."

She rolled her eyes, locked her jaw, and shot the third. This time it landed, but only earned her seventeen points. "Now who's cheating?"

"Don't be a poor sport." He took his place behind the line while she removed her darts from the board, the floor, and the wall.

The bastard got a bullseye on his first shot. If he threw two more, he'd win. If he won, he'd kiss her. She didn't know if she wanted him to miss or make the shot. Losing kind of felt like winning with so much on the line.

As he aimed, she couldn't blink. He was completely focused. Nerves of steel. He threw and she sucked in a sharp breath.

Pivoting slowly, he smiled at her. Another bullseye.

She scowled. Had he been taking it easy on her all this time? She honestly didn't know and felt hustled. Her heart raced as she waited for him to take the final shot.

Maybe he'd miss.

He threw the dart and—

She never actually saw a man smolder with such palpable self-satisfaction, but when Ryan turned to face her, he held nothing back. "And *that's* game." He bowed theatrically.

"You hustled me."

"Hardly. I told you I'd win." Sauntering to the scoreboard where she stood, he leaned over her and chalked in his winning total.

Her shoulders pressed into the wall as he caged her in. The scent of his skin filled her lungs as the warmth of his nearness filled her with a jumble of nervous energy.

"Pardon me." He groaned, as if writing such a large score on the board was some sort of hardship. "Ah, there we go." He dropped the chalk, letting it dangle from its tattered rope. "Now, I'm no mathematician, but I believe I've won the bet."

His gaze dropped to her mouth, and her heart thundered in her chest. Was he going to do it right there, in front of everyone?

She always paid her debts and this was no different, but as she considered all the strangers sitting at the bar and in the booths, she got dizzy. "Ryan, wait."

Leaning close, his warm breath teased her ear and he whispered, "I'll collect my payment tonight."

Tonight? He was going to make her wait until his shift was over? How long? Sometimes he didn't get home until after midnight. Waiting seemed somehow worse than having to pay the piper now.

"I don't want to wait."

Ryan's playful expression sobered and he did a double take. Had she just said that aloud?

"Really?"

The air stilled and the sound of the jukebox fell away. He looked into her eyes the way he often did, and she felt that deep longing Alec had asked about. Yes, she wanted him to kiss her but not here.

Ryan studied her, waiting for some form of consent. His patient façade failed in that moment as nothing but uncensored longing reflected in his blue eyes. "You want me to kiss you?"

She should take it back, but she didn't want to. She wanted him to kiss her, but she didn't want to feel guilty about it. This was a bet. She lost. A debt was a debt. She couldn't be held responsible for what happened. It wasn't like she hadn't tried to win the game. She thought she had it in the bag. He was going to clean her gutters. But she lost.

The guilt and blame tangled up in enough excuses that she didn't question her motives too deeply. She nodded and he stepped closer, grabbing her arm and whispering at a volume so low no one else could hear.

"You don't want to wait until we're alone?"

Maybe they should wait. But if she waited, the guilt would slip past her guard and she'd chicken out. Maybe that was wise to take a minute to cool off and think. Now she was second-guessing herself.

No. They were going to kiss, and she needed it to happen before she came up with a list of excuses. "The loft upstairs."

Her words registered and his hand slid down her arm, his fingers lacing with hers. They disappeared through the entrance to the back hall. Without the crowd that had been clogging the space last time, they made it to the loft door in only a few seconds.

Her heart raced as he swiped a hand over the door molding and located a hidden key, his hands shaking as he slid the jagged metal into the lock. Any longer and she'd back out.

"Hurry."

He looked at her in shock but didn't say a word as the door opened and he pulled her inside. Her back hit the wall and the light from the hall disappeared as they were swallowed by the darkness.

"You sure this is okay?"

His hands cupped the side of her neck as the heat of his breath teased her lips. Her breasts pressed against the hard wall of muscle, and her stomach jolted with a rush of nerves. It had been so long since anyone touched her like that, since she felt a man's body pressing against hers.

"I want to see you." She couldn't handle the dark right now.

He stilled. "Take my hand."

Her fingers traced down his arms and his hand closed around hers.

"The light switch is upstairs. Careful."

Her heart beat louder than their footsteps hitting the wooden stairs. When he reached the switch, the small lamp flipped on. An amber glow chased away the shadows and she remembered the first time he'd brought her there. Maybe they should do a shot of whiskey again.

The mood changed the moment he turned on the light. Maybe they ruined it. He led her to the small love seat near the many canvases stacked along the wall. She sat down beside him and stared at the drafting desk on the other side of the loft, suddenly convinced this was a mistake—too much of a delay.

"Hey." He brushed his fingers along her jaw and turned her face toward his.

A shiver teased up her spine and she sat straighter. He looked into her eyes with that familiar blue stare.

She smiled, torn between an apology and a plea. "Hey."

Tracing his thumb over her full lower lip, he whispered, "I wanna do this right, Maggie."

She nodded. If anything happened, it needed to be right or she'd never get over her instincts that this might be wrong.

He slowly closed the distance, and her lashes fluttered closed. Soft lips pressed to hers, gentle and warm. His fingers slipped under her hair, gently teasing the sensitive skin at the back of her neck.

As his head tipped and his lips coaxed hers open, the warm trace of his tongue over hers sent a lightning bolt of awareness through her. It was both frightening and invigorating.

Her hand tightened on his shoulder, pulling at the flannel threads of his shirt. A spark of need jumped inside of her as her body reclined. Forgetting where they were, she eased back and let her mind slip away.

Her mouth grew bolder, remembering this familiar dance, and her body melted deeper into the sofa. Desire swelled inside of her as fingers glided up her neck. She mirrored his touch, teasing the scruff at his jaw and raking her fingers through his hair.

Warmth swirled low in her abdomen as his body ground into hers, rocking and pleading silently. Her senses came alive as his breath mingled with hers, his lips needy and wanting. Hooking her leg over his hip, she pulled him closer.

"Maggie…"

Her name was a song on his lips. His kisses so different from the ones she'd had before. She wanted to say his name back, but the kiss was too good to stop.

And while she didn't speak it out loud, it rang through her mind. *Ryan… Ryan… Ryan.*

Nash. Her eyes opened and she stilled.

"What's wrong?"

She wasn't sure. She pulled back, but the sofa gave her little room to move.

Ryan sat up. "What happened?"

She shook her head. Everything had been perfect. It was her and Ryan. Just them. But then she was suddenly thinking of Nash.

Guilt poked at her like a glowing iron, but she shoved it away. She didn't want guilt right now. Guilt had her in a headlock every other hour of the day. This was her time.

She tried to focus. "Keep kissing me."

He leaned down, but this time when he kissed her something was off. He pulled away. "Let's not force it."

His words were thoughtful but they mostly made her feel like a failure. "I wasn't forcing it. I was having fun."

"Me too."

But something changed and they both felt it. Ryan wasn't an idiot. He could figure out what happened.

He sat up. She lay on her back, clothes rumpled, hair tangled, and her wool cap missing. Scooting into an upright position, she awkwardly searched for her hat and shoved it on her head. Silence.

"I'm sorry—"

"Did you eat—"

They both spoke at the same time.

Her brow creased. "I don't know what happened," she admitted. "I was enjoying everything and then my brain got involved and I panicked."

He nodded. "It's okay."

But it wasn't. She felt entitled to a few minutes of uninterrupted happiness. Shouldn't choosing happiness be enough? Why was everything so damn difficult?

The longer they sat there the more certain she became that this was not how normal hookups went. Normal girls didn't panic over making out. They didn't take this much work. Who was worth that much effort? Certainly not her.

"I should go."

He opened his mouth, appearing ready to object, hesitated but didn't ask her to stay. "Do you have your bike?"

She nodded. "It's out back."

"I'll walk you down." Maybe he was being kind and noble, but it felt more like he was giving up on her. The sad truth was, she couldn't blame him.

On the ride home she cried, but as she wept, she thought about a study she'd read about the shape of tears. A scientist examined various tears under a microscope and found that, like water, human tears take various shapes linked to the host's reason for crying.

These weren't shaped like Nash tears. They weren't even tears of sorrow. She didn't know how to identify the feelings she was having, which made her wish she knew a scientist who could put her tears under a microscope and make sense of things for her.

CHAPTER 17

*F*riday proved the longest day of the week. Ryan couldn't get his head off Maggie. All day long he caught himself daydreaming, obsessing over the taste of her mouth, the softness of her lips, the way her breath hitched when he kissed her throat, and how soft her body felt under his.

Great, now he was hard again.

His phone vibrated. Another text from Kelly, thanking him again for covering the pub so much lately.

Ryan didn't mind picking up the extra shifts. With all the new furniture he needed, he could use the extra money. But since kissing Maggie last night, he only wanted to go home and start his weekend.

Shutting off the kitchen lights, he tossed a damp rag in the hamper at the back of the bar. "Can I walk you out, Sue?"

"Thanks." Sue turned off the accent lights behind the liquor shelves and grabbed her purse from the back.

He followed her out, locking the door behind them and carrying the last of the trash to the dumpster. "Drive safe."

She waved. "I'll see you tomorrow."

"Uh, actually I'm off tomorrow."

Sue turned and frowned. "You are?"

"Yeah. It's my birthday. Finn's covering."

"Oh. Okay. Then I guess I'll see you Sunday." She climbed into her car. "Happy birthday."

"Thanks." Ryan waited until her car started, a habit he formed when he began working late with her, then started his truck.

The streets were empty at this hour. He barely saw the road the whole way home, his mind lost in fantasies about his neighbor and how they might spend the weekend.

Finn was a lifesaver, offering to cover the bar for him on his birthday. Usually Ryan would want to spend the day hanging out with his cousins, who were his best friends, but this year was different.

He was turning thirty, a milestone, and he didn't want any reminders of the benchmarks he'd yet to meet. He didn't want to feel like a third wheel or sit through a family dinner where everyone had a spouse to the right, and he had no one. And he didn't want to feel sorry for himself. For the first time in a very long time, he was actually happy—and hopeful.

Maggie was amazing. She was funny yet shy, bold yet hesitant, tough yet delicate. He didn't want to get ahead of himself, but every time they hung out, he fell a little harder for her.

Dangerous territory, he thought, remembering the look on her face last night when she broke the kiss. He could guess what happened. She had an attack of conscience.

The whole Nash O'Malley thing was a touchy situation. He didn't want to compete with the guy. One, because he was a ghost. And two, because he was her husband, and he wasn't sure anyone stood a chance of getting her heart when Nash still owned it so completely.

Ryan parked his truck and shut off the engine. Gripping the wheel, he stared up at Maggie's windows, wishing he saw her lights flash on, but the place was pitch black. His mind was racing.

Maybe Maggie would never get over her husband. Maybe she didn't have to. As long as she had a little space in her heart for him, he could live with that.

His conscience nipped with the reminder that he wanted more. But that was before. He made a promise to himself the day he signed the papers for this house, he wouldn't keep getting hung up on everyone else's benchmarks.

So what if most people met their partners and got married in their twenties. And maybe it was still customary in some circles to start a family before thirty. Not everyone had to follow the same set of rules.

He might never get married or have kids. It was time he accepted that. Acceptance was the only way he'd stop feeling like half a man and start feeling whole.

Maggie was exactly what he needed right now. There were parts of her that remained off-limits and that worked for him. It kept him in check. Yes, they were *dating*, but they were moving too slow for anything to be serious.

On the other hand, getting mixed up with someone as fragile as Maggie had a way of making their relationship as serious as trying to dismantle a bomb. One wrong move and he could spoil everything.

Maybe someday she'd get there. She'd be adorable with a big pregnant belly, and she'd make a fierce soccer mom.

His imagination wandered as he made his way up to bed. He could imagine her with a minivan full of sons and sports equipment. She'd be the sort of mom to give the ref an earful when he miscalled a game.

Realizing how far his mind spun, he reeled it back in. Maggie didn't drive, so good luck getting her in that minivan. And they shared two kisses, one she vomited directly after, and the other because she lost a bet. Yeah, he was dreaming.

But he couldn't stop the fantasies from coming, so when he fell asleep, they shifted into dreams full of color and emotion, children with laughter so real he could hear it. When he woke up the following morning, she was his first thought.

"This is bad," he mumbled, stuffing his pillow over his head and trying to steal a few more minutes of sleep. It was no use.

He grabbed a shower, then waited as the coffee pot slowly percolated. Something outside caught his attention and he looked out the window. Maggie climbed on her bike and turned to ride out of the driveway.

He cursed, not wanting to miss her, but by the time he got out the door she was already down the street. Where was she going? She didn't work on Saturdays. He really hoped to spend the day with her.

He went back inside and had his coffee, anticipating her return. While he waited, he ran a load of laundry and started peeling the wallpaper in the dining room. The moment he saw her shadow pass the window, he raced out the back door.

"Morning, neighbor."

She jumped, startled by his overzealous greeting as she parked her bike against the shed. "Hey."

He walked to the fence that separated their yards. "You're out early."

Her gaze dropped as she lifted an old thermos from her bike basket. "Yeah."

She wasn't looking at him. "Do you want to do something today? I don't have to work at the bar."

She hesitated, one hand on the fence gate. "O—okay."

"Maybe we can—" His phone rang and his words cut off. It was his dad, probably just calling to wish him a happy birthday. "Hang on." He turned and answered the call. "Hey Dad."

"Happy birthday, Ry."

"Thanks." He held up a finger telling Maggie he'd only be a minute. "What's up?"

"Just calling to wish you a happy-happy and all that noise. Any plans today?"

"No, just hanging out with a friend."

"Do you plan to stop by?"

His mother had a strange way of making his and Patrick's birthdays her accomplishment, which it was, but sometimes the expectation that they all be together on that day got tedious. "I wasn't planning on it."

"Oh." He sounded disappointed. "I was hoping you could give me a hand with something."

"What do you need?"

"Your mother wants the curio cabinet in the dining room moved to the hall. I'd do it myself, but my back's been acting up."

"You need to do that today?" He glanced back to Maggie and mouthed *sorry*.

"Well, your mother's been riding me to move it for a few weeks. But Pat's been away, and you've been working so much, I haven't found an opening to get a hand."

His dad was always there whenever Ryan needed anything and he hated not to do the same. But it was his birthday, and he really just wanted a day to himself with Maggie. "Did you ask Tristan?"

"He and Luke went to Kelly's art show this weekend."

"Oh. Well, I guess I can take a ride over in a little bit. But can you make sure Mum has it cleaned out before I get there?"

"Will do. Thanks. I'll see you in an hour."

His father hung up before saying goodbye. Ryan pocketed his phone and faced Maggie. "I have to run to my parents' house in a little bit to help my dad move some furniture, but I shouldn't be long."

"Oh." Was that disappointment in her voice?

He wanted to hop the fence and kiss her, but sensed it was too soon. "How do you feel about ribs?"

"Ribs?"

He nodded. "Yeah. I make good barbeque ribs, and there's this little charcoal grill I've been eyeing up at the hardware store in town. I could swing by and grab it after my parents', and we could have ourselves my first backyard barbeque. What do you say?"

She bit her lip. "You don't have any other plans today?"

"Free as a bird." He smiled. "Come on. Have a cookout with me. We'll rent a movie and pig out on ribs and beer in my living room."

"Just us?"

"Just us," he confirmed, wanting her all to himself.

She grinned and nodded. "I'd love to."

"Great." This was going to be the perfect birthday. "I'll head to the grocery store and then my parents'. I shouldn't be more than an hour—two at the most."

"Okay. I'll wait here."

He wanted to go and rush back as soon as possible, but he hesitated. "One more thing." He hopped the fence and crossed her driveway in three long strides, not stopping until he caught her face in his hands.

"Good morning," he whispered, tipping her face up and brushing a kiss across her lips—quick enough to catch her off guard and simple enough that she shouldn't object.

Her eyes lit and her gaze softened when she smiled up at him in surprise. "Good morning."

God, he loved catching her blind reaction before she had a chance to overthink things. Her eyes and smile told him they were on the right track. His body jolted with sharp desire and he gave her a promising look. "I'll be back."

CHAPTER 18

*R*yan spent a fortune at the grocery store, but it was worth it. He wanted to impress Maggie with a good meal and ribs were the only thing he knew how to cook outside of the wax ramen noodle family. After the market, he went to his parents', only to find his mother sitting in a mess of keepsakes and knickknacks, weeping over old pictures in front of the still-full curio cabinet.

"There he is, my first born. Will you look at how adorable you were?" She held up a dated picture. Ryan recognized himself as a baby, sitting in a large stew pot and wearing a potholder on his head.

"Mum, you were supposed to have all this stuff cleaned out. Where's Dad?"

"Your father had to run out." She turned a page in the photo album. "Look at you here! You used to love that baby swing. And look at me. My arms still looked like arms back then. Now, they look more like broken bat wings or a flesh kimono."

"Mum, I don't have time for this." He grabbed an empty box and started loading it with items in the cabinet.

"Careful, love. Those are fragile and should be wrapped."

"They're moving to the hall. I think they can make it."

"They could chip. Here, use some newspaper."

"I'm not wrapping each individual piece just to transport them down the hall."

"Then I'll do it."

He held out the box, and she gave him a pointed look, then turned another page of the photo album.

"Oh, look, it's you and Patrick in your Easter suits."

"Mum! Please. I can't be here all day."

She slapped the picture album down on the table. "You don't have time to reminisce with your mother for a few minutes? For Pete's sake, Ryan, you just got here. Am I so unbearable that you can't even tolerate a polite visit home anymore? Far be it for me to ask for any of your precious time. I only carried you for nine and a half long months and gave you life."

He rolled his eyes. Every time she used that line her pregnancy got longer. "I love my life, mum, and I love you. But I've got meat in the truck, and I have to be somewhere in a little bit."

"Where do you have to be?"

He hesitated, not wanting to mention Maggie. If his mother knew he was dating someone she'd start asking questions, not just to him but to everyone. Rumors would burn through the town like a brush fire. Maggie wouldn't like being the center of gossip. Then his mother would insist on meeting her, and he didn't want to cross that bridge yet.

He let out a sigh. "Fine. I can stay for one hour, but I have to make a phone call."

That seemed to appease her. He went out front to make sure his groceries weren't sitting in direct sun and called Maggie. She told him to take his time.

"I should be back by noon. Two at the latest."

"I'll be here."

When one o'clock came and passed and the cabinet still wasn't emptied, Ryan moved his groceries into the garage freezer. His mother was now polishing her silver, which they never used but she seemed compelled to suddenly clean.

"Mum, you can do that later. Can you call Dad again? I really need to get going."

"Where are you in such a rush to go?"

"I have plans."

"With who?"

"Tristan," he lied.

"No, Tristan's away with Luke. Your father told you that this morning. Try again."

He silently counted to ten, but his frustration didn't abate. "Don't you care that it's my birthday? Did it ever occur to you that this might not be the way I wanted to spend it?"

Her mouth flattened and her expression blanked. She gently closed the silver box. "I see." She stood and batted the wrinkles out of her pants. "Well, you should go then. I'll wait until Patrick comes home. He won't mind moving this for me. He never minds."

"Jesus, Mum. Why do you have to make it some sort of competition? Dad asked me to come help and I'm here. But he's not. As a matter of fact, I've been here all morning. The day's half shot, and you *still*, somehow, make me feel like a terrible son for wanting to do something other than clean out your dining room hutch for hours on my birthday."

Her chin dropped. "You're right. It was thoughtless of me to think you had nothing better to do. Go ahead. Enjoy the rest of your day. We can do this another time."

He hesitated. This felt like a trap. "Thank you."

She nodded. "Maybe this week you can come back, and we can have a nice family dinner."

"Sure." He withdrew his keys and kissed her forehead. "I'll call you this week."

She affectionately slapped his cheek. "Happy birthday, love."

"Thanks."

The front door opened, and his father walked in.

So close.

"I'm home," his dad yelled, coming face-to-face with Ryan in the hall. "Oh, good, you're here."

Ryan gritted his teeth. "I've been here for hours. Where have you been?"

His mother sprang into action. "Oh, wonderful. Ryan was just about to leave, but now you can move the cabinet before he goes. It's almost empty."

Ryan didn't get to the hardware store until three o'clock. By the time he got home, all ambition to grill had abandoned him. As he unloaded the truck and put the groceries away, Maggie was nowhere to be found.

He knocked on her back door, and before she could say anything, he blurted, "I'm sorry. Did I mention escaping Alcatraz is easier than getting away from my mother?"

She laughed. "It's okay. I napped."

"All day?"

She nodded. "It was pretty great."

His gaze dropped to her socked feet, traveling up her baggy sweats to her worn Floyd T-shirt. Jealousy burned through his stomach as he counted each wrinkle in the soft clothes covering her skin. "I want to throw you over my shoulder and carry you back to my house."

The side of her mouth lifted in a half grin. "You do?"

Keeping his eyes on hers, he nodded. "Yeah."

She lifted a shoulder. "Okay."

"Really?"

She bit her lip and smiled. "If that's what you want."

He swooped down and lifted her off her feet. She laughed as he hoisted her over his shoulder, wrapping an arm around the back of her thighs. Shutting the door, he carried her down the driveway and around to his front door, which was locked.

"Damn it." He rotated her to his other shoulder and lugged her to the back. Just as he reached the door, his phone began to ring. "Do me a favor, grab my phone out of my back pocket and throw it in the trash."

He didn't care who was calling. He just wanted to be alone with Maggie.

The ringing eventually stopped when he set her down on the futon in the living room. She smiled, still in her socks and looking completely delicious.

He stared at her, unsure what she'd allow. "I wanna kiss you."

"Okay." Another surprise.

He sat down and yanked her legs over his, pulling her onto his lap. "I never know what you're going to say." Maybe that was part of her irresistible appeal.

He pressed his lips to hers, and the familiar taste of her mouth greeted him. Soft and warm, her tongue teased his. His hand coasted up her back, drawing her closer and then his phone rang again.

"Son of a bitch."

"Maybe it's important."

"It's not." She wasn't wearing a bra and he could tell her nipples were hard by how they pressed at the soft cotton of her shirt. *That* was important.

He turned the ringer off and tossed the phone aside. "Come here."

His tongue swept into her mouth, greedy for more. She straddled his lap and cupped his jaw, kissing him back every step of the way, until his phone vibrated on the cushion and she pulled away.

"Ignore it," he growled against her soft lips.

She turned her cheek. "It's distracting."

He grabbed the phone and frowned. "It's my cousin Finn. Hold on. He's covering the bar." He answered the call, finding it hard to keep the frustration out of his voice. "Finn, what's up?"

"Ry, I'm so sorry to do this to you on your birthday, but all the kids have a stomach bug and Mallory needs my help tonight. I'm not going to be able to cover the pub for you."

His eyes closed and his head dropped back to the cushion. "No problem. I'll figure it out."

"I'm sorry, man. Happy birthday."

"Thanks." He hung up the phone and sighed. "I have to go to work. Finn's kids are sick."

"Oh." She didn't sound overly disappointed. If anything, she sounded like she'd expected another setback. Probably because he was leaving her with the shittiest impression today. First the holdup at his parents and now this. Weren't people supposed to get what *they* wanted on their birthdays?

He opened one eye and looked at her. "I swear this isn't how I wanted today to go."

She slid off his lap. "It's okay."

"No, it's not." He hadn't told her it was his birthday, because he didn't

142

want her to feel obligated to do anything. He just wanted to spend some time with her. So much for getting his birthday wish.

"Ryan, it's fine. We can do something tomorrow."

He caught her hand and brought her fingers to his lips, kissing the tips. "Thanks."

"For what?"

"Just ... being you."

Maggie lingered as he made a go-cup of coffee and got ready for a long night shift at the bar. It was Saturday, so he'd likely be up for the next twelve hours. When he was ready to leave, he walked her to her yard.

"Tomorrow I'm shutting off my phone."

She laughed. "Okay." Rising on her toes, she brushed a kiss on his lips, and he drew back in surprise. It was the first time she initiated it. She smiled up at him. "I know this wasn't what you wanted to do tonight, but ... try to have fun."

"I'll have as much fun as one can possibly have waiting on a bunch of drunks."

"Maybe it won't be as bad as you think."

She was sweet to think so.

When he reached the bar, the lot was packed. "Great."

He wasn't usually such a spoilsport about picking up extra shifts, but nothing about today had gone his way. As far as birthdays went, this was one of the shittiest ones.

He parked in the back and entered through the kitchen. Jackson Browne played on the jukebox. He headed out to the bar to tell Sue that Finn wouldn't be coming in after all.

"*Surprise!*"

Ryan staggered back as fifty loudmouth Irish lunatics screamed at him from the other side of the bar—his mother, father, and *brother* standing right up front. "What? Pat? What the hell is going on?"

Kelly—who was supposed to be out of town—appeared to his left and handed him a shot of whiskey. "Happy birthday, Ry. Now go change your pants. You look like you just shit yourself."

He frowned. "You're supposed to be at an art show." He scanned the crowd and found Luke and Tristan grinning. "And you're supposed to be out of town."

Finn stepped forward, Mallory at his side and four healthy kids hanging off their limbs like monkeys on a tree. "Gotcha."

Ryan blinked, completely confused. "Is this a surprise party?"

"Happy birthday, darling." His mother stepped around the bar and pressed a kiss on his cheek. "It was my job to distract you all day, so you didn't find out about the surprise. This week when you come over you can help me put all that stuff back in the curio cabinet."

He scowled at her. "You're not moving it?"

"Of course not. Who keeps a curio in the hallway? It's a dining room piece, dear."

One by one they all wished him a happy birthday and gave him a hug. Everyone was there—except Maggie. His head was spinning. They completely shocked him.

His brother, Pat, approached with a face full of laughter. "They got you good."

Ryan couldn't believe he was there. "Aren't you supposed to be off playing doctor?"

Pat leaned in and gave him a warm hug. "I'm exactly where I want to be. Happy birthday, bro."

Holding onto his younger brother for an extra second, he got the chance to shut his eyes and let it all sink in. "I thought tonight would suck."

Pat eased back and grinned. "Don't count your chickens too early. I'm pretty sure you'll be puking your socks up before dawn."

"There's the man of the hour!" Sheilagh shouldered her way passed Pat. "Let others have a go at him. No one likes a Ryan hog."

"Devil," he said affectionately, pulling her into a hug.

"I'm so glad you're older than me," she teased.

He laughed. "Thanks." Turning to her husband, he held out a hand. "Hey, Alec, thanks for coming."

Alec, always the proper Brit, shook his hand and did a not so subtle glance around. "Did you come here alone?"

"They told me I had to work."

"Then they surprised you?"

"Shocking, with all the loudmouths in this family, but yes."

Alec nodded. "Well, enjoy yourself. The night's yours."

Ryan was handed beers, shots, and cocktails and instructed to drink each one as it arrived. They sat him at the head of a banquet table, a throne suited for a king as they handed him one gift after another.

Most of the presents were household items—toasters, picture frames, laundry baskets, bath towels. He was grateful for everything.

Music pumped from the jukebox, and the mood only grew rowdier as the hours passed. He didn't get a second to himself until seven o'clock.

Sneaking into the back hall, he plugged a finger in his ear and dialed Maggie. His cousin Kate exited the lady's room just as the call began to ring. Ryan waved and she blew him a kiss. As he pretended to catch it, he realized how drunk he was.

"Hello?"

"Maggie May…"

"Ryan?"

"Yep. You'll never believe what happened to me tonight."

There was a pause then she laughed. "Well, are you going to tell me?"

He smiled and leaned into the wall. Her voice had a way of crawling into him, soothing him. "My family tricked me. All of them. Fuckers."

"How did they trick you?"

"They threw a surprise party for me. I had no idea. And now I'm drunk. No idea how that happened either."

Another pause. "And why would they throw you a surprise party?"

"Because…" The wall was really holding him up now. "They love me and it's my birthday."

She was quiet for several seconds. "Happy birthday, Ryan."

"I'm sorry I didn't tell you. I just didn't want to make a big deal out of it. All I wanted for my birthday was to be with you, but I barely got to see you today." He tripped over his feet and sidestepped into the door. His hand caught the doorknob to the loft and he had an idea. "Will you come here?"

"To the bar?"

"Yeah. Everyone's here, but you're not. I want you to be here. Please?"

"Ryan, I don't know if—"

"I can sneak you in the back like before. You're little. No one will suspect a thing. Please? It's my birthday wish." He blew like he had a cake full of candles in front of him. "I need a cake."

She laughed. "How much did you have to drink?"

"This much." He squinted at his fingers smooshed together and slowly widened the measurement. "A lot."

"Do I have to meet everyone?"

"Nope. Just me. A secret rendezvous."

"Okay. I'll meet you at the back steps to the loft in thirty minutes. Leave the door unlocked."

"You're amazing."

He didn't remember ending the call but nearly broke his neck on the steps to the loft. He unlocked the back door and left the lamp on so Maggie would be able to see her way around.

Pat found him fumbling around in the hall. "You look a little lost, brother."

Ryan smiled and slung an arm over Pat's shoulders, giving his red hair an affectionate tousle. "I can't believe you're here." His brother was his best friend and he missed him terribly over the past several years while he was finishing med school. "You need to move back home. Philly's had you long enough."

Pat laughed. "Christ, you're wasted."

Squaring off with him, Ryan balanced his hands on his shoulders and, through blurred vision, looked him in the eye.

"But I'm serious. I want you to come back. I know you thought she'd come around, but maybe it's time to move on. She doesn't even live here anymore. Come home. You could start your own practice and settle down. Any girl would be lucky to have you. Forget about Julie."

His brother didn't bother denying his affection for Julie Cook. He'd been a goner for her since he sat next to her in kindergarten, but Pat never had the guts to make a move and she'd moved on without him. No one had the heart to tell him she was now engaged. But he'd find out eventually. It was time for him to move on.

"I know it'll never happen. But every time I picture my future, I can't help but imagine her by my side."

He affectionately slapped his cheek and burped. "It's her loss."

Pat reared back and steered him out of the hall. "Well, I'm not going to meet anyone new slow dancing in the back hall of a bar with my brother, you lush. Let's get you something to eat. I have a feeling you could use a cracker or ten to sop up all the booze."

Pat dragged him out to the bar, where more shots took place. Food was served. He might have swallowed a few bites, but he mostly drank. Finn started a dance-off and the music switched to disco. Someone handed out flamboyant sunglasses, feather boas, beaded necklaces, and hats. The room was spinning, but Ryan was having a blast.

"Ryan," his mother called, holding her purse and standing by the door with his father.

He danced over to them and remembered he had a giant purple glitter top hat on his head. "Are you leaving?"

"It's getting late. You stay and enjoy yourself." She leaned in and kissed his cheek. "I love you. There's a freezer full of casseroles at my house with your name on it. Come by and get them this week. And this is for you." She handed him an envelope. "We're very proud of you. Happy birthday."

Despite the alcohol pumping through his veins, her words hit him with the velocity of a speeding train. "I love you too, Mum. Thank you for … everything." He hoped she knew how much she meant to him, and how much it meant that no matter the situation, he could always count on her.

She smiled and comprehension glittered in her faded green eyes. "You're welcome. Enjoy the rest of your party."

He hugged and thanked his dad, but only when they left the bar did he realize the time. If people were leaving it must be late. "Shit. Luke, what time is it?"

His cousin looked at his phone. "Eleven."

"Maggie." He made a beeline to the back, cursing himself all the while.

Relatives called his name as he passed, some even made a joke that he was running to the bathroom to toss, which he almost did along the way. How could he have lost track of time?

He careened into the hall and turned toward the loft door, only to come up short when he found his cousin Kelly leaning against it, arms folded across his chest, and a cocky smile twisting his mouth.

"How's it going?" Kelly asked, his eyes twinkling with mischief.

Ryan caught his breath and eyed the loft door. "Hey. I, uh, need to check something."

Kelly cocked his head and raised a brow. "Funny thing. I was checking my inventory a while ago and heard a noise. I thought maybe an animal got into the soffit or something. You know how the raccoons can get around here."

"Oh, God, please tell me you didn't go hunting."

"Luckily, I don't keep any guns up there. Turns out it wasn't a raccoon but a cute little brunette. Now, how do you think she got up there?"

"Kelly, please tell me you didn't yell at her."

He scowled. "I'd never yell at a beautiful woman. Besides, I remembered her from the other week when she was in here whooping your ass at darts."

"Actually, I beat her."

Kelly chuckled. "Try again. That girl let you win, whether she realizes it or not. I saw you two sneak up here after the match."

Ryan's mouth sealed shut. "Is she still up there?"

A negligent shrug. "Let me give you a little advice, Ry. Girls aren't born tough, the world makes them that way. The more rough and tumble they appear, the more fragile they actually are. If you get a girl like that out of her armor and get her to actually show you her vulnerable side, you owe it to her to take care of her the way she deserves."

If those words came from anyone else, he'd gag over the sheer arrogance. But Kelly was a lot smarter than people gave him credit for, and he knew women. But most of all, he knew Ryan. More than anyone else, Kelly had watched him for years at the bar, botching one date after another. They'd had many late night discussions about why he couldn't seem to make it work with anyone.

"She's different from the others."

"I can tell." He stepped away from the door. "I told her she could hang out as long as she wanted. I'm not sure if she stayed."

Ryan's hand touched the knob, and he met his cousin's gaze. "Will you tell everyone I said thank you?"

He slapped a hand on his back. "I'll take care of it."

CHAPTER 19

Something touched Maggie's cheek and she drew in a breath, but the air didn't smell like home. The faint trace of paint thinner and dust had her opening her eyes.

"You look like sleeping beauty."

She blinked awake. Maybe it wasn't paint thinner as much as it was the scent of whiskey. Ryan's smile filled her view as he leaned over her, his grin lopsided as he stared at her with red rabbit eyes.

"Your breath smells flammable."

Ryan laughed and ducked his head to the cushion of the love seat where she'd fallen asleep. "Sorry. And I'm sorry I lost track of time. *Again*. Today was not really my day."

She smiled and touched the brim of his glittering hat. "It's fine. Did you have fun at your party?" It sounded like it was still going.

"They totally surprised me. And everyone got me things for the house. I'm … overwhelmed."

A pang of envy dove into her belly. "You have a great family that loves you very much."

He nodded. "I don't always appreciate how lucky I am. Tonight was a good reminder, not because of the gifts, but because they were all here, together, for me. I really needed that, but I didn't know I needed it."

She'd never met a man who could express his emotions so openly and honestly. Her hand cupped the side of his beard. "Then I'm glad they surprised you. Good surprises are the best."

He studied her face for a silent moment. "Did Kelly scare the shit out of you?"

She laughed. "Let's just say we scared the hell out of each other."

"Forgive me?"

She nodded. "I don't have a birthday present for you."

148

He'd think it was because she only found out it was his birthday last minute, but the truth was she couldn't think of anything good enough for him. She wanted to get him something special, something he'd touch every day and appreciate, and when he held it, he'd think of her.

"I don't need a present."

"Well, I still wanted to give you something." She hesitated, hoping he didn't find her words corny. "I want to tell you something, Ryan."

"Okay." He kneeled on the floor, his eyes level with hers as she rested her head on the cushion of the love seat.

She drew in a slow breath. "Every day I wake up afraid that something terrible will happen. That fear has made a shell around me, and every year it gets thicker and harder to penetrate. I use it to keep people away. I've pushed all my old friends away. I even pushed my family away. But since you moved in, something's changed. When I wake up in the morning, my first thought isn't what terrible thing will happen today." A shy smile trembled to her lips. "My first thought is … I hope I see you."

He sat back on his feet, making a ridiculous picture with that purple hat and green feather boa around his neck. "Wow. I don't know what to say."

She sat up and pushed her hair behind her shoulder. "You don't have to say anything. I just wanted to say thank you for making my life a little brighter. It's been dark for a really long time."

He glanced at the floor and back at her. "I think that's the nicest thing anyone's ever said to me." He laughed. "That's my favorite gift today."

She scooted off the love seat onto the floor. He hugged her to his side, and she blew at the feathers from his boa when they tickled her nose.

"I should probably take all this stuff off." He tossed the hat and boa aside, revealing more than twenty beaded necklaces.

"What did you have to show to get them?"

He laughed. "Wouldn't you like to know? Want one?"

"Do I need to flash you to get one?"

He stilled and laughed. "I never know what you're gonna say, but I'm learning not to guess." He put a red beaded necklace over her head. "First one's free."

Just like that, those red beads became as valuable as a string of pearls, and she knew she'd keep them somewhere safe, always appreciate them, and think of him whenever she touched them. "Your loss. I would have flashed you for them."

He did a double take. "You liar."

She arched a brow. "Guess you'll never know."

He pulled her to his side, and they slouched against the foot of the sofa, lounging comfortably on the floor. "It's probably dangerous how much I like you," he murmured, casually drawing in a breath of her hair.

"Probably." No point in denying her baggage. She carried it everywhere. "But I like you, too."

He rested his head on hers, and while she should've been figuring out how to get him home safely, she didn't want to stress over anything in that moment. Being there in his arms was exactly the place she wanted to be. So she let her eyes rest and listened to his slow breathing turn to gentle snores.

When she opened her eyes some time later, they were covered by one of the sheets used to drape the canvases along the wall and the sun was starting to rise. It was the first time she'd spent the night with anyone who wasn't Nash.

It didn't feel as traumatic as she expected. On the contrary, it felt nice.

She left Ryan curled up on the floor and quietly slipped out the back. The roads wore a gray mist that morning as she rode her bike to the cemetery. When she got to Nash's grave, she didn't speak a word.

She usually told him about her day and anything that happened, but today she didn't share those details. As she rode her bike home, she tried to understand why she'd been so quiet.

She hadn't held her tongue due to a sense of betrayal toward Nash, which she'd assumed she'd feel. On the contrary, she didn't share the details of her night or the day before because it felt like a betrayal to Ryan.

Those moments were theirs and they were still new and delicate. Realizing she didn't want to share those secrets reminded her of the day she finally grasped she was a married adult and no longer had to answer to her parents about her choices. Nash had been the one to get that through her head, because for a long time into her twenties, she still felt very much like a kid.

Dating Ryan and keeping their relationship private brought about similar feelings. She'd always shared everything with Nash. He got fifty percent of everything she owned right down to her soul. But he couldn't have this.

Whatever this was, this tiny sliver of unbroken heart she'd found and given to Ryan, she wanted him to keep it for himself. He'd never have all of her. He'd never be able to fix the damage done before he came into her life. But he got a small, precious piece of her that may very well be the last piece capable of feeling something other than pain.

He somehow found a private piece of her heart everyone else had missed—including her. It didn't belong to her family. It didn't belong to her grief. It didn't even belong to Nash. She hadn't known it existed until Ryan came along. But last night when he told her about all the gifts his family had given him, she decided this would be her gift to him, as small and intangible as it may be.

Sometimes tiny, seemingly insignificant things grow into enormous things. Maybe her heart could still grow, like a seed in a ravaged forest that sets roots amongst the ash and later matures into a mighty oak. It was a sliver of hope, but in a way, it made her feel more powerful and optimistic than she'd felt in years.

CHAPTER 20

*R*yan had company most of the day on Sunday, so Maggie kept to her house. She watched the many cars coming and going, finding the sheer amount of his relatives dizzying. He often made jokes about his family smothering him like an infestation of locust, but it was clear how much they all loved each other.

Her envy led her to call her sister, which wasn't that bad. They had a lengthy conversation, and for once, they didn't discuss anything sad.

The day had turned out to be warm, so Maggie swept the front porch, hosed off her siding where mud had caked from winter, and turned the soil in the flower beds. The daffodils would be sprouting soon.

"Now, you keep them frozen until you're ready to eat them, then bake at three-fifty for one hour. No need to thaw. Any questions, just call."

Maggie's head lifted as the voices traveled from Ryan's back door. She peeked around the side of the shed and watched as a redheaded woman and burly man stepped onto Ryan's back porch.

"Thanks, Aunt Maureen."

"The house is lovely, Ryan. Frank, let's go! I got soup on the stove." Maggie watched as the rotund older woman hugged Ryan and pried open the door to a vintage Jeep. "Sorry we missed the party, but someone had to watch all the babies."

"That's okay. Thanks for all the frozen meals."

"They should keep you well-fed until the end of summer. Do yourself a favor and eat my dishes first. I'm a better cook than your mother." The woman glared at the back door and yelled, "*Frank!* I haven't got all day."

"I'm coming, woman! For the love of Christ, stop your yelling."

"Bye, Uncle Frank."

The man grumbled and climbed into the Jeep. When it pulled away, Ryan hopped the fence. "Do you think no one can see you hiding down there in the dirt?"

Maggie poked her head up. "I'm not hiding."

"You could have said hi."

She could have but she didn't want to. "Are you expecting any more visitors?"

He shook his head. "Nope. And I plan on kidnapping you and locking my door. I might even give my phone a bath."

She stood and brushed the dirt off her gloves, then discarded them to the ground. "Kidnapping, huh? I'll have to check my schedule to see if I can fit you in. I already have a burglary planned for six, and a bank heist penciled in for midnight."

He sauntered closer, and she backed up toward the shed. "I don't think you understand kidnapping. As the *kidnappee*, you don't get a choice in the matter."

"Huh. Interesting." She reached down to the grass and picked up the hose, angling the nozzle in his direction. "Well, I hope you prepared for a fight, because I'm not going to make this easy."

"You wouldn't."

She sprayed him and he lunged. Her scream exploded into laughter when he caught her around the waist, lifting her off her feet and pulling her to his soaked chest.

Her legs kicked as he hoisted her off the ground. By the time he carried her off her property and onto his, she gave up fighting and saved her strength.

He carried her into his house and slammed the door, locking it behind him. Boxes of household supplies lined the hall and filled the living room. He paused at the cluttered futon and shifted her body to better support her legs, now cradling her in a rescue hold against his wet chest. She looped her arms around his shoulders and waited.

He glanced up the stairs and back to her. "Any objections to seeing my bedroom?"

Her belly tightened and flipped. "Let me see your phone."

He reached in his pocket and handed it to her. She tossed it onto the futon. "To your room we go."

He carried her up the stairs, his breath steady and his strides sure. His house was the identical design to hers, only the rooms were flipped to face the opposite direction.

The master bedroom was sparse with only a double bed and dresser. A simple green comforter lay over the sheets, not a decorative touch in sight.

He tossed her onto the bed, and she bounced into the pillows. "Thanks to you, my shirt's soaked."

He peeled the damp material over his head, and she sobered. Tattoos completely covered his chest and upper arms. Roped muscle carved his torso and chiseled his hips, forming the deep V that sloped into his jeans where strawberry blond hair trailed.

She swallowed and blinked. "You're really in shape."

"Not as much as I used to be. Sitting at a desk all week kills me."

She loved seeing him like this, exposed and revealed. He was beautiful. Different.

She rose to her knees, emboldened by the sight of his body. Without thinking too hard, she pulled her hooded sweatshirt over her head and tossed it to the floor. With the whoosh of her clothes came a shock of brazen pride mixed with trepidation.

His blue eyes went wide. "Holy shit."

"Sometimes it feels like I'll die an old lady, waiting to be normal again." She glanced down at her black bra. It wasn't anything special. No lace or padding, just satin. Her gaze returned to him. "But when I'm with you, I sometimes forget how weird I am. You make me feel slightly normal."

Face notched with awe, he slowly shook his head. "You'll always be different, Maggie. It's what makes you so special." He took a small step closer and whispered, "Maybe stop worrying about your weirdness and just embrace it."

His eyes dropped to her hips where the five lines of a music staff wrapped her skin, unsung notes of pain inked into her flesh for all eternity. His head tipped as he approached, his expression weighing and reflecting the importance of the marks.

The urge to cover herself pinched, but her rigid body didn't move. She wanted him to see her, all of her, including the scars she hid on the inside.

The backs of his fingers softly traced the notes, and she sucked in an audible breath. "What is it?" he rasped.

Goosebumps rose on her skin. "*Thank You* by Led Zeppelin. It was the song we danced to at our wedding."

He nodded with proper deference, his hand slipping away from the sacred notes to drift back to his side. "It's beautiful."

Every breath felt like time shifting mountains, permanently redesigning the world as she knew it. Her chest cramped painfully as something in her heart lifted, and she shied away from the effort caring for someone might take. Like a fractured bone that needed to be rebroken in order to heal, maybe it would be less painful to leave it broken.

"I'm nervous." The confession murmured past her lips on a shaky breath.

"Me too."

Her body trembled with tumultuous energy. She feared so many contradicting things in that moment. She feared the phone would ring with an interruption. She feared losing her nerve. She feared forgetting how to do this. She feared embarrassing herself. She feared disappointing him. She feared she might hate it. But most of all, she feared she might love it.

Everything with Ryan came so easy, almost too easy. It was as if they'd known each other forever even though they really only became friends a month ago.

"We don't have to do anything you're not ready to do."

Would she ever be ready? She wanted him to hold her in his arms. She wanted to be kissed, touched, cherished. She wanted that sanctuary more than her next breath, but he was the only person alive who made her want those things.

She reached behind her back and unhooked her bra, letting it fall down her arms to the bed. No going back now. Her gaze fastened to the green comforter. Waves of jolting adrenaline rolled up her spine as she waited for something to happen. Slowly, her head lifted.

He stared at her, slack jawed. "Maggie, I *really* want this, but I want you to be comfortable with it more."

She slid to the edge of the bed and stood, gently taking his hand and lifting it to her wildly beating heart. "I'm nervous because I want this too. And because I haven't done this in a really long time."

His mouth formed a sympathetic smile. "I feel the need to warn you that I might … disappoint…"

Her gaze lowered. "I doubt that."

He closed his eyes and laughed without humor. "I'm single for a reason."

She reached for his chest, mimicking the way his palm pressed to her beating heart. "I'm almost certain *this...*" She gestured to his body. "...isn't the reason you stayed single all these years."

Her touch drifted across his tattooed chest, tracing dips of muscle and chiseled flesh. He was gorgeous, fit, toned, and so kind and gentle. She slowly explored the topography of his upper body, learning his sensitive parts and familiarizing herself with his many tattoos. She'd ask about each individual one later.

When she glanced at his face again, his eyes were closed, as if no one had touched him like that in years. It hadn't occurred to her that he might have his own reservations.

"Is this okay?"

His lashes lifted and his nostrils flared with a deep inhale. "Your touch feels amazing." His hands balled into fists at his sides.

She smiled and whispered, "You can touch me too."

His gaze studied her for a moment, giving her the chance to revoke her words. When she said nothing, he dove low and sealed his mouth to hers.

His hand sifted through her hair, cupping her head, tipping her back onto the bed as he kissed her with explosive need. His gentle grip closed around her breast, massaging softly as he climbed over her, his weight sinking deliciously into her.

The edge of his thumb teased her nipple as his tongue delved deep into her mouth, seeking, conquering. She arched into his caress, her legs opening and her body cradling his. The press of his erection through his jeans drew a hungry moan from her throat.

The pinch of his fingers over the rigid tips of her breasts set her body on fire. Her touch raked through his hair, and as he dropped his head lower, she held him to her chest, arching in pleasure as he tasted her flesh. She'd forgotten how incredible a man's touch could be, how strong and tempered, yet raw and coveting.

Every lick and pull of his mouth drove her closer to the razor-sharp edge of need, until she feared desire might cut her open. Her fingers flicked open the button of her jeans. Every inch of clothing needed to go. She shoved them down her hips and thighs, pushing her panties away as well.

His clothes needed to go. She reached for his hips, and her fingers stumbled over his belt. His mouth moved to her neck, kissing and nipping at the sensitive spot just below her pulse, sending shivers up her spine and chills across her front. Her toes curled into the bedding, and she lost focus on the belt as his mouth closed over the lobe of her ear.

No one ever kissed her like that before, and it sent off a magazine of shots firing up every nerve ending in her body from head to toe. He noticed her response and chuckled against her ear, the sound easy and rugged, turning her on all the more.

"Ears. I'll remember that," he whispered, kissing a trail down her throat to her collarbone.

His fingers explored lower as his mouth made a meal of every sensitive spot around her neck. The first grazing touch to her sex had her stiffening.

Ryan's arm banded beneath her back, lifting her to him as his other hand paused between her clenched thighs. He looked into her eyes, not in question but something else. It was almost as if they'd made a deal and this was happening, no matter how long it took. There was something so gentle yet authoritative in his stare, her thighs slowly opened for him.

"That's it," he whispered, dropping a soft, approving kiss to her trembling mouth. "I won't hurt you, Maggie. Ever."

He kept his stare locked with hers as he softly teased over her folds. Soft hair and delicate flesh welcomed his touch, and arousal slowly unfurled her tension. She sucked in a sharp breath as he grazed her clit. When his finger slowly penetrated, her spine stretched, and her mind scrambled to stay in the moment.

"Easy. Keep looking at me."

She opened her eyes and gazed up at his piercing blue stare as he stroked slowly, driving that teasing touch over her sensitive flesh. Her breathing shifted and her body tightened. She wanted more and she wanted less. Maybe this was a mistake.

His thumb brushed over her swollen clit, and her breath hitched, her body arching away from the bed and taking his finger deeper. He kept his touch buried inside of her, stroking, slowly at first and then faster as her body tightened.

Lowering her body, he crawled over her. His other hand teased the soft hair at her apex and exposed her clit. His head dropped between her legs and warmth exploded through her.

His mouth worked magic over her flesh as his fingers pushed and teased, deeper, faster, until she was crying out nonsensical words and moaning for more. He shouldered his body lower, spreading her legs and stretching her in ways she hadn't stretched in years. Then all thoughts disappeared and sheer unadulterated pleasure careened through her body.

Her muscles stiffened and fluttered with a release of tension. Ryan gripped her thighs, feasting on her pleasure. Her hands fisted in the bedding as white light burst behind her eyes. Again and again, one stunning sensation rolled into another as he relentlessly pushed her higher.

She gasped and moaned louder, losing all control of her responses as he greedily wrung every drop of ecstasy from her. Her hands pulled at his hair. Her legs squeezed and clenched. When he was finally satisfied, she was empty, and at the same time, she felt completely full.

He lifted his head, strawberry blond hair standing on end, a cocky smirk twisting his mouth. And he had doubts about his abilities? They hadn't even slept together yet, and she was blown away. Literally.

She shut her eyes and savored the sensations running through her body. Peeking through her lashes, she watched him fumble with the drawer and withdraw a condom. She forgot about condoms, but since she wasn't on birth control anymore...

She shoved away those thoughts, knowing they'd quickly spiral to a reality she didn't want to intrude. He shed the last of his clothes, then ripped the foil and shifted closer, the crinkled hair on his thighs brushing her sensitive skin. Her body chilled as his weight came down and he balanced over her.

"You ready?"

Her chin trembled as she looked up at him. Maybe it was the sight of the condom. Or the pause lasted too long and something shifted. Her confidence was gone.

Goosebumps lifted on her arms and torso. Her nipples tightened, but only from the chill.

"Maggie?"

She blinked, her eyes burning with unexpected tears. She didn't want to cry, but words wouldn't come out.

"Hey, hey, hey." His body dropped over hers, warm and comforting as his arms banded around her back and lifted her to his chest. "It's okay. We can stop."

He pulled her to his lap, cradling her close. She sniffled and clung to him, her heart breaking all over again. "I don't know what happened."

"It's okay." His hand rubbed up her spine, the motion so incredibly comforting. He pulled the blanket over them, as if to say the nudity under the covers no longer mattered. "It's okay."

She couldn't explain what happened, so she said nothing. She couldn't control her tears, so she simply cried, unprepared for the intense emotions bottled up inside of her.

Small sniffles mounted and tumbled out of her in wrenching sobs that were humiliating and inexplicable. But Ryan never let her go. He simply held her.

He stroked her back, tucking her hair behind her ears, never asking for explanations or apologies. It was like he understood everything ripping her apart in that moment and respected that it was bigger than both of them.

A jumble of confused memories skated through her tired mind. Her first time with Nash. All the wild places they did it. The last time they did it. It was as if she couldn't focus on anything else until she recalled every single time with him, committed each one to memory, and put it somewhere safe so it could never go away.

Her desire for Ryan remained, but her fickle heart wouldn't let her enjoy it. Her body had closed up like a shell, cold on the outside, unevenly warm on the inside.

They lay there until the sun faded and dark shadows stole the light. Ryan didn't sleep and he didn't speak. Maybe he feared this was the end. Maybe it was. She couldn't bear too much self-examination, because she'd known all along this could happen, and she ignored it, telling herself that with therapy and determination she could somehow bury all the pain and be a normal woman again.

She'd spent two long years dissecting every part of her ravaged soul, and there was nowhere to bury the vast amount of pain left inside of her. Her heart was a hopeless Chernobyl and anyone who came too close would get hurt.

She should have never involved him. She wasn't ready and chances were she'd never be. Detangling her body from his arms, she sat up, her eyes searching the darkness for her clothes.

"Stay."

Sitting on the edge of the bed, her back toward him, she lowered her head. "I can't."

"Why?"

Didn't he see? This was how it would always be. She couldn't move past the obstacles. They were too big, too agonizing, too scary. "I'm sorry

I couldn't..." The words strangled her, and her eyes flooded with fresh tears. "I just can't."

He sat up, his hand pressing softly to her exposed back. "Can't stay or don't want to?"

Choking on her excuses, she physically tensed trying to get the words past the lump in her throat. He was asking for so much more than just one night. "I can't do *this*. I'm sorry. I'm so sorry."

She moved off the bed as he tried to hug her. She couldn't bear his touch, not after leading him on and letting him down. She needed to get her clothes and get out of there.

"Maggie, wait." The light turned on, her shame and nudity exposed in glaring reality.

She covered her breasts and torso with her crumpled shirt and pants. Screw the bra, she could get another one.

"I can't, Ryan. You don't understand what this is doing to me. I'm sorry. I have to go. Please, just let me leave."

The look in his eyes so wrought with rejection and confusion broke her heart. That delicate little sliver of hope she'd found, wilted like it never existed.

"I don't understand." His brow creased and his eyes turned pleading. "We can slow down. I shouldn't have pushed you."

"You didn't." She'd been the one to take off her clothes. This entire evening was her doing. And the worst part was, she wanted him, but she was too fucked up to have him. "I made a mistake."

"What mistake? This isn't a mistake, Maggie."

Realizing they couldn't go backwards and undo what was done, she understood that once this ended there could be no friendship, no pizza takeout, no game days, or movie Sundays. She swallowed against the lump choking her.

"I think you're wonderful, Ryan. But you aren't meant for me. I think you need to find someone else."

"I don't want someone else," he snapped. "Let's talk about this for a second."

She forced her arms into her shirt and yanked on her pants. "There's nothing to talk about."

"There's everything to talk about, Maggie. We have something, whether you're willing to admit it or not."

"Don't you get it?" She snatched her shoes off the floor and moved to the door. "*You* have something. You have this amazing personality and a family that gets you and doesn't want to change you. You're gorgeous, loyal, and dependable. I'm none of those things. I can't even depend on myself. I can't bear my own family, so I'll never be able to handle one as big as yours. Every day I'm paralyzed by social anxiety. It's not like an outfit I can change. It's who I am. Somehow you slipped past my defenses, but you can't stay. *I* can't handle this. So, if you care about me at all, please respect that and let me go."

"I care about you," he rasped in a strangled whisper.

But there was nothing more to say. Holding her shoes, she left his room and didn't stop until she was safely inside of her kitchen.

Her weight sank into the wood of her back door, as she let out a gut-wrenching sob. Her hand slid down the surface until her fingers tripped over the deadbolt. She locked the door, terrified if she let down her guard again, the world would break-in and crush the last of her soul.

CHAPTER 21

"*Y*ou want another beer?"

Ryan only half heard Luke as he stared at the television. His head had been so far up his ass all day, he could hardly recall which game they were watching.

When his cousin's words sank in, he lifted his beer, finding it warm and barely touched. "No, I'm good."

Luke disappeared up the stairs to the kitchen, and Tristan's eyes narrowed on him. "You want us to go?"

"What? No." He checked the score. "The first period's not even over."

"I'm surprised you could tell we're watching hockey. You're barely watching the screen."

The room wasn't near completed, but he'd bought a flat screen and moved the futon downstairs. He'd been going crazy over the last couple of weeks trying not to think about Maggie and failing terribly.

They ended before they even started, and every day that passed without hearing her voice or seeing her face felt like an excruciating lifetime apart. With her, the emptiness inside him seemed less gaping. Without her, he was falling apart. Never before had he suffered such a reaction to one specific female.

"Sorry. My head's on other things."

Tristan made a face that said he got that. "Want to talk about it?"

Of course he wanted to talk about it. He wanted to flip out and throw things. He wanted to demand answers and a second chance. Christ, he even wanted to beg. But at the same time, he wanted to tell the world to fuck off and leave him alone.

"No."

Luke returned and they watched the game, only speaking when something needed to be yelled at the television set.

"You should get a foosball table down here," Luke said during a commercial. His cousin had always been an athlete, so he had an abundance of energy to burn. Even a thirty second commercial could make him antsy.

"Maybe."

Luke studied him for a moment and sipped his beer. "Kelly said you're seeing someone."

Figures. Nothing ever stayed secret for long in their family. "Your brother doesn't know what he's talking about."

"So, you're not seeing anyone?"

"Nope." He finished his tepid beer and stood. "Single as always."

"Were you?" Tristan asked and Ryan's shoulders stiffened.

He climbed the steps. "Doesn't matter. I'm not now."

In the kitchen, he jerked open the fridge and yanked a beer from the shelf. Twisting off the cap, he flung it in the general direction of the trashcan and glared out the window.

She planted flowers. Or old flowers were starting to bloom again. They were the tall yellow ones. Daffodils, he thought.

He glanced at her gutters. They were overflowing with sticks and leaves. He'd planned on surprising her by cleaning them out, even though he'd won the bet and beaten her at darts. Now he wasn't touching them.

He scowled at her shed where she parked her bike. What did she do in that house all weekend? Didn't she get bored? Lonely? Not his problem.

When he returned to the basement, Luke and Tristan stopped whispering about whatever they'd been discussing. The game continued in monotone plays.

"Next week's the Main Street Burger Festival," Tristan said.

Ryan lifted a brow. "And?"

He shrugged. "You like burgers. You should go."

He'd probably stop by but didn't see the need to make a plan of it.

"Luke, isn't that girl from the gym competing?"

"Yeah, she's making some vegan jalapeno concoction. Claims it could convert the biggest carnivore."

"Doubtful," Ryan sneered. Why were vegans always in competition with other diets?

"You got a problem with vegans?" Luke asked.

"No. I couldn't care less what other people eat. But if I go to a burger festival, you bet your ass I'm eating beef."

"Aren't you a little curious?" Tristan asked.

"About veggie burgers? Hell no!" Ryan frowned and then it clicked. "Let me guess, the vegan's single."

"I don't know, is she Luke?"

Ryan rolled his eyes. This was so rehearsed.

"Her and her boyfriend broke up last month." Luke lifted his brows. "She's probably ready for a rebound."

"No thanks."

"Are you honestly saying you'd turn down the chance to get laid?" Luke asked.

He was about to say yes, when he thought about the lonesome reality of his life. "A girl just out of a relationship isn't going to amount to anything meaningful. Like you said, she's probably just looking for a rebound."

Luke scoffed. "So? Are you so flush with pussy you're willing to turn a rebound fuck away?"

"God, I hate when you get crude," Tristan grumbled. "She's a woman, not pussy."

"He knows what I mean." Luke's stare turned probing. "Well?"

Ryan shifted uncomfortably. "I don't even know the girl."

"Her name's Willow. She does yoga every day and doesn't do dairy or meat. She's single and looking for a hookup. What more do you need to know?"

He rubbed his head, wishing a fight would break out on the ice. "I don't know."

"Just meet her. Stop by her booth and try her weird burger and see if anything clicks. She's pretty."

Luke might be in a long committed marriage to Tristan, but before they met, Luke was a womanizer. He wasn't blind when it came to the opposite sex and Ryan trusted his opinion. "Maybe."

"Good enough." The topic dropped and they watched the rest of the game in relative peace.

~

THE MORNING of the burger festival the town bustled with activity, much like it did before any town jubilee. The hosed off sidewalks and thoroughfare of Main Street was cluttered with booths where cars usually parked. The police closed off the main strip and restaurant owners hooked up generators and mobile grills. In a few hours, the streets would smell like red meat man heaven.

The town was voting on a new name and signs were everywhere. Posters encouraged residents to stop by the ballot boxes at the end of Main Street to weigh in. Ryan found the ballots and read over the choices, irritated that Center County wasn't even an option.

Jasper Falls had a nice ring to it. And he recalled learning about Jasper Willcot in high school. He'd been the first settler in their area. That was probably where the name came from. It was better than the other options *Peach Grove* and *Mountain Ville*. He checked off his vote and moved on.

Ryan helped Kelly unload a large charcoal grill outside of O'Malley's. The pub was contributing Bloody Mary's complete with seasoned shrimp and bacon cheeseburger sliders bursting from the tops. It was a town favorite, and no one mixed a Bloody Mary like Kelly.

"You sticking around today?" his cousin asked, scraping and prepping the grill.

"Might as well eat." His eyes searched the booths for the vegan girl, but nothing jumped out. If he didn't see her, he didn't see her. He wasn't even sure why he looked for her in the first place.

"How are things going with the O'Malley chick?"

"They're not."

Kelly paused and glanced at him, then turned back to the grill. "You okay?"

"I'll live."

"Sorry to hear things didn't work out. She was cute."

Cute didn't begin to describe her. "She had baggage."

"Because of Nash?"

Surprised he knew Nash's name, Ryan stopped stacking cups and looked at his cousin. "Did you know him?"

"Didn't everyone? He wasn't hard to miss. I used to try to get him to play at the pub, but he always turned me down. Probably the rivalry."

"You would have let an O'Malley perform here?"

Kelly shrugged. "Business is business. He was insanely talented. It's a shame he died before ever making something of himself."

"Yeah." Ryan returned to stacking the cups under the stand, wondering if he seemed boring compared to Nash and all of his talent. That's probably why it was so easy to walk away.

Once the booth was running and Kelly had the grill going, Ryan took a walk to check out how other people were setting up. The café had a special coffee rub they were selling, and Aunt Maureen was handing out samples of grilled beef. He stopped by to get a coffee but didn't stay long.

At the pizza parlor, Maria and Angela were stirring a large vat of sauce for braciola. It wasn't necessarily a burger, but they were serving it over thick Italian bread and the girls said it counted. He didn't have the balls to argue.

The hardware store was working with a classic small charcoal grill and basic burgers with traditional fixings. They never won, but Ryan secretly preferred their burgers most each year.

A box collapsed on the sidewalk and a woman cursed as large cans of black beans went rolling into the road. Ryan stopped a runaway can with his foot and walked it over to her.

"You lost this."

She looked up at him, strands of pale blonde hair clinging to her golden lashes, and huffed. "Thanks. The box sort of got away from me."

The bottom of the cardboard had caved in and now looked useless, so he picked up another large can and asked, "Where's your booth?"

"Just over there by the salon."

He followed her finger and did a double take. "Vegan?"

She laughed and a soft pink flush crested her high cheekbones. "I know, this is a Burger Festival. But there are lots of people who prefer veggie burgers nowadays, and there's proven health benefits to limiting meat consumption, not to mention the effects cows are having on our environment."

If he wasn't holding two heavy cans of beans, he would have held up his hands in surrender. "I'm not judging."

"Sure you are." She stood and smiled. "But that's okay. In an hour you'll take it all back when you taste my burgers."

He laughed. "Is that so?"

"Scared?"

"Not at all." He followed her to her booth and decided he'd be eating his words to Luke as well. She was pretty.

When the festival started, the street filled with townsfolk. It was the first event of spring and everyone seemed ready to say goodbye to winter. He ran into friends from high school, employees from the lumberyard, regulars he got to know from working at the bar, and plenty of relatives. The only person he didn't see was Maggie, but that was no surprise.

Not wanting to seem too interested, he waited until three o'clock to return to the vegan booth. Willow seemed happy to see him again, and he stayed for a while since she didn't have much of a line.

"So, vegan means no meat or dairy?"

"No animal products of any kind."

He pointed to the creamy cheese spread she'd been mixing on the burner. "What about that?"

"This is actually a mix of nutritional yeast, carrots, oil, and seasoning."

"Yum," he said dryly.

She flicked her gaze to him and smiled. "You'll see."

He really didn't want to, but he agreed he'd taste her burger.

She served the sandwich on a toasted English muffin of a cardboard consistency and topped it with the fake cheese sauce, a leaf of crisp lettuce, and a bright red slice of tomato. It actually smelled pretty good.

He took an experimental bite and chewed. The texture was ... different. But the flavors were explosive. "Wow."

"See?"

He wiped his mouth. "It's got a kick."

"That's the jalapenos."

He ate the entire burger, but when she offered another, he politely declined.

"Hey, Ryan, I thought that was you."

He turned and spotted Ashlynn, Kelly's wife pushing a stroller. "Hey, Ashlynn." He hugged her and bent to the stroller. "And look at this little angel." He sometimes forgot the new babies' names. There were so many.

"She's a handful."

Willow leaned over the counter and spoke in a voice only women could get away with. "Don't let your momma say that. You tell her you're perfect. Aren't you, Bethany?"

Ah, Bethany. He never would have guessed that.

"So, what are you doing over here by the veggie burgers?" Ashlynn asked, then placed an order with Willow. "I'll take a plain veggie and a small order of sweet potato fries, Will."

He'd forgotten Kelly's wife was a vegetarian. Willow started her order then asked, "You two know each other?"

"Ryan's Kelly's cousin."

Recognition dawned. "Oh, then you must be related to Luke, too."

Shit. Had Luke mentioned him the way he'd mentioned her? "I'm related to all of them. All eight thousand of them."

Her smile turned nervous and she quickly turned to Ashlynn, thanking her for the tomato shipment from the farmers' market.

Feeling uncomfortable now that Willow realized who he was and probably knew Luke had tried to set them up, he excused himself and stepped away. His life had become a labyrinth of blind dates and awkward encounters with exes. He was no stranger to navigating his way through uncomfortable situations.

By late afternoon, the streets and sidewalks were full, not only with Center County residents but also visitors from other towns. He'd been about to pack it in and head home when something by the firehouse caught his eye.

Men in blue T-shirts emblazoned with the local fire station's shield worked an extended gas grill. They were a mangy bunch, but there seemed a collective sense of family among them. Women spooned out side dishes to those lined up at the tables, but what caught his eye was the small figure at the end, taking money and handing out napkins.

Maggie's head turned and her stare found his. His heart sank into his stomach as they looked at each other. What was her association with the firehouse? He lifted his hand in a casual wave. It took her a moment but she did the same.

Should he talk to her? Maybe he could get in line and order something. He didn't really have any room left in his stomach, but he'd suffer through another hundred burgers if it gave him an excuse to talk to her and ask how she was doing.

He couldn't walk away without hearing her voice. He grabbed a plate and—

"Ryan…"

Confused by the sound of someone calling his name, he turned. Willow jogged over to the line where he stood. "You left before I could say goodbye."

"Oh. Sorry."

She smiled nervously. "I guess your cousin told you who I was."

"Um, he mentioned you."

Her full lashes flickered, and she bit into her lower lip. "Well, you seem really nice. If you ever want to go out, give me a call." She handed him a napkin with a smiling radish on it and her number scribbled underneath. "I have to get back to my booth."

He watched her jog away in her tight leggings and open back shirt. Swallowing, he turned and found Maggie watching him, her expression blank.

He tossed his plate on the table. This was nuts. If he wanted to talk to her, he shouldn't have to pretend he needed any reason other than he missed her. But when he walked to the end of the table where she'd been standing, she was gone and a woman with jet black hair had taken her place.

"Plates are on the other end. First, get your food, then I'll ring you out."

"Do you know what happened to the woman who was just here?"

"Maggie?" She turned and yelled, "Did anyone see where Maggie went? She's got someone here to see her."

The firefighters looked around, but no one answered.

"Could someone look inside?"

She glanced at the line. "Sorry, we're slammed. She'll probably be back in a few minutes if you want to wait over there."

He stepped out of the way of the crowd and waited on the grass where the woman directed. His stare kept scanning the swarm of people and looking up at the station windows. But Maggie didn't show. After thirty minutes, he gave up.

When he got home that evening, her bike was leaning against the shed. He got out of his truck and hopped the fence. He was done playing hide-and-seek.

CHAPTER 22

*M*aggie jumped from her place on the couch as a fist pounded on her back door. She crept down the hall, recognizing Ryan's tall shadow in the window. Biting her nail, she hesitated, not wanting to answer.

"Maggie, I know you're in there. Open the door."

She pressed her back to the wall, hiding behind the molding of the kitchen breezeway.

"I need to talk to you." He pounded again. "Why did you run away today?"

She hadn't run away. She saw him and finally decided this distance between them was stupid, and she should say something to him. But then that beautiful blonde came running up to him and handed him her number. He clearly knew who she was, since he took the number. That was the kind of woman Ryan deserved to be with, confident, striking, tall… Perfect.

"Goddamn it, Maggie, please open the door."

Her shoulders rounded as she backed further into the shadows. If she opened that door, he'd wear her down. They'd end up right back where they were, until she had her next breakdown and they broke up again. He was better off finding someone else.

His head thunked against the door and his voice lowered. "I wanted to talk to you today."

Her back slid down the wall until she sat on the floor.

"Please open the door." He paused, but when she didn't move, he said, "I wanted to tell you that I miss you, and I can't stop thinking about you."

She looked at the carpet, remembering his smile when he waved at her.

"I know you said you can't do this, but I don't know how to shut off the way I feel about you. And I don't believe that you can shut it off either."

Sorrow unfurled in her chest as a tear rolled down her cheek.

"I can't seem to get over you. You're different. You make me feel different." The doorknob jiggled and her breath caught, but she relaxed when she remembered locking the deadbolt. "You never lock your door."

His shadow shifted and her phone pinged. She pulled it out of her pocket.

Please let me in.

SHE WAVERED, debating if she should just let him in. Keeping him out of her life hurt more than she expected, and maybe if she opened the door, he could take the pain away. He had a way of doing that, of making her feel safe even from herself.

Her phone beeped again.

You're breaking my heart.

SHE DROPPED the phone and shut her eyes, giving in to her tears. It was too much. *He* was too much. She didn't want to feel the things he made her feel. She couldn't handle her own heart, and she had no business being responsible for someone else's.

"Maggie... Please."

Her chest was splitting open, pieces of her falling out. She reached for the phone and wiped her nose. Her fingers trembled as she typed out a reply.

I don't want to see you anymore. Please go away.

SHE HEARD the notification hit his phone and felt his frustration through the wall. Then his shadow disappeared, and she was alone in the dark, a place she knew too well.

CHAPTER 23

The following morning Maggie's chain popped on the way to the cemetery. By the time she had it fixed, she was late for work and had no time to visit Nash's grave. When she got to work, it popped again. Jim tried to fix the chain, but it was shot.

"It's too rusted to use. You need a new one."

She ordered a new chain online, but it wouldn't be there until the middle of the week. When her shift was over, she walked her bike out of the warehouse and through the parking lot. The wind whipped at her clothes.

Jim beeped and pulled his truck next to her. "Get in," her boss ordered.

"Thanks, but I can walk."

He sighed, and the door to his truck squeaked as he climbed out, leaving the engine running. He grabbed her bike and lifted it into the bed of the truck. "I'm not asking."

She glanced at the sky, noting the storm clouds in the distance over the mountains. She had an hour walk ahead of her, and if it rained, she'd be soaked through by the time she got home.

Lowering her head, she walked around the truck, and he opened the passenger door. Once she climbed in, he slammed it behind her. The broken in leather seats of the cab smelled of diesel fuel.

He clambered in behind the wheel. "There's an empty takeout bag on the floor if you're gonna be sick. Buckle up."

A deep breath pulled from the hollow pit of her stomach as she clicked the seatbelt into place. Jim drove with both hands on the wheel and took his time, going slower than the law required.

"You know, after Tina died, I never put up a Christmas tree again.

170

The holidays were her thing. She'd always spruce the house up and make it smell like cinnamon. Said it was her favorite time of year."

Her gaze remained focused on the two-way CB radio all the fire-fighters had in their cars so as not to look out at the road rushing by.

"Wasn't until years later when the kids were all teenagers that they told me how much they missed the way the holidays used to be." The truck turned slowly, and her stomach lurched. "I agreed, saying no one did Christmas like their momma, but that wasn't what they meant. Turns out, they missed spending the holidays with me. For years, I just treated it like any other day. I'd get them a few presents, but then I'd park my ass in front of the TV until I woke up and moved to bed."

The rain started and the sky darkened, casting shadows around them. The windshield wipers kicked on, and she tried to time her breathing to the slow pace, but her heart was beating too fast.

"I can't ever give them those holidays back, Maggie May. And just like me, you're losin' time too. Now my kids are grown and doing their own thing. They've made new traditions."

The truck turned and her mouth watered. She glanced at the bag on the floor and closed her hands into fists.

"At first, I didn't want to participate in holidays without Tina. I made excuses and told them to go on and enjoy it without me, but they insisted."

She recognized her street from the corner of her eye. The rain fell harder, pinging off the metal roof and drowning the windows. The wipers sped up, now moving faster than her heart.

"Turns out, I never stopped loving Christmas. There are parts that remind me of Tina and make me miss her a little bit more, but it's bitter-sweet. Just because she can't celebrate with us anymore doesn't neces-sarily mean we ain't got reason to celebrate. This past year, my oldest gave birth to my first grandchild. And now her sister's expecting." He pulled into her driveway and put the truck in park. "The point is, life goes on, whether we want it to or not. You aren't saving anyone by standing still. You're only missing out and hurting yourself."

Her hands were so tight her knuckles cracked when she opened her fists and unbuckled the seatbelt. She didn't meet his eyes.

"I tried to move on. I can't."

"I couldn't either. Not without my family." He patted her arm through her sleeve. "Maybe give your mom and dad a call. I know they'd be happy to hear from you."

Shutting her eyes against her tears, she nodded. "I will. Thanks for the ride home."

"You go on in. I'll put your bike in the shed before I go."

"Thanks, Jim."

Just as she climbed out of the truck, her vision and hearing muffled by the rain, twin headlights flashed. Ryan's truck pulled into the driveway, casting a spotlight on Jim as he lifted her bike out of the truck bed and tucked it inside the shed.

His hood was up, due to the rain, and before he got back into the truck, he came around and hugged her. "You know I'm only looking out for you, Maggie May. To me, you're still just a little girl playing dollies in my front room with my girls."

"I know."

"Go on and get out of this rain before you catch a cold. I'll see you tomorrow."

Dodging puddles, she ran across the backyard and up the steps. Jim pulled away, and she looked across the driveway. Ryan sat in his truck watching her. She went inside.

CHAPTER 24

$\mathcal{M}$aggie taped the box shut and carried it out to the shed where she'd crammed the others. It was getting difficult to open the doors without risking something spilling out. Furniture, instruments, bags of clothing, and paperwork filled the space from floor to ceiling. Yet, with every box removed, no sense of accomplishment came.

It had been four weeks since her bike chain broke, since she missed talking with Nash for the first time in two years, since her conversation with Jim. She continued with therapy but no longer felt like she was getting anything from the experience, mostly because she refused to talk about the things bothering her.

Right now, she wanted to be angry. Anger was the only energizing response to grief, so she preferred it over sadness. It helped her throw things into boxes and angrily tape them shut. It helped her scrub the kitchen floor and purge closets without thinking too hard. Anger was preferable to curling up in the fetal position and letting the world cave-in.

As she closed the shed door and turned back to the house, she stilled at the sight of a small blue car pulling up at the curb. "Shit."

She moved away from the shed to avoid drawing any suspicions and waited at the back door. Perrin appeared a moment later holding a caddy of coffee.

"I thought I saw you."

"Hey."

Perrin glanced at the shed. "Were you going somewhere?"

"No, just putting some things away. Want to come in?" Her sister hadn't been around since she started painting and purging. She hoped she didn't make too much out of nothing.

"Sure. I have something I want to ask you."

Maggie led her into the kitchen and grabbed the sugar bowl and creamer from the fridge. Perrin loved her coffee extra sweet. She said it was the way they drank it in Europe, but Maggie didn't know.

"The house looks different. Did you move stuff?"

Maggie shrugged. "I've just been decluttering."

Rather than sit, Perrin walked down the hall. Maggie shut her eyes just as her sister gasped.

"Oh, my God. You got a new couch!" Perrin returned to the kitchen. "Your living room looks amazing. When did you do that?"

She shrugged. "Two months ago."

Perrin's gaze dropped. "I didn't realize how long it's been since I visited."

"That's okay. It's not like you missed anything."

She sat at the table. "Maggie, I think it's great that you remodeled."

"It's just a new couch and some paint."

"It's huge." She took her hand. "I'm proud of you."

Maggie pulled her hand back and lifted her cup so it remained occupied. Leaning back in her chair, she asked, "What did you have to ask me?"

Her sister hesitated. "Well, I know you've been upset with me."

She frowned. "I'm not upset with you."

"It's okay. Really. I was avoiding you and you needed some space."

She'd been avoiding her? Maggie supposed it had been a long time between visits. "I wasn't mad at you, Perrin. I just figured you were busy."

"Well, I was. Bran and I took a trip to Jersey to visit his parents, and when we were there, we started looking at houses."

"In New Jersey? Isn't it really expensive to live there?" And why was she looking at houses with Bran?

"It is, but it's beautiful. Especially down the shore where his parents live. Bran recently got a promotion at work, and one of the benefits is that he can now work from home, so he doesn't have to commute every day."

"I'm sorry, you said you had a question for me?"

She smiled and folded her hands on her lap. "Maggie, he asked me to marry him and I said yes."

For a second, her heart stopped beating. "What?"

A smile stretched across Perrin's face, and she couldn't recall the last time she saw her sister so happy. Maybe she'd been masking her happiness so not to rub it in.

"He did it on the beach. It was so romantic. We were walking along, admiring the pretty houses and talking about the possibility of him moving there, when he dropped down on one knee and pulled out a ring. I nearly crapped my pants I was so surprised."

Surprised didn't begin to explain it. "But you just started dating." She barely knew the guy.

Perrin frowned. "Maggie, we've been dating for two and a half years."

Right, because they got together just before Nash died. "Oh."

She leaned forward, folding her hands on the table and Maggie saw the ring. It was enormous and lustrous, catching the sunlight and sending prisms across the wall. "We don't want a long engagement. We're thinking a July wedding."

Her eyes bulged. "*This* July? That's two months away."

"I know, but both our families are small. We could have the ceremony at the church and book a hall for the reception. He wants to move fast so we can focus on the house. Bran put a bid on a stunning Victorian on the beach of Avalon."

"You already picked out a house?"

"I told you, he moves fast."

"I'd say."

She smiled, as if that was one of his best qualities. "Maggie, I wanted to ask if you'd be my maid of honor. I know you hate anything social anymore, but the wedding will be small. Just us and a few close friends and family. Please say yes. You're my best friend, and I can't imagine anyone else standing by my side when I say I do."

Visions of taffeta and strangers flew into her mind. She pictured herself cemented to the bar. A memory of her and Nash's wedding cut in, and she recalled how wonderful Perrin had been that day, how calm and supportive, when everyone else had said they were too young.

"Of course I'll be your maid of honor."

"Thank you!" Perrin startled her by lunging across the table and squeezing her into a tight hug. "I knew I could count on you!"

The next hour passed in a whirlwind of details about Perrin's perfect wedding. Maggie tried to keep up and not panic when she heard things like *maid of honor toast* or *wedding party dance.*

Through it all, she felt under qualified for the job. Yes, she knew her sister better than anyone, but she'd been a shitty friend to her in the last two years. And she hardly knew Bran at all.

"I'm sorry," she interrupted, barely listening to her diatribe about lilies versus roses.

Perrin's voice silenced and she frowned. "For what?"

"Everything. I've been so out of it. I never check to see how you're doing, or if you need anything. If you didn't pop in with coffee every few weeks, we'd never see each other."

Perrin shifted but didn't object or deny how terrible she'd been. "You were going through stuff."

"So were you. You met the man you're going to spend the rest of your life with, and I never even noticed how important he was to you. I feel so stupid and selfish. You're getting married, and I don't know the first thing about the groom."

"That's not true."

Maggie gave her a pointed look, embarrassed to admit how true it actually was.

Perrin mentioned Bran throughout the years, but Maggie only half listened. She'd only met him a handful of times. The most she ever talked to the guy was the night before Nash died.

Maggie's brow tightened. "Do you think there's some rule that says sisters aren't allowed to be happy at the same time?"

"What? Maggie, no."

"It just seems that Bran showed up just when Nash..."

Her sister gripped her hand. "Look at me, Maggie. Nash died because of bad weather and bald tires. The universe isn't punishing you. It's *waiting* for you. We all are."

"I'm trying," she admitted. "I'm trying really hard, but it's killing me. Every day I box a piece of our life up and carry it out to the shed, waiting for some of the pain to go with it but it won't." She sucked in a jagged breath. "It's got me in this chokehold, and I can barely breathe without hurting or fearing I might die of heartbreak."

"Oh, Maggie." She pulled her chair closer and wrapped her in her arms. "Honey, I can't imagine how bad it hurts. You and Nash were everything to each other. No one expects this to be easy. But we all believe in you. You're tough and so independent. We just figured if we gave you time..." She ran her hand over her hair and looked at her with tears in her eyes. "Maybe we gave you too much space. We never meant to make you feel like you needed to get through this on your own."

She wiped her eyes, but more tears came. "It wasn't you. It was me. I pushed everyone away."

"You asked for space. You were entitled."

"I could have been nicer."

"Could you have?" She looked into her eyes. "I think if I lost the love of my life, I would need to be a little mean for a while. I think that's normal."

She caught Perrin's wrist and squeezed. "Thank you for saying I'm normal."

"Oh, honey, you are. You're just a little weird too."

Maggie laughed. "I missed you."

Her sister smiled, then held out her arms. Maggie leaned into her, and when she tried to ease away, Perrin held tighter.

"Not yet."

When they broke apart, Perrin passed her a napkin and took one for herself. They both blew their noses, sounding like a couple of truckers and laughed.

They spent the rest of the afternoon discussing the wedding. Maggie told Perrin she'd taken her advice and started seeing a therapist, and that news filled her sister with hope. She didn't mention Ryan because there was no point when everything ended as abruptly as it had.

As she walked her out to the car, Perrin hugged her again. "So, the engagement dinner is next Friday at that new restaurant in town. They have a backroom for private functions."

"Do I need to do anything?" She wasn't the most girly girl, so she already warned Perrin that she'd need a road map for any expected maid of honor frills.

"No. Mom already started buying decorations, and Bran's family is taking care of the catering. Just wear something nice and be there at seven."

"Something nice like a button down?"

Her sister pursed her lips. "Something nice like a dress and heels. If you need to borrow an outfit, I can come by with a few dresses this week."

"No, I'll find something." She had some old dresses in the spare closet. One of them should fit.

"Good. And don't panic. It's literally just going to be our immediate family and Bran's. His sister's super nice. You'll love her."

"Can't wait." She tried not to sound too sarcastic or terrified.

Perrin squeezed her hands. "Thanks for this, Maggie. It really means the world to me."

And just like that she knew she'd wear anything and say anything and dance to anything her sister asked her to, because that's what sisters did for one another.

CHAPTER 25

*M*aggie tugged at the hem of her dress, wishing it reached her knees. The old floral sundress was something she wore to her sister's twenty-fifth birthday, and it fit as good as it had the day she bought it. However, Maggie seemed to have lost some of the confidence that once helped her fill it out.

She paired it with a kelly green fitted cardigan and matching green peep-toe heels. It had been years since she walked in anything other than flats, so she needed some practice. Luckily, she had a long walk to town, since there was no riding a bike in a dress that was fitted.

Her toes were screaming when she reached the restaurant. She hobbled through the front door and looked for someone to direct her. A hostess appeared, asked if she was with the engagement party, then directed her to the back room.

Maggie veered off when she saw the bathroom, needing a minute to check her toes for blood. She used the facilities and inspected her shoes, expecting to find rusted razor blades in the soles.

Nope. Just plain old shoes.

A toilet flushed and she quickly slipped her high heel back on her foot. Turning to wash her hands, she reached for a towel and did a double take at the woman using the other sink. A fissure of recognition traveled up her spine.

The tall blonde smiled and dried her hands. "Are you Perrin's sister?"

Oh, God. Was she part of the wedding party? Her mind raced to place her, not recalling *how* she knew her or from where but somehow instinctively knowing she didn't like her.

"Yes. I'm Maggie."

Without an invitation, the woman barged through every personal boundary and pulled her into a hug. Maggie stiffened and hated how good the other woman smelled.

"It is so nice to finally meet you. I adore your sister." She let go and Maggie stepped back. "I'm Bran's sister, Willow."

As she smiled, Maggie's memory placed her. She was the woman at the festival. The one who ran to Ryan and handed him what was likely her number. Everything from Maggie's scalp to her toes went numb.

The woman was utterly perfect. Her full lips, her flawless skin, her almost silver blonde hair, nothing appeared out of place. Her legs seemed to start at her perfectly round and perky breasts and extend for miles.

"It's nice to meet you," she said numbly. Did Ryan ever call her? Did they have a history?

Willow held the door, all sun-kissed peach skin and perfected femininity. "Come on. I'll show you where we're sitting."

As Maggie followed her to the back room, she couldn't help admiring her willowy figure. The name suited her.

Everything about her, from the sound of her melodic voice to the delicate scent of her perfume, made her presence pleasant, but Maggie hated her on the spot. If this night had been for anyone other than Perrin, she would have made an excuse and left. But she was her sister's maid of honor and she owed this to her. Besides, how bad could one dinner be?

"Maggie, these are my parents Seth and Mila. And this is my date, Ryan."

Her fake smile fell as she came face-to-face with the one person she'd carefully avoided for the last month.

"Maggie, you made it." Perrin came to her side and gave her a hug. Maggie clung to her, needing the added balance. Her sister leaned close and whispered, "You look incredible."

"So do you," Maggie said numbly. "Where are we sitting?" She needed to get away from that blonde gazelle and her Ryan. Not *her* Ryan. Her neighbor. They were only neighbors.

He blinked at her with an unreadable expression, and she couldn't breathe.

"We're over here. Mom, look who I found." Perrin, thankfully, dragged her away.

For once, Maggie was glad to see her parents. Her mother eyed her outfit and hugged her, pulling her into the seat next to where she and their father were sitting.

"How are things?" her mother whispered. "Perrin says you've started therapy."

"Not here, Mom." Her mother had a habit of offering too much sympathy and personal details in public places.

"Well, you look beautiful. Your sister's so thrilled you agreed to be a part of all of this."

She watched Ryan, where he sat on the other end of the long table. Willow chattered at his side, and he stared at his plate, expression blank.

She supposed he made good use of that number. And while part of her wanted to be happy for him, there was too much bitterness rushing through her veins, preventing her from being the bigger person at the moment.

Someone tapped their fork against a champagne flute. Bran's father stood. "I'd like to make a toast. To my son and his beautiful bride-to-be, Perrin. May the two of you face a life full of celebrations as happy as this one. First, your wedding. And then birth announcements and Christenings…"

Maggie remained numb and emotionless as others dabbed misty eyes and Bran's father listed every cause for celebration in a marriage stretching from the engagement party to the golden wedding anniversary.

"Cheers."

"Cheers," the room echoed.

Maggie smiled at Perrin and chugged her champagne, desperate for it to take effect.

"I'd like to make a small toast as well."

Maggie spit a mouthful of champagne back into the flute, earning a glare from her mother. She shrugged and mouthed *sorry.*

Willow stood beside Ryan in all of her glowing glory, holding her champagne like a celebrity might cradle an Emmy.

"Bran, you and I have always been close. You're not only my brother, but you're also my best friend. I'll never forget the day you traded in all your comics to buy me a ticket to see Bon Jovi, which was probably the best gift I ever received—until now." She raised her glass, and Maggie tried to smother an eye roll. "You've outdone yourself and given me a sister, who I love just as much as you. Thank you."

Maggie frowned as everyone raised their glasses and awed. Perrin stood and hugged Willow, wiping her eyes as if she shared this artificial bond.

That's my sister. Get your own.

She shot back the last sip of champagne and when a server appeared with more, she held up her glass. "Could I also order a martini, please? Extra olives."

Her mother frowned. "Perhaps you should wait until you eat, Maggie."

"Trust me, Mom, it's better if I don't."

Her mother crossed her arms and sat back, making no effort to hide how displeasing she found her behavior. While everyone else indulged in the bubbly stuff, Maggie buried her nose in the business end of a martini glass. Things were going down a little too quickly, and she almost forced herself to stop until she overheard Ryan order a glass of Tully on the rocks.

"Jameson's better," she mumbled, finishing her drink.

"What?" Perrin frowned at her. "Are you drunk? We haven't even eaten yet."

"Don't worry. I'll eat."

Bran leaned around Perrin's shoulder. "It's nice to see you out, Maggie."

Like she was some sort of escaped gorilla from the city zoo. "Yeah, I'm a real crowd pleaser."

Her gaze drifted to the end of the table, where Willow whispered something in Ryan's ear. Her fingers played with his as they rested on the table.

"Is something wrong?" Perrin hissed.

She looked at her sister, remembering that this was her special night and all the ways Perrin had been there for every special moment in Maggie's life. Heat rushed up her neck and her stomach knotted with guilt. She set her empty glass down and pushed it away.

"No. I'm sorry. Nerves."

Her sister frowned, her eyes asking for the truth.

"I'll stop," Maggie whispered.

Dinner was served in six courses. Throughout the entire meal she carried a bowling ball in her stomach, making it impossible to swallow more than a few bites. Her mother watched her like a hawk, commenting on the weight she'd lost and worrying that she wasn't getting enough sunlight or nutrition.

"I saw a study that most Americans are vitamin D deficient," her mother commented after making reference to Maggie's complexion.

Yes, Maggie was genuinely concerned that her lack of vitamin D might be her ultimate demise. "I'll pick up some supplements, Mom."

"It's not a joke, Maggie May. You're not young anymore. Before you know it…"

She turned a hard glare on her mother, daring her to finish that sentence and tell her how unprepared she might be for one of life's fun little shocks.

Her mother returned her attention to her dessert plate. "You understand."

She ground her molars. The woman just couldn't drop anything without that last word. "Yes, I *do* understand."

Perrin turned. "What's going on? Mom, drop it."

"Drop what? I was merely having a conversation about the importance of vitamins."

"Oh, bullshit," Maggie grumbled, flagging down the waiter. "Can I have another martini, please?"

"Well, whatever you're discussing, save it for another time," Perrin hissed.

Their mother set down her fork in a huff. "I see, now that you two made-up, I'm back to being the odd man out."

Maggie frowned. "We weren't in a fight."

"No? What do you call it when a family member disappears for two years?"

Maggie's jaw slackened. She couldn't believe she just said that.

Perrin looked equally shocked. "Mom."

"Well, I'm sorry. You might easily forgive her absence, but I don't. Holidays, Mother's Day, birthdays... Those moments are just gone now."

"Shut. Up." The words came out of Maggie's mouth cold and cruel, but she didn't care.

Her mother blinked, as if she were somehow the victim of this attack. "See how you speak to me?"

The waiter returned with her martini. She glanced at Perrin, her eyes brimming with unspoken apology. "I'm sorry. I tried."

She chugged the chilled vodka in her glass and stood. The martinis and lack of food didn't mix very well with her heels, but she made it work, only slightly banging her hip into the table and alerting everyone to her exit.

Bran's family stared up at her totally oblivious to the dysfunction at the other end of the table. Ryan watched her as well, his brow creased with what she dreaded might be pity.

"Oh." She lifted the untouched champagne flute in front of her sister. "To the happy couple. May you both live—" Her words ceased in her throat, and she tried to think of an appropriate well wish for the soon to be bride and groom. Then she realized she hit the nail right on the head. "I hope you both live to see everything you dreamed come true. Excuse me."

She left the back room without a second glance. When she reached the sidewalk, she gasped for fresh air, trying to force back the tears that threatened to come. She would not be the sloppy disaster that cried in the middle of town.

Withdrawing her phone, she sent a quick text to her sister.

I'm so sorry I ruined your night. I just can't deal with her self-righteous attitude when she doesn't have a fucking clue what she's talking about. I understand if you want to pick someone else to be your maid of honor. I'm sorry.

PRESSING her hand into her stomach, she caught her breath and stumbled in the direction of home. Her phone buzzed.

You didn't ruin anything and I want YOU as my MOH—exactly as you are.
Mom was out of line. I'll call you tomorrow. I love you.

EVEN DRUNK AND HURTING, she knew she didn't deserve such easy forgiveness. Plucking her shoes off her feet, she ambled home but somehow made a wrong turn and found herself sitting in the cemetery alone at night.

She tugged off her earrings and tossed them on his grave, not caring where they landed. "Your wife's become the kind of woman we used to stare at and pity."

She wiped her nose on the back of her hand. "You know, I tell myself all these things like get out of bed, get dressed, no drinking today, don't lock the door in case Nash loses his house keys again. But it's all bullshit."

She wished she had another martini. It was getting cold and her feet were freezing.

"This dress is useless. Oh, and you know what else? I'm going to die from lack of sunlight." She nodded and twisted her lips. "My mom's got it all figured out. So I can probably stop worrying about all the other ways I might go. It's going to be a vitamin D deficiency in the end."

She closed her arms around her knees and rested her head on them. "Do you know she actually had the balls to accuse me of not realizing how fragile life is? What is wrong with that woman? And my dad just sits there, like our dysfunctional pecking is perfectly normal."

She shivered. Her nose started to run, but she had nowhere to wipe it. Her fingers burrowed into the grass, finding the ground cold.

"What am I doing, Nash?"

No answer, per usual. She let out a frustrated breath and pressed a kiss to her fingers before touching them to his name. "I'll see you tomorrow."

She grabbed her shoes and wandered through the cemetery to the front gate. Just as she turned onto the road twin headlights beamed at her, and she lifted an arm to shade her eyes as she squinted. The vehicle moved slowly, and she sucked in a breath when she recognized it as Ryan's truck.

Her heart thundered with confusion. What was he doing there? Why wasn't he with Willow?

His window rolled down. "Can I drive you home?"

CHAPTER 26

*M*aggie looked up at Ryan, her pale face bathed in moonlight and her eyes pink from crying. "What are you doing here?"

He figured she'd ask that. No way to lie his way out of the obvious. "I followed you."

She frowned. "But you were at dinner." Her gaze searched the truck. "Where's your date?"

"She's still at the restaurant with her family."

"You should go back and get her." She pivoted and started walking.

"Maggie, wait." He left the truck running and went after her on foot.

"Go away, Ryan."

"Stop telling me to go away." He caught her arm, forcing her to stop walking. "I want to talk to you."

"About what?"

"Tonight."

She shook her head and looked away. "I'd really rather not."

"I'm not dating her. We went out for coffee once and she asked me to be her plus one for an engagement dinner. I didn't even realize it was her brother's engagement, and I had no way of knowing you'd be there."

"Well, at least you got the whole meeting her parents thing out of the way."

"I don't care who her parents are! I have no interest in her, and I'm not going out with her again."

She pursed her lips. "Oh, come on. I'm a heterosexual woman and even I'm attracted to her."

"She's not who I want."

Her gaze dropped to the road. "Don't do this."

"Come on, Maggie. I'm crazy about you. I can't sleep without dreaming of you. I'm constantly staring at your property looking for you. I had to delete your number just so I wouldn't text you. And tonight, when I saw you—you look like a million bucks by the way—all I wanted to do was kiss you."

Her brow pinched and her head lowered. She shivered and he took off his suit jacket placing it over her shoulders.

"You're freezing." He rubbed his hands up and down her arms, and she didn't push him away. "At least let me take you home." He noticed her bare feet. "Why aren't you wearing your shoes?"

"They're killing me. I can't walk in them anymore."

"Aren't your feet cold?"

"I don't know. I lost all feeling in them an hour ago."

"That's it." She squeaked as he lifted her into his arms and carried her to his truck.

"Ryan, no. I want to walk."

"Just warm up for a few minutes. I left the heat on." He deposited her in the passenger seat, which was much warmer than the street and she stopped arguing. He walked around the front and climbed in the other side. "Music?"

"No."

"Booze?"

She turned her head. "Do you have some?"

Leaning across her seat, he flipped open the glove compartment and caught a thin metal flask that tumbled out. He gave it a shake, noting it was a little more than half full. "Here."

"Do you always drive with an open container? That's illegal you know."

"Get broken down in the dead of winter, in the middle of nowhere, with no cell signal and those laws become gray areas. Take a sip. It'll warm you up."

She tipped the flask back and took a long pull. She didn't gasp or show any signs that the whiskey was too much for her to handle.

"So, Perrin's your sister."

"Yeah."

"She seems nice."

"She is. I'm the mean one."

He smirked. "You're not mean."

"Has your life gotten easier since knowing me?"

He loved her snark. "In a way."

She scowled at him like he was the village idiot. "How so?"

He shrugged. "I'm not guessing anymore about what I want."

"Ryan, don't," she warned.

"What? It's the truth. I'm not going to pretend my feelings changed just because you broke up with me. If anything, they've grown."

185

LYDIA MICHAELS

"We didn't break up. We weren't officially together. You just want what you can't have."

"Maybe I do, but I still want you, so what difference does my reasoning make?"

She looked out the window at the cemetery.

He followed her gaze. "How often do you come here?"

"Every day."

"Is that where you go in the morning?"

She nodded.

He tried to think of something to say after just learning the girl he loved hung out in graveyards on a daily basis. "Does it help?"

She lifted a shoulder. "Sometimes."

"And other times?"

"Mostly it's just sad." She fiddled her thumbs. "Sort of like a dead party."

He looked at her and held his breath so he wouldn't laugh, certain she couldn't have just been making a joke about the cemetery where her husband was buried.

She smiled. "I have a morbid sense of humor."

He still didn't think he should laugh. "A few weeks ago, I saw you riding in a truck with some guy. Who was he?"

"My boss, Jim."

"So, you do accept rides when you have to."

"When my boss orders me to get in his truck and it's storming, yeah, I make an exception."

"Were you in the car when it happened?"

Her gaze dropped to her lap. "You mean Nash?"

"Yeah."

Her head shook. "I was home. I was eating an orange when the phone rang. When I got to the scene, I still had the peel in my hand. He was barely holding on."

Her voice grew smaller with every word. He reached across the seat and took her hand. The force at which she gripped his fingers surprised him.

"They had to cut him out and there wasn't much time. The fire department was there. A lot of them work with me, so they tried to wait as long as they could. Once they removed him from the wreckage, because of the way his body had been crushed and pinned, there was only minutes. I had to decide when we'd said enough goodbyes because the engine was about to catch fire." A tear fell on their entwined hands. "I wish I would have waited a little longer. There was so much I forgot to tell him."

"I'm sure he knew."

She sniffled and another tear fell. "When they pulled him out, he couldn't talk. He just looked at me, and I watched him fight to breathe but his lungs had collapsed. I just held him as he died in my arms."

Her pain seemed so large in that moment, he too felt extreme pressure on his lungs when he tried to breathe. "I'm so sorry you lost him."

She looked up at him, tears flooding her eyes. "Me too."

He lifted her hand and kissed her fingers. "Do you want me to walk you home?"

"What about your truck?"

"I can come back for it." He didn't want her walking alone at night.

She drew in two deep breaths and reached for the seatbelt. "We can drive."

"Are you sure? I don't mind walking with you."

Her head shook. "I'm trying to be normal. You already picked me up in a cemetery, so I'm hoping driving home will even the score."

Another cemetery joke? This time he chuckled.

He drove home slowly, keeping to the back streets and glancing at her every time they stopped. When they reached his house, he put the truck in park.

"Do you wanna come in?"

She shook her head no. "Yes."

"Was that a yes or a no?"

She nodded. "No."

"Can you give me another clue?"

She unbuckled her seat belt and slid across the seat, cupping her hand over the side of his beard. Her breath smelled like sweet whiskey, and her hair smelled like flowers. She pressed her lips to his, and he shut his eyes but didn't deepen the kiss.

When she pulled away, she looked up at him and whispered, "If you keep rescuing me like this, I'm going to forget how to save myself."

"Who said you have to do it alone?"

"The universe." She opened the door and slipped out of the truck.

He climbed out after her and yelled, "I'm falling in love with you, Maggie."

She stilled at the foot of the driveway and slowly turned to face him, her eyes cast in utter confusion as the moonlight colored her pale face in silver and blue. "Why?"

He held out his hands. "I don't know. I just know that the things I feel for you are stronger than anything I've ever felt for anyone else. And it doesn't matter if you ignore me or see me, my feelings keep growing."

"Nothing's changed."

"*Everything's* changed." He tucked his hands in his pockets. "I just wanted you to know, because I figured some things out these past few weeks."

"Such as?"

"I can't shut it off. It's bigger than me and it's bigger than you. So there you have it."

Her lips parted and he held his breath, waiting to hear her reply, hoping like hell she accepted his admission for the truth it was and they could finally move forward and figure this out. But, instead, she simply shook her head and turned.

CHAPTER 27

*A*s Maggie turned away, Ryan cursed himself for complicating an already complicated situation. When it came to women, he was a complete tragedy.

He marched up the back steps and unlocked the door, flinging his keys against the backsplash of the kitchen counter. "Fuck!"

A small knock broke the silence and he stilled. He turned to the back door, finding it vacant. Was he hearing things? The knock sounded again, and he placed it coming from the front door. He raced through the house, flipping on the porch lights and twisting the deadbolt open.

Maggie stood on the door mat, her body dwarfed by his suit jacket and her eyes too big for her face. "I was wondering if you had plans tomorrow?"

He laughed and nearly collapsed in shock. "My day's wide open."

"Maybe we could catch a movie?"

"I'd love to." What did this mean? Was she finally giving in?

"Okay. I'll see you tomorrow." She turned and walked down his steps crossing into her yard.

He smiled and closed the door. Facing his dark living room, he threw his fist in the air and punched. *"Yes!"*

He thought he wouldn't be able to sleep, but he slept more soundly than he had in weeks. The next morning he was up at six, pacing the house, waiting for the day to begin. He was on his second cup of coffee when he heard Maggie get her bike from the shed.

Standing by the front bay window, he watched her ride toward the cemetery. He'd always wondered where she went every morning, but now it made sense. Knowing she'd be gone for at least an hour, he headed out to the garage.

Digging a pair of work gloves out of his truck, he carried the extension ladder around front. Once he had the hose unraveled, he got to work cleaning her clogged gutters.

At some point, when he was elbow deep in muck on the side of her house, she returned. "Um, usually a guy buys a girl dinner before he goes dipping his hands in her gutters."

"I'll buy you dinner tonight. When's the last time anyone cleaned these out? You've got mud as thick as clay in here." He sprayed the hose, trying to loosen some of the debris and she yelled.

He glanced down to where she stood in the driveway, realizing all the mud and wet leaves had sprayed in her direction.

"Sorry."

"How much longer are you going to be up there?"

He gave the house a quick scan. "I have to do the back and the other side."

"You don't *have to* do anything. I thought we were hanging out."

He smirked. "We are."

"This isn't fun. Let's go do something."

He glanced down at her, grinning at the way she propped her hands on her hips. She was as potent and unpredictable as a powder keg—yet damn irresistible. The way sparks flew between them, he knew this could blow up in his face at any moment, but he also knew he'd give his arms and legs just to be near her.

He peeled off his gloves and stuffed them in his back pocket. "Watch out." When she moved a few steps back, he dropped the hose to the blacktop and climbed down. He waited all night to have her in arm's reach again, and he wasn't going to waste any time.

Crossing the driveway, he closed the distance between them and caught her chin, tipping up her face, and leaned in but she turned away.

"Wait, what are you doing?"

He paused and frowned. "Kissing you."

"Um…" She side stepped out of his grip and wrung her hands. "Ryan, I told you last night, nothing's changed."

He frowned. "And I told you *everything's* changed. And then you asked me out."

"I asked you to *hang* out. As friends." Apology flashed in her eyes. "I … thought you understood."

His arm dropped to his side and he took a step back. "Maggie, what is this? What am I to you?"

His mind spun, replaying the events of last night. She let him hold her hand and comfort her. He kissed her fingers. He told her he was falling in love with her. Then she came back and knocked on his door. Technically, she only mentioned a movie. But he assumed…

He was such an idiot.

Her brow pinched as she looked up at him. "I'm sorry if I misled you. I didn't mean to confuse things, I swear. I care about you—"

"As a friend?"

"Well, yeah."

He laughed without humor. "This is just great."

His mind suddenly reminded him of all the facts he conveniently ignored. She'd had a lot to drink last night. She'd clearly argued with her family. She'd been caught off guard by seeing him with another woman. And she'd been distraught when he picked her up at the cemetery. All arrows pointed to needing a friend, yet he'd misinterpreted her words as a green light to something more.

This was why he was single. "I'm an idiot." He raked his hand through his hair and turned his back to her, embarrassed and rethinking his entire existence.

"Stop. It's my fault. I should have been more clear."

He pivoted to face her, figuring if he was gonna go down in flames he might as well get out what he needed to say. "And what do you want, Maggie? Is there any part of you that wants me? Because I'm losing my mind wanting you."

She took a step back, her eyes blinking and her mouth moving before she'd formed an answer. "I care about you."

"What does that mean?"

"It means exactly what I said. You're my friend. I like hanging out with you. I hated not talking to you, and I want to go back to the way things were before."

"Before, we were *dating*."

"Were we?" She shook her head and her jaw trembled. "I tried, Ryan, but I can't date you. You saw what it was like. There are certain things I just can't... I'm broken."

"You're not broken, Maggie."

She was her own worst enemy. She said these things and in her mind they became true, but they had *dated* and it worked. She just spooked when things moved a little too fast.

"You can move on without erasing him."

"No, I can't. We can't do this."

"Why not?" he snapped.

"Well, for one, you have a girlfriend!"

He ground his teeth. "She's not my girlfriend. We went on two dates."

"Does she know that? Before you left last night, did you tell her you were going after me?"

No, he'd lied and said he got a text from a cousin, and he needed to go help his family out in a pinch.

Maggie glared at him. "Like it or not, Ryan, that woman thinks you're in a relationship with her."

"We never defined anything. You're making way more out of her than she deserves. And you're using some chick I barely know as an excuse for something totally unrelated. This is about us—you and me." Their feelings had as much to do with Willow as they had to do with Nash. "Try to take everyone else out of it for a minute and admit how you feel."

She laughed without humor, the sound tired and defeated. "Why are you doing this? That woman was beautiful and she seemed nice. But most of all, she's emotionally available and into you."

"I'm not interested in her."

Her brows drew tight, her eyes full of apology. "I'm sorry." She glanced back at her house. "I think I better take a rain check on the movie."

Stunned, he watched her walk into her house and shut the door. What the fuck just happened?

He paced her driveway, replaying everything that was just said, trying to make sense of it. She used Willow as an excuse, which was bullshit. He pulled out his phone and sent the vegan a text, thanking her for a nice time but explaining he was still into someone else and it wasn't fair to mislead her. SEND.

One obstacle out of the way. Now, for the tricky part.

Maggie had herself convinced she couldn't date. Not just him, but anyone. Yet, she wanted to spend time with him. He wanted that too, but it was pure torture being in her presence and pretending everything was platonic. And he didn't buy her crap about them being in the friend zone. She felt something—

"She feels something," he whispered and paused from winding up the hose.

That was it. She felt something and it scared her. She'd said before she feared him erasing Nash. He'd sworn that would never be his intention and he meant it.

He had no interest in intruding on her memories. But he also wasn't going to let the ghost of her past intrude on their future.

He tucked the hose away and scraped the debris from the gutters into the trash. Once he put the ladder away and washed up, he returned next-door. Standing on her back porch, he drew in a deep breath and turned the knob. The door opened.

CHAPTER 28

$\mathcal{T}$he sound of the back door opening drew Maggie's attention. She paused from folding laundry and listened. Who would walk into her house uninvited? "Perrin?"

She set the laundry aside and stood from the couch, sucking in a breath when Ryan appeared at the doorway to her living room.

"What are you doing in my house?"

"I need to talk to you."

His gaze moved over all the instruments, stopping on the upright piano. When they painted, she had most of the personal items tarped and hidden. Relics of Nash surrounded him now, and she wondered if he could feel the ache of betrayal she felt at seeing him so close to her husband's favorite things.

"Can I sit down?"

She wasn't sure this was the place for them to talk. "Let's go to the kitchen."

He frowned. "What's wrong with here?"

She looked at the Fender guitar hanging from the wall. Too much Nash still lived in this part of the house. It was like he could hear them, and she suspected this was going to be a private conversation.

Ryan drifted to the wall and stared at the framed portrait. It was their wedding photo.

Maggie shifted from foot to foot. "I can make coffee."

Ryan didn't respond to her offer, his attention locked on the photo. "You were a beautiful bride."

Her head lowered. "Thank you."

"You two look really happy."

Her chest tightened. Why was he doing this? "We were."

Turning, he gave her a sympathetic smile. "I love you, Maggie. I lied last night when I said I was falling in love with you. I fell a while ago and I can't undo it."

Her chin trembled. She wouldn't allow herself to respond. This had to be about him, not them or her.

"I know you'll always love Nash," he said, coming closer to where she stood in front of the couch. "I'm okay with that. You can keep on loving him because your love for him has nothing to do with my love for you."

He stood an arm's reach away from her. She trembled with the urge to stretch the distance but forced herself not to move.

"That day you broke up with me," he said softly, looking into her eyes. "You didn't run away because we couldn't make things work. You bolted because things were coming too easily, and it scared you."

That wasn't completely true. She also couldn't get Nash out of her head once she started thinking about him.

"So, when you tell me you can't be with me and only want me as a friend, I have to call you out. I know what we have is more than friendship, Maggie. I know I can make you happy, if you'd just let me try."

Her gaze shifted to the piano. "You don't understand."

"Then explain it to me."

A memory flashed in her mind, and she could almost hear Nash singing. She closed her eyes and could see his back straight as he sat at the upright. A lost memory came to her then, of him sitting on his piano bench, facing her, strumming his guitar and murmuring the lyrics to Cat Stevens's *Hardheaded Woman.*

He used to say that song was about her. Sometimes he'd sing it when they argued. He'd look at her and sing, *"I'm married to a hardheaded woman..."* in Cat's high pitched way.

Eventually, he'd wear her down and get his way. And after all their disagreements, she had no regrets. Giving him his way had made her happy, so happy that, overtime, she forgot how to compromise in favor of herself.

"Sometimes I hear him in the silence," she confessed. "Like just now. I could see him sitting there."

He followed her gaze to the piano. "What did he say?"

"He was singing." True concern flashed in his eyes. "Relax. They're just memories. I'm not seeing ghosts." Though there had been countless times she wished she could.

"I'm not after your memories, Maggie. You can keep all of them and still have something more."

"When we were together in your bed, I was thinking of him."

He noticeably tensed. "At which part?"

"The end. Before I started to cry."

His shoulders slightly relaxed. "That's okay."

No one could be that understanding. "That's not okay, Ryan. Don't you see? He's always with me. I can't do those things with you without feeling like I'm betraying him." *Betraying both of them...* She massaged her temples, feeling the onset of a headache. "It's unfair to both of you."

He caught her hand and pulled her to sit on the couch. "Maggie, I want to know you. Your mind, your heart, all of you. And loving someone means accepting every piece of the puzzle. Nash is a part of you, and I accept that. I'd never get upset with you for thinking of him. You have no control over your thoughts. Those memories exist inside of you, and you're allowed to enjoy them whenever you want."

It was a relief to hear him say such things, because she'd been struggling with her guilt but his acknowledgement wasn't enough. "The first time we kissed, I cried. The first time we fooled around, I cried. That isn't normal."

"People cry. Intimacy is emotional. The fact that it's hitting a cord with you, only tells me you're feeling things as deeply as I am. Do you have any idea how rare that is?"

She shook her head. How could she know? She'd only ever been with Nash.

He took her hand and lifted it, pressing a kiss to her fingertips. "Sweetheart, I've *never* felt this kind of connection with anyone else, and I've been dating since I was fifteen. I know you're scared, but as your friend, I must tell you, letting this slip away is a huge mistake. We have something together. And it's not one-sided."

Her belly turned and twisted. She knew it wasn't one-sided, but Ryan had more experience. He was so confident and collected all the time. She was a basket case, more so when she stood next to someone so flawless.

"Wouldn't you rather be with someone who—"

"No. I only want to be with you."

"But—"

"No."

She smirked. "You're not letting me—"

"Because the answer's no. It's you or nothing."

She shook her head and blurted, "You want someone who's going to cry during sex?"

"No, but I want someone who shares a connection with me so deeply that when I make love to her it puts tears in her eyes."

Her gaze dropped to her lap. "You have an answer for everything."

"One way to shut me up."

She looked at him and her cheeks pulled into a smile at the sight of his challenging boyish grin. Everything about him attracted her, so much so it terrified her.

She hadn't wanted anything for years as some sort of trade off, a bargaining chip that might turn back time and return her to the past. An impossibility she spent a long time trying to accept, but she was finally facing the truth that Nash was never coming back, and she had many years of her life to still live.

But sometimes, closing things away hurt. Same as the boxes she'd sealed up and carried to the shed pained her heart, the memories that played in her mind had become intangible pieces of furniture in an emotional home. They were familiar, but she'd lived with them long enough.

Part of her wanted to feel something new. That meant coming out of her shell and risking vulnerability. Her heart was a fragile, tattered piece of tissue, and she protected it fiercely. The question was, would Ryan be just as protective, knowing how easily she could break? She believed he would.

Her gaze shifted to his lips and back to his eyes. Could she?

The desire was there but equaled in fear. Every time she attempted intimacy she was met with a side of herself she didn't like. A broken, weak side that needed more time and part of her was tired of waiting. Maybe it would be easier if she just pushed through the pain, blindly trusting she'd live through the experience, no matter how much it felt like dying.

"There's no rush, Maggie," he whispered, still holding her stare.

Her heart raced as she slowly closed the distance. He didn't meet her halfway. This was her decision. He'd let her come to him at whatever pace she needed to take, no matter how excruciating the speed.

She loved that about him. But she also hated that she loved anyone aside from Nash. Was that what progress felt like? She'd foolishly expected it to feel like relief, because no one warned her it would be excruciating.

Her eyes closed as her lips pressed to his, warm and familiar, welcoming and safe. And in the comfort of his touch, she found the courage she'd been missing.

It was a special kind of kiss, the sort shared with a vow. It was her unspoken promise to try. As she pulled away, her shoulders felt lighter, as if the weight of her shell had been cast aside.

CHAPTER 29

*I*t started with a movie, a simple harmless drama with very little sexual content. Ryan had bought popcorn and snowcaps, and they shared a cherry slushy. That straw would be the closest they came to the kiss she'd shared earlier.

The next day they went to dinner, and on the walk home, he held her hand. Holding hands was a gateway drug, she should have broken contact. Except, when he held her hand, she felt connected, protected, and safe—treasured. It was much nicer than walking alone.

Each night that week, when she'd pull her bike into the driveway after work, Ryan would be waiting for her on her back porch. Sometimes he had a box of pizza. Sometimes he had a bag of Chinese. One night, he even made dinner—well, he heated up a casserole his aunt had prepared.

For a solid week she worried that things would get heated and panicked that she'd fall face first into another meltdown, but dating Ryan wasn't like the dating she remembered. It was more like hanging out with a best friend.

They teased each other and laughed, gossiped, debated which Star Wars was the best or if a California Roll counted as sushi. They bonded over food, since the time they spent together usually revolved around the shared need for sustenance.

When she thought of Nash, she didn't give in to the rush of shame. She simply let the memory play and moved on. Sometimes she'd get quiet and Ryan would ask what she was thinking. At first she'd say nothing, but after a while that seemed silly. He could tell when she was distracted, and he'd asked her to be honest from the start.

"I was thinking about how Nash and I never ate at the table."

"Never?" he asked, popping a soy-soaked piece of sashimi in his

197

mouth, and not at all disturbed by the mention of her husband. "The salmon's really good. You need to taste it." He rotated the takeout container and pointed with his chopstick to a soft pink piece.

She pinched it between her chopsticks and swirled it in the sauce. "I mean, we had a table, and when we cooked, I'd put food on it, but we always carried our plates to the living room." That was probably why their couch looked like a prop in a paintball field after only a few years.

"Huh. It's like a law in my family that you have to eat at the table. Everyone has to sit down at the same time, and you get smacked if you pull out your phone during a meal."

She paused. "They smack you?"

His shoulders shrugged. "Just in the back of the head. It's more like a love tap."

She arched a brow. "You associate hitting with love? Good to know."

He laughed. "It's not like that. The women in my family are just… They're old-school. My mum and the aunts make sure there's always a place for everyone to belong. Sharing meals together is the glue that brings us all home at the end of the day or week." He popped a spicy tuna roll in his mouth and mumbled, "That's kind of why I'm on my mum's shit list."

"Why?"

"I missed the last seven Sunday dinners."

"Today's Sunday."

"I know. This is much nicer."

She pushed away her plate. "Ryan, why are you avoiding your family?"

"I'm not. I'd just rather be with you."

"But they probably miss you."

"Maggie, I see them all the time. I work with nine of them at the lumberyard, and when I'm at the bar, a few of them are always there. I buy my groceries from the market Kelly and Ashlynn own. I get my coffee at the café where my little cousin works. I order my pizza from my cousin's husband's family. Trust me, just because I'm not sitting down for Sunday dinner with them doesn't mean I'm not seeing them."

She still didn't think it was the same. "What about your mom?"

"I stopped by to visit her this week." He picked at the fried rice. "Besides, you're guilty of the same thing. I never see you with your family."

She closed the takeout containers and tossed them into the brown paper bag. "My family's different. You've seen my mother."

"Okay, but what about your sister? I see her around town sometimes. Once I even saw her eating at the café alone. Why don't you hang out with her more?"

Uncomfortable with the shift in attention, she carried the bag to the kitchen. Ryan followed. She turned on the coffee pot, mostly because she didn't want to sit back down. "We've drifted apart. And she's moving."

"All the more reason to spend time with her now."

"She's busy. They're planning a wedding."

"Aren't you the maid of honor?"

"What do you want from me? We just aren't that close anymore!"

He drew back and lowered his hands to his sides, his fingers still holding chopsticks. "Hey, we were just talking."

"Sorry. It felt a little more like an attack."

His head cocked in confusion, and she shrunk into the wall of cabinets at her back.

"Hey..." His brow pinched in concern. Two steps and he had her cornered. Catching her chin, he tipped up her face and looked into her eyes. "I'm sorry."

"It's okay. I'm defensive because I'm guilty. Perrin's been incredibly patient with me, and I've been the world's worst sister."

"So change."

"It's not that easy."

"Isn't it?" He reached behind her and picked up her phone, holding it in front of her. "Text her. Ask her what she's doing next weekend. See if she wants to hang out. If you want, I'll go with you so there's less pressure."

She squirmed out of his arms. "She doesn't know about you."

"Ah. And the reason for that is...?"

Wringing her hands nervously, she explained, "I don't want her to get the wrong idea."

"Like we're dating?"

Her eyes narrowed. "Like she should lob her bouquet at me in July."

He hugged her and laughed. "Maggie, give her a little credit. I overheard her telling her fiancé how big of a deal it was that you were attending their engagement dinner. I'm fairly sure she'll figure out we're taking things slow."

Slow was an understatement. Middle schoolers got more action than them. "You'd really go with me?" If Ryan was there, she wouldn't feel like she was under a microscope alone.

"Sure."

"What about the whole Willow thing?"

"Do I need to show you the text again?"

"No, but won't it be weird with Bran?"

He kissed the top of her hair. "Ask me if I care."

She smiled, her face pressing into his shirt as she breathed in his familiar smell. "Okay. I'll text her."

Perrin was so excited she didn't want to wait until Friday, so they made plans to meet for Mexican that Wednesday. On Tuesday Maggie made a point to call her and clarify *who* she was dating.

"The guy who was with Willow?"

"Well, he was with me first."

"When?"

She explained that Ryan was her neighbor, and they had been spending time together since he moved in last March. Perrin was stunned to say the least. Maggie expected multiple questions about what their relationship meant, how serious they were, and intrusive questions about intimacy she wouldn't be able to answer, but that wasn't at all what came.

"Is he nice to you?" Perrin asked, her voice soft with concern.

Maggie smiled. "He's amazing. He's so thoughtful and patient. We have fun together."

"You're sure you're ready for this, Maggie?"

Her concern reminded Maggie how sisters never stopped looking out for each other, even when life events kept them apart. "We're not rushing into anything."

"If you're happy, I'm happy for you."

"I'm … happy," she said, testing the word and tasting its truth.

The following night, they met at the local Mexican restaurant. Main Street didn't have as many eateries when Nash was alive. Maggie felt like she'd woken from a coma, realizing how many new options now existed for people with social lives.

The restaurant had brightly painted chairs and a margarita menu four feet long. There was an entire inserted list specifically dedicated to tequila.

"Who knew Center County had such a sophisticated pallet?" she joked.

"You mean Jasper Falls," Bran commented. "Apparently, the votes are in and that one won by a landslide."

Maggie didn't have an opinion on the town name one way or another but wondered if this would finally force her to get new return address stickers, ones without Nash's name. She folded the drink menu and placed it on the table. "I'll take a strawberry jalapeno margarita on the rocks with salt."

Ryan raised a brow. "Aren't you brave?"

"I've got my spicy pants on."

Perrin and Bran ordered one of the specialty tequilas and drank them on the rocks as well. It became clear who the more sophisticated couple was once Maggie and Ryan started speaking like characters from *The Treasure of Sierra Madre.*

The waiter cleared their dinner plates, and they ordered refills of margaritas and chips. He asked if they wanted more salsa to which Ryan replied, "We don't need no stinkin' salsa."

Perrin and Bran watched them with refined judgement as Maggie snorted into her spicy cocktail.

"I kind of wanted more salsa."

Ryan flung his hand into the air like a matador and clicked his fingers. "Waiter! More salsa for my *senorita*." Proud of his Spanish, he grinned widely and said, *"Me llamo es Ryan Clooney. Si y también tenemos queso."*

She laughed again and nearly fell out of her chair.

"I'm not sure what that second part means," he confessed.

Bran leaned forward. "You told her your name and then told her you also have cheese."

Maggie lost it. After that, they gave up on trying to act classy, and Ryan started making up words he thought sounded Spanish. When he made a mess, he needed a *napkin-o*. And he said he couldn't stop laughing because of all the *beverage-ios*. The waiter took pity on him and tried teaching him the correct words, but after five margaritas, it seemed pretty hopeless.

On the way out of the restaurant, Perrin pulled her aside. "Our car's out back."

"Oh, we walked."

"Do you want a ride?"

Maggie scrunched her nose and shook her head, but her neck wasn't doing too good of a job holding her head up. "Nah."

Her sister smiled. "I can't remember the last time I saw you this happy, Maggie."

"I *am* happy." It felt good to say it aloud. "Ryan makes me happy."

"I think he's great for you."

Up front, it was a lovely compliment but something snagged Maggie's attention. Only, she was too drunk to figure out what. Something about *him* being great for *her*... She half wondered if anyone would consider *her* remotely good for *him*.

She hugged Perrin and told her they should do this again sometime. Ryan shook Bran's hand and then looped his arm in hers and steered them home.

"I like your sister."

"Me too," she emphatically agreed. "Remember how the Monkees used to walk? Or was that the Beatles? Or am I thinking of *The Wizard of Oz*?"

"I think we should just think about left-right, left-right."

That was probably the safest option. "I had fun tonight. Although, I don't think I'm going to have fun at work tomorrow."

"Shit. I totally forgot it was a weeknight."

"This is very, very bad for tomorrow morning."

"Let's not think about it yet."

"Okay."

They reached her house and he walked her around back. He stood across from her on the small porch. "Do I get to kiss you goodnight?"

She tipped her head back and smiled, then laughed when her head just sort of bobbled there. "Yes, please."

He cupped her cheeks and laughed. "You've turned into a bowl of Jell-O."

"It's on account of all the tequila."

"I believe it's pronounced *el tequila-o.*"

She snorted. "Tequila's tequila."

Her laughter cut off as his mouth closed over hers. Her skin tingled as his hands swept up her spine and pulled her closer, his tongue stealing into her mouth and kissing her passionately.

She grew dizzy from his touch and hung onto his shirt with tight fists. Her ribs pulled tight against her lungs and her belly swirled with warm wanting.

When he gently pulled away, she clung to his shoulders in drunken awe. "Why do I feel like you're not as think as I drunk you are?"

He bit her lower lip. "I love you. Good night."

He opened her door and guided her inside without ever crossing the threshold. She looked back at him and smiled, her cheeks warm and her body soft.

She wondered how she could like someone so much, despite all the ways she told herself she couldn't. Maybe she didn't know herself at all.

"Good night."

She blew him a kiss and he pulled the door closed.

CHAPTER 30

*R*yan's hand closed around her hip, massaging gently as his mouth pulled at hers. His tongue teased softly, coaxing. And she moaned into the kiss.

They had been making out on the couch for over an hour, just like they had the day before and the day before that. As a matter of fact, it didn't seem to matter what their plans were. The moment they were behind closed doors, they couldn't keep their mouths off each other.

"I really just wanted to know if you had baking soda."

"I know." He kissed down her jaw and to her ear. "I'm checking."

Her head rolled back, and she sighed. She loved when he kissed her ears. "But my fridge stinks."

"I love it when you talk dirty to me."

"I think it's from the Thai leftovers. We're not ordering curry again."

"I'll buy you a new fridge tomorrow." His fingers teased over the belt loops of her jeans.

She giggled and found his mouth, biting playfully at his lips and looping her arms around his neck. He growled and took over the kiss.

The next night, she came over to watch a movie, but they never even got past the Netflix menu.

"I'm obsessed with your mouth," he whispered. "I can't get enough."

"You haven't even seen half the things it can do."

He broke the kiss and drew back. "Oh, really?"

She nodded. "You should see me make balloon animals."

He snarled playfully and toppled her to the sofa.

By the following week, her jaw was sore, and her lips were swollen, as if she'd been eating popcorn for days. She and Ryan needed to cool things down or they were going to hurt each other—literally.

She spent the day thinking of the most *unsexual* thing they could do for dinner and remembered that he claimed to make good ribs. Ribs were not date food, so she suggested he make them Friday night.

She could smell the grill as soon as she got home from work. Ryan smiled from the other side of the fence, a basting brush in one hand and a bowl of barbeque sauce in the other. "Wait until you taste these."

She leaned her bike against the shed. "I'll be over in a minute. I have to change."

"I'll be here."

Working in a subzero warehouse meant wearing winter clothes year-round. She jogged up the stairs and stripped off her hooded sweatshirt, tossing it in the corner by the hamper. She was sweaty from riding her bike in heavy clothes at the end of May, so she quickly rinsed off in the shower.

Pulling her hair into a messy bun, she slipped on a pair of cargo pants and a tank top. Ryan was still at the grill when she returned outside.

"Perfect timing. These are just about ready."

She held the door as he carried the tray of ribs into the living room. Ryan still didn't have a kitchen table so when they ate at his place, they usually used the coffee table in the living room.

He had the round table set with plates and a large empty bowl. Setting the tray of ribs in the middle, he said, "I just have to get something."

She sat on the floor and breathed in the savory scent of pork and barbeque. "It smells amazing."

"Nothing goes better with ribs than coconut, so I picked up pina colada mix."

"Ooh, momma likey."

He tipped the frosty blender over her glass and filled her cup. "Dig in."

The ribs were so tender the meat pulled right off the bone. She moaned as the sweet sauce mixed with savory meat and melted in her mouth. Chasing each bite with a sip of pina colada was a master call.

"Oh, my God, these are the best ribs I've ever had." She tossed the naked bone into the debris bowl and pulled another rib from the rack.

"You've got barbeque sauce on your chin."

"Oh." She used a clean part of her hand to wipe her jaw. "Did I get it?"

"Now it's on your neck."

"Damn it." She put down her rib and reached for a napkin. "How about now?"

He tipped his head and scooted closer. "Let me see."

She handed him her napkin and he dabbed the corner of her mouth, then leaned in and slowly licked her lower lip. He tasted like sweet char-grilled sex.

"I missed a spot," he whispered, reaching back to the bowl of ribs and dunking his finger in the sauce. She sucked in a breath when he dragged the finger down her throat.

"Ryan!"

"Let me clean that up before the ants carry you away." He leaned over her, tipping her back to the floor, and trailed his tongue over the sauce.

Her eyes rolled back, and she arched beneath him. Her plan of keeping their hands occupied lasted all of five minutes.

"More," she whispered, and he dipped his finger again, painting her throat, dragging his touch to the neckline of her tank top. She stretched her arms above her head and out to the side, giving him full access.

His mouth teased over the wing of her collar bone, and his tongue traced the soft swell of her breasts. Her breathing labored as he came dangerously close to her nipples. She couldn't take his teasing anymore. Sitting up, she rolled him to his back and climbed over him.

He caught her hips as she straddled him and took his mouth, kissing hungrily and showing him with the rocking of her body how much she wanted him. His grip tightened, his fingers sliding under the hem of her shirt until he caged her ribs. His thumbs rested just under her breasts, and he broke the kiss.

"What are we doing?" he gasped, his head falling back to the carpet.

"I don't know." She didn't want to think about it. Her mouth kissed down his throat. "Take this off."

He stripped away his shirt and her body seemed to flare with appreciation. She trailed kisses down his front, scooting off his lap and fitting her body between his legs.

"Whoa, where you going?"

She loosened the buckle of his belt and popped the button of his jeans. "I'm kissing you." Her tongue dragged down the slope of his hip. "Lift."

He lifted and she yanked down his pants. The world stilled, and she held her breath for a split second, a thousand comparisons knocking at her mind, but she pushed them away. Breath pushed past her lips as she tried to remember how to do this.

"Come back up here."

"No." She shook her head. They'd been kissing for an eternity. This was where they were. "Just … give me a second."

A second turned into a minute. Ryan folded his hands behind his head and shut his eyes, his face tense. "This is a little awkward."

Realizing how difficult it must be to lie still while someone stared at your most intimate parts, triggered her into motion. Her hand closed around his length, and he sucked in an audible breath. She stroked slowly, familiarizing herself with his velvet smooth skin and the weight of him in her hand.

"You have no idea how good that feels."

She hadn't even started. Leaning forward, she placed a kiss on the smooth tip, and he cursed. "How do you like it done?"

"However you do it."

Bullshit. Everyone had a preference. "I'm good at this. I'm just rusty. But if you tell me what you like, I'll do it."

He tipped his chin to his tattooed chest and studied her for a moment. "Really?"

Half her mouth curled into a smirk, and she lifted a shoulder. "Some girls like crafts. I like blowjobs."

His head fell to the carpet with a thunk. "I have to be dreaming."

"Let's see." She leaned forward and took him into her mouth, moving quickly up and down until the length of his erection was slick with saliva. "Awake yet?"

"No, I think I died and went to heaven."

She laughed and ducked again, this time tracing her tongue slowly up the length of his shaft. He groaned and spread his legs wider, giving her more room.

His hand gently cupped the back of her head. She loved the feel of him holding her to him and hummed happily, dragging her mouth up and down.

"Please don't stop."

Her mouth formed a smile around him. Even during blowjobs, he remained polite. She took her time, teasing and drawing out his pleasure. The more comfortable she became the more pleasure she took for herself as well.

His breathing shifted, and his lungs pumped faster as she increased her speed and the pressure. She stroked and sucked him, making sure to hit every pleasure point. His flesh trembled under her tongue, and he moaned her name. She tightened her grip and worked him faster, her lips curling around the smooth tip and working his release.

He cursed and his body pulsed under her touch as she finished him. Loosening her grip of his tender flesh, she licked over him, taking her time as he breathed through the aftershocks of his climax.

Ryan panted on the floor. She curled into his side and rested her head in the crook of his arm. He pulled her close and kissed her temple then softly chuckled. "You topped my ribs."

She laughed. "Your ribs started it. From now on, consider them an aphrodisiac."

He sighed, the sound full of masculine contentment. "Now, I need a nap. I wish I had a blanket down here."

"Want to go upstairs?"

"No, I don't want to move."

He lay with his pants around his hips, his softening erection completely exposed, and his arm holding her tight. She loved seeing him so relaxed. His comfort eased her.

It only took a few minutes for her eyes to grow heavy and her mind to still. The slow beat of his heart played in her ear while she used his chest as a pillow and peacefully drifted off.

"*Oh, sweet Jesus!*"

The earth moved and Maggie fumbled back, her head colliding with something hard. Ryan sprung to his feet and shouted, "Mum, what the hell are you doing here?"

A shrill female voice pierced the air. "For God's sake, Ryan, put yourself away!"

Maggie's hands flew to her mouth as the woman—presumably Ryan's mother—turned beet red and covered her eyes.

He turned and zipped his pants then pivoted. "Why are you here?"

Maggie scurried behind a sofa pillow and covered her body only to remember she was still fully dressed.

"Colleen had an extra table and chairs," the woman shouted, still shielding her eyes. "Your father and I brought it over for you to put in your kitchen."

"On a Friday night?" Ryan snapped.

"I didn't think you would have company!"

Maggie's face burned. She stood and mumbled, "I'm gonna go."

"Oh, don't leave on our account, dear." His mother rounded the furniture and paused at the sight of ribs and melted pina coladas. "I see you needed the table more than I realized." She returned her attention to Maggie. "I'm Rosemarie and this is Ryan's father—" She scowled at the empty living room. "Where the hell did he go? *Liam!*"

"*What?*"

"Where are you?"

Maggie flinched at the shrill way they spoke to each other, shouting through everyday conversations, as if it were totally normal to scream at walls.

"I'm moving the table like you told me to do!"

His mother scoffed. "Well, get in here and meet Ryan's lady friend." She smiled. "He'll be back in a second. Ryan, you didn't tell me you were dating such a pretty girl."

Ryan rubbed the back of his neck. Nothing, not even his tattoos, hid the way his blush burned down his cheeks and chest. "Mum, this is Maggie O'Malley."

"O'Malley?" A man who resembled an aged, thinner version of Ryan appeared. "What the hell are you doing messin' with an O'Malley?"

"Liam!" his mother snapped. "Ryan, why don't you make a pot of coffee so we can have a nice visit."

"This isn't a visit, Mum."

"I put a bag of groceries on your counter. A bin of coffee's on the top."

Defeated, Ryan sighed and stepped toward the door.

"Don't leave me," Maggie begged, catching his arm. His mother seemed terrifying, and his dad obviously hated O'Malleys.

He took her hand and walked her past his parents. She looked back when they didn't follow. Ryan grumbled a string of curse words under his breath as they marched into the kitchen.

She did a double take of the new table. "This is nice."

"What?" He glanced over his shoulder, as if just noticing the chrome trimmed table sitting in the center of the room. "Oh. Yeah." He rummaged through the bag and unloaded the coffee, slamming cabinets as he hunted for a coffee filter.

"Are they just waiting in there?"

"My mum's cleaning. She'll be here in a second."

As if conjured by his certainty, his mother appeared, her arms full of dishes. "You shouldn't leave meat out, love. Where's your Tupperware?"

"I don't have any."

"Horseshit. Your Aunt Maureen gave you a whole bin of her older stuff."

"I haven't unpacked it yet."

His mother tsked. "Well, maybe you can find it when you go put on a shirt."

Maggie backed to the far side of the room, which also happened to be where the door was located. Her hand fumbled for the knob, her mind solely focused on escape.

Ryan's eyes narrowed on her as his mother began scrubbing dishes. He crossed the kitchen and pulled her away from the door. "We'll be right back."

Maggie skipped after him as he towed her through the hall and up the stairs. A quick glance into the living room told her his father was still there.

"Your dad hates me," she hissed as soon as they made it to his room.

"He doesn't know you enough to hate you."

"Well, he hates O'Malleys."

He pulled a fresh shirt out of a drawer. "It doesn't mean anything."

Easy for him to say. No one gawked at his name. "How long will they stay?"

"If my mother had her way? Forever."

"I'm serious, Ryan. I'm not ready to meet your family."

He sighed and turned to face her. "I'm sorry. I had no idea they'd stop by."

"Obviously."

He crossed the room and hugged her. "Please stay. I know they're a lot, but they mean well."

"Your mother probably thinks I'm a hussy."

He laughed. "My mother thinks you're a godsend. There's literally nothing you can do to avoid being her favorite person in the world right now."

Her anxiety came to an abrupt halt. "R—really?"

"Yeah. Try not to bolt when she starts mentioning her china set and heirlooms she's been holding onto in hopes of one day having a daughter-in-law."

Her eyes widened as he walked out of the room. "You're kidding, right?" When he didn't answer, she called, "Ryan?"

CHAPTER 31

*M*aggie took her time returning to the kitchen. Despite it being eight in the evening, the house smelled of fresh roasted coffee and… Was that cake?

"There she is!" Ryan's mom stood from the vintage table and filled a mug with coffee. "How do you take your coffee, love?"

She glanced at Ryan who only shrugged, as if to say there was no sense in fighting once the smothering started—sort of like being choked to death by a boa constrictor.

"Just black, please."

Rosemarie nodded and put down the creamer. "Would you like a slice of cake? I made cinnamon strudel. It's one of Ryan's favorites."

Discovering his favorite dessert triggered something inside of Maggie. She cherished the information and wanted to taste the cake so she nodded.

"Thank you." She took the warm mug and held it in both hands, breathing in the rich scent, as if she might inhale a bit of courage with the caffeine.

Curious about what one of Ryan's favorite desserts might taste like, she carefully sat beside him at the round table. Rosemarie placed a sweet-scented slice on a plate in front of her.

Ryan grinned and took a large bite from his own serving. Traces of toasted cinnamon and caramel filled the kitchen air with an intoxicating scent.

Maggie sipped her coffee and paused to savor the bold taste. "This is really good coffee."

"It's from Ashlynn's market. She has a machine that grinds the beans fresh."

Maggie didn't know who Ashlynn was and looked at Ryan in question.

"My cousin Kelly's wife," he explained.

Lucky woman, Maggie thought.

Ryan's father stared at her with his arms crossed over his chest. "How are you related to Caleb?"

"Dad, let it go."

"Liam, shut up and eat your cake."

Maggie blinked. Could he really be that serious about disliking her simply because she was an O'Malley? The rivalry was half a century old. She had nothing to do with the bar and found his immediate dislike of her offensive. "He was my husband's grandfather."

Rosemarie coughed into her mug. "Husband?"

"Mum."

Maggie placed a hand on Ryan's thigh, telling him not to bother. The awkwardness was inevitable. "I'm a widow. My husband was Nash O'Malley."

"Oh, dear." Rosemarie's weathered fingers trembled to her mouth. "He was the young man who had that terrible accident a few years back?"

"Yes." Her nerves bolstered with steel as she reminded herself the woman's bluntness wasn't personal, but the empathy in her eyes was.

"I'm so sorry."

Liam's arms uncrossed. "I'm sorry for your loss."

An uncomfortable silence fell over the table until Rosemarie picked up the knife and said, "I think you need a bigger piece of cake."

Maggie smiled, unused to maternal figures whose first instinct was to comfort rather than blame. She picked up a fork and cut into the gooey crumble. "Thank you." As soon as the first bite hit her tongue she stilled. "Oh my God."

Rosemarie smiled expectantly. "Good?"

Maggie covered her mouth. "Delicious."

"See?" Ryan's mother patted his hand. "You two have similar taste. That's a good thing. So, tell me how you two met."

Over the next hour, Maggie consumed her weight in calories and drank too much coffee while chatting with Ryan's parents. Once his father let go of the fact that her married name was O'Malley, he relaxed. He was actually funny, in a dry, take-no-prisoners sort of way.

Rosemarie was lovely. Maggie had never met anyone quite like her. Being near her felt like a hardy hug. She was so at ease with others, she put others at ease too. She took interest in every detail she discovered, down to where Maggie thought Ryan should buy his curtains and where one might buy the best tomato plants this summer. Maggie had little knowledge on either but felt significant simply by being asked.

Once Ryan realized she was enjoying the visit, he loosened up. She loved watching him with his parents. Sometimes they'd bicker over nonsense. Other times they'd laugh over some anecdote from twenty years ago that never stopped being hysterical. She envied their palpable closeness, wondering how some families simply worked like magic while others never blended.

"Well, this was lovely," Rosemarie said as she tucked in her chair. The woman had cleaned the entire kitchen while sharing stories, cake, coffee, and some sort of mythical unicorn dust that made Maggie want her to stay. "Maybe this Sunday Ryan will bring you to dinner."

Magical feeling gone.

"I'm not sure I can make it this week," Ryan said.

His mother turned her sharp maternal glare on him. "Ryan, you've missed enough dinners. You won't be missing another. This Sunday's at Aunt Maureen's and Uncle Frank's. I'll tell them to set out two places." She turned to Maggie. "You'll see that he goes, won't you dear?"

She seemed to have lost the ability to blink. Or speak. But the question sounded more rhetorical than anything else.

"Wonderful." Liam opened the back door. "We'll see you then."

The door closed and Ryan immediately locked it behind them. "Please don't break up with me."

She snapped out of her stare. "What? Why would I break up with you?"

"Were you not conscious for the last two hours?"

"What are you talking about? Your parents are incredible."

He frowned and pointed to the door. "The man and woman who barged in, took over my kitchen, and methodically reorganized all my stuff, you saw them right?"

She rolled her eyes and dumped the last of her coffee in the sink. "You're being silly. Your parents are perfectly nice and normal. Want to see scary parents, try spending ten minutes with mine. My mother has a gift for making you feel responsible for every disaster in your life, and my father only talks when he's looking for a pen to do his sudoku. I liked your parents."

"Really?" He felt her forehead.

"What are you doing?"

"Checking for a fever. I think you might have hallucinated normal people, because I have it on good authority my mother is a maniac."

She laughed and batted his hand away. Why was it so hard for him to believe that she'd like them? "Ryan, they're exactly what normal parents should be like in my mind. But I'm not going to Sunday dinner." Before he could argue or try to convince her, she went into the living room to find her shoes.

"Neither am I."

She pivoted. "You have to. Your mom said so."

He laughed. "I'm thirty, Maggie. I don't have to do something just because my mum says so."

Her brows lowered in a scowl. "But it's important to her. What's the harm in going?"

He leaned against the wall and crossed his arms. "Why do you care?"

She slipped on her shoes. "I don't know. She brought you your favorite cake and cleaned your kitchen."

"I didn't ask her to do any of that."

"Well, you sure seemed to enjoy the three slices of cake you ate." She didn't know why she felt so defensive of his mother. Maybe because she showed Maggie more kindness and acceptance in one night than her own mother had shown her in the past decade. "If I had parents like that, I'd never miss a dinner."

His gaze pulled from hers and drifted to the floor. "You don't know how they can get. If I start going back to family dinners, other obligations will follow. There's also Sunday brunch, and church, and Wednesday dinner, and Friday happy hour with the lumberyard relatives. Summer's coming. They'll want me on the baseball team and at all the potlucks. It's just too much."

"I'm not saying you should do all of that. But it seems mean to do none, especially when your mom clearly misses you."

"I know they seem harmless right now, but you don't know them. It took me thirty years to get some space. Before I moved out, they dictated every minute of my day by where my relatives expected me to be. I never even got to pick what I wanted for a career. Me and my cousin Finn were just thrown into the family business and told we'd take over one day. For the first time, I feel like I actually have some control over my life and I'm happy."

She knew all about control. She knew how misleading it could be and how temporary it actually was. She also knew what it felt like when loved ones disappeared.

"I have no right to tell you how to live your life. But family's important, especially when you're lucky enough to have the kind of family that loves and supports you no matter what. Because one day that support might disappear, and I promise, you'll miss it when it's gone."

He took a moment to process that. "Below the belt, O'Malley."

"Truth hurts, Clooney."

He sighed. "Fine. I'll go to dinner, but I draw the line there. Sunday dinners and that's it."

She smiled and crossed the room, rising on her toes to kiss his lips. "I'm proud of you." When she broke the kiss, she said, "When you said baseball, do you mean a league?"

"Yeah. The bar sponsors it, but this is probably the last year since O'Malley's is going on the market."

She wove her arms around his waist. "And you're sure you want to sit this season out? Could be your last chance to play."

He rolled his eyes. "This is how it happens. There's always some extenuating circumstance that makes me crumble."

She laughed. "It might not be so bad. Baseball sounds fun."

"Really? Would you want to play?"

"Could I? I mean, I am the enemy and all—even though the team shares *my* name."

"Hell yeah, you could play."

She scoffed. "I thought you were against this. *Sunday dinners and that's it.*"

"That was before you were involved."

She hadn't realized she carried that sort of pull. And while she hated social pressure, she loved baseball. Plus, it would get her outside—counteract that vitamin D deficiency her mother had been so concerned about.

While she might have to socialize with the players, there wasn't much small talk that could happen in the outfield. It seemed like a good start. "Count me in."

He kissed her, shifting the mood with a good dose of unexpected passion. He must really like baseball.

"There's just one small issue." He broke the kiss.

Her lashes hung low over her eyes. "What?"

"In order to be on the team, you have to meet the family. So, I guess you're joining me for dinner after all."

CHAPTER 32

$\mathcal{M}$aggie fidgeted as the truck bumped up the unpaved road leading to Ryan's aunt and uncle's home, hidden high on the largest mountain in town. Her eyes stayed mostly closed on the drive, but she never once forgot she was riding in a vehicle.

"We're almost there."

She blew out a forced breath. The house had been too far to walk and too steep of a trek to ride her bike. The good thing about the drive, however, was it made her forget how nervous she was about meeting his entire family.

The truck slowed and he shut off the engine. She opened her eyes and looked out the windshield. Her heart jolted at the amount of four-wheel drive vehicles parked on the lawn. It was like a compound. Then she saw the house and her jaw dropped.

An actual log cabin raised on tall stone pillars and wrapped in an enormous porch dominated the horizon. "That's where your aunt and uncle live?"

"Yup. Growing up, there were nine McCulloughs so they needed a lot of space. Now, they're all moved out and multiplying like rabbits."

"How many are going to be here tonight?"

"Probably most of them."

"Right." He'd tallied them up for her on his fingers and toes that morning, losing count somewhere in the thirties.

"You ready?"

She couldn't move. Her brain told her hand to open the door, but the truck, which had been her most recent nightmare, now seemed her only sanctuary.

"Maggie?"

"I'm thinking." Mostly about how she could get out of this. "How many of them know about me?"

"My parents, my brother Pat, but he won't be there. Then there's Kelly, Luke, and Tristan."

That left twenty-five or so introductions.

He took her hand and rubbed it with his. "I know it seems like a lot, but most of them are kids."

That helped. "I can do kids."

"See? We've got this."

Her stare moved over all the cars and spotted a group of small children pushing each other on a tire swing in the distance. She counted six little bodies.

A large red barn stood on the other end of a wide field beside a colonial style stone house. "Who lives there?"

"That's Luke and Tristan's place. And here comes my cousin Sheilagh and her husband. Come on. I'll introduce you."

A strange mix of dread and comfort spike through her at the sight of her therapist. Alec Devereux had an incredible calming effect over her, but this wasn't the time or place for them to discuss her emotional inadequacies the way they usually did. Here, they had to act like strangers, which was weird.

She'd met Sheilagh McCullough, Alec's wife, at the bar on St. Patrick's Day. The same day she met Sammy McCullough. Would they remember her?

Ryan opened her door and helped her down. He took her hand, and she clenched his fingers in a tight clammy grip. They rounded the truck, and she braced for awkwardness.

"Hey guys, this is my girlfriend, Maggie. Maggie, this is Sheilagh and her husband Alec. Where's Alexia?"

"Luke's getting gum out of her hair. Don't ask. I think we've met." Sheilagh's smile was welcoming. "At O'Malley's, right?"

Maggie nodded. "Right." Her gaze shifted to Alec who stood a foot taller than his wife.

"It's nice of you to join us," he said, giving no clue to the others that they knew each other.

She smiled nervously. Neither she nor Alec claimed it was nice to meet, since they already knew each other fairly well.

They climbed the grand wooden steps to the porch, and Sheilagh walked right in, so they followed. Ryan was tackled by children, before he fully made it across the threshold.

"He's quite popular with the kids. Sort of the fun uncle," Alec commented, hanging back until the mob broke up.

She glanced at him, expressing her nervousness with her eyes but not having the courage to say a word.

He seemed to understand. "I find, at family functions, whiskey works wonders. Maureen keeps it under the sink next to the Windex. I'll join you."

Ryan rose from a pile of clinging children like a sea monster dredging to the banks of salvation. A rosy-cheeked blond boy wreathed his arms around his neck and refused to let go.

Ryan faced Maggie with a smile and gave the boy a squeeze, hoisting him onto his hip. "This is Lennon, my cousin Braydon's youngest."

"Who are you?" The little boy waved.

"I'm Maggie."

"Do you have candy?"

Why hadn't she thought to bring candy? Probably because kids weren't supposed to take candy from strangers. "I'm sorry I don't."

His big blue eyes flashed with betrayal. "Next time you bring some?"

She nodded. "I promise." How could anyone resist those eyes?

Ryan set the boy down and told him to go play with the other children. Voices rose from the kitchen in a cacophony of sound that was too chaotic to translate. They entered the room, and Maggie stared wide-eyed.

Men gathered around the table talking and shouting from one end to the next. Children raced from the hall, through the kitchen, and into the dining room. Women lined up at the counter from adolescents to a very tiny black haired woman who looked about a hundred. In the corner, another ancient woman sat, unphased by all the pandemonium around her.

Pots steamed and dishes clattered as ingredients passed back and forth, and people called for distinct items like salt or scallions. The room was ten degrees hotter than the rest of the house. It looked more like a soup kitchen than any family scene she recalled from her home growing up.

"You made it." A man with golden brown hair slapped Ryan on the back.

"Yeah, I figured I stayed away long enough. Finn, this is Maggie."

She smiled. "You're one of the twins, right?" If she remembered correctly, he also ran the lumberyard with Ryan.

"Right. I'm the handsome one."

A woman screamed, startling her, and before Maggie could fully process what was happening, she was being strangled in a bear hug.

"You made it!" Rosemarie released her and smiled. "I knew you would get him to come. You're a good influence." She clung to her hand in an unbreakable grip. "Come with me. I want you to meet the girls."

Maggie looked back as Rosemarie dragged her away from Ryan. Her first thought was *never go to the second location*. Her second thought was *help*.

"Maureen, Col, stop and meet Ryan's Maggie."

Two women, about the same age as Rosemarie turned from the

counter and smiled widely. One had red hair just like Rosemarie. The other was thinner and blonde.

"Welcome to our home," the redheaded woman said, startling Maggie with another hug. "Can I get you something to drink?"

Maggie vaguely recognized her from the day after Ryan's birthday. "You must be Mrs. McCullough."

"Oh, will you listen to that? Call me Maureen, love."

The blonde sister shouldered her way closer. "It's nice of you to get Ryan back for us. I'm Colleen, his favorite aunt."

"Get the hell out of here, Colleen." Maureen shoved her sister aside. "Everyone knows I'm the favorite." She took Maggie's hand, much like Rosemarie had done, and dragged her toward the table. "Colin, get up so Maggie can sit."

A man with dark black hair and familiar blue eyes stood and offered his seat. Maggie flushed. "Oh, you don't have to get up—"

"Of course, he does," Maureen insisted. "You're our guest." She shoved her into the vacated seat which pushed up to an enormous wood carved farm table. "I'll get you some tea."

"Bring the whiskey, too, Maureen." Alec winked.

She folded her hands in her lap. Every man gathered around the table sat a foot taller than her.

"Well, look who it is."

She sucked in a breath at the sight of Ryan's cousin Kelly. The man looked perfect in every setting. Even that time when he caught her sneaking into the loft, thought she was a raccoon, and tried to hit her with a broom, he still looked perfect.

He flashed a heart-stopping smile at her. "Did you sneak in, or is this visit on the up-and-up?"

"Leave her alone, Kelly," Ryan said, coming to stand behind her. He leaned down and whispered in her ear, "Doing okay?"

She nodded.

Maureen returned with a pitcher of iced tea and a bottle of whiskey for Alec. He subtly filled his glass, topping it off with a hefty splash of booze and then switched cups with Maggie. She was immensely grateful. The whiskey helped her relax enough to breathe normally.

She recognized Sammy from the bar and recalled she was married to the black haired man who gave Maggie his seat. She'd tried to say hello several times, but children kept interrupting, so eventually she gave up and sipped her whiskey and tea.

Ryan made sure to introduce her to all the adults, but there were too many to keep their names straight. Some Maggie recognized and some she didn't.

When dinner was served, the children crowded around two folding tables in the corner, and the adults took up the seats in the dining room and kitchen. Maggie purposely tried to position herself between Ryan and Alec. Alec kept the conversation moving around casual topics whenever Ryan was pulled into a discussion with someone else. She appreciated him going the extra distance to make her more comfortable.

A man named Giovanni sat across from her, beside Mariella, the stunning woman from the café. She was more beautiful than Maggie remembered. But this time she didn't feel as threatened by the other woman's striking good looks.

"They're siblings," Alec whispered. "Colleen's children. Paulie, their father, is a Mosconi. That's where the olive skin and old Italian Mary come from."

"Italian Mary?"

He pointed to the wrinkled little woman with the severe black hair sitting in the kitchen. "Paulie's mother. I think she'll outlive all of us."

The food was delicious. There was pork roast with fluffy mashed potatoes and string beans with butter. But what Maggie really adored was watching them interact. It was like an exhibit at a zoo, an entire species of people reaching over each other, chatting, poking, cohabitating. She'd never witnessed such evident love in such a widely assorted group of people.

By the time coffee was served, she no longer felt the need to top her glass with whiskey. Or the whiskey had already done the trick. Either way, she felt much more at ease.

The kids disappeared with popsicles to the front porch and the volume dropped substantially. The older men and some of the younger ones went into the den to watch television and digest. Maggie was happy to see at least one of the males stayed back to help with the dishes.

"Which one's that?" she whispered to Ryan.

"That's Tristan. He lived with my family when he first moved here. Like a surrogate brother. He's married to Luke."

She was beginning to put names to faces, but Luke and Finn were tricky on account of them being twins. Mariella's cell phone rang, and she excused herself from the table.

"You coming to play in the game next weekend, Ry?" Kelly took the now empty seat across from them.

"Actually, I wanted to talk to you about that. Do you think we could get a jersey for Maggie?"

Kelly's brows lifted in surprise. "You want to put an O'Malley on the O'Malley's team? Whatever will the locals say?"

Maggie rolled her eyes. "Probably that they don't care, on account of that vendetta being fifty years old and stupid."

Ryan snorted and Kelly grinned. "Oh, I like her. But make no mistake, love, people care. Don't they dad?"

Maggie's back stiffened as she sensed Mr. McCullough standing behind her. She slowly turned and sure enough there he was, all six and

a half feet of masculine flannel and work-roughened skin. She shrank
into Ryan's side.

"What's that?" Mr. McCullough asked.

"Maggie here was sayin' no one cares about the O'Malley rivalry
anymore."

Mr. McCullough's dark brows lowered into a scowl. "If no one cared,
the bar would have been renamed. We keep it O'Malley's so they never
forget we own a piece of them."

She glared at Kelly who chuckled. Was he purposefully trying to
make things uncomfortable for her? Her eyes narrowed on him. Challenge accepted. "But I wonder, if they had changed the name, which
name they would have used, McCullough or Clooney?"

"Clooney—"

"McCullough—"

"Mosconi—" Ryan's father and uncles all barked at once, as if
somehow hearing her quiet comment through all the other chatter.

Ryan chimed in. "Uncle Paulie didn't have a chance to get it named
after him. It's always been an Irish pub."

"Aunt Col would have insisted on the bar taking her maiden name,
O'Leahey, before letting it be called Mosconi," Kelly insisted. "And there
was no way you were getting it named McCullough, Dad. You weren't
even there for the full fight."

Mr. McCullough shrugged, his expression unapologetic. "I got what I
wanted."

Ryan leaned close and whispered, "He practically kidnapped my Aunt
Maureen and ran off to elope with her. When they got back to town, my
grandfather took a shot at him."

"He missed," Mr. McCullough barked. "Besides, keeping the pub's
name as O'Malley's served as a reminder to Caleb that he not only lost a
bet fair and square but also that people don't take kindly to others
defaulting on their promises."

She found it interesting that no one mentioned the upcoming sale of
the pub. It would have taken the attention off her name, but she wasn't
cruel enough to bring it up.

Kelly cocked his head and gave her a told-you-so grin. "See? Now
you know just how crazy the old grudge holders are. Still want to play
on our team?"

She rolled her eyes again. "I think if you saw me play, you'd want me
on your team."

"Oh!" Kelly hooted and laughed. "She's no shrinking violet, that's for
sure."

"What brought that up?" Mr. McCullough asked, exchanging his
coffee for a beer.

Maggie's eyes went wide, silently begging Kelly not to—

"Maggie here is an O'Malley."

The kitchen fell silent, and she sank into her seat.

"Alright, you had your fun," Ryan said. "Now, drop it. She was a Harris first."

"You're dating an O'Malley?" Mr. McCullough's tone rumbled through the stillness. "After what they did?"

Maggie lowered her hands and gripped the table, wishing an escape hatch hid underneath.

"Come on, Dad." Kelly laughed. "It was fifty years ago."

"And I still have scars from that fight. Your Uncle Paulie's knee still isn't right. Your mother nearly got her head bashed in with a stool, before I got her out of there."

Unphased, Kelly turned to her and clarified, "And my grandfather didn't totally miss. Dad's got a scar smack dab in the center of his arse."

"That's not a bullet hole, you moron," Kelly's father smacked him in the head.

Her jaw gaped. What kind of crazy family was this?

"He missed," Mr. McCullough snarled.

Ryan's Aunt Colleen laughed. "Oh, I'll never forget the night you came into the pub howling like a banshee and bleeding all over the place. You were a big wuss."

"The man fired a rifle at me! But he missed."

"Sure, he did, Frank," Mrs. McCullough said and snickered.

Thankfully, Mr. McCullough stormed out of the room, and the conversation over the O'Malley rivalry was put to rest. Kelly laughed, but she didn't find it as funny.

Not realizing how serious the older generation took the stupid conflict, her heart thundered. She worried they might truly hate her over a name.

"You're a jerk," she snapped at Kelly and pushed back from the table.

"Oh, come on, love. You gotta have a thick skin if you're gonna hang around this lot."

She carried her coffee mug to the sink and used the screen door to escape the kitchen to the porch. Rocking chairs lined the side of the house, and children's voices babbled in the distance.

Several syrupy popsicle sticks clung to the banister where the kids left them. She was picking them up so they didn't attract ants when the sound of sniffling caught her ear.

Walking quietly along the side of the house, she peeked around the corner. Mariella sat on the porch steps in front of the main entrance, her phone clutched in her hand as she wiped tears from her eyes.

Maggie took a cautious step forward, causing a floorboard to creak, and the woman turned, clearly startled. "Sorry," she apologized then asked, "Are you okay?"

Mariella's beautiful face pinched as she tried to answer, but she could only manage a shake of her head.

Concern drew her across the porch and she lowered herself to the step. "Can I do something?"

Mariella's breath hitched and shuddered. "No. There's nothing anyone can do."

Her brows pulled in concern, and she gently placed a hand on the woman's back, rubbing softly. "Do you want to talk about it?"

"It's too embarrassing."

"Okay."

"I'm an idiot. I should know better."

Maggie had no idea what the issue was, so she just listened and continued to rub her back.

"Every time I fall in love and give someone my heart, they stop wanting it."

She was crying over relationship stuff? How could that be? Mariella was gorgeous. She should have men flocking to her and throwing themselves at her feet. "Whoever hurt you, he doesn't know what he's missing." *He* was the idiot.

"We were in love," she explained. "Every time I came home from college, he'd buy me presents and promise that we would eventually make things work." She wiped at the smears of makeup and tears under her eyes. "He said he loved me."

"Just because a relationship doesn't work out doesn't mean two people aren't in love."

"Oh, I know. He loves me. But I'm not what he wants. I'm too young and too…" She waved her hand, as if trying to think of the right word. "I'm not the kind of woman he wants to marry."

Whoever this guy was, he sounded like a creep. "Then maybe forget him. You seem like a perfectly nice woman to me. And you're so pretty. You shouldn't have to put up with that kind of attitude from any man."

"But I love him. All this time I thought, if he genuinely loved me too, he'd get over his commitment issues." Her voice broke with a sob, and her face dropped to her palms. Just then, her cell phone rang, and she sucked in a breath. "It's him."

"Are you going to answer it?"

Her lips tightened with indecision, and she wiped her eyes, lifting the phone to her ear. "Hello?"

Maggie stood to give her privacy and noticed Ryan waiting at the corner of the porch. How long had he been standing there? She walked over to him.

"I followed you out here to make sure you were okay."

She smiled because that was sweet of him to check on her. "I'm okay."

He glanced over her shoulder to where Mariella spoke on the phone. "Is she?"

"Guy problems."

"I see." He tipped his forehead to hers and smiled. "It was nice of you to comfort her."

"Whoever she's dating sounds like a jerk," she whispered. "She deserves better."

Ryan shrugged. "She never brings him around. And the few times she expected him to attend a family function, he bailed on her last minute. I wish she'd get rid of him."

"Well, you might be getting your wish."

Ryan gave her a look that said Mariella was off the phone and heading their way. Maggie turned. She looked better. "Everything okay?"

The woman drew in a shaky breath and tucked her phone in her pocket. "Maybe. He wants to see me to talk." She wiped at the black smears under her eyes. "I'm a disaster."

"No," Maggie disagreed. "You're human." It was a refreshing discovery. "I'll get you a wet napkin."

She quickly slipped into the kitchen and Ryan's Aunt Colleen sidled up to her at the sink. "Is that for Mariella?"

Maggie looked at the woman, knowing she was likely only concerned about her daughter. But not knowing enough about their relationship, she didn't want to betray Ryan's cousin by saying too much.

"It's okay," Colleen said. "I'm used to it. Her boyfriend's a real *prize*." There was no disguising the contempt behind her sarcasm. "I wish she'd realize how much better she deserves and get rid of him."

Maggie wrung out the paper towel and smiled. "I better get back out there."

Once Mariella had her face cleaned up, Maggie went inside the house. She and Ryan made their goodbyes, and Kelly apologized for pushing her buttons earlier, promising to get her a jersey for the game next week. Maggie had survived the family dinner, but she also felt like she'd run a decathlon.

On the drive home, Ryan held her hand. "So, do you think you could do it again?"

She smiled. "I want to say no, but part of me hopes we do."

He grinned at her in a way that said he felt exactly the same.

CHAPTER 33

*M*aggie sucked in a sharp breath and put down her flute of champagne. "Oh, Perrin."

"Do you like it?" Her sister twirled in front of a wall of mirrors, white taffeta swishing softly.

"You look like a princess."

"It's not too much, though, right?"

"Not at all." Maggie couldn't stop staring. "I might cry."

"No crying. Today's a happy day. Drink your champagne."

Maggie did as she was told. "You're the boss."

She'd taken the day off to do wedding stuff. As the maid of honor, she had certain responsibilities. Basically, she had to be at Perrin's beck and call for the next month and a half. Making herself available seemed easier than remembering all the trivial things she had to do as the bride's right hand. And Perrin was a list queen, so her sister's endless checklists made the job especially easy. Today's objective: find *the dress*.

Maggie glanced at the itinerary her sister had printed out. "Next we have a tasting in town. Shouldn't Bran be there for that?"

Her sister tried on various veils and tiaras. "He's too busy with work. Last night he was at the office until midnight. Besides, he told me to get whatever I thought the guests would prefer."

After the bakery, they had lunch. Perrin asked how things were going with Ryan, and Maggie couldn't hide her happiness.

"You're really into him, aren't you?"

Maggie's cheeks warmed. "He's fun. And he gets me, even when I don't make it easy."

"He seems like a great guy. I'm happy for you."

Maggie smiled. "I'm happy for me too. And you. I'm happy for both of us."

224

Perrin lifted her glass and tapped it to Maggie's. "To us both finally being happy at the same time."

~

THAT SATURDAY she and Ryan returned to the mountain for the first official baseball game of summer. They each wore green O'Malley's shirts, and she was ready to crush the competition.

"I mentioned I have a bit of a competitive streak, right?"

He laughed. "I'd be disappointed if you didn't."

"And who are we playing today?"

"The post office."

"Oh, they're going down."

She pulled her hair into a ponytail and fed it through the back of her baseball cap. The field was a private diamond with actual bleachers, all owned by the McCulloughs.

Maureen, Colleen, and Rosemarie had a table full of snacks for the kids and coolers filled with water for the players. There were people in the stands she didn't know, and a few she recognized from around town.

This time she was prepared for the kids, and when she saw little Lennon, she was sure to slip him a piece of chocolate. Having candy moved her up to the top of the scale as far as cool points went with the little ones.

"This is so awesome," she said, taking in the field. "You guys have actual dugouts."

Ryan grinned proudly. "Yeah, our dads worked on it a lot when we were kids. The aunts insisted we needed a place to get out our extra energy."

His relatives waited in a dugout that looked well-worn. The entire back wall was graffitied with marker. Each couple's name hid somewhere in the mess, adorable and tucked in a heart. She looked for Ryan's name, wondering if it might be with some important ex of his, but she didn't see it. Maybe one day she'd add it for him, with hers.

His relatives filtered in, some ready for a game, others looking like they partied a little too hard the night before. Mariella arrived and Maggie moved to her side of the bench to ask how she was.

"Did you guys talk? You look better."

The woman drew in a big breath and huffed it out with a smile. "I'm wonderful. I dumped him."

Maggie smiled, proud of her. "Good for you. You deserve better."

"I'm finally starting to realize that, but he's not making it easy on me. He keeps calling and showing up at my house. Last night, he wouldn't leave until I heard him out."

"Did it change anything?" Maybe they might actually make it work after all.

"No. He wants to have his cake and eat it too. But I'm not settling. I told him he either decides that I'm it for him and we try a committed relationship, or I'm out."

"I think it's good you're standing your ground."

She glanced at the bench where her phone vibrated. "That's him. He's been calling all day, asking me to give him some time to think things over before I cut him off completely. I'm not answering."

Maggie couldn't understand why a man would want more time when a woman like Mariella was offering him everything. It made her appreciate how much Ryan devoted himself to their relationship.

"Well, you can take out your frustrations on the field. We're going to kick some postal worker ass today."

Mariella laughed. "I'm down."

The game started and Maggie was impressed with how official and organized everything worked. Their team batted first and took the lead, but in the next inning the postal workers tied up the score. It was a good match and a lively competition. By the sixth inning, she was sweating the score.

"Come on, Kelly, knock it out of the park!" she yelled, gripping the fence in front of the dugout.

Kelly swung and cracked the ball. With bases loaded everyone went nuts and the players cleared home plate.

Maggie was up next. Her team cheered as she approached the plate. Out of the corner of her eye, she saw Mariella walk off the field into the parking lot. A sleek black car idled by the fence.

Returning her focus to the game, she lifted the bat and eyed the pitcher. The first pitch was a strike. She honed her attention on the ball and swung again, not hitting it as far as she wanted but getting herself safely to first base.

She glanced at the fence. Mariella was talking to whoever was in the car. Her hands waved as she spoke fervidly. Maggie narrowed her eyes. Was this the boyfriend?

Ryan was up next. He whacked the ball into the outfield, and Maggie hustled all the way to home plate, scoring another run for their team. Unfortunately, Ryan only made it to third.

As she walked back to the dugout, she paused. Mariella was clearly upset, and when she tried to walk back to the field, the car pulled alongside of her, blocking her way. Maggie shifted directions and walked to the fence.

"Mariella, you okay?"

Her friend turned and Maggie could see she was not. Tears streamed down her face and she held out her hands helplessly. Turning back to the car, she snapped, "I have to go. Please leave me alone."

She jogged back to the fence and Maggie scowled at the car as it turned away. But it didn't leave the lot. It parked. "I don't think he listened."

Mariella looked back and scoffed. "That's it." She stomped toward the parked car that was partially hidden by the bleachers. Maggie heard her friend snap at the man and the man begging for her to listen to him.

"I'm through listening. I told you what I want, but you don't want that."

"Why can't you compromise? You're being unfair. I told you, we could have an apartment here, and I'd take care of you. Isn't that enough?"

"No! Don't you get it? I don't want any of those things. I want you to love me. Only me, Bran."

Bran? Blood rushed from Maggie's face as she moved closer to the bleachers. The game carried on, and she heard Ryan calling her, but some sort of trance had her body locked. She had to have misheard.

She rounded the bleachers and staggered to a stop as she spotted her sister's fiancé. This was the man Mariella had been seeing since college? No wonder he couldn't commit. He was marrying Maggie's sister!

Something unleashed inside of her, and she gripped the fence, throwing her leg over the rail and vaulting into the parking lot. "You son of a bitch!"

Mariella turned, her eyes wide as Maggie charged toward the black car. "Maggie, what are you doing?"

"Maggie?" Bran did a double take.

"You cheating piece of shit!" She didn't stop until both her hands shoved into his chest. "How dare you?"

"Maggie!" Ryan leapt over the fence and came running to her side. He frowned when he recognized Bran. "What are you doing here?"

"He's cheating on my sister!" Maggie shoved him again.

"Hey!" Bran held up his hands defensively. "Calm her down."

"Fuck you!" Maggie yelled, chest out and ready to maul. Ryan tried to get between them, but she wasn't having it. "You think you're going to get away with this? You don't deserve either of them!" She swung her hand and scratched his cheek.

"Someone get her away from me!"

More people gathered and Ryan banded an arm around her waist, hauling her back a few steps.

"Put me down!"

"You have to calm down."

"Fine! But put me down!"

"Someone tell me what's going on!" Mariella shouted. Turning her tearful eyes on Maggie, she asked, "You two know each other?"

Ryan set her down in front of the black car, and she panted. "He's engaged to my sister."

Regret flashed in Mariella's eyes, telling Maggie she knew there was another woman but never expected it to link back to her family and those they knew. "I'm sorry."

"You knew he was cheating on you?" Ryan barked, a stunned look on his face.

She held out her hands. "It's complicated. He started dating me first. I'm not the other woman. She is."

Maggie ground her teeth. It took everything inside of her not to lunge at him again. "My sister's too good for you." She turned and kicked his headlight, smashing the glass with her cleat.

"Hey! You're fucking paying for tha—"

His words cut off with a solid whack. Everyone in the crowd collectively gasped. She turned and Bran was on the ground.

Ryan stood over him and snarled, "You're a real piece of shit."

He jogged over to her and adrenaline raced through her veins. She couldn't stop shaking. When he reached her, she looked up at him on the verge of tears. "Please get me out of here."

He took her hand and led her to his truck.

On the ride home, she didn't see the road through her rage, and she didn't speak because she couldn't unclench her jaw.

How could Bran do that to her sister? Perrin had been so happy. She gave that putz two years of devotion, and he'd been seeing Mariella the whole time. He planned to keep seeing her! That was why he wanted to move to the Jersey shore, so he could keep his sidepiece in an apartment back home.

A pinch of guilt nipped when she thought of Mariella as the sidepiece. According to Ryan's cousin, she had a relationship with him first, which made Perrin the mistress. But that couldn't be right, because he was marrying Perrin.

Ryan pulled into his driveway but didn't shut off the truck. She stared blindly at the dashboard. "This is bad."

He didn't disagree. "What are you going to tell Perrin?"

"The truth." She had no choice. "She's going to be devastated."

Maggie knew what it was like to have your entire life planned and have it unexpectedly ripped away. She didn't know if having a target for the blame helped matters or would make things worse.

Ryan's hand folded around hers. "Do you want me to drive you there?"

The last thing she wanted to do was drive to her parents' to break her sister's heart. But she needed to do the right thing. Perrin deserved to find out from someone who loved her, someone who would be there to catch the pieces when her world came crashing down. And she needed to get to her before Bran filled her head with more lies.

Maggie nodded and Ryan put the truck in reverse and backed out of the driveway. She gave him directions to her childhood home, and her blood chilled when she saw Perrin's car at the curb.

"This is going to be terrible."

"Do you want me to go inside with you?"

She shook her head.

"Do you want me to wait in the car?"

"No, I'm going to be a while."

"I can come get you when you're ready. Just call."

She appreciated his thoughtfulness, but she had no idea how bad her sister would take the news. Maggie cringed that the "save the dates" had already been sent and the announcement posted in the newspaper that week. She hated knowing how humiliated her sister would feel.

"I'll probably stay the night. I'll call you tomorrow."

When Ryan pulled away, Maggie took a bracing breath and opened the front door. Her mother lifted her gaze from a novel and frowned. "What are you doing here?"

"I need to talk to Perrin."

"Was she expecting you?"

Because God forbid Maggie show up at her childhood home without a written invitation. "Yes," she lied and walked down the hall to her sister's bedroom. She tapped on the door.

"Come in." Perrin sat on her bed with her laptop open and smiled. "Hey, this is a surprise."

"Hey." She closed the door tightly behind her.

"Is everything okay?" She shut the laptop.

"No. I have to tell you something Perrin, and it's terrible." Maggie took off her baseball cap and sat on the bed.

Her sister's face paled. "What is it?"

She broke the news as gently as she could, explaining how she'd found out and how long she believed the affair with Mariella had been going on. At first Perrin denied it, saying it was impossible for Bran to cheat on her, but as reality sank in, her denial evaporated, and she fell apart in Maggie's arms.

She held her sister and kissed her head as she cried. Maggie was accustomed to heartache, but watching her sister break, somehow seemed worse than her own pain. She cradled her head on her lap as heaving sobs raked Perrin's body.

"Why? Why would he do this to me? I'm so humiliated. Why wasn't I enough?"

Maggie's heart shuddered with empathy. She didn't have any answers. To her, Perrin was perfect. She was strong and loyal and beautiful in a way that exceeded the usual definition. "Sometimes life's just unfair."

"It hurts."

"I know, honey. It's going to hurt for a while."

The door opened. "What's going on?" Their mother stood at the threshold, her accusing glare burning into Maggie. "What did you do?"

"I didn't do anything."

"Then why is your sister crying? What's the matter?"

Perrin continued to sob. The pressure to form an explanation churned incoherent, gut wrenching sobs past her throat. It was too much to bear.

"The wedding's off," Maggie said abruptly, trying to save her sister the pain.

Knowing her mother, Maggie worried she'd somehow catch the blame for what Bran did, so there was no point in hiding the truth. Her biggest concern right now was taking care of Perrin. And knowing how hard it was to explain an unjustified heartbreak, Maggie saved her the trouble.

"What? Says who?"

"Bran's been cheating on Perrin."

Her sister wailed and Maggie rubbed a hand down her back.

"Bran wouldn't do that to her. He loves your sister. You did this. You couldn't handle the attention moving to someone else. You couldn't bear to see your sister happy when you're determined to stay miserable."

Her mother's hateful words took the breath from her lungs. Ice formed around her heart.

"That's not true," she wheezed, stunned by how much her mother's lack of understanding could still crush her. "How could you say such a hateful thing?"

"Perrin was perfectly fine before you walked into this house."

She swallowed tightly. "Sorry, Mom. For once, I'm not the one to blame. Bran is."

"But you had to tell her," she sneered. "Now, look at her!"

"Mom, stop!" Perrin cried. "This isn't Maggie's fault."

Her mother glared at both of them. "You won't be happy until everyone around you is miserable." She slammed the door, and Maggie shook with the reverberation.

"Don't listen to her," Perrin sniffled. "You didn't do anything wrong."

Her sister's words barely penetrated the icy shell protecting her. She didn't comment. Her hand smoothed over Perrin's hair and she continued to comfort her. As her sobs abated, she fretfully mentioned all the things that needed to be done.

"We'll take care of it," Maggie promised, unsure how she'd handle everything.

They needed to get a refund on the hall and the church. They needed to contact all the guests and cancel the flower order. In between each task Perrin mentioned, her voice would die a little more.

Maggie started a list on her phone, promising to take care of everything. Leave it to her sister to have everything booked ahead of schedule. Maggie refused to leave any of the fallout to someone who clearly needed time to mourn—something she understood all too well. And so help her God, if Bran even tried to interfere, she'd murder him.

CHAPTER 34

$\mathscr{R}$yan gave Maggie plenty of space over the next week. Perrin's car became a frequent fixture in front of her house, and he figured she'd appreciate the time with her sister. But when Friday came and her sister didn't show, he expected Maggie to visit him or at least call. She didn't.

On Saturday morning, she left early to visit the cemetery, and he waited on her back porch for her to return. When she pulled her bike into the yard and spotted him, her expression blanked.

While he wanted to respect her and give her time to deal with her family, he also didn't want this trouble with Bran and his cousin to put a wedge between them. It hadn't been the easiest week, and he needed his girlfriend.

She walked through the gate but didn't come to the back door. Instead, she sat on the chair by the firepit. The other chair had been Nash's, and he didn't feel comfortable taking it. She'd know that, so her choice confirmed she was forcing space between them.

"How's Perrin?"

"Hurting. Confused. Sad."

He expected as much. She wouldn't look at him. Her sister's turmoil likely stirred some past fears, and he hated that this felt like a step backwards for them.

"I'd never do what he did."

"I know. You're one of the good ones."

He was glad she thought so. "Perrin will meet someone better."

Maggie nodded. "Eventually. But she'll never get over this. She'll never forget what he did. My sister has always been one of the most trusting people I know, and he took that from her."

"We're all products of our experiences. The bad ones only make us

232

stronger." When she didn't comment, he said, "Maggie, I know watching your sister get hurt scared you. It scared me too. But we're in a different place, and we can't let other people's choices control our own. *We* decide what we want."

"I know that, too."

"Then why are you avoiding me? Your sister hasn't been here in two days."

She folded her hands between her knees and looked at the ground. "Because this made me realize some things about us, and I'm still trying to process them."

"Care to fill me in?"

"You'll get there faster than me."

"What does that mean?"

She looked at him then. "It means, if I tell you, you'll process it faster than I can, and I don't want to feel pressured."

"Pressured to do what?"

"Ryan…" She fidgeted. "I think we should…" Her brow knit tight and her lips pressed into a thin line.

His heart plummeted. "Please don't break up with me."

She drew back. "I'm not. I think we should sleep together."

Not at all what he was expecting, he felt his mouth open and close, but words wouldn't come out. He finally blurted an off pitched, "*Now?*"

She shrugged. "Not right this second but soon." Her palms dragged over her face and she blew out a breath. "Last week when I went to my sister's, I realized how lucky I am to have you. Not that I didn't already appreciate you, but I realized you're more than my boyfriend. You're my best friend. I trust you more than I trusted…" She looked away.

His heart seemed to literally tremble at the significance of her words. He saw her as his best friend, too, which was why the thought of losing her terrified him.

"I know I can count on you, Ryan. You would never do anything to hurt me. You give up your own free time to take care of me, even when I don't ask you to."

"That's what you do when you love someone."

Her smile was sad. "The fact that you believe that just proves how special you actually are. Bran loved my sister and he loved your cousin, but he still hurt them both. People are incredibly selfish. I loved Nash with all my heart, and he loved me. Do you know how many times I asked him to clean out the gutters? You're the first person who ever actually did it, *and* I didn't even ask you to."

"They needed it."

She pressed her palms flat over her knees, a nervous tell that said she had something important to share. He held his breath when she looked up at him with tears in her eyes.

"You replaced the bulb on the front porch."

Should he not have? "It was burned-out."

"I know." She blinked and a tear tumbled down her cheek.

His heart broke, wanting to catch that tear before it fell and another soon joined it. "Maggie, I don't understand why you're crying."

"I'm crying because I'm happy. For the last two years, all I did was wish for a way to turn back time, because I thought the only way I could ever feel happy again was to go back to the way things were. The more time that passed, the harder it became to remember what happiness felt like. I was so afraid of something else happening, of life getting one more degree sadder, that I pushed everyone away. Some people were toxic, and it was good to get away from them, but other people... I lost all my friends, because no one could understand what I was feeling. Perrin was the only one who waited patiently for me to come around. And then you showed up and pushed your way past my defenses."

"I'm not sorry." He'd never apologize for getting close to her. She was his everything.

She smiled through her tears. "And that's why I love you. I know you'll always do what's best for me, even when it's the least easy thing for you. No one's ever loved me like that. Ever."

What she wasn't saying spoke volumes. His breathing labored as he stared at her, grasping the implication of her words. It was the greatest compliment of his life, because he knew how much she loved Nash, and he might never fill the guy's shadow but to say that Ryan loved her better...

His vision blurred and he blinked. What the hell was happening to him? He cleared his throat and glanced away.

He'd been so careful not to get ahead of himself. Rather than rush into hopes of a future and let his family intrude, he'd kept Maggie to himself as long as possible. It terrified him, bringing her to Sunday dinner, but she managed like a champ and everyone got along great with her—they even broke her balls, which was how his family generally showed affection. She fit in like she belonged, and he wanted her to belong to him but feared she never would.

Even now, he could feel his heart running ahead as it tried to beat out of his chest. "What does this mean?"

She lifted a shoulder and smiled. "It means I'm in. I can't imagine going back to a time when my life didn't include you. And I don't want to keep looking backwards, when there are so many good opportunities ahead of us."

His bones trembled and his breath shook. "Get over here."

She slowly crossed the patch of grass and climbed onto his lap, looping her arms around his neck. He stared into her eyes and for the first time, dared to see his future there. "I love you so much."

"I love you, too."

He kissed her and didn't stop kissing her until he carried her into his house, up the stairs, and dropped her onto his bed.

CHAPTER 35

"*W*ait." Maggie covered his mouth before he could kiss her again. Everything he was doing felt incredible, but she had to explain her conditions. "I've thought about this moment for a long time. Since the last time we... When I freaked out."

He kissed her palm and pulled her hand away from his mouth. "It doesn't have to be right now. I just need to be close to you."

She scooted out from under him. "The thing is, I don't want to make too big of a deal out of the first time we do it."

He frowned. "But it is a big deal."

"I know, but the more of a production we make out of it, the harder it is for me to go through with it. I think we should just get in there and get it done."

"*Get it done?*"

"Yeah. Just do it so there's no going back."

He shifted his weight and sat up. "That's not happening."

"But—"

"Maggie, I love you. I'm not just going to *get it done*. This isn't like testing a cake with a toothpick."

"God, I hope not, because that would be really disappointing."

"You've already seen me."

Another reason they should get the first time over with quickly, she hadn't had sex in over two years. Her lady bits might scream from the shock. "I just think the first time should be fast. In and out. We can make it nice the next time, when it doesn't feel like there's so much riding on it."

He stood and walked out of the room.

"Wait. Where are you going?"

"For a walk."

She scrambled off the bed and followed him into the hall. "Are you mad at me?"

"I'm not exactly happy with you."

Her footsteps staggered. His disappointment hurt more than expected. "You can't get mad at me for how I feel."

"I'm not mad. I'm … frustrated."

"Why? Most men don't care about foreplay anyway."

At the foot of the stairs, he pivoted and scowled at her. "How would you know?"

Her jaw opened and closed. "Porn?"

His face twisted. "What the hell sort of porn are you watching?"

She shrugged. "The guy kind."

He scoffed and shook his head. "First of all, I don't like being compared to other guys. Second, I *like* foreplay—sometimes more than the main event—especially with you. I like feeling close to you. I want that connection. Third, if you can't handle that then maybe we're rushing things."

She stared after him as he disappeared toward the kitchen. Her heart thundered. She liked the connection too. But sometimes it was too much.

She found him putting on his boots. "You make me feel like I'm in debt."

He dropped his foot, ignoring the untied laces. "What?"

"Did you ever have a friend that was so good and kind they made you feel like a fraud?"

"No."

"Well, that's how I feel with you. You do everything right, Ryan. I'm a disaster, especially next to you. And you're so thoughtful of others." She shifted uncomfortably. "Of me."

"You're thoughtful too—"

"No, not like you. I'm too busy trying to navigate my own crap to think about other people as much as you do. And the way you help everyone… It's everything about you. Half the time, I don't even know why you're with me. You … overwhelm me. Sometimes I feel like I don't belong with you, but I can't seem to give you up, so I selfishly stay and worry that one day you'll wake up and realize you could do so much better."

"Maggie, that's never going to happen. Do you know how stunned I am that I even have the right to touch you? To kiss you? You say I over-whelm you. Well, I'm the lucky one. My life was nothing before you came along. It was empty and sad and so fucking lonely. I could find *company*, but it got old real quick. I got tired of lowering my standards to pretend at something was real when everything I found was so clearly fake. I didn't want to settle, even when everyone else acted like I should." He rubbed the back of his neck and flushed. "I couldn't. Every girl I dated wasn't right for me, and I knew it. I knew there was more, and if I was patient, I might one day fall in love. Then I found you."

She threw her hands out in front of her. "You see? How the hell am I supposed to follow that? Debt!"

He stood from the table and caught her hands. "No. It's not *debt*. It's gratitude. I feel it too, every time you look at me or laugh at one of my stupid jokes. It's nothing to be afraid of."

"You make me feel so much." She shut her eyes and pressed a hand over the ache in her chest. "I don't know how to fit it all inside when all that's left of me is a little, fragile piece of my heart."

He pulled her close and hugged her to his front so her back was to his chest. "You do the same to me." He kissed her head, rubbing his palm over the ache. "The heart's a muscle. It gets stronger the more you use it."

"Mine's just a little sore. Recently, it's been getting more use than usual."

He chuckled. "But look how strong you're getting."

Making love to Ryan would be intense. She feared bursting into tears when the emotion had no place to fit. She feared losing all control and making a fool of herself. She feared letting anyone that close to her again. And then she turned and looked into his eyes and realized he had already broken down her walls and worked his way inside.

"Be gentle," she whispered, rising on her toes to press her lips to his.

His hands softly cupped her face. "Always."

He carried her up the stairs as if she were a precious gift. When he laid her on the bed, his eyes never left hers as he removed their clothes. Soft kisses pressed into her flesh, waking her heart and sending it into the clouds with every heavenly touch.

Her body writhed under each caress, slowly unraveling. His strong hands held her through every ripple of pleasure, and when her body quaked in completion, he kissed her, whispering how beautiful she was.

Tears wet her lashes when he filled her. The intimacy stole her breath as he waited for her to adjust, never once taking his stare away from her face.

"I love you," he whispered.

"I love you, too." Her knee hooked over his hip, and she kissed him.

Slowly, he rocked into her, his shoulders bunching with muscle as his body flexed over hers. Her breath hitched the deeper he drove, and her mind tumbled into a swirling majesty of pleasure.

She clung to him, needing and wanting the closeness she spent so long fearing. Every caress of his skin seemed to sew up an old wound. Her heart swelled and ached like a muscle strained.

As he drew closer to his release, he kissed her neck, finding her ears and sending chills down her spine. Her toes curled into the blankets, and her nails dragged down his back. He moaned against her throat, his strokes quickening and driving deeper. She cried out, her own pleasure a direct result of his.

Shoulders shaking, he dropped his head to her chest. She cradled him close to her and kissed his temple. As he curled into her, wrapping his arms around her body and pressing their bodies closer, she considered that this might be the first time in her life she made love to a man.

Everything was different. The unspoken significance loomed over both of them. Did he know that it would be like that? Was it like that for him with other women? She had no comparison, because it was so very different from all her times with Nash.

He kissed her cheek and rolled to his side, still holding her tight and spoke her exact thoughts, "I've never felt anything like that before."

She turned to look at him, relieved and hoping his statement was true and not some nonsense men spout after climaxing. "Really?"

He nodded. "That was … intense."

Her throat tightened around a lump, and her vision blurred. "It was perfect."

He pushed the hair away from her eyes and kissed her nose. "I thought so, too."

They fell asleep in each other's arms, and when they woke, they made love again. When the sun came up, she considered sneaking out and going home to make coffee and do her usual morning routine, but something kept her next to him. It was the first time she intentionally chose not to visit the cemetery. And it was the first time she didn't feel guilty for putting herself first.

CHAPTER 36

"*T*he worst part about not moving to New Jersey is that I have to stay in this small town, where everyone knows my humiliation. I can't even get my coffee at the café anymore, because that's where *she* works." Perrin scoffed and sipped the cup of subpar coffee Maggie had made her. "Did she have to be so damn gorgeous?"

Remembering the day she thought Mariella might be one of Ryan's exes, she sympathized. "Just remember that she was as much the victim as you. He's the asshole."

"Oh, I know he's the asshole. And I'm making sure everyone else knows, too."

Maggie didn't think revenge was the healthiest approach, but who was she to tell someone how to cope with trauma? "I know a good therapist."

Perrin rolled her eyes. "No."

Maggie laughed, also remembering how hard Perrin had insisted therapy would help, which it had. "Maybe you just need to say screw him."

"I wish that did the trick. I tell myself I'm better off finding out what a creep he is now, rather than marrying him and living a lie, but then I think about how stupid he made me look and I feel like such a fool."

"You're not the first woman to get cheated on, Perrin."

"I know. I've been reading all these affirmations trying to feel better. *No setback will ever be as big as your comeback,*" she said in mock agreement and stuck out her tongue. "But I don't have a comeback. He still gets to move away into a beautiful house and start a life where no one knows how much of a scumbag he is. And I get to keep living with my parents and washing hair at the salon."

"So, move out of Mom and Dad's and look for a new job if that will make you feel better."

"Where? Getting paid from somewhere a few doors down on Main Street isn't going to really change anything. At least at the salon I get to talk to people."

Unlike Maggie, Perrin was a people person. Maggie preferred to stay behind the scenes, which was why she worked at Restaurant Supply. She had no real affinity for food goods, but it was easy, brainless work and no one expected her to be Miss Congeniality on the job.

"Well, you can't keep this negative attitude," Maggie said, rising to top off her coffee. "People will start thinking I'm the pleasant one and then we'll really be fucked."

Perrin slouched back in her chair. "I always thought I'd do something cool or have life figured out by now."

Maggie frowned. "You're twenty-six. You've got plenty of time to figure things out."

"I can see it now. In another decade, I'll still be washing hair at the salon. I'll be twenty pounds fatter, still single, and wishing I had done something with myself when I was this age." She sat up. "Oh, God, what if I regret letting Bran go because he's the best I could do?"

"Don't make me smack you. Bran is a dick wart, and you're lucky to be rid of him."

She laughed and crossed her arms. "Fine."

She hated seeing her sister so down on herself. "Perrin, if there's something you want to do, do it. If you need money for classes, I can help you." She had the money from Nash's life insurance sitting untouched in an account.

"I don't know."

"Well, what do you want to do? Stop thinking in terms of obstacles and try to imagine the life you want."

Her sister shrugged. "Dad thinks I should take after him and be an accountant. I always thought I'd be a good business owner, but I never knew what kind of business I should go into."

Maggie made a face like she tasted a burp. "Ew. You'd hate accounting."

"I know. I need to be around people."

Maggie had a thought but then pushed it away. It was too extreme and too much for Perrin to handle on her own. Or was it?

She considered how much money she had in the bank and wondered how much an investment like that would cost. "How would you feel about going into business together?"

Her sister perked up. "Really? Doing what?"

She hesitated, not wanting to get too far ahead of herself before actually considering if this was something *she* wanted. "I'm just thinking out loud, but I know of a place for sale in town. Everything's already set up.

The seller just needs a buyer. They're willing to sell it as is, company name and all."

"What is it?"

Maggie bit her lip. This was crazy. Wasn't it? "The O'Malley's Pub."

Perrin looked at her like she'd lost her mind. "The bar? Have you ever even been in there?"

"I've been in there a couple times. It's a regular bar."

"It's a dive."

"So? People love a good dive bar. It's always packed."

"Is it even for sale?"

Maggie nodded. "The owner is switching careers and with the revitalization happening around town it's the right time to sell."

Perrin sat back, a look of stunned shock on her face. "You're serious? You'd actually consider buying that place?"

She thought about how sad Ryan was when he told her they'd listed it on the market last week. He said it was the end of an era. He toyed with the idea of taking it over because no one else in his family wanted the responsibility, but he couldn't do it. He was taking over the lumberyard, and while he might be able to take a few extra shifts at the bar, he couldn't manage both jobs full-time. He seemed desperate to find someone who would keep the pub alive.

Life was short, and Perrin and Ryan were the two most important people in her world. She'd do almost anything to see them happy. "I'd consider it. As an O'Malley, I might be able to negotiate a decent price."

Perrin rolled her eyes. "Or they might jack up the price. Isn't there a big rivalry between the owners and your in-laws?"

She waved her concerns away. "That's old news. Besides, I know the owners, and their wives like me."

"Who are the owners?"

"Ryan's parents and his Aunt Colleen and Uncle Paulie."

"I thought that hot guy owned it."

"No, he just manages it. It was Paulie and Liam who won the pub in a hand of poker against Caleb. Their family's been running it for the last fifty years."

She shook her head. "Wait a minute. What about your job? You hate anything with more than three people."

"I'm getting better. Besides, I wouldn't be the one running the social end of things. I could keep a nine to five schedule handling the administrative stuff, sort of like a silent partner."

"You mean owner. I have no money, Maggie."

"But you'd make money if you had a bar. And in time, we'd be equals. It would be like a loan."

Perrin stood and paced the kitchen. "Are you seriously considering doing this? Like, for real?"

Maggie shrugged. "If you think it would make you happy, sure. The money's just sitting there."

"Maggie, this is a big deal." She raked her fingers through her short blonde hair. "A *really* big deal. I mean, this could be *huge.*"

She smiled. Seeing her sister light up after weeks of tears was a beautiful sight to behold. "Then let's do it."

Perrin spun on her heels and caught Maggie's shoulders. "For real?"

"I'll look into it."

"Oh my God, we're buying a bar!" She screamed and jumped up and down, rattling Maggie's teeth with her excitement.

"First, I have to see what they're asking. Let's just keep this between us for now."

Perrin dropped into the chair across from her and squeaked. "I won't tell anyone."

"Especially not Mom," Maggie said with complete seriousness. "If we do this, it's *ours*, Perrin. She and Dad keep out of it."

"Agreed."

Perrin had always been the easier child and therefore, the favorite. But since Maggie's last run-in with her mother, she made a difficult decision. She wasn't going to feel guilty anymore if she couldn't get along with the toxic people in her life, her mother being top of the list.

It was fine if Perrin kept a relationship with their parents. Maggie wouldn't expect anything less, since they treated her differently. But she was finished pretending anything about their relationship was normal.

Her mother had never liked Nash. Even when he was a kid, she used to call him *that boy* and make reference to the way he dressed. Whenever Maggie mentioned his talent, her mother would make a snide comment about low rent musicians wasting their lives away on foolish potential that would never pay the bills.

Her parents refused to offer their blessing when Nash proposed, angry that he hadn't come to them first. They made no secret of disapproving of the wedding, thinking she and Nash were both too young and foolish to know what was best. And when Nash died, Maggie saw the relief in her mother's eyes. Only when Maggie didn't bounce right back and find a more suitable husband, did her mother realize she still wouldn't get what she wanted.

After Perrin left, Maggie peeked out the window and saw Ryan's cousins were still over. It was game day, and she figured she had a few hours before he came looking for her. Just enough time to run an errand and do some research about the bar.

On account of the game, O'Malley's had a full lot. She pulled her bike around the back and walked to the front. Van Morrison played on the jukebox, and she shivered as a memory of Nash crept through her mind.

A woman tended bar. Maggie pulled herself up on the rail and waited to get her attention.

"What can I get you?"

"I'm looking for Kelly McCullough."

The bartender eyed her from top to tits. "Who should I say is asking?"

"Maggie O'Malley."

The bartender's brows lifted. "O'Malley?"

Maggie raised her chin. "That's right. He knows who I am."

The woman left the bar and disappeared into the back. Maggie blew out a shaky breath. She should have ordered a drink.

The bartender returned and Kelly followed. Seriously, was there a day when he just looked average? She climbed off the bar ledge and walked over to him.

"Maggie, everything all right?"

"Everything's fine. Could I talk to you privately for a minute?"

Curiosity flashed in his eyes, and he waved a hand for her to follow him to his office. Every time she walked through that hall, she remembered how Ryan had saved her from a panic attack. Now, the pub didn't seem so scary.

Boxes cluttered the dated office. A large dry-erase board hung on the wall with the schedule drawn in. She noted that the bartender on duty went by the name Sue.

"What's up?"

She figured it best to get right down to business. "How much would it cost to buy the bar?"

He blinked, his blue eyes going a bit wide. "Who's asking?"

"Me."

He sat back, crossing his arms over his chest and studied her. "You have that kind of money, or are you asking for your in-laws?"

She frowned. "First of all, my in-laws are perfectly nice people, and I'd appreciate it if your family stopped acting like they were lepers. Second, this has nothing to do with them. No one knows I'm here."

"What about Ryan?"

"I'd appreciate it if we kept him out of this."

Kelly pinched his chin, folding a finger over his mouth as he continued to study her. "You're serious about this?"

She nodded. "I know your aunts and uncles own it outright, but I figured I'd come to you first. I thought you might be able to put in a good word before I approached them."

"Being that I no longer have the time to run the pub and no one else wants the job, they have no choice but to sell—so having a good word won't make a difference. It has to go. What would you do with the property if you bought it?"

"I'd run it."

"You'd keep it as a pub?"

"Yeah. My sister and I would."

"And the name?"

She narrowed her eyes. "The name belongs to me more than it ever belonged to you."

"Touché. But I have a feeling you won't be an O'Malley forever."

His comment threw her. "What?"

He smirked. "Call it intuition." Sitting up, he knocked a knuckle on the desk causing her to flinch. "Here's what I'll do. I'll mention your interest to my Aunt Col, since she's the boss over there, and I'll see what she thinks. Knowing you plan to keep it a pub, she might come down on the price. Or she might not. I can never predict what she'll do. That will give you about two days."

She frowned. "Two days until what?"

Kelly laughed. "Until word gets out. Aunt Col's the tightest lipped, but she's really no better than the others. Once she tells Aunt Rose, Aunt Rose will tell my mother and then your secrets will be shot to shit. So, if I were you, I'd move fast or come clean with Ryan. No one keeps secrets for long in this family."

"Great." Pressure mounted in her chest.

CHAPTER 37

"*I* can't go in there." Perrin paced on the sidewalk in front of the home Kelly sent them to visit. It was the house of Colleen Mosconi, wife to Paulie Mosconi, Aunt to Ryan, and mother to Mariella.

"Perrin, we have to. They're expecting us." They were standing on a sidewalk in the middle of a neighborhood. People were going to get suspicious.

"What if *she's* in there?"

"We're not here to see anyone but Colleen. This is business."

"You go. I'll wait for you back at the house and—"

"No." Maggie put her foot down, blocking her sister's incessant pacing. "You're supposed to be my business partner. If you can't do that, then we can't do this. What are you going to do when someone you don't like walks into the bar and you have to serve them?"

"It'll be my bar. I can tell them to leave."

"What year are you living in? That's not how business works, and you can't act like that in a town as small as this. People will talk and the bar could go under. You have to handle this like an adult."

Perrin stilled and blinked in confusion. "When did you turn into the sensible one?"

Right around the time her sister lost her mind. "It's a give and take. We keep each other in check. Now, pull yourself together, because in about five minutes, I'm going to make the biggest investment of my life, and I need you by my side."

Perrin swallowed and nodded, straightening her shoulders. "Okay. Let's do this."

They walked the path to the house, and Maggie blew out a nervous breath as she rang the bell.

"I'm not speaking to her if she's here."

"Just pretend you don't know her—Hello." Maggie smiled widely as Colleen opened the door.

"Perfect timing. I just made a fresh pot of coffee. Come in, come in." She held the door and led them into the house. "Paulie, Maggie's here."

"This is my sister, Perrin."

Colleen turned and her gaze softened as she offered a friendly but guarded smile. It was clear she knew Perrin's role in the Bran saga and decided she'd been as much a victim as her own daughter. "I figured we'd meet in the dining room."

The house was a mix of cream and greens. Every end table and coffee table wore a sheen of polish that reflected the porcelain sculptures and vases on display. As they followed Colleen through the home, Maggie spotted the little woman with black hair spying on them, the one Alec told her was Italian Mary.

"My mother-in-law," Colleen said. "Ignore her. She's like a piece of furniture I can't convince my husband to throw out."

Perrin gave her a wide-eyed look and Maggie waved it away. She'd seen Colleen taking care of the woman at family dinner, the way only a loving daughter would handle a parent. She might make jokes, but it was clear she cared for her mother-in-law deeply.

A long table with cherry finish dominated the dining room. A pile of large manila folders waited in a neat stack at the head, and a tray of coffee with all the fixings sat in the center. Colleen waved them to have a seat on the side against the wall as she filled the chair at the head of the table.

Paulie appeared and Maggie introduced herself and her sister, again. His first question wasn't much of a surprise. "Now, explain to me again how you're an O'Malley."

She'd prepared for this. "I'm the widow of Nash O'Malley, grandson of Caleb."

He sat across from her. "And you're dating Ryan, but he doesn't know you're here?" He appeared to disapprove of the secrecy more than her name.

"Only because I didn't want to give him false hope before finding out if I could actually do this."

Colleen lifted the folders and tapped the edges on the table like a gavel, calling their meeting to order. "Enough of the inquisition, Paulie. Half the good things in your life wouldn't have happened if I hadn't gone ahead and laid the groundwork first. It's a good woman's job to plan for the future. That being said, I've talked to my realtor and explained that this will be a private sale. That allows us to come down on the price a little bit." She removed a sheet of paper and slid it across the table. "This is what we're asking."

Maggie's heart stilled at the price. It was twice as much as she'd assumed. "This is…" Her mouth went bone dry. "This is everything?"

"Well, there's the cost of inspection, and the legal fees for signing over the LLC. You'll need a broker..." Colleen continued to talk about all the extra expenses, but Maggie's ears muffled, as if water was closing over her head.

Perrin's hand pinched her thigh under the table, bringing her back to the present. Maggie cleared her throat. "This is a lot more than I expected."

Colleen and Paulie exchanged glances, and Perrin looked at her in ill-disguised panic. "I thought Kelly explained the appraisal."

"We didn't discuss price." They should have. What kind of person goes into a buyout not knowing how much money she'd need? A stupid person.

"There are additional costs because you're buying out the business, not just the property."

She frowned. "And if we just bought the property?"

"Then you wouldn't be able to call it O'Malley's."

Perrin sat up. "But it's her name. You can't trademark a name."

"O'Malley's Irish Pub," Paulie clarified.

"Then we'll call it something else." Perrin's voice had turned defensive, and Colleen sat back, her arms crossing with disapproval. "We'll call it O'Malley's Bar. Or maybe just call it Maggie's Place. We don't care about the name."

"Relax," Maggie whispered. "The name's important. O'Malley's has an established clientele we don't want to lose. People don't like change. It scares them."

"Even if you didn't buy the business, you'd only skim twenty thousand off the price. Also consider that we've included all the assets, the pool tables, jukebox, kitchen equipment, stools, and everything else not nailed down. We could sell those items on consignment and lower the price another hundred thousand, but if you're planning on running a bar, you'll need them anyway."

She was right. They weren't trying to rip them off. They were trying to work out a fair price. Maggie looked at Colleen. "Can you pretend for a minute that I'm not an O'Malley and this isn't a business meeting?" She drew in a deep breath. "Pretend I'm your daughter. Would you tell me this is a good investment?"

Colleen smiled. "I'd tell you that the pub brought our family generations of joy. It was the backdrop to every celebration and the landing point when any of our children came home. It kept food on my family's table and gave us enough to live generously with others. It kept us close and kept us laughing. This is the end of an era for us and watching the doors close will be like burying a dear friend, one whose time ended too soon. O'Malley's is a fine running establishment that could still make many more generations of memories. But sadly, with all the people in our family, we still have no one interested in running it." She smiled. "I think you'd be wise to buy it, Maggie. I think it will add to your life in ways I could never explain in one business meeting, ways that make a person of any income feel rich on even the poorest of days."

Annnnnnd sold.

Maggie tried to hide her dying urge to sign the papers. She'd started this venture to lift her sister's spirits, but now, it became something she wanted for herself as well. Maybe even for Ryan.

She breathed with uneven, intense breaths and swallowed. "I have to speak to the bank." The only way she could manage the price would be to borrow against her house. That wasn't a sure thing, but it was her only hope. "Could you try to keep this quiet for another day or two?"

Paulie blew out a breath that sounded like a laugh. "In this family?"

"Please?" Maggie looked Colleen in the eye. "I need to make this decision on my own. Ryan would... He'd try to talk me out of it." Even though deep down she believed he wanted to see the bar saved, he'd think she was risking too much.

"I'll do my best," Colleen said and closed the folder.

CHAPTER 38

hy did people always want what they couldn't have?
Maggie sat on the stained red couch stuffed into her shed and stared at the wall full of boxes. Memories. Pieces of her past. Some still felt familiar, but others just felt like … junk.

She lifted the lid of a box and found all of Nash's socks. Why would she keep these? She sniffed one and scrunched her nose. It didn't smell like him. It smelled like dust and cardboard. He wasn't here anymore than he was in the cemetery.

She looked out the glass window of the door toward her house. She and Ryan never slept there. Something about being inside made her feel like the walls had eyes. She had no regrets about moving forward with Ryan. She loved him. But something about her home held her back, entrenched in memories that sometimes weighed her down, when outside of the house she often felt lighter.

A knock on the door startled her. Ryan looked through the glass. "What are you doing?"

"Thinking."

He opened the door. "Do you want to be left alone?"

She shook her head and scooted over, offering him a place to sit. "No. How was work?"

He rolled his eyes. "My dad needs to retire. At least Uncle Frank stays out of the field and Finn can call the shots. I'm in the office and my dad is constantly micromanaging everything I do. Today, he asked me if I knew how to use a program we've been using since I graduated. I installed the damn thing." He sat beside her on the couch and glanced at the box of socks, as if it were a perfectly normal thing to store. "By the way, he's coming over tonight to watch the game."

She laughed. "You do realize that you just went on about how much he's getting on your nerves at work."

He shrugged. "That's work. He's my dad. We always watch the College World Series together."

And that was another reason why she loved him. Ryan might get frustrated, but he never stayed angry at those he loved. "You have fun with your dad. Perrin's coming over to help me with some things."

"You two are welcome to join us. Luke and Tristan are stopping by, too."

"How about I come by after Perrin leaves?"

He lifted a brow. "How about you come over right now?" Just then his father pulled up. "Damn it. My parents always have the worst timing."

She laughed and shoved him to his feet. "You invited him. Go say hello so he doesn't come looking for you."

He leaned down and kissed her slowly. "That's a little preview of what's coming tonight."

"Can't wait."

When he disappeared, she reached into her pocket, pulling out the printout from the bank. Due to some hard times just after Nash had died and before the life insurance paid, her credit wasn't as great as she thought. She didn't use credit cards anymore and she didn't have a car payment or a mortgage, so there was no way to quickly fix the dings in her record to create better credit. That meant the bank saw her as a risk on a refinance.

But there was still one other option. Maggie didn't want Perrin's input or anyone else's. She hadn't discussed anything about the bar with Alec at therapy. This needed to be her decision and hers alone. As she stared at her beautiful little home with the firepit in the back and the daffodils dancing along the fence, she knew her mind had been made up.

Perrin's car pulled up at the street and Maggie stood, closing the lid over the box of socks and carrying it down to the curb. That night, while Ryan was in his basement cheering with his father and cousins, she and Perrin emptied her shed. Maggie kept a shoebox of items she felt were most important. A few of Nash's guitar picks, his Led Zeppelin T-shirt, his favorite coffee mug, and the last grocery list where he wrote *I love you* on the bottom.

Seeing her shed empty and all her treasured belongings on the curb filled her with a sense of purpose and certainty. This was moving forward. She couldn't carry all the pain with her, and she didn't want to. Funny how keeping the things that made her happy somehow kept her sad. She carried her shoebox into the house and set it on the stairs.

Perrin waited on the couch with her laptop. "You're sure about this?"

Maggie handed her a beer and took a long sip of her own. "I'm sure."

"You want to watch?"

She sat down beside her sister and looked at the screen of her computer. Perrin clicked the mouse and the sale went live. A photo of Nash's Fender guitar filled the auction page with all his other instruments.

Maggie had told Perrin she needed to do something to get over what had happened to her. It had been good advice for both of them. Deciding to buy the bar was both terrifying and exciting. It helped having a partner.

Her decision to sell her house to get the rest of the money wasn't an easy one, but the right choices are rarely easy.

"That's it?" Maggie asked.

Her sister gave her a familiar smile, one reserved for difficult decisions that came with delayed relief. "Now, we wait."

"What if no one bids?"

Her sister glanced at the screen. "The auction just started and there are already two people who marked the guitar as a favorite. They'll be back."

In moments like this, her sister's confidence far outweighed hers. "Thanks for helping me with this."

Perrin smiled. "We're a team. Sisters usually are."

Maggie divided Nash's instruments. Half were being donated to the school's music program and the more valuable pieces were being sold at auction. Perrin was a great help in finalizing such arrangements, which proved a special kind of painful when it came time to actually let the items go. But Maggie knew she would breathe easier without the constant reminders of her past cluttering her future.

The auction bids continued to grow. After Perrin left, Maggie continued to box up items. Some went into the trash. Others were bagged for Goodwill. All the necessities would be going with her to her new loft apartment on top of the pub.

"Maggie?" Ryan's voice called from downstairs.

She pushed the box under the bed and went to the top of the landing. Ryan stood at the foot of the steps. "Hey."

"All your stuff's out front."

Her stomach flipped with a subtle urge to carry it back to the shed, but the feeling quickly passed. "I know."

"Why?"

She shut off the hall light and came downstairs. "It was time to let go of some things."

He studied her closely. "Are you okay?"

"I am. I wouldn't have done it if I wasn't ready."

He hugged her and kissed her head. "That's a big deal."

She smiled, glad he realized. "Let's go to your place."

That night they made love, and Ryan fell asleep in her arms. She couldn't sleep so she spent hours staring at the ceiling, picturing how she would decorate the loft. Because she'd be downsizing, it forced her to only take with her what she absolutely needed, and that sort of minimalistic simplicity came with an unexpected dose of clarity. For the first time in a long time, she could see her future clearly, and she liked the view.

CHAPTER 39

*M*aggie turned the last page of the buyout contract. The bank had agreed to a short sale, since her investment was contingent on the selling of her house. That meant that once she signed the paperwork, the bank would then own the property and she would be renting from them for the next thirty days as she moved out of her home. During that time, they'd list the house on the market and sell it for about ten thousand more than they paid for it. Maggie and Perrin would get the bar and everyone would be happy.

"Any questions?"

She looked at the woman sitting across from her. A bank representative and Maggie's only advocate in this decision. "I assume this is all boilerplate?"

"Everything's exactly as we discussed. Once you sign, the check is endorsed, and the money will clear your account in twenty-four hours. You'll be able to stay in the home until July twentieth."

That sounded right. Same as the last time she had it explained. Maggie's hand shook as she lifted the pen. She didn't hesitate because she thought she could get a better price on the house or because she was second guessing her decision to buy the bar. She hesitated because there remained a flicker of concern that this was a mistake.

Delaying her decision was clearly self-sabotaging. The idea that she might be giving away something she needed made no sense. There was nothing she needed in that house. Not anymore. It was four walls and a lawn. The memories didn't live there. They lived in her heart.

She scribbled her name across the first blank line and turned the page. There were about thirty places she needed to sign, and each one passed like a bullet through her lungs. When she signed the last blank, the woman took the papers and smiled.

"Congratulations." She handed Maggie an endorsed check. With that and the insurance money, she would now have enough to buy the bar and live comfortably for a while.

When she left the bank, she texted Colleen Mosconi confirming that she was ready to sign the papers. Maggie's excitement was only curbed by the remaining details.

She needed to give her notice at Restaurant Supply, and she needed to tell Ryan. Now that the sale was imminent, his parents would find out she was the buyer, since they were partners with Colleen and Paulie.

She'd been warned about how fast word could travel in a family that size, yet somehow she hadn't been prepared. When she rode her bike into the driveway, she saw Ryan sitting on her front porch—not the back where he usually waited for her. Four feet in front of him, a FOR SALE sign stood plunged into the ground.

She climbed off her bike and leaned it against the fence. "Hey."

He stared at her, his face blank of expression. "Busy day?"

"I was going to tell you, but I wanted to wait for the right moment."

"And when was that?" He laughed without humor. "When the house sold?"

"Ryan, it's not what you think."

He stood and scowled. "Maggie, I try to be patient with you, and for the most part I think I'm pretty understanding. But this…" He waved an angry hand at the FOR SALE sign. "This is bullshit."

She wondered if he heard about the bar. "Ryan, do you know?"

"Do I know what? All I know is my girlfriend put her house up for sale without even mentioning it to me. What the hell, Maggie? I thought we were closer than that."

Her stomach knotted. "Can you not yell at me?"

He dragged a hand through his hair and paced. "I just don't understand this. Where are you moving?"

"I … found a loft apartment in town."

"A loft." He scoffed. "I like you living next to me."

"I like that too, but I needed to make this move for myself. I was holding onto the past with the house. This was a really hard decision, but the second I sold it, I felt this incredible relief like I'd done the right thing."

He pivoted. "Wait. *Sold* it? You already *sold* it? To who?"

"The bank. It's a short sale. They're relisting it."

He shook his head, face stunned. "You can't even decide if you want sausage or broccoli on your pizza without having a full conversation about it, yet you did all this without even mentioning it to me."

"I wanted to surprise you."

"Well, color me fucking shocked."

"Ryan, I had my reasons."

"Yeah, I'm sure you did. But you never thought to discuss them with me."

She frowned. "I didn't want other people's opinions deterring me from what I wanted."

"And what is it you want, Maggie? Because you clearly don't trust me to let you decide for yourself."

"That's not true."

"If it wasn't true, you would have told me—" His phone rang, and he glanced at the screen.

"Who is it?"

"It's my mother." He silenced the call.

"Answer it."

His eyes narrowed. "We're in the middle of something."

"Ryan, answer the phone."

He huffed and brought the phone to his ear. "What is it, Mum? I'm in the middle of something." He paused. "No, I'm standing." He frowned. "Mum, just tell me. Is everyone okay?" He waited. "Oh." He moved to the steps and sat down, his anger shifting to disappointment. "That fast? I thought it would take months to find a buyer."

He glanced up at her and covered the phone. "They found a buyer for O'Malley's." His attention returned to the call. "No, it's Maggie. Yeah. We're just talking. Why would she?" He frowned and glanced up at her, then he glanced at the FOR SALE sign and his face paled. "Mum, I'll call you right back."

He ended the call and stared at the ground. The silence stretched for a solid minute. "You said the bank already bought the house off of you?"

"Yes."

"I know what our houses are worth. That's not enough to..." He shook his head and looked up at her in confusion. "Maggie, what did you do?"

"Nash had a life insurance policy, but it wasn't enough."

His chest lifted with each breath as he stared at her. "Enough for what? Please tell me you didn't—"

"I'm buying the bar. The papers are all drawn up, and I'm signing them tonight. I didn't want you to talk me out of it."

He looked at her with a blank expression of shock. "Why?"

She shrugged. "Because it meant something to you, and I didn't want to see you lose something you loved." She smiled apologetically. "And also, because I wanted it."

"You ... bought the bar?"

"Well, I still need to give your family the check, but yeah, it's mine as soon as I sign."

A disbelieving breath punched out of him. "You sold your house to afford it?"

She nodded. "I'm really okay with it, Ryan. This is a good move for me. Perrin's going to help me run it, and I can live in the loft on the second floor."

"Fuck that."

She flinched. "W—what?"

"I want you to live with me. I like that I see you each morning before I leave and that you're the first person I see when I get home. Anything else feels like a step backwards."

Her heart jerked wildly in her chest. Moving in was a big deal. It meant living in a life of compromise, but more importantly, it meant opening herself up to another person and not always having a place to escape and catch her breath. It meant growing closer and caring more deeply. It meant entwining her life with his, in a way that wouldn't be easily untangled.

"Will you move in with me?"

She stepped back and tried to catch her breath. What if she wasn't ready? What if this led to emotional landmines?

Or, what if living with Ryan made her as happy as hanging out with him did? Their life would be one long sleepover. They could actually plan ahead and grocery shop like a normal couple, instead of debating over takeout each night. Her furniture would mix with his. They could maybe get a dog. There were so many possibilities. The only thing that scared her was how badly she wanted all of those things.

"Are you sure that's what you want?"

His eyes turned pleading. "I love you, Maggie. You're all I want."

Her heart warmed and she smiled up at him. "Then yes."

A smile jumped to his face and he hugged her, lifting her off the ground. "Yes?"

"Yes! Let's move in together!"

His mouth found hers and he kissed her, sealing the deal. Her body slid down his, bringing her feet back to the earth. He looked at her and laughed. "I can't believe you're buying the bar."

She laughed with him, still a little stunned herself. "Did you think we were going to let you all keep it? It belongs in the hands of an O'Malley."

He arched a brow. "Careful. You might not be an O'Malley for long if I have my way." He left her gaping on the front lawn and yelled, "Come on. My mum's putting out cake and coffee. She said to get there before it's all gone."

Her chest warmed as she watched him glance back and smile. Four months ago, she thought she had her future figured out. She could see it as a bleak, dark road ahead. But then Ryan showed up, letting a little light in, and her heart had been healing ever since.

She jogged after him and took his hand. Their arms swung as they walked towards town. They smiled at the neighbors they passed, waving and saying hello to strangers and friends. She was finally alive again. Living. All because this beautiful man rescued the last of her heart and brought her back to life.

EPILOGUE

*M*aggie pounded on the door to the loft. "Let's go, Perrin. It's five of five."

Her sister barreled down the stairs of the second floor, into the back hall of the pub. "My shift doesn't start until five."

"Would it kill you to get out there a few minutes early? Sue's slammed."

Her sister rolled her eyes and hooked a left into the pool table room. "You're a nag."

"I heard that!"

"I wasn't whispering!"

Maggie returned to her office and reviewed the schedule for the weekend. Everything looked right. She grabbed her purse under the desk and shut out the lights.

"Hey, Maggie May, come have a beer with me." Jim called from the bar.

Unable to resist her old boss, she climbed up on the stool to his right. Sue uncapped her regular and slid it in front of her. "Thanks."

"So how are things?" he asked.

"I can't complain."

"You look good. Happy."

She pressed the mouth of her beer to her smile and took a sip. "I am."

Perrin filled orders behind the bar and teased the regulars. It was nice to see her sister's smile had returned, too. Her beautiful sister wasn't hard up for attention, as every single man in town now waited for her to notice them every weekend. She had found her calling, and Maggie might have found hers, as well.

Maggie liked the office work. It made her feel good to manage a business and plan things behind the scenes. She especially loved giving young musicians a chance to perform. But most of all, she loved the sense of family she found within O'Malley's.

Arms reached around her waist, startling her until she recognized Ryan's scent. She leaned her weight into his chest and smiled up at him.

"You started without me." He kissed her cheek and climbed on the stool to her right. He leaned around and shook Jim's hand. "You keeping an eye on her?"

"I think that ring on her finger's doing the trick. Haven't seen any men sniffing around."

Maggie's gaze dropped to the diamond weighing down her left hand, giving her fingers a wiggle, never growing tired of how it glistened in the light.

Ryan had proposed at exactly the right moment, when the Eagles won the Super Bowl. She'd flung herself off the couch and into his arms, screaming with excitement. He pulled out the ring and made the day one of the best in her life.

They were getting married next June. Perrin was planning all the details, and Maggie insisted she keep things on the small side—as small as things could be when her fiancé had a family the size of Texas.

She couldn't wait. They planned to say their vows in front of a lake on his cousins' property. Then they would have a small reception at the pub. Ryan's mother was a big help when it came to planning the food and menus. Maggie loved how she kept a positive attitude through even the dullest arrangements. She also loved that Rosemarie would soon be her mother-in-law and looked forward to one day calling her *Mum*.

Ryan laced his fingers with hers. "How about some music?"

She smiled. He'd been trying to narrow down the options for their first dance. Every day he hit her with a new choice, each song a translation of his feelings for her. "Okay."

Holding onto her hand, he walked her to the wall and slipped a dollar into the jukebox. A quick beat of drums started, and the humming voices of The Beach Boys followed. Ryan gave her a twirl and pulled her to his chest.

"Well, it's been building up inside of me for oh I don't know how long..." His off-key voice peeled into her ear with terrible pitch and she squinted. *"Don't worry, baby... Everything will turn out all right..."*

Cupping her hand to his, she moved across the floor with him, never doubting for a moment that as long as he held her hand everything would turn out fine.

Faces around the bar swirled as she laughed and clung to him, savoring this temporary moment and appreciating its value all the more because she knew life was fleeting and impermanent, but true love could outlast a lifetime.

THE END
www.LydiaMichaelsBooks.com

CLAIM YOUR GIFT, A FREE BOOK!

NOTABLE TITLES BY LYDIA MICHAELS

www.LydiaMichaelsBooks.com

Follow Lydia Michaels on Instagram and Facebook!

Don't stop here!

Grab your free books and keep reading...

What to Read Next?

FREE Books

Almost Priest | Calamity Rayne | Sacrifice of the Pawn | Blind | Forfeit | First Comes Love

Billionaire Romance

Falling In | Sacrifice of the Pawn | Calamity Rayne

Small Town Romance

Wake My Heart | The Best Man | Love Me Nots | Pining For You | Almost Priest

Emotional & Heartwarming Romance

La Vie en Rose | Simple Man | Wake My Heart | Sacrifice of the Pawn | Forfeit

Romantic Comedy

Calamity Rayne

Erotic Romance

Breaking Perfect | Protégé | Falling In | Sugar

Dark Psychological Romance

Hurt

First Books in Binge Worthy Trilogies and Series

Almost Priest | Falling In | Wake My Heart | Forfeit | Original Sin

Paranormal Vampire Romance

Original Sin

LGBTQ+ & Menage Romance

Broken Man (MM) | Breaking Perfect (MMF) | Forfeit (MMF) | Hurt (Non-Consensual) | Protege

Sexy Nerds

Blind | Untied

Teacher Student, Workplace, and Age-Gap Love Affairs...

British Professor | Pining For You | Breaking Perfect | Falling In | Sacrifice of the Pawn

Single Dads or Teen Moms

Simple Man | Pining For You | First Comes Love | Intentional Risk

Non-Fiction Books for Writers

Write 10K in a Day: Avoid Burnout

Other Titles by Lydia Michaels

Wake My Heart

The Best Man

Love Me Nots

Pining For You

Falling In: Surrender Trilogy 1

Breaking Out: Surrender Trilogy 2

Coming Home: Surrender Trilogy 3

FREE! - Sacrifice of the Pawn: Billionaire Romance

Queen of the Knight: Billionaire Romance

Original Sin

Dark Exodus

FREE! - Calamity Rayne: Gets a Life

Calamity Rayne: Back Again

La Vie en Rose

Breaking Perfect

FREE! - Blind

Untied

FREE! - Almost Priest

Beautiful Distraction

Irish Rogue

British Professor

Broken Man

Controlled Chaos

Hard Fix

Intentional Risk

Hurt

About the Author

Lydia Michaels is the award winning and bestselling author of over forty titles. She is the consecutive winner of the 2018 & 2019 *Author of the Year Award* from *Happenings Media,* as well as the recipient of the 2014 *Best Author Award* from the *Courier Times*. She has been featured in *USA Today, Romantic Times Magazine, Love & Lace,* and more. As the host and founder of the *East Coast Author Convention,* the *Behind the Keys Author Retreat,* and *Read Between the Wines,* she continues to celebrate her growing love for readers and romance novels around the world.

In 2021, Michaels released the groundbreaking, non-fiction series, *Write 10K in a Day,* to commemorate her career in the publishing industry. She looks forward to many more years of exploring both fiction and non-fiction writing, teaching about the craft, and learning from the others in the author community.

Lydia is happily married to her childhood sweetheart. Some of her favorite things include the scent of paperback books, listening to her husband play piano, escaping to her coastal home at the Jersey Shore, cheap wine, *Game of Thrones,* coffee, and kilts. She hopes to meet you soon at one of her many upcoming events.

You can follow Lydia at www.Facebook.com/LydiaMichaels or on Instagram @lydia_michaels_books

THE BEST MAN

Chapter One

"Drink! Drink! Drink! Drink!" The heavy pounding of many exuberant hands thumped down on the littered table, rattling empty bottles and jostling what was left of the cheesesteaks they ordered earlier.

Pat tipped back his shot and chugged hard, nearly choking himself on the thick taste of black beer and Irish cream. He was getting too old for this shit.

He slammed down his empty glass and roared like a champ, but his victorious cry was cut short by a belch that seemed to come from the deepest part of his soul. As a full-fledged medical doctor, he had it on good authority that his liver might not survive the next week. Tomorrow, he'd be back home in Jasper Falls, reunited with his crazy Irish family, celebrating the end of this chapter in his life as well as his brother's wedding. His insides would surely be fermented by then.

"Keep it down, Heaves!" his best friend, Jo, yelled, angering his sour stomach all the more with a hard smack on his back.

She'd called him Heaves ever since they were children, when they broke into his parents' liquor cabinet. They drank so much it was a shock they hadn't ended up in the hospital. He'd spent the next several days dry heaving, and Jo spent the next fifteen years not letting him live it down.

"No more." He waved a hand over his glass as Dina attempted to refill it. "I have to drive in a few hours."

He squinted at the clock on the wall, debating if it was two or seven in the morning. He misplaced his glasses sometime around the cheesesteak feast. No one did cheesesteaks like Philadelphia, though it was up for debate who made the best sandwich. To commemorate his last night in the City of Brotherly Love, they ordered several from all the greats like Geno's, Pat's, Tony Luke's, and even Shank's. He definitely *did not* want to see his dinner return.

"We're gonna head home," Jeff said, his arm slung over Shay's shoulders as they staggered for a hug goodbye. "Don't be a stranger, man."

Pat kissed Shay's cheek and gave Jeff a thumping, manly hug. "I won't. Give me a call sometime next week and let me know how you make out at the animal rescue. Don't let Shay talk you into one of those little dogs people carry around in their purses."

Jeff laughed. "You got it."

"We should go, too," Dina said, nudging Brian, who had passed out on the table an hour ago.

The parade of goodbyes lasted several minutes, and soon their little apartment overlooking Broad was empty. Jo smiled at him, her dimpled cheeks the same as they were when they were children, mischievous and a great disguise to whatever was going on inside her always moving brain.

"What?" he asked, sensing she had something to get off her chest.

"Nothing." She shrugged. "I just can't believe you're leaving me."

"You always knew this would eventually happen."

"I know, but I got comfortable here. I like living with you."

He looped an arm over her shoulder and pressed an affectionate kiss on her cheek. "You know I'll be back."

"It won't be the same. I know how Jasper Falls works. Once you return, you get sucked in, and you never leave. You'll open your practice, be the town hero after you patch up a few scraped knees and stitch a busted face or two, then you'll forget all about your friends in the big-city."

He scrubbed a hand roughly over her short brown hair, mussing the stylish way she had it parted. "With that outlook, I might as well be living in a Norman Rockwell painting."

"You love that small town cheese-dick shit."

"True." His mouth hooked into a half smile.

After years of med school and finishing his residency, his life could *finally* begin. It seemed surreal that it was actually happening. His title and credibility had changed in a blink, yet he still felt like the same, unsure guy but with a lot more credentials and money. It almost felt fake or undeserved. He had a lot to prove, once he moved back home, and he wanted to make his family proud.

His mother was over the moon to claim one of her sons was a doctor. And since Doc Jones passed, their hometown was hurting for a replacement. He'd always dreamed of owning his own practice, something that usually took years to establish. But in a small town like Jasper Falls, where everyone knew everyone and people rarely trusted outsiders or big fancy hospitals, his practice would be a welcome addition.

He helped Jo gather plates and trash, only slightly stumbling toward the kitchen. "I'm going to hate you tomorrow. Whose idea was it to shoot Fireball?"

Jo laughed. "Yours."

"I'm an idiot."

"That's what I said. Where did you even find that bottle?"

He paused and scrunched his brow. "I think my brother gave it to me as a graduation present."

"From Penn?"

"No, from high school. Does alcohol expire?"

They finished cleaning up the table. There wasn't much to put away, being that most of his belongings were boxed up by the front door.

"Am I making a mistake?" he asked, staring at the pile of boxes marked *KEEP* to take home.

"No. You've always wanted this. And just think, you get to see Ryan every day. It'll be like old times."

He did miss his brother. "I can't believe he's getting married."

"To Maggie O'Malley no less. I never thought I'd see the day that an O'Malley married a Clooney."

"She's not, technically, an O'Malley." His brother's fiancée was an O'Malley by marriage. She was also the youngest widow in town—but she was about to marry into the biggest—and craziest—family in Jasper Falls.

"Everyone's getting married," Jo commented, plopping on the broken in couch, where Pat spent most of his nights after returning home from the hospital, too exhausted to find his bed.

He collapsed next to her and rested his head on her shoulder. "Not us."

She snorted. "I doubt I ever will."

He laced his fingers with hers, admiring the diamond ring on her right hand. It was the only feminine thing Jo owned. They found it stumbling home from the bar one night.

"You never know. Your soul mate could be out there somewhere."

"Oh, please." She lifted her hip and fished her phone out of her back pocket. "Speaking of which… Listen to this."

She opened her voicemail, flashing the screen with a list of calls from her mother and hit play.

"Josephine, it's impolite not to return someone's call, especially your mother's. I found a dress online that would look lovely with your eyes and hide your tattoos. I'm sending you the link. I think you should buy it for the wedding."

"A dress?"

"Wait," she said, scrolling down the voicemail page. "There's more."

"Josephine, I ran into Rosemary Clooney at McGinty's, and she said

Ryan hasn't received your RSVP for the wedding yet. This reflects poorly on the family. I hope you've sent it by now."

She pursed her lips and narrowed her eyes at him. "You told Ryan I wasn't coming, right?"

"I mentioned it, but we still think you're going."

"Pat, I'm not going."

He lifted his chin at the phone, gesturing for her to play more.

She hit play on the next message. "Josephine, I spoke to Elise Wiseman today after mass, and she says that Tobin is looking for a date to the wedding. I gave her your number to pass along. Hopefully you answer the phone when he calls."

Pat scrunched his nose. "Tobin Wiseman?"

"I know. Even if I *was* into guys, I'd find him gross."

She played a few more messages, each one a testament to why she escaped her controlling, critical mother and ran away from her conservative family years ago. At least in Philly, she could be herself.

If he didn't know Dee and Rodger Cook, he'd advise her to *come out* to her family. It wasn't like the Cooks were all bad. Jo's older brother Garret was cool, and her younger brother Smith was fine, just at that post pubescent preadult indifferent stage. And Julie... Well, Julie was perfect, aside from her wretched taste in men.

But Jo's parents were a special kind of challenging. They lived in a bubble, got their news from unreliable sources, believed in actively repenting for their sins, and placed way too much emphasis on what others thought, especially when it came to their children.

He never understood why Jo earned such a difficult rap. She was no different than the others, but when it came to her mother, there seemed no pleasing the woman, especially where Jo was concerned. Maybe, on some level, Mrs. Cook already knew Jo's secrets. Sometimes, her expectations and criticism seemed more like an ongoing punishment than any twisted form of love.

Coming from a warm family like his, the Cooks' coldness chilled him to the bone, so he understood why Jo kept her sexuality to herself—at least where her family was concerned. Here, in the sanctuary of their little loft apartment, located in one of the most diverse cities in the world, Jo was *out* and proud.

He wished she felt confident enough to be herself at home. With the way things were, she'd never go back.

"I'll call her tomorrow and break the news that I'm not going. That should occupy my morning with a lengthy lecture, followed by an afternoon of undeserved guilt, and a long evening of drinking alone."

"Don't drink alone."

"But you're abandoning me." She pouted. "And Jeff and Shay will be busy with their new dog."

Together, they always had a partner they could count on, and he hated the idea of leaving her alone. He sat up and faced her. "Come home with me, Jo. Just for the wedding. I promise it won't be that bad. We can crash at my house most of the time."

She didn't immediately say no. "I do miss Rosemarie's cooking."

"It's not too late. I could call ahead and put in a menu request."

She hesitated, then shook her head. "No. I don't have the strength to deal with my mom. If I go home, she'll insist I take a date to the wedding. So help me God, if Tobin Wiseman tries to stick his tongue in my mouth, I'll be the new *Heaves*."

"What if there was a way to go home *and* get your mom off your back?"

"How?" She challenged him with heavy skepticism in her dark eyes.

The truth was, he had plenty of friends and family in Jasper Falls, but no one like Jo. Jo was his best friend. He wanted her there and couldn't imagine picking a new place to live without her skeptical input and dry cynicism guiding him away from every money pit. Plus, he wanted to see her sister, Julie—even if that meant having to stomach Lance.

"Tell your parents *we're* dating."

She burst into laughter, as if the idea were too hilarious to conceive.

He scowled. "It's not *that* unbelievable."

"No, I know, but…" She laughed harder, holding her stomach and falling back in a fit of unladylike snorts and cackles. "Me and you… I can't…" She wiped tears away from her eyes and blew out a breath. "Could you imagine?"

"Well, I clearly don't find it as difficult to imagine as you do!" He got up and went to the kitchen to take an aspirin.

"Pat, don't be mad!"

"I'm not mad. But I'll also never offer to be your boyfriend again."

"Oh, no. Whatever will I do without a fictional boyfriend?"

He narrowed his eyes and tossed back two white pills, chasing them with water. "You're mean."

"One of my best qualities."

"I guess I'll go to the wedding alone. Which is fine. I need to get laid."

"You're so cliché."

"Why? Because I want to hookup at my brother's wedding? Weddings are a great place to meet women."

"You know everyone on the guest list."

He shrugged. "Maggie could have some out-of-town relatives. I'm just looking for a one-nighter."

"Guys are so gross."

He shrugged. "If you feel so morally offended, you could prevent it by being my date."

"I'd be saving a woman a night of regrets and probably an STD test."

"Ouch." He laughed. "Come on, Jo, please…"

"Don't give me that look! You know it's my kryptonite!"

He fell beside her on the couch and did his best puppy dog stare. "If your mom thinks we're in a relationship, she'll stop trying to fix you up with every unclaimed penis in Jasper Falls."

~~"She'll know we're lying. Everyone knows we're just friends."~~

"I can be convincing. Before I decided to be a doctor, I toyed with improv. I could be the best boyfriend in the world, if the right girl ever gave me a shot."

Something knowing flashed in her eyes. "You know she'll be there with Lance."

His playful mood evaporated. "I know. It's expected."

Jo studied him for a long minute. It was no secret he'd been in love with her twin sister Julie his entire life. But, as a young boy, he'd been awkwardly shy and scrawny. He was the redhead with freckles that all the girls immediately lumped into the friend zone. By the time he filled out and got over his awkward adolescence, Julie had started dating Lance—the town douchebag. They'd been together ever since.

It was something they didn't discuss. Something he needed to put to rest if he ever wanted to move on and actually find a wife, preferably one who wanted him and was available. But he wasn't ready to retire the fantasy of Julie in his bed, arms, and future just yet—even if it was delusional and impossible.

"You'd be doing *me* a favor, actually. If we pretend we're dating, I won't have to come up with excuses about why I'm still single."

"Don't do that to me. Don't pull the favor card."

He shrugged. "Please?"

She groaned. "I hate you."

Sensing victory, he smiled. "Should we pack now or after we wake up?"

KEEP READING…

ACKNOWLEDGEMENT

I especially thank my devoted editor, Theresa Kohler, and my amazing beta team for their enthusiasm surrounding this story, and their wonderful feedback. Lauren Campbell, you are a true original when it comes to loving my Irish characters. Loren Brake, you police my settings and commas like a true law enforcer. Perrin Larton, thank you for being so thorough and loaning me your beautiful name. Dawn Wallingford, you're a savior when it comes to character placement. And last but not least, Michele Dyson, you excel at emotional feedback and always keep me laughing. Thank you, ladies, for sharing your talents with me and taking part in my writing process.
Xo, Lydia

THANK YOU FOR READING!

www.LydiaMichaelsBooks.com